# DISCIPLE

# Books by E. G. Lewis

## The Seeds of Christianity™ Series

*WITNESS* — Book One

*DISCIPLE* — Book Two

*APOSTLE* — Book Three

*MARTYR* — Book Four

## The Mountain Memories Trilogy

*PROMISES* — Book One

*LOST* — Book Two

## Christian Non-Fiction

*At Table with the Lord* - Foods of the First Century

*All Things Christmas* -  The History & Traditions of Advent and Christmas

*In Three Days* -  The History & Traditions of Lent and Easter

## About the Author

Writing has always been a major part of E. G Lewis' life. A former newspaper editor and publisher, his articles have appeared in many national and regional magazines. He also wrote and directed corporate training films.

He has a graduate degree in Economics from Ohio State University and worked in  management and corporate planning before deciding to become a fulltime novelist.

He and his wife, Gail, an editor and writer, live on the Southern Oregon Coast with more pets than they need.

# DISCIPLE

## Book Two
### of
### The Seeds of Christianity™ Series

A Novel

by

E. G. Lewis

**Cape Arago Press**
North Bend, OR
www.capearagopress.com

ISBN-10: 0-9825949-2-5
ISBN-13: 978-0-9825949-2-6

1. Fiction: Christian—Historical 2.Fiction: Christian—Biblical

*Disciple* is set in sight-saving Georgia 11 point type for your reading ease.

I want to offer my heartfelt thanks to all those who facilitated my research by graciously sharing their knowledge and expertise. They supported my goal of accurately depicting everyday life in the era during which Christianity came to be. Without their help and guidance, The Seeds of Christianity might never have germinated.

This book is dedicated with love to my wife, and best friend, Gail.

*"He that hath found a good wife, hath found a good thing, and shall receive a pleasure from the Lord."*
                                                    — Proverbs 18:22

## Praise for The Seeds of Christianity™ Series

A friend once told me, "When I read historical fiction, I want to learn something." If you share that viewpoint, this is the series for you. Mr. Lewis weaves the lore seamlessly into the adventure, blending meticulous research and practiced storytelling into a delightfully satisfying tale you won't soon forget.
> —Bruce Judisch http://brucejudisch.blogspot.com/

The story will keep you glued to your seat turning pages long into the night. And the characters are just wonderful! I love Rivkah and feel like she's family now!  I highly, highly recommend that EVERYONE read this book. You will be moved by God and E.G. Lewis' writing as much as I was..I am sure of it!
> —Michelle Vasquez  http://michellevsblog.blogspot.com/

*WITNESS* is worthy of so much more than a 5 star rating. It's an emotional story full of fiction but also full of actual events...
> —Molly Edwards  http://buuklvr81.blogspot.com/

You will rejoice and cry at various times..this is a novel that will transport you to a different country.
> —Isabelle Lusier http://canadianladybugreviews.blogspot.com/

The author did a wonderful job on weaving history and fact together to make a fast paced and gripping book.
> —Sarah Bailey http://quivermom.blogspot.com/

It was a gripping story, not in a who-dun-it manner but rather in a way that made me want to learn what happened next, to be part of their story.
> —Wyndy Callahan http://wynsbooks.blogspot.com/

This book delves into the humanity and depravity of both the Jewish and Roman peoples, medicine, the military and economics...and all with a bit of humor.
> —Tammy Litke http://threedifferentdirections.com/

# Historic Personages Mentioned in DISCIPLE
Name, Meaning, Biblical Reference, Modern Equivalent

## Yeshua's Family
Yeshua: Iesous...Jesus
Mother: Miryam...Mary
Foster Father: Yosef...Joseph

## Others
Andrew bar Yonah: Apostle Andrew, brother of Simon Peter
Annas: Former High Priest and Caiaphas's Father-in-Law
Caiaphas: High Priest at the time of the crucifixion
Gamali'el: Teacher and Head of the Sanhedrin
Matthias: Apostle chosen to replace Judas Iscariot
Mattithayu bar Alpheus: Apostle and Evangelist, Matthew, Levi
Netan'el bar Tolmai: Apostle Nathaniel aka Bartholomew
Nikademus: Secret Disciple of Jesus
Phillip: Apostle, friend of  Netan'el bar Tolmai
Shau'ol: Saul...the Apostle Paul
Simeon the Cananaean: Apostle Simon Zelotes
Simon Petros: the Apostle Simon Peter
Stefanos: First Christian martyr, Stephen
Thaddeus: Apostle aka Jude
Thomas: Apostle, Didymus, the twin, Doubting Thomas
Yaakov bar Alpheus: Apostle James the Lesser
Yaakov bar Zebedee: the Apostle James the Greater
Yaakov the Just: James, first Bishop of Jerusalem
Yohan bar Zebedee: the Beloved disciple and Apostle John
Yohan Marcus: Evangelist and companion of Peter, John Mark
Yosef Barnabus: Apostle and companion of Paul, Barnabus
Yosef of Arimathea: Secret disciple of Jesus

## Fictional Characters
Name, Meaning, Modern Equivalent


### Rivkah's Family
Rivkah: A snare...Rebecca
Shemu'el: God has Heard...Samuel
Their Oldest Son: Yo'el...Yahweh is God...Joel
Yo'el's wife: Tzipporah...Bird...Zipporah
Their Son: Shemu'el...God has Heard...Samuel
Their Oldest Daughter: Hadassah...Myrtle Tree...Esther
Hadassah's Husband: Hebel...Breath...Abel
Their Granddaughter: Sarit...Lady...Sarah
Their Middle Son: Yaakov...Supplanter...James
Their Youngest Daughter: Channah...Grace...Hannah
Their Youngest Son...Yudah...Praise...Judah/Jude

### Others
Channah's Friend: Eleana...God has Answered...Ilana
Idriya: Midwife, Siphrah's replacement...Duck
Pavlos: The Autistic Giant...Small
Phaidra: Eleana's Midwife...Bright
Rivkah's friend: Rachel...Ewe...Rachel
Shemu'el's friend: Atticus...of Athens...famous Roman name
Atticus' Wife: Marcelina...dedicate to Mars...Marcella
Siphrah: Hadassah's Midwife...Beautiful

~ **1** ~

Rivkah's skin prickled at the sound of their coarse laughter.

Tossing a damp towel over the dough she'd been kneading, she whipped off her apron and raced to the window. Ear cocked, she huddled beside the window's hide covering.

The jumble of voices, though indistinct, grew steadily louder. Somewhere beyond the hill a rooster crowed and chickens squawked in fright.

The tromp of hobnailed sandals on the road winding through the cluster of small homes in their settlement made her heart pound. Rivkah strained to decipher their conversation. She caught a smattering of words and phrases. Among them *meretrix*, the Roman word for prostitute.

Expletives, grunts of acknowledgement and additional coarse laughter followed.

Soldiers. Roman soldiers on the march.

*Why here? Why now?*

Rivkah lifted the worn corner of the window covering. Peering through a green curtain of fig leaves, she watched six Legionnaires descend the hill toward her home. Six professional soldiers could decimate her small community much as they had when Herod the King sent them in search of infant boys. The memory made her shudder.

She eased back the hide cover and glanced into the sleeping area.

Though it was already mid-morning, her husband, Shemu'el, dozed on the bed. The night before he'd sprinkled medicine from the vase shaped like a poppy pod into his wine to help him sleep. His right leg, broken weeks earlier, remained encased in a heavy plaster cast. He sighed in his sleep, coughed, and brushed away a fly crawling on his forehead.

Rivkah waited until he resumed snoring, then crossed to the front of the house. She pressed her back against the wall between the door and the front window and eased the bolt across the doorframe.

Shafts of sunlight cut through the clouds of yellow dust billowing around the soldier's feet. Their insignias indicated they were part of the Jerusalem detachment stationed at Antonia Fortress, the military garrison adjacent to Herod's Temple. But Bethlehem was miles from Jerusalem and this little shepherd's settlement farther still.

*Why were they so far from home?*

The soldiers were 50 cubits from the path leading to their door and closing fast. She knew she had to do something...but what?

Carrying their arms loosely, they laughed and chatted as they walked. Their pace had the cadence of a drum roll. From long habit they maintained the Imperial standard of 3.6 Roman miles per hour regardless of the terrain.

So long as their swords remained holstered she allowed herself to hope they were merely passing through. Undefended women were at risk anytime soldiers moved through the countryside. Bad things happened to a woman left alone.

Despite his handicap, she knew Shemu'el would rise to defend her. Better he sleep undisturbed. On his best days, he could barely hobble on his walking sticks.

Rivkah ran her eyes around their modest home searching for a weapon, any weapon. She spotted a sickle hanging above the door. The week before her middle son, Yaakov, had sharpened its crescent-shaped blade in anticipation of harvest. Twisting to her left, she reached up and snatched it off the hook.

Her stomach lurched.

They were outside now. The men drew even with the path

leading to her home and continued on without missing a beat.

Rivkah released her breath and, for the first time, relaxed a little. Sickle in hand, she ran to the window beside the bed. Her foot brushed the night pot as she passed and its white pottery lid clanked against the bowl.

Shemu'el woke with a start and glanced around. "Heh? Wha..."

The after effects of the narcotic he'd taken dulled his mind and slowed his reactions. Digging an elbow into the bed, he used it to leverage himself onto his side. His right leg, encased in a cast, thumped onto the bed.

Finger to her lips, Rivkah spun to face him. "Shhh!"

Shemu'el shook his head, clearing the fog in his brain. His brow knitted as he watched his wife crouch beneath the window clutching the sickle like a battle axe.

"What is going on?" he whispered.

She fluttered her hand at him and stared at the soldier's backs until they marched out of the settlement.

Shemu'el, now fully alert, heard their footfalls fading in the distance. "How many?"

"Six." She continued watching from the window. "Just passing through. They're on their way out now."

He grabbed her arm and jerked her around. "Why didn't you wake me? What if they came to the door...broke into the house?"

Rivkah shrugged, trying to appear calmer than she was. "You and I both know there is little you could have done."

He released his breath in a huff. "I am still the man of this house. You should have woken me."

"Why? So you could challenge six men and be killed?"

Rivkah carried the sickle into the kitchen with her. Setting it aside, she tied on her apron.

"All I have are loaves from last evening." She pointed to the mound of dough hidden under the cloth. "The soldiers interrupted my baking."

Rivkah filled a cup with warm apple peel tea, swirled in honey, and carried it to him.

Shemu'el took a sip and nodded appreciatively. "What is done is done. I know you've had to shoulder additional responsibility while my leg heals, but in another week or so all that will end." He took another sip. "Fortunately, no harm came of it."

In the kitchen Rivkah filled a plate with bread and soft cheese. She was stretching for a plum when a terrifying thought stopped her. Their youngest daughter had taken the sheep to pasture that morning. Channah was alone in the meadow and six soldiers were headed in her direction.

"Channah!" The plate slipped from Rivkah's fingers and crashed to the floor.

"What about her?"

Ignoring the shards on the floor, she grabbed her veil and swept it over her head. "She is out with the sheep. I must find her."

"You cannot go alone. Help me up." Shemu'el waved his arm and rocked in the bed, trying to rise.

Rivkah snatched up the sickle and raced out the door leaving him to fend for himself.

## ~ 2 ~

Shemu'el's protests died against the slamming door. Fuming, he groped under the bed for his walking sticks. He shoved one under each arm, planted them on the floor, and rocked forward with all his might. The added weight of his cast increased his momentum and he sprang off the bed staggering like a drunkard.

Sweat beaded on his forehead as Shemu'el teetered around the small room trying to avoid the shards of his breakfast on the floor. Once he achieved a tenuous equilibrium, he hobbled over and buried his hand in his tool kit. Rummaging around, he pulled out one of his carving gouges.

He settled onto a stool and set to work. Rivkah could hardly complain about plaster chips and dust on the floor, he thought, glancing over at the plate's shards.

Shemu'el stretched out his leg and scratched a line down each side of the cast. In a perfect world he would've given the leg another week to heal and asked his oldest son, Yo'el, to cut away the cast.

And in a perfect world Roman soldiers didn't ravish innocent maidens while they tended their sheep.

Shemu'el rolled his shoulders, easing out the kinks. The muscles in his jaw tightened in concentration. Cupping the gouge's handle in his right hand, he moved it around his palm until he found a comfortable spot.

Easy enough to do. Etch two lines down the cast, one on each side. Slice through the plaster to weaken them then shatter the cast along one side by prying up on the other.

How many casts had he removed when he was a slave to Evodius the *Medicus Cohortis*? Fifty? A hundred? More than he could count. But he'd never been both patient and physician until today.

Tiny chips of plaster spurted from the tip of the gouge as Shemu'el inched it along the cast. He worked with deliberate slowness, keeping the tip of the gouge on his guidelines. Chalky plaster dust coated the stones beneath his leg by the time he finished.

Shemu'el breathed a sigh of relief. Halfway there. So far, so good. Now came the tricky part, cutting through the upper layer of cloth without accidentally slicing an artery. He took out his sharpest cutting blade and went to work.

Pale skin showed through the crack when he finished.

He inserted the pry. Leaning back in the seat, he gently tested the handle. The pry bar sank into his thigh, but the cast refused to budge. The handle sprang back when he released it. Impatient to be on his way, he gritted his teeth, closed his eyes and slammed his hand down with all his might. He roared in pain when the metal pry bit into his leg.

Shemu'el hurriedly stripped away the outer wrappings, sending cloth, plaster and bindings flying. A growing blood-red stain saturated the underlying wrap. He nicked the cloth with his blade and ripped it across. Gathering the torn scraps, he folded and tied them around his thigh as a makeshift bandage.

Shoving a walking stick under his armpit, he heaved himself up. A bolt of lightening flashed up his leg when he put his foot on the floor. Bright colors danced before his eyes. Waving one arm for balance, he made a wobbly circle before collapsing on the floor.

Several tries later, Shemu'el finally managed to stand on the leg. Ignoring the pain and plaster dust in his hair and beard, he stuffed his shepherd's rod into his girdle and headed down the road after his wife and daughter.

Rivkah found the sheep wandering aimlessly in the meadow. Lingering dust from the Legionnaires' passing hung in the air far down the road. She scanned the field, but saw no sign of Channah. Dropping the sickle in the grass, she cupped her hands around her mouth and shouted, "Channah!"

She listened for a few moments, then called again.

"Over here," a tiny voice answered. "Have the soldiers gone?"

"Yes." Rivkah swiveled her head. "Where are you?"

"In the brambles."

Rivkah walked over to the wall of thorny vines. "Channah?"

"How are the sheep?"

"They'll be fine." Rivkah peered into the tangle of branches. "How did you get in there?"

"I burrowed in from the back. Fear gives you amazing powers."

"Well, the soldiers are gone. You can come out now."

"I can't. The branches closed behind me." Channah sounded near tears. "I'm trapped."

"Stay where you are, I brought the sickle." Rivkah attacked the vines with slashing strokes, sending leaves and branches flying.

"How did you happen to have the sickle?" Channah asked when she crawled out the opening her mother hacked in the brambles.

Rivkah shrugged. "It was handy."

They gathered the sheep and started back to the house. A short time later Rivkah noticed Shemu'el's wobbling silhouette rising over the brow of the hill. Leaving Channah around the bend with the sheep, she rushed ahead to meet him.

Her heart went out to him as he limped toward her, grim-faced and scowling. Parts of his face and beard were ghostly white. His clothes were covered with yellow dust from falling on the road. He'd given up trying to walk and resorted to dragging the foot of his bad leg along in the dirt like a stubborn donkey that refused to be led.

Rivkah ran to meet him. "What are you doing here?"

Shemu'el patted the club tied at his waist. "I came to help you and Channah." He scanned the fields. "How is she?"

"What about your cast?"

His eyes narrowed. "I took it off. Where are Channah and the sheep?"

"Your cast should have remained on at least another week. Why didn't you wait at the house?"

The veins in Shemu'el's forehead bulged when he frowned. "You and Channah needed my protection."

Rivkah ran her eyes over him, surveying his disheveled appearance. White dust puffed out of his beard when she touched his cheek. "Did you stick your head in the flour bin?"

He refused to meet her eyes. "It's plaster dust from the cast. I tripped the first time I tried to stand up," he said, gritting his teeth. His eyes were full of masculine defiance.

She struggled to contain her pity, knowing it was the last thing he wanted. "More than once based on the way you look."

Shemu'el grabbed her arms. "Forget about me. What matters is Channah. Where—" He stopped in mid-sentence as Channah and the sheep rounded the bend.

"She is fine," Rivkah whispered, "And so am I." Seeing the state on his cloak, she wondered how many times he'd tumbled to the ground, but knew better than to ask. "Does it hurt when you walk?"

"Just a little." He moved his foot in the dirt and, despite his best efforts, winced in pain.

Rivkah threw an arm around him and kissed his dusty cheek. "Rest your arm across my shoulder so we can get you back home where you belong."

# ~ 3 ~

*"Why do you seek the living among the dead?
Remember how he told you, while still in Galilee, that
the Son of Man must...be crucified, and on the third
day rise."*

— Luke 24:5-6

## Jerusalem, several days later—

Someone called Rivkah's name from across the marketplace. She turned and saw Miryam rushing toward her with open arms.

"It is good to see you, my friend." Miryam reached to hug her. "How have you been?"

Rivkah took a step back, resisting her embrace. When their eyes met, Rivkah looked away.

Miryam touched her coarse gown. "You are wearing sackcloth."

"And you are not."

"I do not understand. Has someone died?"

"Has someone died?" Rivkah struggled to control her rising anger. "Yes, someone died. Your son! Look at you. You wear a fresh tunic while I am dressed in sackcloth. I have ashes sprinkled on my head. You have washed your hair and anointed it with oil. Each night since his crucifixion I have recited Torah verses on Yeshua's behalf. Why do I, merely his friend, honor the 30 days of *Shloshim* while you, his mother, have ceased mourning?"

"It is not as you imagine," Miryam said. "After they placed Yeshua in the tomb I stumbled home grief stricken. Friends brought me the *se'udat habra'ah* and I ate my bread and eggs of consolation alone in the darkness. Though it was *Pesach*, a time when mourning is prohibited, I sat on a stool in my room and wept for three days."

"And then what?"

Miryam snatched Rivkah into her arms and kissed her cheek. "And then my room was suddenly filled with light and

Yeshua stood before me."

Rivkah began to tremble. "His ghost visited you? How can this be?"

Joyful tears sparkled in Miryam's eyes. She shook her head. "It was no ghost, my friend. Yeshua lives. His Father in heaven raised him up from the tomb just as he predicted. I held him in my arms. He told me not to mourn, but to rejoice."

A shiver passed through Rivkah. She experienced the same unexpected surge of hope she'd felt the first day of the week after Yeshua's crucifixion. She and her son, Yaakov, were on the road home from Jerusalem and she had noticed the fields filled with lilies.

"So the feeling I had on the road is true. His death was not the end of all that we hoped for." She lowered her eyes. "I feel so foolish dressed this way."

"Nonsense. You did not know. Now you do." Miryam caught her by the hand and pulled Rivkah away from the stand. "This fruit will still be here when you return. Come home with me. I have so much to tell you."

She tugged Rivkah through a confusing labyrinth of streets. Leaving the stands of fruits and vegetables behind, they passed through the market of wool buyers and sellers of cloth. Turning one corner and then another, they eventually entered the bazaar of the fishmongers.

"This way." Miryam led her into the front portion of a two-story stone building.

A shipment had just arrived and they were forced to step around workmen unloading barrels from a cart parked beside the shop's open door. The men hoisted the heavy containers onto their backs and weaved between customers to complete their delivery. After stacking the barrels of dried fish on the shop's wooden floor, they returned to the cart for more.

Miryam led her toward the back of the shop. They wove through a maze of merchandise, passing crates of spicy fish sauces from Rome and Alexandria and baskets of fish from the Great Sea. On the way, she paused to speak to some clerks sorting fresh fish.

As they spoke, the man pulled another wiggling fish out of a large clay jar and inspected it. Satisfied, he passed it to the man beside him who opened it with a quick slice of his knife and gutted it. The third man stuffed the fish with damp moss, wrapped it in grape leaves, and packed it.

"Fresh fish?" Rivkah asked. "Here in Jerusalem?"

A man's deep voice chuckled behind her. "Nothing but the best at Zebedee's Fish Market."

She watched as the intense young man stepped around her to check the last fish the man placed in the basket.

He shook his head. "This will never do." He quickly replaced it with a larger one. "How many times have I told you, nothing but the pick of the catch for the High Priest's household?" He brought his hands together in a loud clap. "Hurry! His servants are waiting. Caiaphas has a banquet planned for this evening."

The man's expression softened when his eyes returned to the women. "Imma Miryam, how was your trip to the market?" He rested an arm on her shoulder and bent to kiss her cheek as any son would do. "You found many bargains, I hope." A spark of recognition flashed in his eyes. "And who is this with you?"

"You remember Rivkah, wife of Shemu'el. She was at Golgotha the day they crucified Yeshua." Miryam turned. "Rivkah, this is Yohan bar Zebedee, my new son and benefactor."

"Oh, and about the fish," Yohan said. "During the cooler months fishermen at Jericho transfer their catch into jars of cold water. Before dawn these fish, fresh from the Jordan River, are loaded onto wagons and rushed through mountain passes to Jerusalem where they command a premium. But in this heat they won't last forever."

Grinning, he turned to help the men.

Miryam led Rivkah out a side exit to a stairway. "Up here," she whispered. "This is where I live now."

Leaving the hustle and bustle of the shop behind, the two women climbed the narrow stairway. They entered a simple loft with whitewashed walls and pine floor. It had a small sitting room and tidy kitchen in front and two bedrooms in the back.

Yohan's deep voice resonated through the floorboards as he directed the workmen in the shop below.

"Who is this young man who called you mother, the one you introduced as your son?"

"Yohan was Yeshua's loyal disciple and most beloved friend. Both he and his older brother, Yaakov, were with him from the very beginning. While he hung from the cross he charged him with my care."

Rivkah glanced around the plain room. "Are all your needs met?"

"I am well cared for." Miryam chuckled. "One thing we never lack is fish. Although I must confess the smells one encounters living above a fish market differ greatly from the sweet perfume of wood shavings."

"Has Yeshua visited others as well?"

"Oh, yes. Many of those who loved him. He appeared to Miriam from Magdala when she went to the tomb on the morning after *Shabbat*. And to his disciples, of course, a number of times...both here in Jerusalem and in Galilee."

She motioned Rivkah into a seat and offered her dried fruit from a pottery plate. "He appeared to others along the road to Emmaus." She sighed with satisfaction. "The list grows and grows."

"Where do you think this will lead?"

Miryam shook her head. "I do not know what God has planned for us. Those who knew Yeshua are ecstatic, yet terribly afraid. None of us knows what to expect from one day to the next."

She rocked from side to side, crossed her arms and hugged herself. "But my son lives. I held him in my arms and kissed his cheek just as when he was a young man. For now, nothing else matters."

"Where are his disciples now?"

"They fear the Great Sanhedrin will order their arrest. When they tired of cringing behind bolted doors and creeping through dark alleyways, they left Jerusalem and scattered.

"Yohan, of course, remained behind because of me and his

father's business. His older brother, Yaakov, returned to Capernaum to help their father, Zebedee. Andrew and Simon have gone back to their nets as well. Mattithayu also returned to Capernaum, not to fish, but to write."

"He is a scribe?"

"No. He was a tax collector before Yeshua called him to be a disciple. He has begun collecting all of Yeshua's sayings on a scroll. When he finishes, Mattithayu says it can be copied and distributed to keep the memory of those teachings alive."

Miryam stared away into the distance. "You are correct; our story is far from over. Yeshua promised to send a Comforter...a Counselor who would teach us all things."

"Who will this Counselor be? How will we recognize him?"

"No one knows. All we can do is wait and wonder. In my heart, I feel we should not be dispersed as we are now. We draw strength from each other. I am hoping that during the pilgrim feast of Pentecost his disciples will return to Jerusalem so we can again gather as a group."

## ~ 4 ~

*"I am a Jew, born at Tarsus in Cilicia, but brought up in this city at the feet of Gamali'el, educated according to the strict manner of the law of our fathers..."*

— Acts of the Apostles 22:3

Sweat beaded on the young man's forehead as he raced through Jerusalem's crowded streets. Down the hill he ran, robes billowing as he wove in and out between foot traffic and plodding donkeys.

Startled passersby slowed to watch and wonder. Some imagined him a criminal fleeing a crime. Others merely shook their heads and chuckled. They'd seen this handsome stranger make similar dashes in the past.

*Pesach* had come and gone and, as the month of Nisan drew to a close, a calming lull settled over Jerusalem. The crush of Passover pilgrims had vacated the surrounding hillsides and headed home. Shopkeepers and businessmen, having just completed their most lucrative selling season, happily counted their profits.

Things felt normal again and the city acknowledged it with a collective sigh of relief. Now the merchants busied themselves replenishing their inventory in anticipation of the influx of worshippers at the next pilgrim feast, Pentecost.

The ruling elite also noted the change and congratulated themselves. "Watch and wait," Caiaphas, the High Priest, had counseled. "Time heals all wounds."

And, just as he predicted, events of the recent *Pesach* gradually receded into the background as the day-to-day necessity of earning a living replaced the turmoil that accompanied Yeshua's crucifixion.

But this particular young man knew how mistaken Caiaphas was. This comforting period of normalcy was only the calm before the storm. Soon, very soon, Jerusalem's foundation would be shaken to the core. Rocked until the city split apart.

If, what he had heard proved true.

The street on which Stefanos ran bordered the city's aqueduct where late winter rains flowed fast and deep. He gazed up at Herod's Temple. A wonder of the Roman world, its white Melekeh limestone walls sparkled in the morning sun.

When Stefanos reached the base of the hill, he slowed long enough to gulp in a few breaths and mop his damp forehead. Then he joined the crowd on the broad north-south walkway leading to the Temple. Rows of wooden stands, packed tightly together and shaded by faded awnings, lined both sides of the concourse. On his left, the Temple Mount's Western Wall towered like a sheer cliff.

Stefanos passed under the eighty-foot arches supporting the upper walkways and hurried through the bazaar. He ignored the merchant's pleas to stop and examine their merchandise.

*Let the pilgrims buy their overpriced souvenirs*, he thought, with a dismissive glance. No one but a pilgrim would be foolish enough to patronize the swindlers who rented space from the Temple aristocracy.

The crowd in front of him came to an abrupt halt. Catcalls and frustrated shouts echoed off the surrounding walls.

Stefanos ground his teeth and clenched his fists. He was already late and had no time for this. Taller than most, he rose to his tiptoes and peered over the crowd.

Ahead, a distraught woman stood in the midst of the angry throng fingering a tattered cloth purse which had sprung a leak. Her simple clothing labeled her a country dweller.

And a poor one at that, Stefanos noted.

Two children crawled on the ground around her, groping between people's feet to retrieve the coins that spilled from their mother's purse.

Stefanos forced his way into the crowd, elbowing people aside. "Make way. Make way, make way."

A rolling *denarius* wobbled to a stop at his feet just as he reached the tiny circle of pavement surrounding the woman.

An unkempt man in a dirty cloak saw it at the same time.

Grinning at his good fortune, he leaped for the silver coin.

Stefanos stepped on the man's hand, pinning his fingers to the ground.

Grimacing in pain, the man muttered curses.

Stefanos eased his sandal back.

The man scooped the coin up and clutched it to his chest. "It's mine. I saw it first."

Stefanos grabbed the man's wrist and pried his fingers open. "It's hers and you know it."

He snatched the coin out of the man's sweaty palm. Then, ignoring his angry glare, Stefanos stepped to the front of the crowd and raised his arms. "Give the children room."

At his command, the crowd took two steps back. The children scurried about easily collecting the spilled coins. Several people bent to help them and the children returned to their mother with happy faces.

When Stephanos lowered his arms the crowd surged past like water released from a dam. He rested a hand on the woman's shoulder. "Over here." He guided her to a shady spot beside the Temple wall.

She stammered her thanks, then stared down at her cloth purse in dismay. Two fingers poked through a gaping hole in one of its many patches. The children, their hands folded over the precious coins they'd gathered, watched in silence.

Stefanos untied the tooled leather pouch he wore at his waist and handed it to her. "Use this."

Coins jingled inside the purse when she took it from him. The woman rocked the expensive purse in her hand and looked up at him with questioning eyes. "But your money is still in it."

"Take it with my blessing, little mother." The silver denarius sparkled in the sun when he held it out to her. "And this, I believe, is yours as well."

She opened her new purse wide. The children giggled as they dumped their treasure in. When she turned to thank him, her benefactor had already melted into the crowd.

Myriad conversations buzzed around him. Words and phrases in multiple languages reverberated off the cool stone wall, blending into gibberish.

Stefanos climbed the stairway to the Temple's upper level. He cared nothing for other's conversations. More pressing things weighed upon his mind.

Unbelievable things.

He'd overstayed his time with Yohan Marcus and risked being late for class. He knew he should have been concerned, but strangely enough he was not. After their meeting, class no longer held the same important as it once had.

All entrances to the Temple emptied into the Court of the Gentiles, forcing every visitor to cross it. Stefanos stepped out of the stairwell and into the courtyard. Far to his left a gray ribbon of smoke rose from the place of sacrifice into the cloudless sky.

Knots of pilgrims, drawn to Jerusalem from the Empire's distant provinces, paused to spin in awestruck circles as they gawked at the Temple's magnificence.

Breaking into a run, Stefanos crossed the wide esplanade with long strides. His mind remained fixed on the strange tale Yohan Marcus had told him earlier that morning.

Running violated protocol and he risked detention by the Temple Guard as a rabble-rouser, but the morning's delays left him no choice. It was either run or arrive late for class. He moved through the crowd mumbling apologies.

After crossing the Court of the Gentiles, Stefanos took the steps two at a time and rushed along Solomon's Portico toward a cluster of students gathered for the day's lesson. His teacher, the esteemed Rabbi Gamali'el, stood to one side tall and austere.

Stefanos slowed to a walk and adjusted his robes. After taking several deep, cleansing breaths, he ran a smoothing hand over his chestnut-colored beard. He stopped before the teacher, bowed slightly, and placed his hands on Gamali'el's shoulders. Then, as custom dictated, the disciple leaned forward and kissed his master's cheek.

Still bent forward, Stefanos whispered, "Rabbi, I must speak with you about a matter of extreme importance."

Despite the urgency in the young man's voice, the older man's placid demeanor remained unaffected. "After the examination, Stefanos. Lessons first, then discussion."

"After the examination then," he said, fixing the appointment.

Taking a seat on the stone walkway beside his friend, Yosef Barnabus, Stefanos swept his cloak around him and spun to the ground cross-legged. Like Stefanos, both Yohan Marcus and his cousin, Yosef Barnabus, were Hellenistic Jews. They belonged to the *Diaspora*, Jews dispersed to the four corners of the world who had come back to Jerusalem to live, work or study.

Stefanos nodded a quick greeting to Barnabus, and leaned close. "I have something to tell you." He winked. "You will not believe it when I do."

Conversation ceased when Gamali'el stepped into their midst.

"*Shalom Aleichem*, my disciples. Today my commentary shall be on the upcoming *Shavo'ut*, the Feast of Weeks, or Pentecost, as it is often called." The old man smiled. "And, as usual, following that we shall have our weekly examination."

The young men surrounding the rabbi were divided evenly, half Hebrews and half Hellenists. The Hebrews, all born and raised in the land of Israel, sat in a group on his right. They were the sons of wealthy merchants and influential priests. Their father's wealth, influence, or both, purchased them the privilege of studying at the feet of the esteemed Gamali'el, Head of the School of Hillel and *Nasi* of the Great Sanhedrin.

The Hellenists sat on Gamali'el's left. Like Stefanos, these Greek-speaking Jews came from far and wide. The only exception was Sha'oul of Tarsus, the son of a Cilician tentmaker, who insisted on sitting with the Hebrews even though everyone knew he did not belong there.

A keen observer of persons, Stefanos enjoyed watching his teacher conduct the weekly examinations. He smiled as the thin, gray-haired rabbi swirled in circles and lobbed questions at his students. He moved around the group, hand darting out, finger pointing like an arrow, shooting questions like a Roman archer.

The longer he watched him work, the surer Stefanos became that these seemingly random choices were, in fact, not random at all. How else to explain the way each student received a question designed to test them to the maximum?

An ominous silence descended around him.

Stefanos glanced up. A quiver of panic clawed at his stomach when his eyes met Gamali'el's.

"Well, Stefanos, what say you?"

Stefanos lowered his head and stared into his lap. "Could you repeat the question, Rab?"

"Daydreaming again?"

"Praying, Rab. Always praying."

His teacher waited until the laughter subsided then repeated the question. "Is the child of an unmarried woman always considered a *mamzer*?"

"It cannot be determined if the child is a mixling without knowing who fathered it." Stefanos breathed a silent sigh of relief. Quick thinking had saved him once again.

"On whose authority do you make such a statement?"

Like bricks in a wall, Pharisaism consisted of a series of carefully crafted opinions, each supported by the others which preceded it. Only the most esteemed rabbis, such as Gamali'el, dared break precedent with the past.

"Your own, Rab. Both you and Rabbi Eliezer ruled that if the mother names the father, her testimony is sufficient proof. And only by knowing the lineage of both parents can the child's caste be determined."

"Truly spoken."

Stefanos glanced across the circle of students and locked eyes with Sha'oul. Rather than seeing the empathy of one student for another, it surprised him to see a look of delight on the young man's face.

Clearly, Sha'oul had enjoyed watching him struggle.

The thought made Stefanos' pulse pound, but he swallowed his anger. He had more important things on his mind.

## ~ 5 ~

*"When the day of Pentecost had come, they were all together in one place. And suddenly a sound came from heaven like the rush of a mighty wind..."*
— Acts of the Apostles 2:1-2

The hope Miryam expressed to Rivkah became a reality. Fifty days after the *Pesach*, all of the Twelve returned to Jerusalem to celebrate *Shav'out*, or Pentecost. The Twelve, along with the women and some of Yeshua's other disciples, gathered in the upper room above Aristopolus and Miryam's home where they'd eaten a last supper with their Master. Early on the first morning of the feast the Holy Spirit descended upon them as fire and wind.

Inspired, Simon preached the word and 3,000 believed that first day. After the feast ended pilgrims from all over the Roman world returned to their home cities carrying the good news of Yeshua's resurrection with them.

The number of believers in Jerusalem increased greatly. So much so that in a short while the upper room could no longer accommodate all who came to worship. Aristopolus' neighbors began to complain about the crowds. Faced with this unexpected problem, the Twelve met to seek a resolution.

"Why must we have a meeting place? We can go to the Temple as a group and worship together there," Andrew said.

"We are no longer welcome at the Temple since the day I healed the crippled beggar, Abijah," Simon replied. "Yohan and I were hauled before the Great Sanhedrin where Caiaphas threatened us for preaching Yeshua's name."

"We do not need this Temple, or any temple," Thomas said. "Yeshua told the Samaritan woman at Jacob's well a time was coming when his Father would not be worshipped on the mountain or in the Temple, but in spirit and truth."

Simon nodded in agreement. "Truly such a time has come. Our presence in Jerusalem is driving a wedge. Being neither fish nor fowl, we are not welcome in the Temple or at any of the synagogues. Some of the merchants treat our people as if they were Gentiles and refuse to conduct business with them."

Netan'el bar Tolmai combed his fingers through his curly black hair as he gathered his thoughts. "We need to find a place where Yeshua's followers can feel at home. Where we can be among people of like mind. A place where we can celebrate the breaking of the bread as the Master commanded us to do."

"A synagogue is what we need," Mattithayu said. He smacked the flat of his hand onto the table. "There is our answer; we need to form a new synagogue here in Jerusalem." He glanced around the room at their skeptical faces. "Why not? We have the necessary funds."

He spun in his seat to face the head of the table. "Simon, did you not tell us a number of believers have deposited funds with you for the Lord's work?"

"Well, yes they have, but how do we know this is the best use of those funds?"

Yohan, the youngest among them, glanced around the table. "We have more than the minimum needed for the *minyan*. Each man here qualifies as an elder of the synagogue's ruling body."

"That is all well and good for now, but the Master told us to go to the ends of the earth preaching his message," Yohan's older brother, Yaakov, said. "What happens when none of us remain to administer things?"

"It is not as if we had an ownership interest," Simon replied. "The building would no more belong to us than the movement itself. There are no masters here, only servants. Everything ultimately belongs to the Lord. When the time comes for us to leave, we can appoint others to act in our stead."

The only thing required to form a synagogue was the desire and a common interest. The more the men talked, the more their enthusiasm grew.

"Why shouldn't we have our own synagogue?" Thomas asked. "Everyone else does. Every neighborhood has a convenient meeting place close to home."

"Each ethnic group has its synagogue," Yohan said. "Why

the Hellenists have several where they read the Septaguint, the Greek translation of the Hebrew Scriptures."

"The craft guilds have them as well," Netan'el said. "Look around you. Potters, Millers, Carpenters, Stonecutters, Tentmakers, and Sellers of Cloth, Wine and Oil all have places of worship within their section of the working city. Even former slaves have a place to gather, the Synagogue of the Freedman."

"We are not the only outcasts in the city," another added. "Workmen whom polite society barely tolerates have the Synagogue of the Tanners, the Butchers and the Fullers. Why not us?"

When everyone had their say, Simon led them in prayer. Afterwards, they sat quietly awaiting the Lord's direction. When the time came to vote, the idea of forming a synagogue passed unanimously.

Simon rose and circled the table. He stopped beside Yaakov, one of the Lord's brethren, and rested a big hand on his shoulder.

"As we are called away to other parts of the world, one of our group must remain behind to shepherd the believers in Jerusalem. I nominate Yaakov here to be that person, the leader of the synagogue of Rabban Yeshua *HaMashiach*."

The others, recognizing Simon's selection as an inspired one, responded enthusiastically. Who better to lead the Jerusalem believers? Everyone in Jerusalem, even those who refused to recognize Yeshua as the *Mashiach*, acknowledged Yaakov's dedication to the Law. How could they not? He spent hours each day at the Temple kneeling in prayer.

They all crowded around Jerusalem's first leader and congratulated him.

The search for a suitable location began the next day. They settled on a building in the lower city near the pinnacle of the Temple. Mattithayu, the one with the greatest financial acumen, negotiated the transaction and the group set about adapting it to their needs. Now, like fifty or so other groups within the holy city, The Way of Yeshua had its own meeting place.

## ~ 6 ~

The mood among the students at the School of Hillel lightened once Gamali'el's examination ended. The midday sun warmed the breeze as the students gathered their belongings and broke into small groups.

"I visited your cousin, Yohan Marcus, this morning," Stefanos told Barnabus. "He introduced me to Yohan bar Zebedee from Capernaum."

Barnabus nodded. "The fish merchant's son. I know him. He and his older brother, Yaakov, were disciples of Yeshua from Nazareth."

Rabbi Gamali'el waited a few feet away.

Leaving his friend's side, Stefanos hurried over to his teacher. "Rabbi, may I speak with you privately?"

Gamali'el pointed to a shady spot under the colonnade. "Over there."

Sunlight filtered through the stoa's lathing casting dark bars of shadow around them as they conversed in hushed tones. "Are you familiar with Yeshua...the Nazarene...the one whom they crucified during *Pesach*?"

His teacher did not answer right away. Learned rabbis such as Gamali'el seldom attacked a question straight on and never without first considering its subtle implications.

"Am I not the *Nasi*? How could the leader of the Great Sanhedrin be unaware of these events?"

"I have a friend," Stefanos paused for a moment, nibbling his lip. "A friend of a friend, actually. This person said Yeshua's body is no longer in the grave. He claims he has risen from the dead, that he is the long awaited *Mashiach*. Is such a thing possible?"

"Absolutely not!" Sha'oul shouted. "Everyone knows his disciples bribed the guards and stole the body."

Neither Stefanos nor Gamali'el had noticed the little man slip up behind them.

Stefanos whirled to face him. "How could you possibly

know that? Your words are nothing but malicious gossip started by..."

He left the thought unfinished, preferring not to name names. Instead, he turned his focus on the short man in front of him. "Or are you saying you do not believe in a resurrection?"

"Of course the dead shall rise again." Sha'oul swung his arms in a wide circle. "The prophets foretold it; only a fool would deny the resurrection. What do you take me for, an unbelieving Sadducee?"

Hands on his hips, Stefanos glared down at him. "I take you for someone who intrudes into private conversations when you are not invited."

"You and I both know this has nothing to do with the dead rising. All this talk about Yeshua being the *Mashiach* is dangerous." Sha'oul's eyes shifted to their teacher then back to Stefanos. "That Nazerene was an itinerant...a nobody." He motioned toward Gamali'el with a broad smile. "His stature could never approach that of our esteemed teacher. Besides, everyone knows, in addition to being a great rabbi, the *Mashiach* will also be a great warrior. Yeshua was neither."

Sha'oul hunched forward and wagged his finger in Stefanos' face. "Be wary, brother, you walk a fine line between truth and blasphemy."

Stefanos suppressed a chuckle. Sha'oul's actions reminded him of the old hag who chided him for throwing apples when he was a boy.

"Is not all of the *Halakhah* open to interpretation?" Stefanos looked to their teacher for concurrence.

"Of course men can discuss the laws," Gamali'el said softly. "Reasonable men can discuss all topics."

"Anyone who proclaims Yeshua to be the Son of God is not reasonable," Sha'oul shouted. "You blaspheme!" He rent his cloak. "I will send you to *Sheol* myself so the angels can pitch you into the lake of unquenchable fire. There you will burn with the rest of the blasphemers and idolaters, unbelievers, adulterers, procurers, murderers and thieves."

Eyes bright with righteous indignation, Sha'oul gave a

mighty shout and launched himself at Stefanos. He charged like a runaway bull. Head down and legs churning, Sha'oul flew past Gamali'el and drove his head into Stefanos' stomach.

Caught unprepared, Stefanos doubled over and fell backwards.

Sha'oul's momentum sent them both sprawling across the steps. They bounced and rolled, swinging at each other as they tumbled.

Once they rolled to a stop, Stefanos easily shoved his smaller assailant aside. He rose and dusted himself off. "Have you lost your mind?"

Sha'oul answered by leaping up from the pavement and taking a wild swing at him.

Stefanos, who'd trained in the gymnasiums of Alexandria, ducked the blow and landed a solid punch of his own.

Sha'oul's head snapped back. His eyes widened and he yelped in pain. Bringing a hand to his face, he staggered back and collapsed in a heap. When he raised his head, blood dribbled between his fingers.

"Satisfied?" Stefanos asked, frowning down at him.

Sha'oul remained on the ground, dusty and bedraggled, using his torn cloak to dab away the blood dripping from his nose and lip.

"Why must you harass observant Jews? If you are so anxious to fight, join the *Cananeans* and fight the Romans."

"Ha! Me a Zealot? Only in your dreams. You would enjoy seeing me up on a cross like that *sheker*, Yeshua, wouldn't you?"

"How could you, of all people, possibly know whether Yeshua was a false *Mashiach*, or not?"

Ignoring his injury, Sha'oul leaped to his feet and curled his hands into fists.

The two men circled each other. With fists raised and jaws set, they prepared to do battle once more.

Barnabus watched and shook his head in dismay. Big and brawny, he stepped between the two men and shoved them apart. Their confrontation ended as quickly as it began.

Gamali'el marched over and frowned at them both. "I

cannot believe you are fighting within sight of the house of God. You bring shame upon all who know you. Another incident like this and someone else will take your place in the School of Hillel."

Neither man dared look at the rabbi. Grabbing his cloak with both hands, Sha'oul tugged it out of Barnabus' grip and stormed away. He paused at the top of the walkway and glanced back. He held Stefanos' gaze for a moment then turned and left.

Barnabus, Gamali'el and Stefanos stood in a semi-circle, watching him go.

Gamali'el's mouth wrinkled into a frown as the short, bandy legged man disappeared from view. He sighed. "Many times I have compared my students to fish."

"Fish, Rab?"

He chuckled. "Yes, fish. The nets come up from the depths writhing with all manner of life. The first thing a fisherman must do is sort his catch. Some are unclean and are thrown away. Others are inedible; they discard these as well. Some have little value and are barely tolerated. And, lastly, there are the few... those of great worth that one rejoices to find in his net."

Gamali'el shook his head. "Sha'oul shows great promise, but some days I think it would be best for everyone if he were pitched back into the sea from whence he came."

He took a step closer and touched Stefanos' arm. "That man is dangerous. Heed my warning and keep your tongue in check around him." He adjusted the blue-edged *tallit* on his shoulders and smoothed his gray beard. "He may criticize the beliefs of the Sadducees, but Sha'oul is firmly in Caiaphas' grasp."

He paused, giving them a moment to digest his words. "It is hardly a secret that the little man from Tarsus harbors great ambitions."

Barnabus laughed. "His will be long and difficult climb to power. Not only is he not a member of the Jerusalem establishment, but he's a Binyamite as well. Sha'oul can never become a priest."

"Truly spoken,' Gamali'el said. "So he seeks an alternate path to power. He believes he has found it in the Great Sanhedrin."

Both men's eyes widened.

"Sha'oul attends every public meeting," Gamali'el continued. "He sits on the back bench, observing and taking notes. No doubt imagining the day when his talents are known and appreciated. The day when he is asked to become a member of the council."

"Perhaps he even dreams of someday being *Nasi*," Stefanos said.

"He very well may. Meanwhile, never discuss Yeshua of Nazareth in his presence again. Anything spoken around Sha'oul will certainly find its way to the High Priest's ear."

He glanced around. Lowering his voice to a tight whisper, Gamali'el said, "I have more to say about Yeshua, but not here. Better we meet in private, far from Sha'oul's prying eyes and curious ears."

## ~ 7 ~

*"Therefore go and make disciples of all nations, baptizing them in the name of the Father and of the Son and of the Holy Spirit..."*

— Matthew 28:19

Shemu'el called from the road.

Grabbing her veil, Rivkah swept it over her head and ran to the door wiping her hands on her apron.

Two strangers stood beside him. A tall, stocky man in a traveling robe with the large hands and weathered complexion of someone accustomed to working outdoors and a petite woman with a pleasant smile.

"Come quickly, my dove. We have guests, important guests." Shemu'el rested his hand on the man's muscular shoulder as if they were old friends. "This is Andrew. He came looking for you."

"Looking for...me?" Rivkah swallowed hard and started toward them.

The stranger met her halfway and grasped her shaking fingers. Her hand disappeared in his when he closed the other over hers. She detected no lust in his eyes when he looked at her, only brotherly love.

"It is good to meet you, Rivkah. Your friend, Miryam, the Lord's mother, insisted I come see you."

"Who are you?"

"One of Yeshua's disciples. My brother, Simon and I spent our lives fishing Lake Gennersaret. Then one day, while we were mending our nets, a stranger, a traveling Rabbi, called us to follow him. He said instead of us being fishermen, he would turn us into *fishers of men.*" He chuckled. "We were so shocked, neither of us bothered to ask what he meant."

"And this Rabbi was Yeshua?"

"Yes." Reaching back, he took the woman's hand and brought her forward. "This is my wife, Tabitha. We came to tell you and the people of your settlement the good news."

After supper everyone gathered at the settlement's meeting site to hear Andrew speak. They took their places as usual, men in the front and the women and children off to one side.

Andrew took one look and shook his head. "This will never do." He began waving people into new places. "There should be no divisions among the children of God. Come together by family groups. Wives, join your husbands; youngsters, follow your mothers."

Rivkah sat with her father on one side and Shemu'el on the other. Their sons, Yo'el, Yaakov and Yudah rested in front of them. Yo'el's wife, Tzipporah, swept her cloak around her and dropped down beside him. Channah sat at Rivkah's feet with Yo'el and Tzipporah's son, baby Shemu'el, in her arms. Imma Sarit, Shemu'el's mother, sat on his left flanked by his brothers, their wives and children.

Rivkah glanced around at her family, friends and neighbors. It felt strange to be sitting with the men. Strange, yet natural. Maybe the way it was meant to be.

It thrilled this community of shepherds to hear Andrew say Yeshua had called himself *The Good Shepherd*. From its very foundation Israel had been a nation of shepherds. Over and over again, God spoke through the prophets of his desire to be a shepherd to his people.

When the fledgling nation of Israel left Canaan and migrated to Egypt, they were a nation of sheep herders. But the Egyptians were farmers, growers of crops who depended on the annual cycles of the Nile River for their sustenance. They esteemed farming and looked down upon animal husbandry.

Over generations the Egyptian way of thinking infiltrated the Israelites. By the time of Moshe, people who once considered sheep herding a noble occupation now scorned shepherds. Even David, a man after God's own heart, a shepherd boy himself and Israel's greatest king, could not reverse this prejudice.

Although Yeshua spoke of many occupations in his parables, he never ascribed any to himself except that of a shepherd.

The following day, Andrew spent the afternoon telling them about the things Yeshua said and did. As evening came he invited all who wanted to join the Way of Yeshua to gather early the next morning at a wide spot in the creek where the water pooled. He chose this location because they always tried to use flowing, that is living, water for baptisms.

Shemu'el and Rivkah, their family, and others from the settlement who chose to commit to The Way of Rabban Yeshua, arrived carrying towels. The women also brought hair ribbons and combs to prepare themselves after their baptism.

Early morning fog hung over the meadows and frogs croaked in the rushes.

"This rite of baptism feels very familiar," Tzipporah said as they waited.

"Like going to the *mikvah* each month after our time of *niddah*?" Channah suggested.

"With one difference. Unlike the *mikvah*, which temporarily removes uncleanliness and must be repeated each month, the baptism of Yeshua cleanses you forever."

"Andrew said baptism marks us as one of Yeshua's own just as surely as the notches we place in the ears of our sheep," Channah said.

Leaning close, Rivkah whispered, "It's very much like a circumcision."

Channah turned to her open-mouthed. "A what?"

"Think about it. In baptism Yeshua provided us with an indelible mark available to all...boys and girls, men and women."

"Better this than the knife," Channah said with a shudder.

Accepting of the Way of Yeshua *HaMashiach* proved to be both simple and difficult. Instead of hundreds of rules and regulations, he left just two commands: Love the Lord your God with all your heart and mind and soul, and love your neighbor as yourself. Easy enough to say, but oh so difficult to do.

Andrew and Tabitha arrived with towels and broad smiles. He opened his arms to the group. "*Shalom Aleichem*. Welcome, my brothers and sisters."

They prayed and sang a Psalm, then Andrew began moving among them with a container of oil. He paused in front of Rivkah.

"May you always walk in the protection of the most High God." Taking one of her hands, he commanded, "Do the work of the Lord. Your hands are now his hands. May all whom you touch feel the love of Yeshua."

Wetting his thumb with the anointing oil, Andrew traced the immortal mark of Yeshua's cross on her forehead. He stared into her eyes. "Keep your mind and heart on the Lord Yeshua," he said softly. "Honor him with every thought and deed."

Andrew moved around the small group praying and anointing each man, woman and child. By the time he reached the last of the group the sunrise glowed red-orange along the eastern horizon. He gathered the men and boys, leading them over the hill and out of sight. The women and young children remained behind with Tabitha.

"When you step into the water, I will have some questions for you," Tabitha explained. "Each of you must answer for yourself. Mothers, you may answer for infants and young children if they are unable to."

Rivkah wore no jewelry other than her wedding ring, which she had never taken off since the day Shemu'el slipped it onto her finger. To encourage the others, she agreed to be the first one baptized. Shedding her clothing, she stepped into the cool water.

Tabitha gave her a reassuring smile. "Rivkah, do you renounce Satan and all his works?"

"I do."

"Do you believe in God, the Father Almighty?"

"I do."

"And do you believe in Yeshua, the only Son of the Father, who was conceived of the Spirit and rose from the dead?"

I do."

Placing her hand atop Rivkah's head, Tabitha eased her into the water. "I baptize you in the name of the Father and of the Son and of the Holy Spirit."

The world disappeared as Rivkah sank beneath the surface.

Tabitha held her there for an instant then released her hand.

Rivkah rose and blinked into the light. Rays of morning sun sparkled off of water droplets clinging to her eyelashes. She felt an unexpected sense of peace and inner content. Like arriving at your destination after a long journey.

Rivkah stepped onto the bank and quickly dried. After she dressed, she began helping with the children and holding infants as their mothers prepared for baptism. When Tabitha finished, the happy group sang Psalms as they retreated over the hill.

While Andrew baptized the men and boys the women kindled fires and prepared a celebratory meal.

After the men returned and everyone ate their fill, Andrew gathered a few loaves and a cup wine.

"For generations we Jews have celebrated the tradition of *Pesach*," he said.

Nods and affirmations arose from the newly-baptized believers.

"But now we have a new sacrifice and a new covenant. As the Lamb of God, Yeshua shed his blood so that all may live. Just as the lamb, after it is sacrificed, nourishes the believer, so too, Yeshua nourishes his followers with his flesh and blood in the sacramental form of bread and wine."

As Andrew consecrated the bread of the Lord's Supper, Tabitha lifted her hands to the sky and, in a clear soprano, led the group in Hosannas.

They ate the bread, then passed the cup from one to another so all might drink from it. Children received a sop of bread dipped in the wine.

Before Andrew and Tabitha left he laid hands on the new believers, bringing the Holy Spirit upon them.

Rivkah and her friends discovered being part of The Way of Rabban Yeshua gave women new freedom. Not that they no longer adhered to the Law. They did. And not that they no longer honored and respected their husbands. They continued doing that as well.

In his ministry Yeshua treated women in a new, freer way, giving them a dignity they never had before. To him women were independent beings whose ideas and contributions, though different, were equal to any of his male disciples.

This subtle sense of empowerment carried over into The Way. Whereas Judaism relegated women to a subsidiary role and automatically elevated men to the superior position, this was not always the case among Yeshua's followers. Women could, and did, participate fully in the community of believers.

## ~ 8 ~

"Be quick about it, Yudah. We do not have all day." Shemu'el pushed aside the window's hide covering and stared at the peaks along the eastern horizon. "The sun will be over the mountains soon."

Knowing the air would be chilly until the sun came up, Rivkah hurried down the path after them, fussing with their cloaks as they walked.

"Don't forget about your waterskin." She adjusted the bag's strap on Yudah's shoulder. "Be sure to drink enough water and make your father stop to rest. And I want both of you to eat the meal I put in your satchels. Half of the time your father gets so busy he forgets to eat."

She gave Shemu'el a nervous glance. "Are you certain you will be all right? Perhaps I should accompany you...just in case."

His condescending snort made her regret asking.

"I worry about your leg." Glancing over Shemu'el's shoulder, she watched red clouds creep across the morning sky. "I only want what's best."

"My leg has healed."

"Of course, but are you certain you can manage the long walk to Jerusalem and back? You have never gone such a distance since you broke your leg."

Shemu'el grasped his staff with both hands, extended his arms straight out, and did several deep knee bends. "See. Good as...No! better than new."

He grabbed hold of his youngest son's shoulder and gave the slim youngster a shake. "Do not fret. I have mighty Yudah along to assist me."

Without warning, Shemu'el released his son, dropped his staff, and threw his arms around Rivkah. She gasped when he pulled her against him and gave her a long, lingering kiss.

Yudah cleared his throat and stared at the ground. When his father continued holding his mother close, he tiptoed away to wait for him at the sheepfold.

Rivkah staggered when Shemu'el released her.

"And you worry," he said with a satisfied grin. Shemu'el gave her a quick peck on the check. "*Kol Tuv*, my dove. We shall be home for supper."

"May you also be well," she said as he left.

Shemu'el and Yudah followed a familiar route, one the boy knew well. Outside of Bethlehem, they stopped at the tollbooth to pay their livestock tax and road tolls. As always, Shemu'el dug in his purse for the coins and then for the next mile muttered about being taxed to death.

They'd left the settlement early hoping to get the sheep to the Temple before the sun reached its full height. They crested the last hill and gathered the sheep by the side of the road so they could rest after the long climb. Standing side by side, the two of them stared down on Jerusalem while the sheep milled around them nibbling grass still damp with dew.

As they walked, they watched the gold roof of the Temple sparkle in the morning light until it disappeared from view as they descended into the valley. The road from Bethlehem led to the south side of the city and their sheep went to the northeast side of the Temple, so they circled the city walls following the Hinnon Valley.

Shemu'el stationed Yudah at the head of the flock and he trailed behind, rounding up any stragglers. The road made a wide, sweeping curve past Herod's palace and then turned a sharp corner, leading them to Tower's Pool. They stopped again to rinse the dust of the road off their faces and water the sheep.

Refreshed, they continued north following the city wall. They crossed the road leading to Emmaus and passed the place of tombs.

Shemu'el pointed to a dark cave cut into the limestone hillside. The tomb's rock cover, big as a millstone, remained shoved aside over a year after the Resurrection. "There is the place where they buried Yeshua, our *Mashiach*."

Yudah stared into the gaping darkness of the open tomb with fear and wonder. Like his father, he bowed his head in respect as they passed Golgotha, the place of crucifixions.

"Not much further," Shemu'el said, as much to himself as to the boy. He had begun kneading the muscles of his right leg as they walked.

They followed a well-trod path around the high walls of Fortress Antonia. Far above them, a sentry in a knee-length, gray military tunic walked his rounds along the battlements. Yudah heard the man's hobnailed *caligulea* clack against the stone walkway and glanced up.

Sensing his stare, the soldier looked down at the boy. Their eyes met for instant before a frightened Yudah jerked his away. He walked on certain he could feel the soldier's gaze boring into his back, but afraid to turn and check.

"Look Abba," Yudah said.

He ran his fingers along the finely cut margin of the massive foundation stones supporting the wall beside them. Like every Jew, the Temple's splendor awed him each time he came. Far ahead, barely visible beyond many other shepherds and their lambs, were the Pools of Bethesda where the sheep were washed before they went to the buyers.

Shemu'el stepped into a small patch of shade next to the wall's foundation. Easing himself to the ground, he sighed and leaned back against the base of the Temple mount. "We can eat while we wait."

Yudah slid the bag off his shoulder and joined his father.

The two of them sat in the shade eating the meal Rivkah packed. Across the Kidron Valley, neat rows of olive trees marched up to the *gethsemane*, oil press, on the Mount of Olives. The tree's silvery leaves shimmered in the sunlight with every gust.

When their turn came, Yudah whistled the lambs forward and directed them into a temporary pen for inspection. Off to one side, Obadiah, the overseer, sat at his table, head down, recording each transaction. Shemu'el smiled as he studied the teetering stacks of clay tablets on the table where the old priest worked. It'd been this way as long as he could remember. Some things never changed, he thought.

"*Shalom Aleichem*, Obadiah," he called.

The old priest quit scratching notations on the papyrus in front of him and raised his gray head. He squinted at the smiling man with the staff for a moment before a look of recognition washed over his face.

"Shemu'el! *Aleichem Shalom.* I became so engrossed in my record-keeping that I did not see you come in." Obadiah waved at his assistant standing in the pen with Yudah and the sheep, halting the inspection.

Shemu'el gave him a confused look. "Is anything wrong?"

Obadiah came toward him shaking his head and waving away his concerns. "Merely a formality. Something new Caiaphas instituted."

Shemu'el felt the hairs on the back his neck prickle. "Something new, you say." He tried to keep his voice level, masking his rising apprehension.

Used to roomier pens at home, the crowded sheep began bleating in protest. Yudah moved among them patting and calming as he watched the old priest and his father confer.

"Have you heard the unbelievable rumors that have grown up around that Nazarene?"

Shemu'el rocked on his staff and flexed his right knee. "Yeshua, the prophet Caiaphas killed?"

"Caiaphas killed no one," Obadiah said indignantly. "You and I both know only the Romans crucify." The old man combed his fingers through his white beard and sighed. "I sometimes forget the everyday working man does not understand things as clearly as we do here at the Temple."

Shemu'el folded his arms across his chest. "Yes, I am sure things appear different from the inside."

"They do. They certainly do."

"I spend my days with the sheep, not in the marketplace, and they seldom have much gossip to share. Why don't you tell me about these rumors?"

Obadiah cleared his throat. "It has, uh, come to our attention that the man's disciples bribed the guards placed at his tomb and stole Yeshua's body."

Shemu'el rocked forward, nearly dropping his staff. "Stole the body, you say? Why would anyone do such a thing? Handling a corpse renders a person unclean."

Obadiah grinned. "I see you recognize our dilemma. His disciples now claim he rose from the dead. They preach that he was the *Mashiach*."

"Which, of course, could never be."

"Exactly."

Shemu'el nodded and stroked his beard. "I see your difficulty. It would be unacceptable for the High Priest to have killed Israel's *Mashiach*." He glanced at his not-yet-inspected sheep bleating in the pen and shrugged. "But all this is Caiaphas' problem, not mine. My concern is my sheep...and getting home for supper."

"True enough," the old priest said, "and Caiaphas has dealt with the problem. You understand, of course, that all sheep sacrificed in the Temple must be pure and unblemished."

"As mine are."

"Perhaps...perhaps not."

"Meaning?"

"Yeshua's disciples gather converts everywhere, even in the rural districts. The Temple cannot purchase sheep from *Meshichim Y'hudim*, they would be unfit for sacrifice."

"You're saying believers in *Mashiach* Yeshua can no longer bring their sheep to the Temple?"

"I knew you would understand. Caiaphas instituted this test so we do not unknowingly purchase sheep from *minim*, heretics." Obadiah tossed an arm around Shemu'el's shoulder and walked him toward the pen. "None of this presents a problem for a good Jew like yourself. I ask the questions. You answer, and all is well."

"Questions? What questions?"

Obadiah looked him in the eye. "Shemu'el bar Yo'el do you

follow the teachings of Yeshua of Nazareth? Are you a member of what is called The Way?"

Shemu'el drew his shoulders back and stood tall. "Yes. I know Yeshua to be the risen Son of the Most High God, the *Mashiach* promised to our forefathers over the ages."

The old priest gasped and leaped away as if he'd seen a snake. He stared at Shemu'el for a long moment then angrily shook his head. "Caiaphas was right; you people are everywhere." He pointed to the pen and shouted, "These lambs are unfit for sacrifice. The Temple will never purchase your sheep again. Take your animals and go."

"They force everyone selling sheep to take an oath," Shemu'el explained as he related the day's events to Rivkah.

"How did you reply?"

"How do you suppose? I could not deny Yeshua before men for material gain."

"But you returned without the sheep, where have they gone?"

"I sold them to one of the traders in the Jerusalem sheep market." Shemu'el's expression turned grim. "I am thankful you were not there to see it. It would  have broken your heart. Our lambs, so clean and healthy, mingled in a pen of worn out ewes whose teeth were mostly gone."

He crossed his arms and scowled. "They will surely fetch him a premium price."

"The way you say that must mean he paid you no premium."

"Premium? Ha! He paid me less than half what they were worth. He might as well have stolen them from us."

"Then why did you sell them to him?"

"What could I do, bring them home? The market for sheep has plummeted. Since the drought good pasture has been scarce and many shepherds are thinning their  herds. There  are already too many sheep in Jerusalem and now Caiaphas' program puts a further glut on the market."

"Where will the sheep go?" Rivkah asked.

"Where they always do, into people's stomachs. The lower prices will entice people who rarely taste meat to visit the butcher. Meanwhile the traders, knowing the Temple continues to turn people away, bid next to nothing. If I had not sold our sheep, there were others in line behind me who would have."

A puzzled expression settled onto Rivkah's face. "What a strange circumstance. Our world seems to be dividing into those who believe in Yeshua and those who do not."

"Reminiscent of the way the Temple separates the sheep from the goats." Shemu'el slapped the meager amount he received for the sheep onto the table. "Hard times are surely coming. Shop carefully. This is all we have."

## ~ 9 ~

*"Blessed are you when people revile you and persecute you and utter all kinds of evil against you falsely on my account."*

— Matthew 5:11

Several weeks after the incident at the Temple, Shemu'el went to the marketplace in Bethlehem. Since they no longer had a ready market for their lambs, he had turned to woodcarving in an attempt to earn a living. He took a number of beautiful bowls with him in hopes of selling them on market day. If that failed, he planned to trade them for needed supplies.

One of the village elders passed his little display and paused to look at the bowls. "Nice." He turned the bowl in his hands, running a finger over its delicate carving. "And very well done."

Shemu'el thanked him for the compliment. "I am sure your wife would love it."

"Perhaps." The man sat the bowl aside and reached for another. "Tell me, have any of those fanatics visited your settlement?" He held the bowl at arm's length, balancing it on his fingertips as he examined it in the light.

Shemu'el shook his head. "We have seen no Zealots."

"Zealots?" The man laughed. "Oh no, I meant the followers of the Nazarene preacher. We had two of them come by here several months ago, a man and his wife. They attended our synagogue and, as a visitor, we invited him to speak. He insulted our hospitality by claiming this Yeshua, the one whom they crucified, was the fulfillment of the prophecies, the *Mashiach*."

Shemu'el let the man examine his wares without comment.

The elder picked up another item. "Excellent workmanship. I had no idea you were a wood carver. I thought your family raised lambs for the Temple bazaar."

"The bottom has fallen out of the market."

"Has it? I heard the Temple pays the same price they always have." The man locked eyes with Shemu'el. "Am I correct in thinking you still sell to the Temple?"

"We once did."

The man tossed the bowl back at Shemu'el with a sneer. "As I suspected; you are one of them." He gave him an icy stare and spat at his feet. "Take your wares and leave, *Raca*. There is no place here for people like you. We do not tolerate *minim* and *meshunadim* among us. I will make certain no one purchases your bowls."

Shemu'el started to protest that he was neither a heretic nor apostate, but the man spun on his heel and left before he could say a word.

Rivkah rubbed the back of Shemu'el's neck while he complained about the unfair treatment he received in Bethlehem.

Channah looked up from her mending. "Maybe someone could mix a few of our lambs into their flock and sell them for us."

Her father gave her a wry look. "That would only work if we chop off their ears. Our mark is on every one of them."

"Perhaps we could enter into a partnership with someone in the settlement, all of the new lambs could carry their mark," Yaakov said.

"That is not a partnership, it is a scheme. Deceit is never a solution."

"But our cupboards are nearly bare." Channah glanced into the pantry at their meager stores. "We must do something or we will all starve."

"A man's ways are in full view of the Lord. Better we starve honestly, than prosper by trickery," Shemu'el said, ending the discussion.

"This edict of the High Priest seems so unfair," Rivkah whispered as they lay in bed that night. "No other sect in Judaism faces the discrimination we do."

"It is of no consequence, my dove. In troubled times such as these a man must follow his conscience." Shemu'el gave a frustrated sigh. "Channah is right about one thing, we cannot go on like this much longer."

Shafts of moonlight illuminated Rivkah's face. Shemu'el brushed her hair aside and kissed her forehead. She nestled into his embrace. Resting her head on his strong shoulder, she listened to the comforting rhythm of his steady breathing. While Shemu'el dozed, she wrestled with the unfairness of life.

The Hebrew natives of Jerusalem happily traded with Hellenistic Jews. Pilgrims from Africa, Parthia and Gaul were treated with respect when they visited the Temple. Day in and day out Zealots and Essenes, Pharisees and Sadducees, followers of the school of Hillel and followers of the school of Shammai, all worshipped, worked and co-operated with each other.

It seemed there was room for everyone except the followers of The Way of Yeshua. Miryam told her the Temple Guard harassed Simon and Yohan each time they took their place on Solomon's Porch and preached the good news to the people.

*Why them? Why us?*

The answer lay in plain sight. Yosef Caiaphas might be the one passing the regulations, but everyone knew who held the reins. Even though he'd been out of office for more than twenty years, wily old Annas remained the power behind the throne. He'd read the handwriting on the wall and it said if Yeshua's teachings prevailed, the source of his wealth and power would disappear.

They couldn't enrich themselves with profits from the sale of animals and birds. Their moneychangers could not cheat the people when they came to the Temple. Knowing this, he had plotted and schemed to kill Yeshua.

Now that the deed was done, he did not want Simon, or Yohan, or anyone else mentioning Yeshua's name ever again. He once said, "Sever the head and the thing will die."

But it was not to be.

The following day, Shemu'el asked Rivkah to walk with him in the meadow. She went, already knowing what he planned to say.

"After a lot of soul searching, I have decided we can no longer make a living here in this settlement," Shemu'el said.

"It is hardly a secret, even the children know."

He stopped and turned to face her. Taking her in his arms, he hugged her tightly. "I am sorry, my dove. This is not the way I imagined our life would end up."

"What will we do?"

"We must find a living from something other than sheep. I was trained as a physician and blessed with a natural gift for carving wood. Both of these skills would be in demand in Jerusalem." He paused to catch a tear on her cheek. "I could support my family in Jerusalem. I am certain of it."

Though Rivkah knew the truth of his words, she hated to leave her home and the little settlement where she'd spent her life.

The preparations began slowly. She and Shemu'el worked afternoons sorting through their possessions, keeping only what was necessary. What they didn't need, they sold or gave away.

One corner of the house gradually filled with boxes, baskets and packages crammed full of essentials. Shemu'el detached his cupboard of medicinal herbs and ointments from the wall and added it to the growing pile. He hammered out the pins holding Rivkah's loom together. Broken down and bundled, it became a manageable package for transport to Jerusalem.

Gathering his tools and carving knives, he stuffed them into the worn *loculus* he'd carried home from Antioch. The old military traveling case, its brass clasps and fittings darkened by age, had become a fixture in their household. So much so that Rivkah could not look at it without being reminded of Shemu'el's time as a Roman slave.

She chuckled to herself as she watched him straighten the sides yet another time. Each time he did, the tired leather, butter-soft from years of use, slumped to the floor. Without contents to define its shape, the *loculus* had no more form than their lives.

Shouts from the bedroom broke the afternoon's peace. Channah, their middle daughter, stormed up to her mother with her hands on her hips.

"Imma, tell Yaakov to leave me alone."

Yaakov leaned around the doorway. "Channah is packing everything she owns."

Before Rivkah could reply, Channah spun around and shook a fist at her older brother. "Mind your own business. You are not head of this household."

"Abba said we must travel light."

The stress of the move affected them all. The children bickered constantly. Shemu'el had grown distant and moody and, though she tried not to, Rivkah had begun losing her temper with him and the children.

Shortly after they married Shemu'el planted a fig tree near the entrance to their home. Over the years the tree grew and thrived, its branches spreading wide. Whenever Rivkah needed time alone to sit and think, she crawled under the fig tree.

Shemu'el found her there the morning they departed for Jerusalem. "Come, my dove," he said, extending his arm. "Everything is ready. It is time we left."

Grasping the hand he offered, she came out from beneath the curtain of branches. "I want to walk through the house one last time. I won't be long."

He gave an understanding nod.

By habit, she put her fingertips to her lips and touched a kiss to the *mezuzah* on the side of doorframe. The dark burnish of the little bronze scroll case stopped her in her tracks. Hadn't it been bright and shiny just yesterday? Yes, she thought, it *was* shiny once, many years ago when she and Shemu'el were young and newly-married.

She stepped into the empty house, remembering the day Shemu'el carried his new bride across the threshold. The house smelled of fresh-cut timbers and new plaster then. Closing her eyes, Rivkah took a deep breath and savored the familiar scent.

It smelled like home.

Moving around the rooms, she straightened the covers on the windows and touched marks on the walls. Each one brought back memories of the children when they were young. The tart, acidic smell of vinegar wafted around her when she opened the pantry door. A circular stain on the floor identified the spot where a large crock of pickled cucumbers always sat.

She ran her eyes along the thick beams supporting the roof, recalling the day Gavriel and Simeon hauled them in as a wedding present. They were freshly peeled then and nearly white. Now they had the golden hue of aged wood and soot stains above the area where she cooked.

The unfairness made her ache. Rivkah stood in the middle of the room with tears rolling down her cheeks. Her fingers closed into tight fists. She wanted to scream and kick and claw. What would happen, she wondered, if I sat down in the middle of the room and refused to go?

In her heart of hearts she knew it would change nothing. Drying her tears, Rivkah lifted her chin and walked out the door, never looking back.

A new life, a better life, awaited them in Jerusalem, she told herself. Believing in the goodness of the future brought her a much needed peace. Later she would realize how foolishly optimistic those thoughts had been.

# ~ 10 ~

*"Now there was a man in Jerusalem, whose name was Simeon, and this man was righteous and devout, looking for the consolation of Israel, and the Holy Spirit was upon him."*

— Luke 2:25

"They say Yeshua claimed to be the eternal son of the Most High God, that he blasphemed before the High Priest. Is it true?"

Barnabus and Stefanos sat with Gamali'el in the atrium of his home, resting beneath the spreading branches of a myrtle tree. Water gurgled in a fountain beside them. Here in the garden, safe from the prying eyes and ears of Sha'oul, the Rabbi could speak his mind.

Gamali'el's face remained an inscrutable mask. "And what, my dear students, would constitute blasphemy?"

Stefanos replied without hesitation. "Blasphemy is the act of taking on the rights or attributes belonging solely to God."

"When Caiaphas asked, 'Are you the *Mashiach*, the Son of the living God?' Yeshua responded, 'I am.'" Gamali'el stared at his students. "How would you judge this reply?"

Barnabus' back stiffened. "Such a statement merits death. How can anyone say he was treated unjustly?"

"Yet many do. Explain this seeming contradiction."

Stefanos and Barnabus stared at each other.

"You have presented us with an impossibility, Rab" Stefanos said. "Both sides cannot be correct."

Gamali'el chuckled. "A solution stares you in the face, yet neither of you recognize it. Years of schooling has closed your minds to the obvious."

Resting his elbows on his knees, their teacher leaned forward. The chatter of birds in the nearby bushes nearly covered his soft question. "Would it have been blasphemy to acknowledge the truth of Caiaphas' words?"

Barnabus gasped and a shiver danced along Stefanos' spine.

Gamali'el turned to Stefanos. "Did the schools of Alexandria teach you nothing? Who was this Yeshua? Think!"

"A carpenter, a rabbi, a healer...the *Mashiach*, perhaps?" Stefanos sputtered.

"Yes, yes, yes and yes. Surely your instructors required you to study the writings of Philo. They must have. Or are you, perhaps, among those he termed the *uninitiated*. Those incapable of understanding the deeper meaning of his teachings?"

Stefanos gave his teacher a blank stare.

Like a shepherd driving his sheep, Gamali'el prodded them to the solution. "Surely both of you know what Philo said regarding the *Logos*, the Word."

"He said when the Torah speaks of the angel of God visiting the patriarchs, it was in fact the *Logos*," Barnabus replied.

Excitement lit Stefanos' eyes. "He defined the *Logos* as the only begotten Son of God, the means by which the universe came into being, the immanent and transcendent personification of God to mankind."

"Truly spoken," Gamali'el said. "Over the years our people's understanding of the *Mashiach* has grown as writers and thinkers shaped, refined and defined his nature. Now, in the fullness of time, the *Logos*, the Word made flesh, came among us."

The two students mulled this over in silence for several moments.

"How long have you understood this?" Stefanos asked in a timid voice.

Gamali'el drummed his fingers on the bench. "How long?" He leaned back and cleared his throat. "Let us simply say, long before the events of the recent *Pesach*."

The old man shook his gray head in wonderment. "For some reason God intertwined our two lives, Yeshua's and mine, as tightly as threads in a tapestry. You see, his reach extends even to my father, Simeon, son of Hillel."

"Your father could not have known him. He was but a child when your father died."

"In his private hours my father devoted himself to studying the prophecies of the *Mashiach*. One day, while at prayer, the *Shekinah* surrounded him and the Spirit revealed he would not pass from this life until he saw God's Anointed One. Transferring leadership of the School of Hillel to me, he spent his remaining days in the Temple. Praying. Waiting. Watching."

Both men inched closer.

"Thirty-three years ago my father, Simeon, heard the *Kol Yahweh*, the voice of *HaShem*. 'There,' it whispered to his heart. 'That child is the one for whom you watch and wait.'"

"What did he do?"

"He approached the young woman carrying the infant. He held the child, blessed him, and told her he was destined to cause the rising and falling of many in Israel." Gamali'el shook his head. "Strangely enough, she seemed to already know. I watched from the shadows thinking him a fool. In reality, I was the fool and he far wiser than the entire cohort of priests."

"Why didn't he shout out the joyous news?"

"Knowing all things come to fruition as they are destined, he spoke only to the child's parents."

"Did he tell you any more?"

"Enough for me to know Yeshua was the one whose birth the prophets foretold." Gamali'el leaned back against the tree. "I will never forget how my father's face glowed that evening. He died a truly happy man."

He rocked forward and brought his hands together with a clap. "But you came to discuss resurrection, not blasphemy. Correct?"

"As I said, my friend's friend insists Yeshua has risen from the dead."

"And why not? He has."

"So he was the *Mashiach*?"

Gamali'el chuckled. "No, he *is* the *Mashiach*."

A servant entered the garden carrying refreshments.

"Are you familiar with Herod's massacre of infants in the area surrounding Bethlehem?" Gamali'el asked, sipping his wine.

Being from the *Diaspora*, neither Barnabus nor Stefanos

knew of the event.

"During his reign Herod committed so many atrocities that, like merging creeks, they blend into an endless river of blood. Even those who knew of the killings had only a rudimentary knowledge of the motivation behind them.

"You see, many months after the incident in the Temple, Herod called me to his palace along with the other priests and teachers. A delegation from the East, accompanied by a cavalry escort, had appeared on Herod's doorstep seeking the one whose birth the prophets foretold."

"The *Mashiach*."

"Precisely. After the Parthians left, Herod called us to inquire about those prophecies." He shot them a conspiratorial grin. "I, of course, neglected to mention what my father had told me. Meanwhile Herod, believing the *Mashiach* came to depose him, tried to strike him down but failed."

"Did your paths cross ever again?"

"One final time, when Yeshua was about twelve years old. He came to the Temple as a pilgrim during *Pesach* to be examined and declared a man. After his examination he began to question the teachers of the Torah. He came day after day. The Temple buzzed with tales of this young man's extraordinary wisdom. I sat in on some of the sessions. Never have I seen such insight in one so young."

"How long did he stay."

"Longer than planned. His mother returned for him three days later." Gamali'el chuckled. "You should have seen the look on her face. I have often wondered what she said to him on the way home."

Their teacher drained his cup. "And now, hearing these things, you two will no doubt leave the school of Hillel to align yourselves with The Way of Yeshua *HaMashiach*."

Barnabus and Stefanos squirmed on the bench, afraid to confirm the rabbi's words.

"I do not condemn you; I congratulate you. You have chosen the better part. Go, and take my blessing with you."

"Rab, you spoke of your father's belief, but never

mentioned yours," Stefanos said, as he rose. "Yet you send us away with a blessing?"

"Stefanos, the one who always requires proof, demands a declaration. Do you not know a man's actions count for more than his words? Great things can sometimes be accomplished in secret. Let the troops go forth to battle, someone must remain to guard the camp."

"So you *are* a believer then?"

"There are more of us than you imagine. The day of his crucifixion the Lord called Nikademus and Yosef of Arimathea from their secret places. Who knows? Someday he may call me as well. Until then I shall remain where I am, serving in secret and awaiting his call."

## ~ 11 ~

Shemu'el and Rivkah entered Jerusalem with optimism, believing Yeshua had called them. After much searching they found a place to stay in the lower city. The children groaned when they saw the tiny house they would now be forced to live in.

Wedged between two shops, the single story tan brick building backed up to the city wall. Instead of the lush orchard they'd grown up with, the house's small backyard left room for only one spindly apple tree.

During the day street noises seeped in through the front windows. Urgent cries of merchants calling out to shoppers, the braying of pack animals, and the constant chatter of the crowds reverberated from daylight to dusk. At night Roman guards walked their rounds on the battlements above their roof. The clatter of hobnailed sandals accompanied by the clang and clank of armaments serenaded them in their beds.

Jerusalem sat at the crossroads of the Eastern Empire and pack trains arrived with merchandise every day except *Shabbat*. In the pre-dawn darkness strings of camels from Idumea, Arabia, Egypt and points beyond, came through the city gates. Most of these caravans entered by the Water Gate, a short walk from their new home.

As a child Rivkah found the jingle of camel bells enchanting when her father's merchant friend, Sidonius, stopped to visit. In Jerusalem she grew to hate their incessant clinking. Each morning before sunrise the cursing of camel boys in a multitude of languages jarred them awake. Camels plodded past their windows huzzing and groaning and littering the street in front of the house with their droppings.

Despite the setbacks, Rivkah tried to make the best of their situation. "Viewed properly, everything can be a blessing," she told the children. They had no money to buy firewood, but the Lord provided camel dung, which they could collect and dry in the backyard. "A free source of fuel for our stove and oven," she said with a smile.

The children took a less enthusiastic view of this blessing when Rivkah sent them into the street each morning with bushel baskets to fill.

A deep despondency settled over the household. Though Rivkah never admitted it, she too longed for the quiet solitude of their old home. She missed seeing birds nesting in the trees, hearing the gentle lowing of the sheep, and harvesting fruit and vegetables from their garden. The little yard in back barely afforded them enough space to step outside and relax in the cool of the evening.

While Rivkah fretted over their living arrangements, Shemu'el had worries of his own. In their settlement he had confidently assured her his skills as a healer and physician would be welcome in Jerusalem. He found that not to be the case.

A few days after they arrived, he presented himself to the Guild of Physicians for certification. They began by testing him on his knowledge of the human body, treatments, medicines and the like just as Gnaeus Valerius, a Roman Physician to the Legions, had done in Antioch many years before.

In an effort to speed the process along, Shemu'el took one of the examiner's hands. Placing his fingers behind the man's shoulder, he said, "Scapulus."

He moved his hand down the arm, identifying, and naming in turn, the humerus, radius and ulna, carpus, metacarpus and each of the digiti. He named and discussed the major organ systems of the body and surgical techniques used to treat various wounds.

The leader of the group nodded appreciatively. Most of the others made no comment; only a few could have replicated his feat.

"You say you lived in a settlement of shepherds near Bethlehem?" their leader asked.

"Yes, for over twenty years."

He frowned and stroked his beard with narrowed eyes. "How did a shepherd manage to accumulate such a knowledge of the healing arts while living in the countryside?"

"When Quirinius governed Syria I served as assistant to Evodius Scipio, the *Medicus Cohortis* to *Legio XII Fulminata*."

The group shrank back.

"You willingly served the Romans...our oppressors?"

"Surely some among you remember the protest under Procurator Sabinus when the Romans set fire to the Temple cloisters. I was in the Temple court the day of the protest, captured, and taken away in chains. I became Evodius' slave and served him for eight years. In his testament, Evodius stipulated his slaves be freed upon his demise. I received my certificate of manumission from Quirinius' own hand."

The room buzzed with interest.

"So you traveled with the army?" a voice in the back asked.

Before Shemu'el could answer, another said, "And treated the soldiers if they were wounded in battle?"

"Yes, yes," Shemu'el said. "That is precisely what I did."

One of the younger men gave his fellows a sly wink. "Well, at least we can be sure he's not a Zealot."

The men's laughter caused Shemu'el's cheeks to burn.

"He is no Zealot; he is a collaborator," another called out.

"I am neither," Shemu'el insisted. "I took the Hippocratic oath to treat all who needed my care and I honored my oath."

"In other words, you helped the Romans subdue your own people."

"I did not. Surely you must understand I had no choice," Shemu'el said in desperation as the men turned away to confer.

In the end, they admitted him to the Guild of Physicians. But the taint of their prejudice, some might call it jealousy, doomed him to failure. The only patients Shemu'el got were the hopeless cases...those too far gone to recover or those for whom there was no hope, patients other physicians refused to treat because of caste or uncleanliness, and patients too poor to pay.

He ceased trying to make a living as a physician and began going into the market square each morning to stand with the common laborers looking for work. When he was lucky enough to find a day's work, he received a single *denarius* as his pay.

## ~ 12 ~

One morning, a few months after their move, Rivkah answered the door to find her friend, Rachel, on the stoop burdened down with bundles.

"What in the world are you doing here?" Rivkah hugged her. "Don't just stand there. Come in, come in."

"Binyamin is delivering sheep to the Temple. I came with him so we could visit."

"How did you find us?"

"Caleb gave me directions." She pointed down the street to her right. "I left Binyamin with the sheep and entered through the Water Gate."

Rivkah marveled at the pile of baskets and bundles Rachel unloaded on the floor of their front room. "What are all these packages?"

"Things from home. Your fig tree is heavy with fruit, so we picked these for you." Rachel handed her a large burlap sack of ripe figs. She dug into another basket and passed her a heavy stone jar. "Elisheva sent perfumed lotion for you and Channah." A bolt of cloth appeared next. "Devorah heard I was coming and sent this." She pulled out another parcel. "For you from Yohanna."

The largess seemed unbelievable. Nearly everyone in their little settlement had sent something.

"Thank you, Rachel." She kissed her cheek. "And you carried it all this way."

Rachel mopped her brow. "Actually, I made Binyamin carry it until we reached the gate. I took it from there." She glanced around their humble home. "So, how is it living in Jerusalem?" Rachel's tone said she knew the answer before she asked.

"Things are very different here." Rivkah touched a sleeve to her eye. "Some days I wish with all my heart we could go back home."

Raised voices and threats from an argument on the street came through the front window.

Rachel covered her ears. "Are things always this loud?"

Rivkah sighed. "We seldom have a moment's peace...and no privacy. We never even use the roof. At night, the soldiers walking their rounds can stare down onto it. Back in the settlement, before the children came along, on hot nights Shemu'el and I often slept on the roof," she blushed slightly, "and lay in each other's arms."

"Why do you think the children came along?" Rachel laughed at the expression on Rivkah's face. "Do not look so embarrassed. Binyamin and I did the same. Everyone does." Rachel's eyes twinkled. "Those were the days."

"Yes, there is nothing better than being young and in love."

"How about Shemu'el, has he found work?"

"He tried being a physician, but the Guild did not welcome him. He treats our fellow believers who attend the Synagogue of Rabban Yeshua *HaMashiach*." She shrugged. "Other than that, he finds work wherever he can."

"Have you told him you are not happy here?"

"He knows."

Rachel frowned. "The two of you remind me of Liat."

Rivkah had not thought of Liat in a very long time. Liat was the ewe lamb her father gave her when she was eight years old. The first sheep she owned and the foundation of a flock that had supported their family for over 20 years.

"What on earth do you mean?"

"Liat never stayed where she belonged. One time a lion almost got her. The last time she wandered away, some bandits ate her for dinner. You and Shemu'el are a couple of runaway sheep that need to be herded back home."

"We did not leave our settlement because we wanted to. Have you forgotten? We were forced out."

"You did not have to leave. Binyamin and I do not reject Yeshua's teachings. One can remain a faithful Jew and still follow his Way."

Rivkah understood what Rachel meant. People held differing opinions about what a belief in Yeshua's *Mashiachship* entailed. Many people, like Rachel and Binyamin, saw it as a doctrinal difference, which in no way affected their status as observant Jews. Much the same as Pharisees who believed in the resurrection of the dead and Sadducees who did not.

"You may believe that," Rivkah said, "but Caiaphas and the Temple hierarchy see things differently."

"Rivkah, we have been friends all our life. We played together when we were little girls. And now, suddenly there is this," Rachel moved her hands around each other as if shaping a loaf, "this...thing coming between us. You are on one road and I am going down another. How did we end up on separate paths?"

"We each must do what our conscience demands. I wish with all my heart things were different, but life is the way it is."

Rachel smacked her hand down. "Nonsense. Your house remains empty. Give up this life and come back home."

"How would we live?"

"Go to the Temple authorities and confess your error in judgement. I am sure they would re-instate your franchise to sell lambs in Annas' market. It is not too late to rebuild your flock. Your friends will help if you let them. Binyamin has an extra ram. He is yours. Take him with our blessing."

"It is very tempting to do what you propose, but we cannot. I love you like a sister, Rachel, and pray my words will not offend you. Though you came in kindness, the devil has put these words in your mouth. I do not know what path others will take, but as for me and my house, we shall serve the Lord Yeshua."

The front door opened and Shemu'el stumbled in covered with mud.

Rachel caught herself staring and forced her eyes away.

Rivkah put a hand on Shemu'el's forehead. "You feel as if you are on fire. Have you had enough water?"

"I drank what I could," Shemu'el muttered. He staggered across the front room heading for the bedroom.

Rivkah raced into the kitchen. "I will bring you vinegar water to drink. Take those dirty clothes off and rest while I draw a pan of water so you can wash."

While Rivkah took Shemu'el something to drink, Rachel poked around the kitchen, found a pan, and filled it.

"Does he always come home like that?" Rachel whispered when Rivkah returned from the bedroom.

"He spent the day digging a trench." She shrugged. "He takes whatever he can get. The work is never easy, but it is not usually this bad."

Rivkah knew it embarrassed Shemu'el to have Rachel see him in that state. For the sake of his pride, she let her think things were better than they were. He would not want Rachel to know about the week he came home each day with his hands wrapped in bloody rags from carrying rocks in a quarry.

Rachel rose and hugged Rivkah tightly. "Binyamin is probably waiting at the gate. It need not be like this. Promise me you will think about coming back home. Talk it over with Shemu'el after he has rested." She gave her a poke. "Maybe tonight when you are in bed."

For Rachel's sake Rivkah pretended to consider it, but in her heart she knew it was too late to turn back. They'd follow this road they were on to the end.

# ~ 13 ~

*"And Stephen, full of grace and power, did
great wonders and signs among the people."*
— Acts of the Apostles 6:8

Additional turmoil descended upon Jerusalem the following year
when all of Judea suffered a severe drought.

The first harbinger of impending trouble occurred in the
month of Nisan when, shortly after *Pesach*, farmers began
harvesting their flax fields. The earliest crop to ripen, flax
provided the first tangible measure of the drought's effect. No
one anticipated such extensive damage.

Word spread across the countryside like smoke on the
wind. Soon everyone knew the flax crop had failed. There would
be no linen this year except for imports from afar, which
commanded premium prices.

Frightened, the people began praying for early rains. Bad
enough to have a drought cut into production, but without
moisture the following year's seed would not germinate. And no
germination meant no harvest...and no seed for the year after.

The next month the barley harvest confirmed what
everyone already knew. A dark cloud of gloom settled over the
region. A few weeks later the wheat kernels came in shrunken
and withered.

The months of Tammuz and Aviv came and went. Again it
was *Rosh Chodesh*, the first day of the new month. Elul came, but
the usual celebrations that accompanied the harvest of figs and
grapes did not. As the month of Tishri loomed and with it *Rosh
Hashanah*, preparations for Yom Kippur, the Day of Atonement,
took on a special sense of urgency.

And then there was a ray of hope. The first rains came not
early, but at least on time. Farmers began to hope the following
year would be better. The droughty weather had put everyone on
edge and the growing division between the other Jewish sects
and The Way of Rabban Yeshua continued to widen.

Despite increasing antagonism from the authorities, Simon and Yohan continued going to Temple each day to preach on Solomon's Porch. Among their regulars was Abijah, the man crippled from birth whom Simon cured. He became one of their biggest supporters.

Day after day he grabbed Simon by the hand and tugged him over to where a man or woman lay on a litter. "Come and lay your hands upon my friend," Abijah would say. "Do for them what you did for me."

Their fame spread with each cure and before long people with all sorts of illnesses and disabilities began crowding the area along Solomon's Portico.

Most of these people survived by begging and had developed a retinue of pathetic and annoying behaviors designed to facilitate their cause. Some survived by sprawling beside a shop's entrance and wailing. In this way they extorted payment from the shop's owner in exchange for crawling away and pestering someone else. Others cursed those who passed by without flipping a coin into their cup. Those who could walk chased after passersby flailing withered limbs at them until, in desperation, they dipped into their purses.

The Temple Guard did not take kindly to this motley congregation of misfits and tried to put a stop to it. Eleazer, the Captain of the Guard, appeared one day accompanied by a dozen armed men.

He waved his arms to disperse the ragtag crowd. "No begging allowed in this area,"

Yohan approached him. "No one here is begging. These people are simply listening."

"Very well." He spun around to face the crowd. "No listening in this area."

"My friend, teachers have always spoken to their disciples here on Solomon's Porch." Yohan pointed toward the school of Hillel and similar groups. "Would you have us believe all of these must also cover their ears?"

Eleazer opened his mouth to reply, reconsidered, and scowled instead. Avoiding Yohan and Simon's eyes, he slapped the end of his club into his palm as he searched for a resolution. "One way or another I want these people out of here. If they do not leave, I will haul both of you before the Great Sanhedrin."

"Again?" Simon rose from the steps where he'd been conferring with a blind woman. "Surely they have weightier matters to consider than the disposition of these unfortunates."

Eleazer drew himself to his full height. "As captain of the Temple guard, my order stands. Go!"

Simon descended the stairs with an easy gait. "Why all this anger, Eleazer?" He rested his arm on Eleazer's shoulder and motioned toward the beggars cowering around them. "What harm have these people done?"

Eleazer shoved Simon's arm away. "Do not touch me."

"What do you fear, Eleazer?" Simon extended his arms, displaying empty palms. "The only weapon I carry is the word of God. I intend you no harm." He gave him a reassuring smile. "Surely we can deal with this in a more reasonable manner."

The two men negotiated a compromise. Those who sought healing no longer congregated along the steps when Simon and Yohan were teaching. Instead, they gathered outside in the courtyard beside the *mikvahs* at the Temple's south entrance. This worked well since those who had illnesses and deformities were considered unclean. If they were cured, the priests required them to bathe in the *mikvah* before pronouncing them cleansed.

Each day, a crowd waited outside the Temple when the men finished teaching. Cripples with twisted, weak legs the way Abijah's had been, those with withered hands, stooped women whose backs were bent with age, and others with a variety of illnesses. They all pleaded for a moment with the apostles hoping they too might be among the fortunate ones who were healed.

Despite the animosity of most of the city, the Synagogue of Rabban Yeshua *HaMashiach* flourished. Following the dictates of the Lord, they ministered to the widows, orphans, sick and poor among them. Each time they met, members brought offerings to share with those in need. Some brought food — meat, grain, oil, wine and fruit — others deposited coins in the common purse.

The task of administering this outreach to the needy quickly overwhelmed the Twelve and so they appointed *diakonoi*, servants, to assist them in the task. As at the school of Hillel and everywhere else in Jerusalem, a cultural divide existed between the Hebrews and the Hellenists.

One day, Perseus, one of the Hellenists in the congregation cornered Yaakov after prayers. "Why are the needy among us not getting their fair share of the Synagogue's resources?"

"The *diakonoi* distribute equally to all," Yaakov said.

Perseus' body tensed and his face reddened. "You know that is not true." He smacked a fist into his palm. "There is a famine raging in the city. We have widows and orphans among us who need food and they are not getting it."

"Are you saying these people are being overlooked?"

"In a manner of speaking, yes. Oh, they get something from the basket all right, but only after the choicest morsels have gone to the Hebrews. Is this how Yeshua said it should be? Give to your friends first and treat the poor Hellenists as if they were dogs begging for scraps?"

"How can we make this right, my brother?"

"Insure the goods are distributed fairly." Perseus spun on his heel and stormed away.

The Twelve addressed his complaint by selecting additional deacons from among the Hellenists. Stefanos was one of those chosen and the matter would have ended there were it not for his ongoing feud with Sha'oul of Tarsus.

He, like Barnabus and Stefanos, had left the school of Hillel to pursue other interests. But unlike them, Sha'oul allied himself with Caiaphas, the High Priest, not The Way of Yeshua *HaMashiach*.

At first, Stefanos failed to notice him as he went about his work. Sha'oul was a shadow in a doorway, a quick movement in Stefanos' peripheral vision, the sound of rushing feet or the flutter behind a bush. As Sha'oul became better acquainted with Stefanos' daily routine, he grew bolder. Eventually he stepped out from the shadows and trailed behind him in broad daylight.

Having had enough of Sha'oul's nonsense, Stefanos confronted him. "Do you think I cannot see you back there scurrying in and out of alleyways like a sewer rat?"

"Why do you care so much about what I do?"

"You are the one trailing me. I should be asking that of you."

Sha'oul motioned to the baskets in Stefanos' arms. "There is a famine in the city and food is dear. Do you imagine I have not unraveled your scheme?"

"Have you now?"

"This movement of yours, this *Way*, is as transitory as the morning fog. All too soon you will meet failure eye-to-eye." Sha'oul spat in the dirt and sneered up at Stefanos. "Go ahead, buy your converts with foodstuffs if you like. See what it gets you."

"We gain new members from among the Jews every day. Even from among the priests and Pharisees," Stefanos said.

"You are nothing but a wolf thinning the flock. Take them with my blessing. Every winemaker must filter off the dregs. Any Jew who would trade their covenant for a few loaves and a jug of oil is no Jew at all."

Stefanos gave a confident chuckle. "Soon all of Jerusalem will follow The Way of Rabban Yeshua *HaMashiach*. Who will you report your suspicions to then?"

Sha'oul waved his hands above his head. "If all Jerusalem converts, may God rain down fire and brimstone upon this city and its inhabitants just as he did on Sodom and Gomorrah."

Stefanos took a step closer. "If you would only listen to what I have to say."

"Do not touch me. You are the Evil One." Sha'oul's finger shook when he pointed. "There is a famine now and people go hungry. What will become of this *Way* of yours once the famine ends and these people no longer require your baskets?"

The little man hunched his shoulders and stared down his thin nose. "Hmmm? Hmmm? What then, my Greek friend. What then...hmmm?"

"The poor will always be with us. We feed the hungry, clothe the naked, comfort the sick and bury the dead as Rabban Yeshua commanded."

The mention of Yeshua's name sent Sha'oul into a frenzy. He covered his ears and danced in a circle, screaming, "Be gone Satan. Do not speak that blasphemous name in my presence."

Stefanos left him and continued on his route.

But Sha'oul clung to him like a bad odor. "You seek to gain their support through gifts as if these people were donkeys who could be drawn aside with a handful of salt. Keep your gifts," he thundered. "Lies and sorcery have failed you, and so you turn to bread. Mark my word, this will also fail."

Sha'oul dogged Stefanos' path each time he made his daily distribution, growing bolder with each passing day. He began trailing behind him shouting, "Woe! Woe to you. Woe to all who follow The Way."

"How are things among your people?" Barnabus asked one evening.

Stefanos laughed and related Sha'oul's antics of doom and woe. "Loneliness is one thing I never worry about when I am making my daily rounds." He glanced over his shoulder and rolled his eyes. "Wherever I go the prophet Ezekiel is never far behind crying out his Woes."

The little man from Tarsus feared Stefanos' strength and athletic abilities. The incident at the School of Hillel when Sha'oul allowed his zeal to overwhelm his good judgement had ended in disgrace. Sha'oul had no desire to repeat such an embarrassing moment.

He came to understand that his war with Stefanos would always be one of words. Knowing this emboldened Sha'oul and his behavior grew increasingly outrageous. Things reached a head one afternoon when Stefanos paused to address a group of men at a fountain. Sha'oul began heckling him from the other side of the street. One thing led to another and the two men engaged in a debate. Despite Sha'oul's superior knowledge, Stefanos easily bested him.

Once it became clear that he could not escape the predicament he was in, Sha'oul burst into a rage and stormed away.

Fists had failed.

Threats had failed.

Now debate had failed.

There was only one way left.

Sha'oul began plotting against Stefanos' life.

## ~ 14 ~

One evening, after the family returned from the agape meal, Channah picked up her sewing basket and retreated to her room. Rivkah's intuition told her they needed to have a mother-daughter talk. Poking her head around the corner, she asked Channah to accompany her to the well.

She gave her mother a wary look, but put aside her needles and grabbed the water jar.

The two of them walked the first block in silence. As they waited to cross a street, Channah glanced at the horizon and sighed. "Look at the sunset. I have never seen such a lovely sight."

"Yes," Rivkah agreed, "it is a pretty sunset." She reached over and touched Channah's arm. "There are some things I want to discuss with you."

Channah smiled. "Of course you do. Why else would you ask me to carry the water jar when you go to the well?"

"And this bothers you?"

"Oh no." Channah laughed and patted her mother's hand. "I learned your tricks long ago." A bemused smile curled the corners of her mouth. "But that is what mothers do, isn't it. I suppose someday I will ask my daughter to accompany me to the well so we can talk."

"*Your* daughter?"

"Well, you do expect me to have children, don't you?"

"Of course I do, but you are not even betrothed. Could this have anything to do with Stefanos?"

Channah's eyes brightened at the mention of his name, and she turned her head away to hide her grin. "You have noticed the way he looks at me, haven't you?"

That evening, as usual, Stefanos had helped serve the Lord's Supper. Rivkah noticed nothing special in his treatment of Channah, but she knew this was not what her daughter wanted to hear.

"You believe he has feelings for you."

"I knew it." Channah giggled. "If you saw it, everyone must have. How can I hide what everyone knows?"

They were still some distance from the well. "Let the water wait." Rivkah directied her to a seat beside a fountain.

Channah rocked on its low wall and tapped her feet on the ground. She leaned close and whispered, "Isn't Stefanos beautiful?"

Her daughter's words surprised her. "Beautiful? I am accustomed to hearing women referred to as beautiful, not men."

"That may have been true in our little settlement, but things are different here in the big city. My friends and I decided it can be applied to men as well. His strong, masculine form, his face like a Greek god, his manly voice and kind eyes." She squeezed her mother's hand. "Trust me, Stefanos *is* beautiful."

Fearing she might swoon and pitch into the fountain, Rivkah slipped her arm around Channah's shoulder. "Clearly you have thought about this quite a lot."

"I think of nothing else," she confessed in a throaty whisper. "I shivered this evening when our fingers touched. My heart thumped inside my chest like a drum. I imagined everyone in the room hearing it. When he looked into my eyes and said, 'Channah, I offer you the cup of salvation.' I thought I would melt."

"Those are the words of the sacrament, my dear. He says that to each and everyone of us."

"Not the way he said them to me. Have you never noticed how he pronounces my name? Stefanos grew up speaking Greek, not Aramaic. He adds the softest lilt when he says my Hebrew name." She adjusted her veil and turned aside. "But I suppose you could never understand."

Channah jumped up, grabbed the jar, and marched away leaving her mother sitting beside the fountain.

"Wait!" Rivkah ran to catch up. "Very well. I will admit Stefanos is a handsome young man, a very handsome young man. Has it occurred to you other girls might also find him attractive?"

"I am no longer a girl, Imma." She lifted her head and tossed her scarf over her shoulder. "When will you understand I am a woman."

Channah took long, angry strides.

Rivkah nearly ran to keep pace.

"Besides, I can satisfy Stefanos in a way no other woman will." Seeing her mother's eyebrows shoot up, she quickly added, "I meant he and I are *b'shert*, destined for each other by God. Just as you and Abba were."

The sky had turned dusky gray by the time they reached the well. Lamplight shone through the windows of the homes they passed. A number of women had also come to draw fresh water before nightfall, forcing them to wait in line. When their turn came, Channah filled the slim jug and swung it onto her shoulder.

"Alexandria is a center of learning. The best and the brightest are schooled there. Stefanos is one of them and he is falling in love with me." She gave her mother a sidelong glance. "Why do wish to dash my hopes? Do you find pleasure in crushing my dreams?"

"That was never my intention. I only want you to accept the reality of the situation so you are not hurt if those dreams do not come true. The Lord has called Stefanos to his service. His lot in life may be a hard one."

The remnants of earlier tears glistened in Channah's eyes. "I do not care. The Lord destined us for each other. I will help him carry the load."

"He is also too old for you."

"He is hardly older than Abba was when you two wed."

"True, but the differences in your ages is much greater."

Channah shifted the heavy jar to her other shoulder. "It makes no difference. I am more grown-up than any of my friends. Even though they have become women, they sometimes behave like little girls."

"What about the cultural differences? Stefanos is Greek and you are Hebrew. He comes from Alexandria, has traveled throughout the Empire and studied in some of the finest schools."

"Can't you see how much we are like you and Abba? He

lived in Antioch and had seen the Roman world, while you spent your entire life in our little settlement outside of Bethlehem." She gave her a smug grin. "At least I have lived in Jerusalem, which is more than you had done when you married."

Rivkah contemplated her daughter's hopeful expression, wishing there were a way to make her see the impossibility of her dream. She wondered if this was how her father felt when she was Channah's age. Did he feel she pursued a hopeless dream by clinging to her love for Shemu'el when everyone believed him forever lost? She prayed for the right words.

"What would you have me do?"

Channah gave her a confused look. "Do? It is all in God's hands, there is nothing you can do."

"Perhaps we could invite Stefanos to join us for supper one evening. Let him enjoy a meal you prepared so he could see how well you cook. It would give you a chance to learn more about him and let your father come to know him better."

The jar wobbled on Channah's shoulder, splashing over the top and wetting her cloak. "You would do that for me?"

"I will suggest it to your father. That is, if you want me to."

"Yes, oh yes, I want you to very much."

They turned the corner onto their street. Channah leaned close and whispered, "How was it the first time you and Abba lay together?"

"One thing at a time. We will talk about lying with your husband after you are betrothed."

Channah gave her an impish smile. "Very well, I will ask Hadassah. After all, isn't that what older sisters are for?"

Like most fathers, Shemu'el found it difficult to imagine his youngest daughter possessing the needs and desires of a grown woman. He preferred living in the past, when he was the only man in her life and she crawled into Abba's lap to hear his stories. Despite these misgivings, Shemu'el approached Stefanos after prayers and invited him to dine with them.

To Channah's delight and dismay, Stefanos agreed.

She planned and re-planned the meal, worrying over minor details such as whether she should blend spices into the cheese, or sprinkle them on top.

"It makes no difference," Rivkah tried to tell her.

"Of course it does. Everything must be perfect." A look of fright swept across Channah's face. "What if they do not eat their cheese with sweet spices in Alexandria?"

"We are in Jerusalem. He does not expect to eat as they do in Alexandria."

Channah licked her lip as she thought. "Stefanos stays in the home of Aristopolus on the city's west side. Can you ask Aristopolus' wife, Miryam, what dishes Stefanos prefers?"

Channah served a delicious meal the night Stefanos visited. Her older brother, Yaakov, ate with the men and she threatened his life if he did or said anything to embarrass her. Her younger brother, Yudah, not as easily intimidated, dined with his sister, Hadassah, and her family.

After he finished his honey cake, Stefanos stepped into the kitchen and complimented Channah on the fine meal. They spoke for a few moments then he took his leave.

"Did it go as you hoped," Rivkah asked as they watched him disappear into the night.

"I was so nervous I thought a flock of birds had invaded my stomach. Did my hand shake when I sat the plate in front of him."

"If it did, he did not notice."

"It would have been better if you and Abba had left us alone."

"Even the Romans do not allow young men and women to be alone until they are betrothed."

"I sensed Stefanos would have liked to take me in his arms and, perhaps, even kiss me." She stared at her feet. "But he could not because you and Abba were here."

"One step at a time, young lady." Rivkah rested an arm over Channah's shoulder. "Kisses come later...much, much later."

She watched her daughter walk to her bedroom, each step as buoyant as a feather floating on the wind. Years ago, Rivkah had been warned, *Love makes women foolish.* Full of the confidence only the young possess, Channah gave her emotions free rein and rushed in without a backward glance.

Slow down, Channah, love of my heart, Rivkah prayed. In your rush to capture the rose of happiness, you may find you have grasped a handful of thorns instead.

# ~ 15 ~

Each day a group of women met at the synagogue to sort donations and prepare baskets for the daily distribution. Late in the afternoon, with everything ready, the *diakonoi* arrived to take those goods and distribute them to needy recipients.

Shortly after Stefanos' visit, Channah volunteered to help.

It warmed Rivkah's heart to see her daughter offering her time to assist others. Channah's generosity, however, turned out to be far less benevolent than Rivkah imagined. One day she glanced out the window and noticed Channah and Stefanos walking toward the house together.

She quickly unraveled her daughter's motives for volunteering at the synagogue. How could she have overlooked the fact that being at the synagogue each day when the deacons came in provided Channah with a respectable way to interact with Stefanos?

In an instant it all became clear.

They began speaking to each other when he came by to pick up his baskets. Nothing serious, just shoptalk. Eventually her devious daughter happened to mention that Stefanos' path to the Hellenist's neighborhood took him past her street. A few days later, she had him walking her home.

"He suggested it," Channah insisted, when Rivkah questioned her about it.

"He did, did he?"

"Oh, yes. Stefanos said it is not safe for a maiden to walk the streets un-chaperoned."

"And this would be the reason he walks with you each afternoon?"

Channah lifted her shoulders and gave her a wide-eyed look of surprise. "What other reason could there be?"

What other reason indeed. Did she think her mother had never been young?

A week later Rivkah found her usually happy daughter moping in a corner. "Such a long face. Your Uncle Caleb sheared his sheep and sent us a large package of wool. If you have nothing to keep your fingers occupied, perhaps you could spin some of it. Your little brother is outgrowing his cloak and I must weave him another."

Channah sighed and pulled a large handful from the bundle of fleece. Taking a carding comb in each hand, she released her frustration on the helpless tuft of wool. Once she had the leaves and grass combed out of it, she rolled the wool off the comb and sat it aside.

She was starting on another wad when Rivkah caught her eye and smiled.

Channah frowned back at her and attacked the wool with as much vigor as she had expended on the first batch. This went on for a short while until she whined, "I am tired of carding wool, there must be something else I can do."

"Put the wool aside for now. I have some rose hips and berry leaves steeping in a pot. I will pour us each a cup. How does that sound?"

Channah supposed it might be all right.

"Do you have cramps in your abdomen? Should I get you a little of your father's decoction of willow bark?"

Channah stared into her cup. "I feel fine. You know very well it is not time for my womanly cycle."

"Your mouth says you feel fine, but your actions say another thing entirely. You have not been yourself for several days now."

Channah rocked her cup, watching little waves rise and fall. "If you must know, Stefanos is not making the daily distribution to the Hellenists."

"You need not fret about the poor. Demetrios is taking care of them until Stefanos and Phillip return from their mission."

"Demetrios is an old man, why would I be interested in what he does?"

Everything dropped into place.

"I thought you volunteered to help at the synagogue so you could assist the needy."

"Well, I did. It's just that..."

Rivkah found herself laughing even though she tried not to. "It's a much more enjoyable task when you are preparing baskets for Stefanos instead of Demetrios. If it has become too much of a burden, perhaps they can find someone else to take your place."

A terrified look swept over Channah's face. "Oh no, I will continue to do it. I want to."

"Because Stefanos returns right after *Shabbat*."

Channah couldn't suppress her grin.

To Channah's great delight, Stefanos and Phillip returned on time. They brought glowing reports of many souls won over to The Way of Rabban Yeshua. More importantly, at her insistent pleading, Shemu'el again invited him to visit on the third day of the week.

During the meal Stefanos complained of a young man named Sha'oul who, like him, had once been a student at the School of Hillel. Sha'oul trailed him each day as he made his distributions.

Channah brought a basket of bread to the table. "Why is he so troublesome?"

"He distorts my words and tries to turn the people against me. Whenever I preach to them of Yeshua, he heckles me."

Channah frowned and returned to the kitchen. "How can he tolerate such a person?" She swung her fist in a swift, upward arc, striking an imaginary opponent. "Stefanos need not put up with this. He is big and surely strong enough to make this awful person leave him alone."

"Yes, he is," said Rivkah. "However, I believe Yeshua said we should love our enemies."

Channah answered her with an angry snort.

Stefanos proved to be bright, engaging and always ready with an interesting tale of life in Alexandria. Over the next months his visits became a regular, and enjoyable, event in their household.

One week, Shemu'el was called away on a medical emergency and the boys were busy with other activities when Stefanos arrived. Rivkah, Channah and Stefanos had a quiet dinner together. After they ate, she left the two young people in the front room while she worked on her loom.

Rivkah wove for a time before she noticed there were no voices coming from the front of the house. Leaving her loom, she went to the doorway. She walked barefoot and neither of them heard her footsteps.

The room lay in purple shadows. Though the sun had slipped below the horizon, Channah hadn't bothered to light the lamps.

The two of them stood beside the window, silhouetted by the dying sun. Stefanos had his arms around her. Resting a hand on his shoulder, she nestled her head against his chest. Rivkah watched him lift Channah's chin and tenderly kiss her.

They were beautiful together. A picture of the love the Greeks and Romans sought to immortalize with their indecent statues. Seeing them like this brought back memories of being in Shemu'el's arms when she was a young girl and the stirrings it caused. Her daughter kept insisting she was a woman, with a woman's needs and a woman's desires. If Rivkah ever doubted those words, she no longer did.

She begged God to give the two of them all the happiness this world had to offer. She wished with all her heart she could leave them be...slip away and do nothing. It would have been easy, but she knew she must not.

She was the mother now and understood the yearnings of youth. Whether she wanted it or not, her task was to extinguish the flame before they were scorched. And to do it in such a way to, hopefully, leave some embers smoldering.

They leaped apart when Rivkah cleared her throat.

"Imma, you startled me." Channah gave her an anxious

look. "Why are you sneaking around the house on your tiptoes?"

She turned her hands one over the other, looking everywhere but at her mother.

"Oh, look at how dark it has suddenly become." Channah raced into the kitchen for a taper. Rushing back into the room, she quickly lit every lamp.

Red-cheeked, Stafanos pulled himself up to his full height. "Sister Rivkah," he stammered, "I did not hear you come in."

Swallowing a chuckle, Rivkah made her voice as stern as possible. "When no one watches, do the young men of Alexandria take liberties with maidens to whom they are not betrothed?"

He sighed deeply and ran his eyes along the floor. "It was not as it appeared." His voice was barely more than a whisper. "I would never do the things you suggest."

"I saw what I saw."

Channah stepped in front of him. "It was not his fault. He could not help himself. I beguiled him with my feminine wiles and—"

Stefanos took her by the shoulders and eased her aside.

"I beg you, do not blame your daughter. The fault was mine, not Channah's. Over the last several months we have become friends, good friends. We were looking out the window enjoying the sunset and, and—" He folded an arm across his chest and scratched the back of his hand as he searched for words to complete his thought.

Stefanos looked at her straight on. "You are correct, Sister Rivkah. I have dishonored your hospitality and behaved inappropriately. Please accept my deepest apologies. I will go to Simon before this night is over and confess my sin of lust."

Rivkah glanced over at Channah.

She wore a bright smile at his mention of lust.

Her mother's stern frown erased the grin.

"And, if he requests it," Stefanos continued, "I will resign from my position as *diakonos*."

Now what had she done? Rivkah only wanted to bank the coals, not extinguish the flame. "I do not think this need go so far as confessing to Simon, or anyone else. Instead, this evening in the quiet of your room, both of you should examine your conscience. If you feel you have sinned, confess it and ask God's forgiveness. The Lord knows what was, or was not, in each of your hearts."

Both of them visibly relaxed.

"One other thing," Rivkah said. "What has happened in this room must stay in this room. Take care that word of this never reaches her father's ears. Do you understand what I am saying?"

Stefanos apologized again, thanked her for the meal and prepared to leave.

She saw him out and, as he left their doorstep, called his name.

He glanced back over his shoulder.

"Will we see you again next week?"

Sweet relief washed over his face. "Oh yes, Sister Rivkah, you may count on it."

Channah grabbed her mother's hand when she returned. "Did you hear him say I incited his lust?"

"You what?"

Channah chuckled. "You need not pretend with me. We both know what he meant. My friends and I discuss these matters." She gave her mother a knowing wink. "I understand all about the ways of men."

"Do you and your friends also discuss the fate which befalls a young woman who makes it a practice to incite a man's lust before they are married."

Channah's face flushed bright red. "I just meant—"

"I know what you meant. Now go to your room and pray about it."

The two of them had lit a powerful spark, unleashing a flame, which if not controlled could consume them both. Even though she was secretly happy for them, Rivkah hoped her words were sufficiently harsh to dampen the flame...at least for a little while.

At that moment, her only concern was that they not blunder into indiscretion.

## ~ 16 ~

One morning, after Shemu'el had gone to the marketplace seeking work and returned empty-handed, someone knocked at the door. He half-heartedly crossed the room, wondering if a member of the Synagogue lay ill or injured. Such emergencies were the only work that came calling.

He opened the door to find a pudgy man in brocade robes on his doorstep. A Nubian slave hovered beside him, fluttering a fan of ostrich feathers to disperse the heat and odor of the street.

Could he be some petty official come to harass them?

"I am Menashe, the vintner," the man said.

"A wine merchant."

The rotund little man puffed out his chest. "The largest seller of wine in all Jerusalem." Menashe studied Shemu'el's homespun clothing for a moment. "And you would be Shemu'el, the former shepherd."

"Yes. What can I do for you?"

"A woman by the name of Miryam resides with the fish merchant, Yohan bar Zebedee. She told my steward you carve in wood."

Shemu'el stepped onto the stoop and closed the door behind him. "You have heard correctly." He rubbed his hands together in anticipation. "What would you like me to carve for you."

"Better if I show you. Come." He flicked a finger at Shemu'el as if he owned him. Menashe clambered onto a waiting donkey. "Walk beside me. I will explain as we travel to my home."

He led Shemu'el to an elaborate estate in the wealthiest section of Jerusalem's west hills. Menashe took him into a large banquet hall and pointed at the ceiling. "I have long thought that a carved piece," he held his hands apart, "about this tall, running around the upper wall where it meets the ceiling would make the room more attractive. Can you do it?"

"I can." Cupping his chin, Shemu'el ran his eyes around the room. "What would you like carved into this wood?"

Menashe shrugged. "You are the artist. What do you suggest?"

"You said you earn your living crushing grapes and selling wine, correct?"

He gave a proud nod.

"Suppose I carved a grapevine running around the room? Do you have something I can sketch with? I will show you what I have in mind."

Menashe clapped his hands. A house slave appeared and he dispatched her to fetch drawing materials.

Shemu'el unrolled the papyrus across a tabletop. He thought for a moment, then traced an undulating line the length of the scroll. He drew a second below it, mimicking its wavelike curves. He tapped the scroll. "This would be the vine."

The merchant hovered beside him, stroking his oiled beard as he watched the design take shape.

Shemu'el added leaves, tendrils and shoots. When he completed them, he glanced back over his shoulder and lifted an eyebrow.

Menashe smiled his appreciation.

Returning to the papyrus, Shemu'el began making a series of circles. "And every so often, a bunch of juicy grapes waiting to be plucked." He leaned aside so the man could see.

"I love it." Menashe hurried across the room and poured two cups of wine. He handed Shemu'el one. "To seal our agreement."

He waited with an expectant look as Shemu'el sipped the wine.

"Good," Shemu'el said. He swirled it on his tongue. "Very good, indeed."

Menashe grinned. "It comes from my vineyards in Galilee. This year the rains came at just the right time." He took a small sip and held it on his tongue for a moment before swallowing. "It is still a bit young, but already it displays the hint of greatness. When can you have the carving ready?"

Shemu'el returned bursting with enthusiasm. "I still have my carving knives," he said as they ate. "Menashe and I agreed on cedar. I will have to contract for some boards." His brow knitted. "Leandros' son now runs his father's wood shop. I wonder if he has any?"

He squinted up at the ceiling, ignoring his food as he planned the work. "And a pattern. I will need to develop a repeating pattern. I measured the room twice. Any seams can be hidden behind grape leaves."

Shemu'el reached over and clapped his middle son, Yaakov, on the back. "You can work as my apprentice. Tomorrow you and I shall go to the vineyards and walk the rows, studying the vines."

He and Yaakov returned with their arms full of grapewood. Shemu'el held up a piece for Rivkah to admire. "Look what I found. I asked if I could take some of their prunings. They did not mind once I explained what I wanted them for." He pointed to another. "Look at this tendril, the way it curls back on itself." He snatched one out of Yaakov's arms. "And this one."

He spread a stack of grape leaves out on the table and glanced at Yaakov beside him. "These all appear the same, but when you examine them closely you can see minute differences. Each one is unique...as ours shall be."

Picking up a stick of charcoal, he motioned his son closer. "These will serve as our template. Bring my papyrus. I must record them before they wither from the heat."

Shemu'el unrolled the long sheet of papyrus he brought from Menashe's. Stretching it out across the table, he drew and redrew his patterns until they satisfied him. He arranged pieces of branches in a semi-circle in front of him, scrutinizing each knot and knob. He spun them around, held them upside down, and turned them this way and that, searching for just the look he wanted.

"Can I see it yet?" Rivkah whispered.

Her voice sounded almost childlike, reminding him of times when they were youngsters sitting in the meadow with the sheep and she watched while he carved.

He moved aside so she could see.

"It's lovely."

Shemu'el grinned. He hadn't been this happy since Obadiah turned him away at the Temple.

"This is the answer to our prayers. When Menashe invites his friends to dine with him, they will see the new molding crowning his room. Soon they, too, will want something similar. This is only the beginning, my dove. Over time, my reputation as a woodcarver will grow. More commissions will surely follow."

He pulled her close. "I have felt like half a man since we lost our contract with the Temple. All that is about to change. Soon I shall be able to support my family once again."

She put a finger to his lips. "I share your excitement, but it is very late."

Shemu'el extinguished the lamp, darkening the room. He pulled her close and kissed along her neck.

"Not in the front room," she whispered. "What if the children wander in?"

With his tools ready and his plans drawn, Shemu'el and Yaakov set off for Leandros' wood shop. They returned a short time later, bitter and disappointed.

Shemu'el banged his fist on the table. "I cannot believe his son refused me credit. The bowls I carved for his father probably put food in his thankless mouth and clothes on his ungrateful back."

"You were a boy when you carved for Leandros," Rivkah said as she kneaded his shoulders. "How old is this son of his?"

Shemu'el thought for a moment. "A few years older than our Yo'el. Less than thirty."

"So he had probably not yet been born when you worked for his father."

Shemu'el ran his fingers through his hair. "True, but the old men in the back of the shop remembered my bowls." He stared down at his hands. "I offered him more than the wood is worth as a premium if he would carry me until I collected from Menashe. He knew I have a commission."

"Perhaps you should request funds for the boards from Menashe."

"I already tried. I would not have gone to Leandros' son if Menashe agreed to advance the funds."

"What did Menashe say?"

"He said I have never worked for him before and a craftsman who cannot afford to buy materials is no craftsman at all."

"What will you tell him now?"

Shemu'el hung his head. "I do not know. When we left our settlement, I believed we could make a life here in Jerusalem. If I back out of this contract, it will destroy my reputation. No one will ever ask me to carve for them again."

They joined hands across the table and prayed for a solution. They prayed not for wood or money, but for direction. "*Ask, and it will be given,*" Yeshua once said. If he wanted Shemu'el to be a woodcarver, he would show them a way. If not, a forest full of wood wouldn't solve their dilemma.

Shemu'el's face brightened. "I know. The Synagogue of Rabban Yeshua *HaMashiach.*"

"What about it?"

"I am not working for myself alone. I also work for the synagogue. I will ask the council of the Twelve to advance funds to purchase my boards. After I carve them and install them in Menashe's house, I can return the money along with my tithe."

Though it embarrassed him to go before the Twelve and beg for money, Shemu'el did it. They deliberated for a few moments, then agreed. Confident of Yeshua's blessing, he purchased the boards and set to work.

He built stands in the small yard behind their house. Each morning, Shemu'el and Yaakov carried the boards outdoors and placed them across the stands. Once they smoothed the wood with *pumicis*, he cut the boards to size and numbered them on the back so they fit together properly.

After transferring his pattern to the boards, Shemu'el began carving. Each day at noon, the two of them came in for their midday meal with curls and chips of wood in their hair and clinging to their tunics. No matter how many times Rivkah insisted they brush off outside, Shemu'el and Yaakov left a trail of wood shavings across her kitchen.

Each evening Shemu'el cooked up a stain from a mixture of tree bark, roots, peels and nut shells and tested it on scraps of wood. One evening he came in with a piece of wood in his hand and a broad smile on his face.

"I have found it." He held the scrap in the light for Rivkah to admire. "The perfect color. What do you think?"

The wood had a rich brown cast, the color of roasted almonds. Turning it, she noticed red undertones. "It is lovely. I am sure Menashe will be pleased."

"I plan to take him a sample in the morning. If he approves it, Yaakov and I will begin staining the boards. Once it dries, I can apply the finish and deliver them." He brought his hands together. "Then I shall collect my fee and repay the synagogue."

He picked Rivkah up and twirled her in his arms. "At long last, things will be good again."

# ~ 17 ~

*"And they stirred up the people and the elders and the scribes, and they came upon him and seized him and brought him before the council..."*

—Acts of the Apostles 6:12

As was their custom, on the second day of each week Rivkah and Channah went to the west hills to sew. Women from the synagogue met in the upper room above the home of Aristopolus to stitch clothing for the poor.

Yeshua and the Twelve ate their last meal in the room where the women now sewed. The Comforter, the Holy Spirit whom Yeshua promised to send, had also appeared there on Pentecost as roaring wind and tongues of fire.

Aristopolus, his wife, Miryam, and their son, Yohan, surnamed Markus, were all members of The Way. Stefanos resided in their home as well; although, to Channah's great disappointment, he was gone when they arrived.

The morning passed quietly. The few words spoken between long, nervous pauses consisted of idle small talk or comments about children and the weather. The budding romance between Stefanos and Channah had become a poorly kept secret. Everyone expected him to approach Shemu'el for her hand in marriage and no one wanted to break the spell by mentioning it prematurely.

For her part, Channah glowed with happiness. As usual, Stefanos would be coming to supper the day after next. Maybe he would ask her father then.

Rivkah hoped he would. Having Stefanos for a son-in-law would make any mother proud. It would also be a milestone for the synagogue, the first union within their congregation.

That night, as most nights, memories of Stefanos' kiss robbed

Channah of her sleep. She passed each day counting the hours until it was time to go to the synagogue to assemble the day's baskets and spent each night remembering their time by the window. She longed to be in her beloved Stefanos' arms again and feel his lips pressed against hers once more.

The next morning, Channah slipped away saying she had an errand to run. Rather than buying thread, or visiting a friend as she told her mother she planned to do, she secretly met with Stefanos. They chose a grassy spot near a grove of olive trees where they could sit together and be alone.

His eyes sparkled with mischief. Hands behind his back, he asked, "Left or right?"

"Do you imagine me foolish enough to fall for such obvious trickery? If I say 'Left,' you transfer the item to your right hand, and, if I say 'Right,' you transfer it to the left. You are no better than the little boy who cups a sparrow in his hand asking whether it is dead or alive."

"Suppose one hand held silver bracelets and a golden necklace dripped between the fingers of the other?"

The tree beside them moved in the breeze, causing leafy shadows to dance around them.

She leaned forward and brushed a kiss across his lips. "Gold or silver mean nothing to me compared to your love."

"You surely must be a little curious."

She folded her hands in her lap. "Very well, have it your way. Right."

Stefanos brought out his right hand and offered her a succulent bunch of grapes.

"Grapes? What happened to my gold and silver?" Though she tried to sound disappointed, Channah found it impossible to be displeased with anything Stefanos did.

"I promise these will be the best grapes you have ever eaten. Close you eyes." He plucked a grape and fed it to her.

She smiled in appreciation. "Where did you find such delicious grapes?"

"I grew them myself."

"I don't believe you."

"You call me a liar?"

"N-o-o, I simply said I don't believe you."

"One evening, while walking in Aristopolus' vineyard, I decided to prepare a special treat for my beloved Channah. Selecting a shoot near the back, on the last row beside the wall, I tied a strip of red cloth around it and asked the vine-dresser to leave it alone.

"After the vine flowered, I carefully removed half of the fruit. Then I thinned the remaining bunches so each grape had enough space to grow big and sweet. I watered the vine and broke away any leaves that shaded the fruit. They are beginning to ripen, so I picked a bunch for you. Several more remain."

They sat side by side, plucking grapes and feeding them to each other. Stefanos spit his seeds to the side.

Channah spit hers straight ahead in long arches.

"Let's see if we can hit that rock jutting from the ground," he suggested.

Stefanos popped a grape into his mouth and so did Channah.

His seed fell wide of its target. Hers hit the mark.

"Amazing. Can you do it again?"

She could and did.

"How about the tree over there?"

Channah narrowed her eyes and sighted the tree. Drawing in a deep breath, she pursed her lips and sent the seed sailing. She grinned when it bounced off the trunk.

Stefanos hugged her. "She carries neither sling nor bow. Yet armed with only a handful of grapes, she strikes terror into the heart of man and beast."

Channah rolled her eyes. "And what do I do when all the grapes have been harvested?"

Stefanos thought for a moment. "How accurate are you with a raisin?"

Laughing, she threw her arms around him and rested her head on Stefanos' strong chest.

He kissed the top of her head. That morning, as usual, she had rinsed her hair with citron-scented water after she bathed.

Many times, alone in his bed at night, Stefanos thought of Channah and recalled the subtle fragrance of her hair. He rested his cheek against her head and breathed deeply of her essence.

When he lifted her chin, Channah's kiss tasted of the grapes they'd shared.

"Tell me again about life in Alexandria," she begged.

He opened his mouth to speak, but noise and shouts from the street below interrupted. He lurched into an upright position.

Channah rolled onto her knees.

Together they watched an angry mob snake along the street below. The group stopped, waiting while a bow-legged man rapped on doors.

"Who is that strange little man?"

"It is Sha'oul."

Hearing the name told Channah all she needed to know.

"They are stopping at every house I serve. He is searching for me."

Channah clutched his arm tightly. "Look, his men have weapons and ropes. They mean to do you harm. They have not seen us yet. We must run, escape while we can."

Stefanos held Channah by the shoulders and stared into her eyes. "Sha'oul's quarrel is with me. You are not part of this. I want you to take shelter in the olive grove while I go down and try to reason with him. You will be safe hidden among the trees."

She thrashed against his strong grip. "No. We must see this through together. I will remain by your side come what may."

He relaxed his hold on Channah. Drawing her into his arms, he tenderly kissed her. "If you love me as you say, you will do what I ask. I could not live with myself if they harmed you because of me."

She tried to protest, but he placed a finger to her lips. "Please, Channah, time is short. Go while you can."

She hesitated a moment longer then, blinking back tears, bolted for the trees.

Stefanos chewed his lip as he watched her flee. Seeing her safely hidden, he turned and headed down the hill to face Sha'oul and his mob. With each step he whispered a prayer for her safety.

Up above, Channah bent a branch and peeked between the leaves.

The men saw Stefanos coming and began screaming insults.

She watched him approach the belligerent mob and speak to them calmly.

Sha'oul waved his arms and shouted in Stefanos' face. Encouraged by Sha'oul's behavior, one of the men swung a fist.

Unprepared, Stefanos absorbed the full force of the blow. He staggered back and toppled over.

Channah put a hand to her mouth to stifle her frightened cry. Tears trickled down her cheeks.

The men jerked him up and tied his hands behind his back. Looping a rope around his neck, they led him away like an animal.

Channah ran a parallel path between the trees. When the mob turned a corner, she circled ahead of them and joined the shoppers at the next cross street. When they approached, she slipped into a doorway and hid in the shadows.

Falling in behind, she trailed behind at a safe distance. When Channah overheard their plans she broke away and made a wild dash for home.

## ~ 18 ~

*"But they...rushed together upon him. Then they cast him out of the city and began to stone him; and the witnesses laid down their garments at the feet of a young man named Saul."*

— Acts of the Apostles 7:57-58

Channah burst into the house wide-eyed and sweating. Her hair had come undone and hung around her face in damp ringlets.

"Sha'oul," she gasped, and sank to the floor. She knelt with her head down, panting for breath.

Rivkah ran to the kitchen and brought her water.

Channah's fingers shook as she held the glass. She took a deep breath, put it to her lips, and gulped it down.

"What happened to you?"

Channah waved away her question. She whipped off her veil and used it like a towel to mop her damp face. Running her fingers along the sides of her head, she gathered her flyaway hair and tied it back.

"Sha'oul and his henchmen have taken Stefanos prisoner."

"How do you know?"

"I watched it all from the trees."

"You told me you planned to walk to a friend's house. What have you been doing behind my back?"

She shook her head. "Not now, Imma." Here words came in frenzied bursts between gulps for air. "Nothing matters but Stefanos. I followed...listened...heard them say they were taking him to the Temple. They'll try him before the Great Sanhedrin."

Channah heaved herself up. "Something terrible is about to happen. I can feel it." A look of desperation distorted her features. "We must do something. I cannot abandon him."

Their path took them through the bazaar of the fishmongers. Seeing Miryam near the front of the Zebedee's shop, Rivkah asked her to accompany them.

Miryam took one look at Channah's face and ran for her

purse without waiting for an explanation.

"What has happened to Stefanos," Miryam asked.

Shouts from the street below drowned out Channah's reply. Hurrying down the hill, they saw Stefanos in the midst of the mob. The men jostled and cursed him as they shoved him along.

"What did I tell you?" Channah raced toward the crowd calling his name.

She'd nearly reached the intersection of streets when a hard blow threw Stefanos sideways. He lurched in her direction and fell to the pavement, striking his head.

His captors quickly surrounded him.

Channah watched in terror as they pummeled him.

One of the men shoved his way through the group. Grabbing Stefanos by the wrists, he hauled him to his feet.

"I must go to her." Leaving Miryam, Rivkah ran to protect Channah.

Stefanos' head wobbled and his eyes rolled in their sockets. He stumbled like a drunkard, struggling to regain his balance.

Channah shouted his name.

He turned at the sound of her voice. Bleeding cuts, welts and bruises marred his once handsome face. They stared into each other's eyes. For a brief instant the pain and the mob and the shouts fell away. He smiled and mouthed her name.

Then his captors closed around him and tore him away from her.

Their shouts muffled her anguished scream. She grabbed at the men's cloaks trying to make her way to Stefanos.

Rivkah took her by the arms and restrained her.

Miryam arrived to help.

The mob moved north toward the Damascus Gate, circling and lunging at Stefanos like a pack of wild dogs.

The two women closed around Channah, hugging her tightly.

Wide-eyed and shaking, Channah limped along between them. She swept a sleeve across her face. "Stefanos is a peaceful man. What could he have done to provoke such violence?"

Just then a little man jogged by. He trailed behind the mob

making it appear he wasn't part of them. The midday sun reflected off his prematurely bald scalp. He carried his robes hiked-up around his spindly legs, skipping and trotting to keep up

Deciding the men holding Stefanos were slacking off in their duty, he dropped his robes and swirled a fist in circles above his head. "Blasphemer!" he cried in a shrill voice. "All who blaspheme must die. Stone him! Stone him!"

"Sha'oul," Channah gasped. "There is the evil man Stefanos complained about."

"How can you be certain?"

"Stefanos pointed him out to me once. I would know the little maggot anywhere."

Sha'oul reached down for his robe. As he did, his sandal caught in a crack in the pavement. He careened across the street and caught himself on a wrought iron gate. Straightening, he carefully adjusted his cloak and ran after the mob shouting encouragement.

"I wish he had fallen and split his head open like a pomegranate," Channah muttered.

"Do you know anything about that man?" Rivkah asked Miryam

"Channah is correct; his name is Sha'oul. He is a tentmaker from Tarsus, in Cilicia. Stefanos complained about him to Yohan one day when he returned from making the daily distribution. He said Sha'oul has been trying to incite the people against believers by claiming we are somehow responsible for the current famine."

Footsteps pounded behind the women as they approached the Damascus Gate. Looking back, they saw Miryam's protector, Yohan, running toward them. His face was flushed and sweat beaded on his forehead.

"Imma Miryam, are you all right? I heard the shouting from the shop, saw the crowd heading north, and remembered you left with Rivkah. I was worried about you." He took a deep breath. "Worried for all of you."

"It was kind of you to come, but you should not have worried." Miryam mopped his damp face with the hem of her veil. "We are never without protection."

He pointed toward the mob. "I know those men. They are Cyrenians, Alexandrians and Cilicians from the Synagogue of the Freedman. Sha'oul of Tarsus has whipped them into a murderous rage. They hauled Stefanos before the High Priest and accused him of blasphemy."

Yohan touched their shoulders, exerting light pressure. "It would be better if you returned with me to the shop."

Channah planted her feet and refused to be moved. "No! I will never abandon Stefanos to those thugs."

"You would be safer at the shop, my men are there to protect you."

"They would not harm women," Miryam said. "If anyone is at risk, it is you. You are the one who goes to the Porch of Solomon each day to preach." She made shooing motions with her hand. "It was kind of you to come, but you can go back to your work. For Channah's sake, we must see this through to its conclusion."

"The Master entrusted you to my care. If you stay, I stay." Stepping in front, Yohan led the way.

The men slammed Stefanos against the huge blocks supporting the archway of the gate. He thudded against the wall and crumpled to the ground.

Channah broke free. Calling his name, she ran to help him.

Yohan quickly overtook her. Placing his hands on her arms, he gently, but firmly, turned her aside. She thrashed and fought as he marched her back to where the others waited.

The bandy-legged man, Sha'oul, circled the mob with arms extended, grinning as he collected the men's cloaks. When his arms were full, he leaned back against the city gate to watch. Men continued tossing their cloaks at his feet for safekeeping.

Struggling to his knees, Stefanos blinked the blood and sweat out of his eyes and stared up at him. "Brother Sha'oul, you should not be here. Have nothing to do with this evil venture. The Lord Yeshua sees into the heart of every man. He knows your motives. Do not let the demon of jealousy seduce you into sin and everlasting condemnation. Go now. Run from this vile deed."

Sha'oul's expression darkened at this unexpected rebuke. He stared at his former classmate in silence for a moment, then looked away.

Stefanos lifted his eyes to the sky and smiled. His face glowed bright as the morning sun. "Look!" he cried. "I see the heavens opened and the Son of Man standing at the right hand of God. The *Mashiach*, the *Christos*, comes for his lowly servant."

The crowd began shouting curses, drowning out the rest of his words. Two burly men grabbed Stefanos by the arms and drug him to the precipice.

Channah's terrified shriek echoed down the street. She collapsed against her mother as he disappeared over the edge.

Stefanos bounced and pitched down the rocky hillside, landing in a heap beside a boulder.

A semi-circle of men inched forward. Clutching stones to their chests, they waited and watched for movement.

Stefanos lifted his bloodied head.

The men raised the stones above their heads and cast them down on him. Two men inched through the crowd sideways, sharing a huge rock between them. They swung it back and, on a count, flung it over the side at him. They grinned and dusted their hands as they watched the boulder thunder down the sheer cliff toward Stefanos.

He turned his eyes heavenward as stones pounded his broken body. "Lord, do not hold this sin against them," he prayed. Then his head drooped and his eyes closed.

The men continued to watch his lifeless body, checking for movement. Channah stared blankly, looking but not seeing.

Miryam shook her head as they turned to leave. "And so it begins already."

"I don't understand," Rivkah said.

"Yeshua told his disciples a servant is not greater than his master," she explained. "He warned that just as they persecuted him, his followers would also be persecuted." She gave a quick backward glance over her shoulder. "None of us is safe now."

# ~ 19 ~

*"Devout men buried Stephen, and made great lamentation over him."*

— Acts of the Apostles 8:2

The mob remained for a time, checking for any further movement.

A widening circle of blood soaked the sleeve where Stefanos' injured head rested against his arm.

"He's dead," someone hollered. Satisfied that they had accomplished their gruesome task, the men retrieved their cloaks and drifted away.

Sha'oul waited until everyone left, then moved to the edge a final time. He stared down at the bruised and blooded form of the once handsome Stefanos. A fellow student. A man who had called him brother and forgiven him his sin. He glanced around, making certain no one watched. For an instant it appeared he intended to whisper prayers for the dead.

Instead Sha'oul muttered a curse and spit into the abyss.

Late that afternoon a hooded man moved through the city leading a donkey laden with bundles. Looking neither left nor right, he traversed the main thoroughfare with measured steps. When he reached Herod's hippodrome he led the donkey into the shadows of its arched entryway and waited.

A few moments later another man, shorter by a head, materialized from the shadows. He too wore a cowl pulled over his head.

"Welcome," the shorter man said. "You are now a member of our *Chevra Kadisha*."

"It is a privilege to be counted a member of your holy society. There is no greater mitzvah than burying the dead."

"True enough. When you bury the dead, the person you serve can never say, 'Thank you.'" The second man eyed the bundle tied to the donkey's back. "Do you have everything?"

"All has been taken care of. I sent two servants ahead. They will meet us at the gate." The tall, thin, gray-haired man glanced back at the lengthening sun. "Time is short. We must be on the move."

The two of them conferred in furtive whispers as they continued north. A short time later a third person emerged from an alleyway and fell in step beside them. The three men followed a predetermined route, communicating, more often than not, with hand signals and gestures rather than words.

High above them, soldiers walked the battlements along the city's north wall. Reaching their destination, the little group sank into the cool shadows of the city gate. The taller of the three gave a soft whistle. At this pre-arranged signal a door beside them swung aside. A moment later, the men and the donkey slipped out of the city unnoticed.

They conferred in hushed whispers with the waiting servants. Armor clanked and the tramp of feet and gruff voices echoed above them. The men had timed their arrival to coincide with the changing of the guard and used this diversion to rush into the valley.

Down and down they clambered, weaving around rocks and between boulders. Pausing to catch their breath, they watched a camel caravan on the road above approach the Damascus Gate. While the guards concentrated on admitting these new arrivals, the men rushed into the gorge and retrieved Stefanos' corpse.

Laying his broken body across the donkey's back, they hurried away. A narrow path led them back up the bank and onto the Emmaus Road. They'd gone only a short distance when one of the servants said, "Here is the aqueduct, Rab. We can use its cool, pure water to wash away the blood, purifying the remains."

The taller man shook his head "When a person dies a violent death, and his lifeblood has saturated his clothing, there is no *taharah*. The corpse remains unwashed because blood is part of the body and cannot be separated from it in death."

They continued on to the place of tombs. Opening the bundle on the donkey's back, the men removed a folded packet of cloth. Woven of pure bleached linen, it was without hems signifying the impermanence of life, and had no pockets, indicating you took no worldly goods with you when you left this life. Working together, they unfurled it out on the ground.

"There," the taller man said, indicating where he wanted the servants to place the body.

The three men knelt beside Stefanos' corpse, one on each side and one near the head. A servant brought them bags of spices. Scooping some out, they anointed the body for burial. They spoke softly and, out of respect for the dead, never passed anything over the body as they worked.

After anointing the body, they straightened Stefanos' clothing, arranged his hands and aligned his feet. Then they wrapped the linen cloth around him forming a shroud.

The first rays of sunset could be seen against the western sky by the time they placed Stefanos' body on a burial bench inside Gamali'el's tomb. Throwing back their cowls, the three men knelt on the chamber's stone floor. They recited the prayers of the dead, imploring God to send angels of mercy and bidding Stefanos to go in peace, rest in peace, and arise in his turn at the end of days.

Rising, the tallest of the group approached the burial bench. "You were taken from us too soon, my friend and disciple," he said softly. He rested a hand alongside the young man's head. "Of all the fish that ever came into my net, you were by far the best of the best. Intercede with the Father for those of us you leave behind. More will join you soon enough."

Gamali'el traced the immortal mark of Yeshua's cross on the young man's forehead and turned aside, wiping his eyes.

The men left the tomb and waited while the servants released the chock. The stone rolled across, sealing the opening. Their helpers and the donkey melted away without a word, leaving Gamali'el, Yosef of Arimathea and Nikademus to walk back into the city together.

# ~ 20 ~

Rivkah prepared the *se'udat habra'ah* and Channah ate her bread and eggs in silence. She remained in her room the first three days of *Shiv'ah*, weeping and praying. On the morning of the fourth day she emerged with ashes on her head wearing a sackcloth smock. The left shoulder of her cloak, the one closest to her heart, hung loose where she'd torn it in her grief. She completed the ritual first week of mourning curled in a corner, rocking and moaning as she recited Torah verses on Stefanos' behalf.

Though she wore the sackcloth for the rest of *Shloshim*, her month of mourning, Channah gradually resumed her daily tasks. Channah and Rivkah were preparing the evening meal when Rivkah's hair came undone and fell across her eyes. She puffed a breath up at it, moving it aside until she could clean her hands.

"I need a comb," Rivkah said. "Can I use yours?"

"It's in my bag on the table." Channah remained at the counter, slicing vegetables.

The bag seemed unusually heavy when Rivkah picked it up. Opening the drawstring, she felt for the ivory comb. Instead, her hand touched a hard, cloth-wrapped package.

It thumped against the tabletop when she pulled it out. "What is this?"

Channah's head snapped around. Tossing aside her cucumber, she ran toward her mother waving her hands. "Do not open that. I said you could get my comb, not rummage through my possessions."

Despite her protest, Rivkah untied the cord. "What could you possibly have in your purse that your mother should not see?"

Shivers of fear raced up her spine when she folded back the wrapping. Rivkah stared in shocked silence, a thousand questions running through her mind. A slim dagger with a handle formed from a piece of antler lay in front of her. Rainbows sparkled off its polished steel blade.

Channah slid the package across the table and quickly refolded the cloth. "Have I no privacy?"

"Do you know what that is?"

"Yes, a *sicarius*." She scooped it off the table and shoved it back into her bag. Channah fished out her comb and slapped it down on the table. "Here is the comb you wanted."

"Where did you acquire such thing?"

Channah snatched her bag off the table and headed for her room. She spoke over her shoulder as she walked. "I got it the same place you get anything, in the marketplace."

She returned a moment later and resumed slicing as if nothing out of the ordinary had occurred.

Rivkah crossed the room and took the paring knife out of her hand. "Why does my daughter carry a *sicarius* in her purse?"

Channah's brow knitted. She chewed at her lip, struggling to find a plausible explanation. "Because I wanted to," she finally said, lifting her chin.

"That is no reason."

"Very well, if you must know, I bought it so I would have it when I wanted it."

Rivkah pounded her fist on the counter. "For what purpose?"

Both of them were now shouting.

"Stand here and I will demonstrate for you." Channah took her mother by the shoulders and placed her in the center of the room.

"Someday, when I am walking on the street, or in the marketplace, or in the Temple courtyard, Sha'oul will pass by. And when he does, I will begin trailing him."

Rising onto tiptoes, Channah silently inched toward her mother. "I'll match my steps to his steps, slowing when he slows, speeding up when he speeds up, all the while moving so quietly that he never knows I am there."

A sly grin curled her lips as she reached into her imaginary purse. "And when the time is right, my hand will slip into my bag and my fingers will close around the handle of my *sicarius*."

It frightened Rivkah to listen to her daughter describe her

plot in such cold, unemotional tones.

"When Sha'oul least suspects it, I will rush up behind him and exact my revenge." She made a sudden leap forward and grabbed her mother's left shoulder.

Rivkah's head instinctively snapped around.

Channah put her mouth close to her mother's ear and whispered, "This is for Stefanos." Then she plunged her imaginary blade between the ribs below her mother's left breast.

Rivkah spun away from her. "Murder? You plan to commit murder? You cannot do this."

"I can. The Torah says, 'an eye for an eye, a tooth for a tooth.' Sha'oul is responsible for Stefanos' death." Channah's expression hardened. "He must die for what he did."

"Listen to what you are saying. Do you honestly believe you can kill another human being?"

"Could I kill another human being? No." Channah tossed her wavy hair aside. "But Sha'oul is not a human being. I will slaughter him like the pig he is."

"What kind of a memorial is that?"

"The only one I can offer Stefanos." Malice burned bright in Channah's eyes. "Sha'oul thinks he consigned my beloved Stefanos to the fires of *Gehenna*, but in the end he will be the one who burns."

"And what about Channah? What will happen to her? This is a fool's errand. The Commandment of God says, 'Thou shalt commit no murder.' Do you wish to dwell in *Gehenna* alongside Sha'oul?"

"Someone must do something. Stefanos' death cannot go unrequited."

"'*Vengeance is mine*,' says the Lord. This is madness. Your grief drives you to think crazy thoughts. Would Stefanos want the woman he loved to become a killer? He is in heaven with the angels and saints. If you want to see him again you will put this nonsense aside."

Channah turned away without a word. She walked to the counter, picked up another cucumber, and resumed slicing.

## ~ 21 ~

"Careful. Easy now. We do not want any scratches."

Sunlight sparkled off the pristine finish of the board Shemu'el eased out the backdoor of the house. His middle son, Yaakov, on the other end, followed his father into the yard where they placed it face-up on one of the stands. They wrapped the board carefully and packed it into the back of the cart beside the others.

The cart and donkey belonged to Zebedee's fish market. Shemu'el borrowed it the day before. Yaakov spent the previous afternoon scrubbing and re-scrubbing the sides and floor of the cart. He did a good job. Even with his face next to the cart's floor, Shemu'el hardly noticed the fishy smell.

As an extra precaution, they spread fresh straw across the bed of the cart. Not only did it provide a buffer between Menashe's molding and the floor of the cart, it padded them during transport.

They put in the last board and secured the load with ropes. Before they left Shemu'el added a sack of forged nails. He grabbed the donkey's lead and gave him a slap. They were off to deliver their boards.

Yaakov tossed the rope handle of his father's toolbox over his shoulder. It held Shemu'el's glue pot, a horsehair brush and a quantity of freshly made hide glue, dried and broken into crystals.

The day before, while Yaakov scrubbed the cart, Shemu'el went to the tanners and purchased odd scraps of rawhide. From there he went to the butcher and procured a couple of hooves. When he returned, he made a smelly concoction of water, hooves and rawhide and, over Rivkah's objections, cooked it in the backyard.

The toolbox Yaakov carried also contained a sack of individually carved grapes, leaves and shoots.

Shemu'el drilled holes through the boards at regular intervals. When they installed them in Menashe's dining room, he planned to secure them to the wall by driving nails through those holes. Then, using his glue pot, he'd attach a leaf, shoot or grape to conceal his work.

When her *Shiv'ah* ended Channah began to haunt the streets of Jerusalem. Looking like a wild woman in her tattered sackcloth dress, torn cloak and flyaway hair streaked gray with ashes, she relentlessly searched for Sha'oul.

Channah relived the tales Stefanos told her as she stalked her prey. She'd never seen the Great Sea, tasted the faint saltiness its breeze left on your lips, or walked its sandy beaches with waves breaking across her bare feet. Yet she felt she had because she'd sat beside Stefanos as he described those moments to her.

Following her usual route, she passed the former palace of the Hasmoneans and headed for the Temple. Always on the lookout, her eyes flicked back and forth, watching, checking... hoping today would be the day she encountered Sha'oul.

Channah grew increasingly familiar with life on Jerusalem's streets. She came to recognize every shop and shopkeeper. Even the beggars who lingered on the street corners nodded to her when she passed.

She walked her route reliving dreams of life with Stefanos. She imagined standing on a hill with the wind whipping at her hair, listening to the call of gulls and staring across the seemingly endless expanse of the Nile Delta. Channah had never seen fishing boats unloading their catch along the breakwater at Alexandria's harbor, or watched an Imperial galley, resplendent with its gilded figurehead and silver-trimmed gunwales, arrive amid trumpet fanfare with crimson banners flying. Knowing she probably never would, she treasured the small sketch of the ship Stefanos once made for her.

As she walked the streets searching for Sha'oul, Channah's fingers regularly slipped into her bag and touched the wrapped handle of her *sicarius*. The dagger's heft became the ballast that gave her life balance, the center around which her dream of revenge orbited.

Stefanos once promised they would someday retrace a trip he took with his father. As she hunted Sha'oul, Channah imagined herself accompanying Stefanos to the plateau near Memphis where they would see the Great Sphinx, a gigantic statue of a resting lion with the face of a man, and the huge limestone pyramids it guarded. From there, he said, they would take a barge down the Nile, traveling south to Thebes and the *Ta-sekhet-ma'at*, the Great Fields, which formed the royal necropolis known as the Valley of the Kings.

Like a fine etching, she had carved each detail into her memory making the trip seem real. Yet late at night, in the darkness of her room, she acknowledged with tears that the only trips she would ever take would be imaginary ones.

Channah reached the city wall, the end of her route, with no sign of Sha'oul. She turned toward home with a disappointed sigh.

True to her pattern, she climbed the Temple steps and entered the Courtyard of the Gentiles. She paused there to scan the worshippers as they entered and left. She wondered how the Temple complex compared in size to the library at Alexandria. Like Herod's Temple, Stefanos had said the Alexandrian Library was the largest in the world. Within its walls were thousands upon thousand of texts...all the wisdom of the world.

And because of Sha'oul, she would never see it.

Channah descended the steps and wove a random path through Jerusalem's streets. She'd nearly written the day off when her heart leaped in her chest. Through the crowd she saw a short, bandy-legged man coming toward her. Spinning aside, she stepped into a merchant's stall and pretended to examine his merchandise.

Her right hand slipped into her bag. A satisfied gleam lit her eyes when her fingers touched the dagger's handle.

Sha'oul approached, pulled alongside, and continued on his way without even a glance.

Channah watched him out of the side of her eyes. A moment later she melted into the press of shoppers and fell in behind him. With her long legs she could easily have overtaken him. Instead, as she'd assured her mother, Channah sped up when he sped up and slowed whenever he slowed.

She fingered the bony texture of the dagger's handle as she walked, stalking him as patiently as a lion pursued its prey.

A commotion erupted on a side street and the crowd came to a sudden halt.

Two steps later Channah saw the reason. An over-burdened camel had plopped itself down in the street and refused to rise. A frantic camel boy circled the animal waving his arms and spewing commands. He tugged the lead rope with all his might, but the rebellious animal wouldn't budge. Unable to overpower him, he kicked the camel's flanks in frustration.

Sha'oul, being shorter than most, could not see. He scurried around the fringes of the crowd hunting for a spot where he could observe the proceedings. Finding one, he crossed his arms and began to chuckle at the young man's misfortune.

Channah crept closer.

Sha'oul laughed with the crowd when the unruly camel spit on its handler.

Inches behind him, Channah patiently waited. She couldn't have planned things any better. The camel provided distraction and the maze of streets and alleyways offered myriad escape routes. Her fingers trembled as they tightened around the handle of her *sicarius*.

Sha'oul leaned to one side to get a better view of the street. They were so close his cloak brushed against hers.

Channah sucked in her breath and waited, hoping he hadn't noticed. Sweat beaded on her forehead. She'd practiced this moment until it became instinctive as the steps of a dance, the dance of death.

She lifted her left arm, reaching for Sha'oul's shoulder the way she'd done with her mother. Revenge will be sweet, she thought, sweeter than honey in the comb.

# ~ 22 ~

*"And on that day a great persecution arose against the
church at Jerusalem..."*

— Acts of the Apostles 8:1

Shemu'el reined the donkey to a stop outside Menashe's home.
Handing the lead to Yaakov, he bounded around the cart and
rang the bell at the gate.

A servant appeared.

Shemu'el smiled. "I have come to install the crown boards
your master ordered."

The servant shook his head. "Rab say he no longer want the
boards you bring."

"There must be some mistake." Shemu'el gestured at the
back of the cart. "Your master commissioned me to carve these
especially for him. The work is complete. Let me in so I can
install them."

"Rab say no boards. I only do what he tells me to."

Shemu'el grabbed the wrought iron gate and shook it hard
enough to rattle it on its hinges. "I said, let me in!"

The man shrugged and turned away.

Shemu'el thrust his arm between the bars and snagged the
back of the man's cloak. Nearly jerking him off his feet, he
slammed the man back against the bars. "You will get Menashe
out here right now, or I'll rip you and this gate apart to get to
him."

The quaking servant motioned with his hands and nodded.
"I go get Rab for you now."

Shemu'el released him.

The man motioned with the flat of his hand "You wait here."
He gave Shemu'el a wary glance and smoothed his clothing
before heading to the house.

Shemu'el straightened when Menashe came down the walk.

The heavy-set man stopped several cubits from the gate and
frowned. "Why have you mistreated my servant?"

"I only insisted upon seeing you." Shemu'el chuckled and pointed toward the cart. "Somehow, the silly man got the idea you didn't want to take delivery of these beautiful carvings you commissioned."

"He spoke correctly."

The ground dropped away beneath Shemu'el's feet. A quiver of fear clawed at his stomach. "How can this be? We made an agreement. We drank wine on it."

"You rendered the contract invalid when you failed to identify yourself. As an observant Jew, I have no dealings with heathens and unbelievers."

Shemu'el glanced around angrily. "Heathens? There is no one here but me and I am certainly no heathen."

"No, you are a heretic, which is even worse. Take your material and vacate my premises." Menashe dusted his hands. "I want nothing more to do with you."

"How dare you call me a heretic; there must be some mistake."

"Do you deny attending the Synagogue of Rabban Yeshua? Are you not a member of this thing they call The Way?"

"No. Yes, but..." Shemu'el gave a hopeless shrug.

"If you darken my door again, I will report you to the authorities." Menashe pointed down the street. "Now be gone." Turning, he headed back to the house.

Shemu'el pushed his arm between the bars of the gate and stretched toward him. "Just take a look at them. These boards are the loveliest I have ever carved. Think about what you are doing. As a businessman your word is your bond. We had an agreement."

Glancing back, Menashe scoffed. "Did we now? Go tell the priests and see if they will enforce it." He watched Shemu'el turn away from the gate, called "Raca!" and spit on the ground.

Shemu'el snatched the reins out of Yaakov's hand. "Come, we are not wanted here."

"What will we do now, Abba?"

Shmeu'el stared at the road as if he hadn't heard the question. What could he tell his son? That in an instant his dreams had turned to ashes? What would they do now? Take them home, he supposed. Maybe find someone else who would pay something for them.

In the meantime, he had to empty the cart. Yohan needed his cart and donkey back to make deliveries.

While Channah visited her friends, Rivkah went to Zebedee's Fish Market to share a midday meal with Miryam. She avoided details when Miryam asked about Channah, preferring to say only that she continued to mourn.

"I have something to share with you that may bring her some peace," Yohan said as they ate. "As usual, after the mob finished with Stefanos they left his broken body in the valley. Certain devout men crept into the valley and recovered Stefanos' remains before the Sanhedrin's burial detail arrived."

"Where did they lay him to rest?"

Yohan shifted on his seat. He swallowed the last bit of fish and swept his tongue around his mouth. "Is it necessary for you to know?" he asked, taking a sip of wine.

"Forgive me. He loved my Channah and she loved him. Had Stefanos lived they would undoubtedly have married. I never imagined any reason why I should not know."

"One cannot always discern the presence of fish in murky waters." He broke a loaf and dipped a piece into a bowl of seasoned oil. He chewed it absentmindedly, trying to decide what to do or say next.

Noticing Yohan's discomfort, Miryam placed her hand over his. "The choice is yours, my son, but Rivkah will not betray secrets. I believe Channah deserves to know."

Yohan nodded. "This group I mentioned carried Stefanos's corpse to the place of the tombs where they prepared his body for burial. After reciting the prayers for the dead, they placed him in one of the *kochim* in Gamali'el's sepulcher and rolled the stone over the entrance."

"Gamali'el? The leader of the School of Hillel and Nasi of

the Sanhedrin? What will happen when he finds out Stefanos is resting in one of his burial niches?"

Miryam brought up a hand to cover her grin.

"He already knows," Yohan grunted. "Gamali'el organized the party that recovered Stefanos' body."

Rivkah stared from one to the other trying to make sense of what he'd said.

Miryam leaned close and rested an arm around her shoulder. "You see, Yeshua always had powerful friends. From the very beginning there were those who came in secret, Jew and Gentile alike. Individuals whose wealth, power, or position prevented them from expressing their beliefs openly. We refer to them as the *hidden ones*."

"Afraid of what might happen if they were seen with us," Yohan continued, "they sent their servants to our camp at night." He motioned to the other side of the room. "The Lord frequently met with them here in these rooms. But sometimes events force them to ignore the consequences and step forward."

"Do you recall Nikademus and Yosef of Arimathea, the two men who came to Golgotha carrying orders from Pilate and cloths and embalming spices?" Miryam asked.

"In the grief of the moment I never questioned their presence."

"Both are members of the Great Sanhedrin," Yohan said. "They risked their positions by approaching Pilate. Jairus, the leader of the synagogue at Capernaum, also came in secret. But when his daughter grew deathly ill, he humbled himself at the Master's feet begging him to cure her. Though she was dead by the time we reached their home, Yeshua took her by the hand and restored her to life."

"And Gamali'el, he is one of these hidden ones?"

"Yes. He will reveal himself at the proper time...or maybe never at all. They are known to the Lord, which is all that really matters."

Miryam called Rivkah aside after Yohan returned to the shop. "I have something for you," she said with a conspiratorial wink. "For Channah, actually."

She offered her a crumpled scroll.

Rivkah hesitated, afraid to touch the dirty, stained papyrus.

"It belonged to Stefanos. He had it hidden next to his body the day he died. Gamali'el discovered it when they prepared him for burial. He passed it on to me, trusting I would know what to do with it. Everything will become clear once you open it."

She placed the scroll in Rivkah's hand and folded her fingers over it.

Rivkah untied it and gasped when she saw the words of the *Shir HaShirim*. Looking closer, she noticed Stefanos had begun altering the text of Solomon's Song of Songs. Beside each phrase spoken by the *Lover* he wrote, Στεφανος, *Stefanos*, and next the *Beloved's* reply, he added Γδανα, *Channah*.

Blinking back tears, Rivkah hugged her. "Thank you," she whispered over the lump in her throat. "I will see that she gets it."

# ~ 23 ~

Killing Sha'oul turned out to be more difficult than going through the motions with her mother. Channah's hand fluttered in the air when she reached for him. Spots danced before her eyes. The street, the buildings, the merriment of the crowd faded into a background of swirling colors. Knowing she was about to collapse and frightened she might fail, she lurched at Sha'oul.

Her hand grazed his shoulder and snagged in the fabric of his cloak. As the ground rushed up to meet her, Channah's fingers tightened around the cloth in a desperate attempt to break her fall.

Without intending to, she pulled Sha'oul down on top of her. The fingers of her other hand remained hidden in her bag around the handle of the *sicarius.*

"*Kill him while you can.*" An evil voice inside her head said.

Channah lay motionless on the pavement as her world spun out of control. Like so much of her life was this too a dream? A nightmare gone awry?

Sha'oul quickly rolled onto his knees and apologized profusely. "You wear sackcloth. Your mourning must have made you weak." He mopped her sweaty brow with his sleeve and brushed dust off her cheek. "How can I assist you?"

Channah blinked up at him in dazed confusion. She seemed to be watching her life instead of living it. Why was Sha'oul kneeling over her? Shouldn't he be dead in the street? Nothing made sense. Things had somehow...come apart. She fumbled to untangle her hand in the purse.

Sha'oul rose to his feet and offered her his hand.

Channah lifted herself into a sitting position and held her throbbing head.

A merchant rushed out of his shop carrying water.

Sha'oul took it from him and knelt beside her, offering her the cup.

Channah took the cup with both hands and drained it. Her moment of opportunity had come and gone.

The reluctant camel in the middle of the intersection rose and plodded away. The crowd dispersed leaving Channah and Sha'oul alone.

He helped her up.

She rocked on her feet.

Sha'oul gripped her elbow, steadying her. "Where do you live? I will accompany you safely home."

She touched her hand to the spot where her head hit the pavement, checking for blood. "It is very close, you need not trouble yourself."

"It is no trouble. I only wish I had noticed you stumble. I might have broken your fall."

"You do not understand," she stammered. Channah handed him the empty cup and raced away.

Shemu'el left Menashe's estate feeling more defeated than when he'd been turned away at the Temple. Shoulders slumped and chin resting on his chest, he shuffled down the hill toward the old city.

Yaakov plodded along behind. He chewed his lip and stared at the pavement, fearing anything he did or said might make their situation worse.

They stopped where two streets crossed and waited for the foot traffic to clear the intersection. To their left, the street led to the Synagogue of Rabban Yeshua *HaMashiach*. To the right, it led home. Shemu'el thought about how quickly he'd taken funds from the common purse. He recalled his confidence and how certain he was the Lord smiled on this endeavor.

In retrospect he wondered why he had interpreted Menashe's commission as a sign of divine approval. Now here he stood, humiliated, and unable to repay the loan.

Yaakov tugged at his sleeve. "We should go now, Abba. Please, people are staring."

"It is good that you are paying attention."

Shemu'el hesitated an instant longer then gave the reins a sharp tug. To his son's surprise, he turned the donkey in the direction of the synagogue. He pulled the cart off to one side when they reached the building and handed the reins to his son. "Wait here."

The door swung aside when he tested it. Following voices, he found Simon and Yaakov in a small back room.

They looked up when they saw him.

Shemu'el fell to his knees before them and bowed his head. "I have sinned against you and all the members of this synagogue. I took funds from the treasury and now I am unable to repay them."

"What has happened, my brother?" Simon asked.

Shemu'el thought for a moment before answering. What had happened was he dreamed of being celebrated for his artistry, of getting more and greater commissions, of becoming renowned...even wealthy, perhaps.

"I succumbed to the demon of pride," Shemu'el said. "When you agreed to advance me the money to buy wood, I took it to be a sign of Yeshua's blessing. Instead, I have squandered the group's resources for my own gain. Menashe broke the contract, calling me a heretic. With no funds to repay my debt, I must throw myself to your mercy."

Simon helped him up. "Save the confessions for now. Do you have the boards with you?"

Shemu'el did.

"Bring one of them to us so we may see it."

Yaakov and Simon admired the board in Shemu'el's hand. They ran their fingers over the wood marveling at the intricacy and lifelike realism of the carving and its lovely finish. After they conferred brieflySimon announced, "You shall install them in our sanctuary."

"I do not understand."

"The Lord once told us he was the vine and we were the branches. Without our connection to him, we can bear no fruit." Simon lovingly patted the board. "This is an appropriate adornment for our synagogue." Chuckling, he threw an arm over

Shemu'el's shoulder. "You did not misinterpret the Lord's hand in this project; you merely confused the ultimate recipient of your artistry."

"It is very kind of you to try and help me out of this dilemma, but they will not fit. I cut them to size expressly for Menashe's banquet hall."

"Measure and see."

Shemu'el went to the cart and retrieved his measuring chain. With his son's help, he measured the room as Simon requested.

When they finished, Yaakov watched his father's brow wrinkle as he studied the figures he'd scribbled. "What is it, Abba?"

"I do not trust these results. There must be a mistake." He motioned his son over to him. "We will measure again starting with this wall. This time hold the chain exactly as I instructed you."

"I always do," Yaakov muttered under his breath as he walked into the corner.

To Shemu'el's surprise and delight, the sanctuary had the same dimensions as Menashe's banquet hall. Where the dining room was long, but not wide, the synagogue's sanctuary was wide, but not deep. The boards would fit perfectly.

"Leave them here overnight along with your tools," Simon suggested when Shemu'el reported his findings. "You and the boy can begin the installation in the morning."

Channah's mind raced as she ran from Sha'oul. Terrified, and hurting in body and spirit, she moved blindly through the streets and alleyways. She turned corners randomly and followed streets without paying attention to where they led.

Her burning lungs eventually forced her to stop. She looked around in dismay. Somehow, instead of heading into the lower city where she lived, she found herself in the upper city beside the Tyropean Valley.

Water, cold and deep, ran in the aqueduct beside her. Cupping a hand, she scooped some out and splashed it on her face. Its coolness against her burning cheeks refreshed her.

*How could she have let Sha'oul get away?*

Fate presented her with not one, but three chances and she missed them all. The brutal reality was she couldn't kill Sha'oul no matter how much she hated him. It was one thing to talk of slaughtering him like a pig, to practice in her room behind closed doors, to imagine shoving the blade deep into his flesh, and quite another to actually do it.

Stefanos was gone and her plan to revenge his death had failed. Once her life seemed perfect, her future unlimited. And now? Now she had nothing. No Stefanos and no satisfaction. Life had no meaning.

She hated herself. It would have been one thing to try and fail, but she did not even try. She was a sham, a fraud...a pretender. Stefanos' death would go unavenged.

I should have found a way to keep him from going to face Sha'oul and his thugs, she thought. Then a horrible notion crossed her mind.

*Had I not been there, Stefanos wouldn't have gone down the hill.*

He died to protect her. Channah began to sob. She was the one responsible for Stefanos' death, not Sha'oul.

She once told her mother, "An eye for an eye, a life for a life." She decided she would offer her life in payment for his.

Channah selected an isolated spot where no one could see her, rolled up her sleeve, and dug out her *sicarius*. She held the dagger in her right hand and plunged her left arm into the cold water. She'd keep it there until it numbed so she wouldn't feel the blade slice through her skin, releasing her lifeblood.

Her hand grew deathly white in the flowing water. Only a few moments longer and her heartache would be over.

Channah removed her arm and made a tentative prick. The blade stung and several drops of blood appeared. Hardly the way the blood spurted when Abba slaughters the lambs, she thought, and plunged her wrist back into the water.

She heard a soft mewing beside her.

Ignoring it, she kept her eyes tightly shut and focussed on the cold water swirling around her hand. Just a little while longer...

Something touched her toe.

She flicked her foot forward, kicking whatever it was away.

The mewing returned a few moments later. She felt a soft, tickling touch on her ankle.

Channah kicked at it again. "Leave me alone," she yelled. "Can't you see I'm busy?"

The mewing became a plaintive whimper.

Channah sighed in frustration. Opening her eyes, she saw a frightened gray kitten huddled beside her.

"Go away," Channah snarled. "I do not want you around me."

The kitten meowed.

"Be gone!" Channah swung out her foot, sending the little animal rolling head over heels.

She closed her eyes again and tried to center her thoughts. Images of Stefanos came to mind and she wept great, wrenching sobs.

Something grabbed her ankle.

She glared down at the kitten attacking the thong of her sandal. Channah waved the *sicarius* at him. "Do you have any idea how sharp this is? Leave me alone before I slice you into pieces."

The kitten's tiny head popped up. He watched the silvery blade flash back and forth in the air then leaped to grab it.

Channah jerked the knife away. "No!"

The kitten curled into a shivering ball and began to cry.

Her plan forgotten, Channah pulled her arm out of the water and dropped to her knees. "What have I done now? Did I hurt you?" She scooped up the kitten and pressed it to her cheek.

"I did not mean to hit you with my knife. I only wanted to scare you. Please do not be hurt."

She turned the little animal over and over in her hand, examining it for cuts or scrapes. To her great relief the kitten appeared unharmed. She rocked back into a sitting position.

"You should not be here with me," she warned. "I am not safe. I bring harm to those I love."

The kitten cocked his head and stared up at her. His yellow eyes seemed to say, "Tell me about it."

Channah poured out her pain of losing Stefanos. She talked and talked until she ran out of words and tears. Then she re-wrapped the *sicarius* and stuffed it into the bottom of her purse.

Rising to her feet, she picked up the kitten and slipped him into her cloak. He nestled against her bosom and dozed as she walked home. She decided to call the kitten *Elpis*.

*Hope.*

## ~ 24 ~

Rivkah was in the bedroom when the door opened. She recognized the sound of Channah's footsteps and called, "Where have you been?"

"Out. Walking and thinking."

"You promised to be here when I retur–" Shocked by Channah's appearance, she froze in the doorway. "What happened to you? You're bruised and your clothes are dirty."

"It is not important."

"The last time you told me something was not important a man ended up being stoned to death. I am your mother. You sit down right now and explain what is going on."

"I tripped and fell." Channah took off her veil and held it at arm's length. "Oh, I see what you mean. It looks worse than I thought."

"Did you hit your head?" Rivkah stepped closer. "Let me have a look at you. What are these scraps on your cheek and forehead? And your clothes. How can you walk around like that? What will people think of us?"

"No one saw me. I came in through the Water Gate."

"Why were you beyond the city walls? You said nothing of this when you left."

"I did not plan on going out, I just did. If I wash and change clothes, Abba and the boys will never know." She caught her mother's eye. "Unless you tell them."

Channah started for her room, but stopped. "Oh, I almost forgot." She slipped her hand into her cloak and rertrieved a gray ball of fluff. "Look what I found."

"A kitten?"

"Actually, he found me. I felt sadder than I ever have in my life. I went to sit beside the aqueduct and, while I thought about Stefanos, this little kitten appeared out of nowhere. He is a gift from Stefanos, a messenger sent to comfort me and let me know life will be good again someday."

"And you want to keep him."

"His name is Elpis."

"You named him, Hope?"

"Yes. He brought me hope when I needed it most." She looked into the kitchen. "Do we have any milk?"

"I have some I planned to clabber for cheese." Rivkah sighed. "Or use as kitten food."

Channah threw her arms around her and kissed her cheek. "Thank you. I will take care of all his needs." After putting some in a bowl, she glanced down at the smudges on her cloak. "Come, Elpis. You can eat while I change."

A short time later Rivkah found her lying on her bed dangling a piece of yarn for the kitten to bat at.

Rivkah brushed aside wisps of dark hair clinging to her forehead. "How are you feeling?"

"Better than yesterday," Channah said with a slight smile. "I am still drinking my tears by the bowlful, but having Elpis here somehow makes things better."

"Have you had anything to eat?"

Channah shrugged. She'd eaten little since Stefanos' death.

"I have warm loaves and crushed berries sweetened with honey. Will you have some?"

Channah pushed her bread around the plate, preferring to play with her food rather than eat it. "Every night I dream about my beloved Stefanos lying among strangers in an unmarked grave."

"What would make you think such a thing?"

"That is what they do with those who have been stoned. Paid workmen who care nothing about them drag them away to the Field of Criminals." Channah's fingers quivered. She lowered her head and tears splattered her plate. "My Stefanos lies in cursed ground where no one prays over him."

"Why must you assume these things?"

"I went back the next morning." She ran her fingers through her hair. "I cannot explain why in any way that you will understand. It makes no sense, I know. But I, I just needed to go back and see if he was there."

"And he was not."

Channah broke her loaf into pieces, arranging them in a line. "Yes, he was gone." She dabbed some berries on a piece and ate it half-heartedly. "The workmen must have come for him. What other explanation can there be?

"Yesterday I noticed a small myrtle tree sprouting in the backyard," Rivkah said. "They are known as the tree of life. It is of modest size, but very hardy. We could dig it up and replant it as a memorial beside Stefanos' grave."

Channah stared at her food with a sullen expression on her face. "How I long for the solace that would bring, but we both know what the Jews do with those who have been stoned."

"True. However, the followers of Yeshua view things differently."

Channah's head snapped up. "You know where they laid my love?"

Rivkah nodded.

Channah reached across the table and touched her mother's hand. "Let me find a pot to put the tree in."

Rivkah started to put the myrtle tree into the hole they'd dug, but Channah stopped her.

"Wait. There is something I want to do first." She reached into her bag and took out the *sicarius*. Unwrapping it, she held it up for her to see. "I do not need this after all."

She placed it in the bottom of the hole and tossed a handful of dirt over it. "Better to bury it here along with all the evil thoughts that accompanied it." She smiled. "Now put it in."

Channah lovingly packed soil around the roots of the sturdy little tree. Rising, she shaded her eyes and squinted into the sunny sky.

"Stefanos can look down on it from his seat in heaven and remember our time together." She ruffled her fingers through its shiny leaves, brushing away dust from the planting. "The sun and rain will nourish this tiny tree, allowing it to grow as our love would have. It will remain here always as a token of what might have been."

Before they left the house, Rivkah suggested Channah gather flowers to leave at the graveside. Taking a basket, she disappeared for a short while and returned with it overflowing.

Basket in hand, she knelt before the huge stone that sealed the chamber's opening. She had cut branches covered with the puffy white blossoms of the Acacia tree and stalks of Horsetail overflowing with multi-colored flowers. Between them, she carefully wove feathery-tipped stems of Papyrus, Horse Mint, and Willow Herb. When the arrangement satisfied her, Channah placed this spray of foliage on the ground in front of the grave.

She glanced back over her shoulder. "I will never be able to repay your kindness. Can we pray for him before we leave?"

They knelt together, joined hands, and bowed their heads.

"My daughter," Rivkah said, after they brushed their knees, "each of our lives is a story we write as an offering to God. Stefanos' life is over. His scroll has been rolled up and tied with a ribbon. His was the privilege of being the first to lose his life following in Yeshua's footsteps.

"Your scroll, on the other hand, remains open on the table waiting for you to write your story upon it. You cannot do it by retreating from life. Despite the pain, you must force yourself to live."

"I will try, Imma. I will try."

"I have something that might help."

Turning away from the place of the tombs, they walked side by side along the road leading back into the city. Rivkah pulled out the stained scroll Miryam gave her and handed it to her daughter.

Channah opened it, read for a moment, then gave a heaving sob. It took her several minutes to regain control. Once she did, she wiped her eyes and kissed her mother's cheek.

# ~ 25 ~

*"...and you shall be my witnesses in Jerusalem and all
Judea and Samaria, and to the end of the earth."*
— Acts of the Apostles 1:8

Lamps flickered in the evening breeze sending shadows dancing across the walls. Simon looked at the eleven men gathered around him in the small room behind the synagogue's sanctuary.

"We have preached the good news here in the Temple and in the surrounding towns just as the Lord instructed. Meanwhile, Sha'oul and the High Priest persecute us and all those who convert to The Way. The time has come for us to leave Jerusalem. Stephanos' untimely death makes it doubly clear how vulnerable we have become."

The men around the table murmured their agreement.

"Before the Lord left us, he commanded us to go to the ends of the earth making disciples of all nations. So, with this in mind," Simon unrolled a map of the world and spread it across the tabletop, "I felt it our duty to persevere and carry the gospel to other lands before some, or all, of us fall prey to Caiaphas and his thugs."

"The Lord once compared us to leaven hidden within a bowl of meal," Thomas said. "In each place we stop we must seek out good men and women, wholesome believers who can be counted on to carry forward the teachings. That way the good news will continue to spread long after we are gone."

Simon's thick finger tapped the map. "My destination when I leave Jerusalem is the capital of the Syrian province, Antioch on the Orentes. Once I have established a firm foundation there, I plan to extend my reach into Pontus, Galatia, Cappadocia and Asia Minor."

Yohan rose from his seat. "Despite the danger, I intend to remain here in Jerusalem with Imma Miryam. Where the Lord's mother is, I will be as well. I am confident he will let no harm come to us."

"So much for Yohan and myself. Now it is time to decide what the rest of you will do." Simon produced an oblong bowl filled with small scrolls and sat it in the center of the map. "I have prepared ten lots. We shall let the Lord himself determine where each of you are to serve. After praying for guidance, draw from the bowl whenever you feel ready."

Mattithayu drew first. His scroll read *Northern Israel*. The irony of his assignment escaped no one. Rather than being allowed to make a new start among strangers, the Lord sent him back from whence he came. The former tax gatherer, despised as a collaborator by most Jews, had been called to work among his own people. Without a moment's hesitation, he grabbed a marker and drew a crooked circle around the land that once comprised the upper reaches of Herod's kingdom. He wrote his name inside this circle.

"When I leave Jerusalem," Mattithayu said, "I shall return to my home in Capernaum. From that base, I plan to carry the word to our brothers in Iturea, Galilee, Samaria and even to those the Master visited in the Decapolis."

Andrew, Simon's younger brother, chose next. The Lord destined him for Bithynia, Thrace and the northern kingdom of Scythia, bounded by the Black Sea.

Phillip went to Asia Minor and his close friend, Netan'el bar Tolmai, reached into the bowl and plucked out Armenia. Thomas chose next. His scroll directed him to the Parthian Empire, a huge territory based in Babylon and stretching from the Tigris to the Indus River.

Yohan's older brother, Yaakov, would minister to Jews in Southern Israel: Judea, Gaza, Idumea, and Tyre and Sidon in Phoenicia. Simeon the Cananaean, a man who disavowed the way of anarchy to become one of Yeshua's disciples, found Egypt, Cyrenaica, and Africa written on his scroll. Years later, when Simeon had traversed these territories, he would make his way to Gaul and from there to Britannia.

The other Yaakov among the Twelve, brother to Mattithayu, drew Persia. Thaddeus, sometimes called Judas, plucked out Edessa and Northern Mesopatmia.

This left a single scroll in the bottom of the bowl. Feeling he ranked last in seniority, Matthias, the man they chose to replace Judas Iscariot, humbly waited until all the others took their turn before choosing. Scooping up the final scroll, he read it aloud.

"The Lord grants me the privilege of serving him in the region of Colchis in the Caucasus Mountains. As soon as possible, I shall gather my wife and children and journey to where he sends me."

The process of division ended as quickly as it began. The assignments were all made, the world divided among the twelve of them. Soon they would each leave home, friends, extended family, and most importantly, each other behind and take to the road.

This was a pivotal moment in each of their lives. What began as a simple response to the invitation, "*Come. Follow me,*" had grown into a life-changing commitment. As they scattered to the far corners of the known world, the Twelve of them would never again meet in a conclave like this.

The power of the moment lingered in the air like sweet perfume. They glanced at each other, awed by the gravity of what they had just done and unsure what to do or say next.

Simon moved about the room. He grasped each man's hand, then pulled them into a bear hug and kissed their cheek. "Though we may never see each other again in this world, someday we shall be together again in the Father's house in the mansions the Lord has prepared for us."

The others turned to their fellows, emulating Simon's emotional farewell.

"We have slipped the noose Caiaphas would place about our necks," Yohan said with a smile.

The men were still murmuring their congratulations when a series of hard knocks rattled the synagogue's outer door. Before anyone could answer, angry hands flung the door aside. It banged against the wall and the sound of running feet slapping against the tiles reverberated in the outer hallway.

The Twelve glanced up to see Sha'oul leering at them from the doorway. "In here," he shouted. He waved an arm, directing those behind him. "I have found them. Hurry lest they try to escape."

Armed men, whom they all recognized as members of the Temple Guard, crowded around Sha'oul brandishing clubs, ropes and swords.

"Escape is impossible," Sha'oul said with a sly grin. "We have men watching the back door."

Simon crossed the room. "*Shalom Aleichem*, my friend."

He rested a beefy arm on the smaller man's shoulder. Sha'oul nearly disappeared in the husky fisherman's hug. He thrashed and struggled like an unruly child trying to escape a parent's loving grasp.

"Keep your vile hands away from me," Sha'oul shouted when he at last pushed free. "I know your tricks. You rely upon the power of Beelzebub." He fidgeted from side to side and shook out his clothing as though he had something crawling on him. He continued muttering to himself and running his eyes around the ceiling as he adjusted his cloak.

The guards behind him looked away, pretending not to notice his strange behavior.

Simon looked over Sha'oul's bobbing head and smiled. "*Shalom Aleichem*, Eleazer. Have you all finally recognized the error of your ways and come to be baptized?"

Eleazer gave the twitching Sha'oul a disgusted sneer. "Your humor may frighten him, but it will not distract me from my assigned task." He drew himself up. Sucking in a deep breath, he said, "The high priest has issued warrants for all of you. If you do not come peaceably, we will bind you and take you there by force."

"And what will this arrest accomplish?"

Sha'oul forced himself between the two men. "Make jokes and laugh if you like, but we finally have you all." The little man gave Simon a malevolent grin. "Cut off the head and the snake will die."

Simon shook his head. "Oh Sha'oul, you poor misguided fool. Caiaphas already tried that when he had Yeshua nailed to a tree. You know as well as I that he failed. Yeshua has risen and

sits at the right hand of the Father, waiting for the day when he
will return to judge the quick and the dead."

"He blasphemes," Sha'oul cried in a shrill voice. "Arrest
him. Arrest them all. Take them to the prison." He scurried down
the hall, arms folded above his head to protect himself from the
lightening bolt he feared might descend upon him any moment.

That night, as the Twelve prayed and sang hymns in the city's
dungeon, an angel of the Lord appeared to them. Bright light
filled their cell and the angel commanded, "Men of Galilee, arise."

The Twelve rose from the damp stones leaving their
shackles still attached to rings imbedded in the walls.

"Follow me," the angel said. He led them out of their cell,
down the dark corridors and through the prison's outer gate into
the light of the morning sun.

High above them, a *shofar's* blast from the pinnacle of the
Temple signaled the opening of the Temple gates. Confused and
frightened, the men blinked in the sudden brightness as they
stretched and rubbed their wrists and ankles, trying to chase
away the numbness in their hands and feet.

The angel pointed at the stairway leading to the Temple.
"Go, stand in the Temple courts and tell the people the full
message of this new life."

# ~ 26 ~

*"But a Pharisee in the council named Gamali'el, a teacher of Law, held in honor by all the people, stood and ordered the men to be put outside for a while."*
— Acts of the Apostles 5:34

"I want my prisoners, and I want them now!" The scrolls beside Caiaphas jumped when he pounded his fist on the tabletop.

"But I already told you they are not there," Eleazer said. Bleary-eyed from being up most of the night and then dragged from his bed after only a few hours sleep, he shuffled his feet and stared at the patterns in the floor.

Caiaphas's brows lowered. His dark eyes turned cold and hard. He glared at his Captain of the Temple and shook his head in dismay. He had been lax in his handling of The Way and now, having resolved to make up for that laxity, everything he tried seemed to come undone.

Wondering what to do next, he left the befuddled Eleazer to yawn and scratch and went to the window. Despite the cool morning breeze, he sensed the day's coming heat. Something in the Court of the Gentiles caught his eye.

*What's going on down there?*

Caiaphas watched the crowds abandon the moneychanger's tables and the temporary corrals of the sellers of animals. A sea of people flooded the east side of the courtyard in front of Solomon's Porch.

He frowned and turned away from the window. Whatever it was, he could deal with it later. Right now he needed to finish with his incompetent Captain.

"Last evening you came to my home and assured me Yeshua's disciples were locked away in the public prison."

"As God is my witness, I personally latched their shackles to the rings in the wall. I went there this morning with Rueven after he roused me from my bed. The men were gone."

"How did they free their shackles?"

Eleazer shrugged. "Their chains remained intact...still locked to the prison wall."

"Impossible. A man cannot shed his shackles the way a serpent sheds its skin."

"I will take you there and let you see for yourself. I left orders that nothing be disturbed."

"What sort of fool do you imagine me to be? I give no credence to this elaborate ruse you have designed to cover your ineptitude." Caiaphas scowled. "I have better things to do, such as finding myself a Captain of the Temple who can keep hold of his prisoners."

Eleazer opened his mouth in rebuttal, but a guard bursting into the room cut short his reply. The man raced over to his Captain. "The men you arrested last evening are in the Temple court preaching to the people."

Caiaphas glanced out the window again. A wave of dizziness swept over him when he saw the mass of people along the courtyard's east side. "Raise the guard. Arrest them and bring them to the hall of the Great Sanhedrin. I will end this once and for all."

Caiaphas demanded the Twelve cease preaching the name of Yeshua in Jerusalem.

Simon, with the others gathered in a semi-circle behind him, politely pointed out they must obey the commands of God, not man.

Sensing that Caiaphas intended to send the men to their death just as he had done with Stefanos, Gamali'el, the Nasi of the Great Sanhedrin, rose to speak.

The room quieted.

Known for his wisdom and intellect, Gamali'el seldom entered into the court's arguments and, when he did, his insights were profound. He glanced around the room at the assembled priests and elders, carefully avoiding eye contact with any of the

Twelve.

"Remove these men from the courtroom," he said with a sweep of his hand.

Gamali'el waited while Eleazer lead the prisoners out. Their lives, and the life of their fledgling movement, now rested in his hands. He knew two things for certain. If the other members of the Sanhedrin suspected that he, too, was a believer, his arguments would fall upon deaf ears. And secondly, whatever argument he raised must be convincing enough to sway even the most cynical members of the assembly.

"Men of Israel," Gamali'el began. His deep voice carried across the room, drawing them to him like fish into a net. "Let us take care what we do with these men. Why invest them with an importance they do not have?"

He rose to his full height and stared down into the faces of those along the first rows, the oldest and wisest of the assembly. If he swayed them, the rest would follow their lead.

"Do you recall earlier days when Theudas arose pretending to be someone special? Four hundred men joined him." His eyes moved around the room as if searching for something...someone. "Where are they now?" He lifted an empty palm and shrugged. "Gone. Either slain or dispersed. In the end, it amounted to nothing.

"Later, Judas the Galilean attacked the armory in Sepphoris and drew away some of the people. He has also perished and any followers he had are scattered like seeds carried upon the wind."

Grabbing the sides of the podium with both hands, Gamali'el leaned forward and drove home his final argument.

"Are these followers of Yeshua any different?" He moved his hand pretending to brush something aside. "I say, keep away from these men. Leave them alone. For if this plan or this undertaking comes from men, rest assured, it will fail. But if it be from God," he said, his voice rising, "all the nations of the world gathered together cannot overthrow it."

Gamali'el paused to run eyes around the room.

The entire assembly rocked forward in their seats as the tension built.

When he spoke again Gamali'el's voice was whisper soft. "Do we dare risk placing ourselves in opposition to the will of God?"

"Do you think this marks the end of the persecution?" Yohan asked Simon as they limped back to the Synagogue of Rabban Yeshua. They, like the others, had been flogged then released.

"We may have won a battle, but the war will never end. This is only a respite before the next round of combat. The Lord was with us today. Gamali'el and his arguments bought us some badly needed time. We must use it wisely, gird our loins, and prepare for the work which must be done." His face softened. "But I did garner one piece of good news from Eleazer as he lashed my back."

"You conversed with him while he beat you?"

He grinned at the younger man walking beside him. "Only while he rested between strokes. He told me Sha'oul will be leaving Jerusalem soon."

"He and his threats are going away?"

"For a time at least. Eleazer told me Caiaphas gave Sha'oul warrants to carry to the synagogues in Damascus. He is gathering a deputation to travel there with him. If they find any followers, men or women, in the Synagogues of Damascus, they have orders to bind them and bring them back here for trial."

"So with Jerusalem snatched away, Caiaphas has chosen to attack elsewhere."

Simon nodded. "You have said it."

"How many times will Gamali'el be able to outfox the High Priest," Yohan wondered aloud.

"And what will become of us when he cannot?"

## ~ 27 ~

*"A man was going down from Jerusalem to Jericho, and*
*he fell among robbers..."*

— Luke 10:30

Rivkah opened the front door wide. "Come in, Simon. Welcome."

Simon winced when he stepped over the threshold. He crossed the room with slow, deliberate steps and eased himself onto a stool.

"How are you feeling?"

He gave her an uncertain smile. "Better. The binding Shemu'el wrapped around my ribs allows me to breathe almost normally and his salve has speeded the healing of the sores left by the whip."

A sudden coughing fit seized him. Grimacing in pain, Simon crossed his arms over his chest and hugged his bruised ribs.

Rivkah handed him a basin from the kitchen and ran to the yard to summon Shemu'el.

Simon coughed bloody sputum into the bowl then rocked back on the stool wheezing and gasping for breath.

Shemu'el took the bowl from Simon and sat it aside. "Still coughing up blood, I see."

"It gets better with each passing day," Simon whispered.

"Or at least that is what you would have me believe."

A look of understanding passed between them.

"Take off your tunic and let me have a look."

Simon began to lift the tunic then stopped. A sense of uneasiness filled the room. He glanced from Channah and Rivkah hard at work in the kitchen to Shemu'el.

"Around here." Shemu'el led him into the hallway out of the line of sight.

The women chopped and sliced while Shemu'el poked and prodded. A short time later, after several of Simon's painful groans, the two men returned to the front room.

"Simon, you will be staying for supper won't you?" Rivkah

asked over her shoulder. "Yohan gave us some fresh fish. I have it over coals in the backyard." Jerusalem's upper class were usually the only ones lucky enough to enjoy fresh fish. She thought for a moment and chuckled. "But then fresh fish is probably not the treat to you it is to others."

"Nothing sounds better."

The boys sat at the table with the men and Channah and Rivkah served them. The rest of the meal consisted of simple fare...all they could afford. If it disappointed Simon, he never let on.

"I came because I wanted to discuss something with you," Simon said to Shemu'el. "The time has come for us to leave Jerusalem."

"Are you sure this is the best strategy? Like an army, we must present a united front. Our strength lies in our numbers."

"It has never been a question of *if* we would leave, only when. Our task has been set before us. We are to be the Master's witnesses to all the world. The twelve of us divided the world into portions and had just finished drawing lots when Sha'oul and his henchmen arrived. The others are preparing to leave as we speak."

"A good general does not disperse his troops. We should not be separated one from another," Shemu'el said.

"The incident with Caiaphas and the Sanhedrin illustrates how vulnerable we have become. Had Gamali'el not come to our rescue, all twelve of us could have ended up in the valley floor like Stefanos. If the seed stock is destroyed, there can be no harvest. By dispersing we sow the seeds of our survival."

Rivkah moved around the table pouring wine as the men talked. "Listening to you makes me feel as if we are in a race for our lives. Have we now become markers in a game of Hounds and Jackals?"

Channah sat a fruit plate in the center of the table and laughed "Well, one thing is certain, everyone knows who the jackal is."

"What of those whom you leave behind?" Shemu'el asked.

"Most of the believers have also chosen to leave," Simon

replied. "We are forming caravans for mutual safety. My final destination will be Antioch on the Orentes."

"If everyone leaves, what will become of the synagogue?"

"The affairs of the Synagogue of Rabban Yeshua *HaMashiach* have always rested in Yaakov's capable hands. He will remain behind to minister to the needs of those who choose to stay. Unlike us, he is beyond the High Priest's reach. Even our most fervent enemies acknowledge his dedication to the Law and refer to him as *Yaakov the Just.*"

With the meal complete, Rivkah took a seat beside Shemu'el.

He kneaded his brow as he considered Simon's proposal. "I sense the reason you are bringing this up is that you would like us to accompany you to Antioch."

Simon nodded.

With an arm on his wife's shoulder, Shemu'el pointed to the children gathered around the table. "Rivkah, the children...none of us have adapted well to life in Jerusalem. Though we've been here over two years, it still feels like we left our little settlement only yesterday. A second move would undermine the little headway we have made."

"Why worry about your accomplishments? Whatever progress you have made will be swept away in the coming persecution." Simon placed a hand on Shemu'el's arem. "Have you forgotten your experience with Menashe, the wine merchant? It is not going to get better, my brother, only worse."

Shemu'el supposed if they had to leave, Antioch might be an acceptable destination.

"Good!" Simon slapped his hands down on his knees and grinned. "Phillip has been preaching in Samaria and converted many there. We need to lay hands upon them so they too may receive the Spirit. We can travel through Samaria on our way to Antioch."

"Never!" Shemu'el shouted. His face grew bright red and veins bulged in his neck. "It was the Samaritans who cursed us as we staggered along in chains on our way to slavery. They threw rotten vegetables at me and spit upon me. They are a vile people, half-breeds and collaborators who do not deserve the Lord's salvation. What next? Do you plan to also accept *goyim*?"

Leaving the table, Shemu'el stomped to the other side of the room. He turned his back on Simon and stared out the window with clenched fists.

With his back turned, Shemu'el could not see the shocked expression on Simon's face. The big fisherman took a deep breath and lowered his eyes in prayer. After a moment he rose and crossed the room.

"Shemu'el, this is not the way of Rabban Yeshua," Simon softly said. "We are all brothers in the Lord's eyes."

"All Jews are brothers, children of Avraham. Yeshua came to bring salvation to the Jews. The rest of them...the Samaritans and the Gentiles?" He gave Simon an angry stare. "They are mongrel dogs conspiring to steal scraps of food from the children's plate and should be treated as such."

Simon placed his arm around Shemu'el's shoulder. "Walk with me, brother."

Neither man said a word as they left the house.

Rivkah hurried to a window as soon as the door closed. She watched them head toward the Water Gate. Shemu'el, slimmer, but nearly as tall as Simon, clenched and unclenched his fists as they walked. The two men disappeared through the gate and out of the city.

Simon couldn't know the depth of pain and humiliation Shemu'el suffered in Samaria, Rivkah thought. No one could. Over the years she learned that just the mention of Samaria never failed to upset him. The thought of returning touched a painful place deep within his soul, releasing memories buried there for over twenty-five years.

Rivkah whispered a prayer asking Yeshua to walk with them and help Shemu'el accept the wisdom of Simon's words.

"Rivkah mentioned what happened in the Temple when

you were young. I am very sorry you suffered as you did, but Yeshua commanded us to love our neighbor as ourselves."

"I do love my neighbor," Shemu'el protested. "If one of my neighbors requires some oil for a lamp or barley for meal, I give it to him. If I roast a goat or a lamb, I invite my neighbors to share it with me. If a neighbor loses a sheep, I help him search. What more could anyone ask of me?"

They came to the heavy stone watering troughs which gave the Water Gate its name. Simon stopped and sat. He rubbed the kinks out of his neck then glanced over at Shemu'el. "You lived in a small settlement of shepherds outside Bethlehem, correct?"

Shemu'el acknowledged with a nod.

"Who were your neighbors?"

Shemu'el thought for a moment. "Well, there were my brothers and my brother's families, of course, and Abba Yaakov, Rivkah's father, and her aunt, Tamar. Her cousins and their families. Gavriel and Simeon and their families and—"

Simon's raised hand stopped him. "In other words, all close friends or extended family?"

"Yes, pretty much."

Simon smiled. "It was the same in Bethsaida where my brother Andrew and I grew up. Everyone knew everyone else's business." He shrugged. "There's no such thing as a secret in a small town, is there? I suppose it's the same in every village throughout Israel. Most people find it easy to love their neighbor when that neighbor happens to also be their cousin, or a close friend."

"True, but that's the way things have always been. And we are not talking about my neighbors, we are talking about Samaritans."

"Rabban Yeshua once told us a story. There was a man on his way to Jericho who was attacked by bandits. They beat and robbed him and left him for dead. A Levite passed by, saw him, and went on. A priest passed, saw him, and went on. A Samaritan saw him and stopped. He gave him water, treated his wounds, and put him on his donkey. He took the man to an inn where he gave the innkeeper some coins for the man's care. When he left, he promised to repay any additional cost on his return trip. Now, who would you say was this man's neighbor?"

Shemu'el stared at his feet. "The Samaritan, I suppose." He watched a camel train come toward them and ran his tongue around his cheek.

Simon laid his rough hand on Shemu'el's shoulder. "It was no co-incidence the Lord chose a Samaritan for his story. He said even the Gentiles love their friends, but we must do better. We must also love our enemies."

"That is all well and good for Yeshua. He was the *Mashiach*, the son of the Most High God. He could forgive the Roman soldiers as they drove spikes through his hands."

"He was also a man like you and I."

"If it were anyone else, maybe, but not the Samaritans. This is asking more than I am capable of giving. What if those we go to see happen to be the same people who threw garbage at me?"

"What if they are? All sins can be forgiven. I denied the Lord three times and yet he forgave me. He would have forgiven Judas Iscariot, who betrayed him to Caiaphas, had he only asked."

"I can never forgive the Samaritans for what they did. I still say it is too much for you to ask of me."

"The Lord demands this of you, Shemu'el, not me. He never said it would be easy, only that we must do it. Remember the prayer he taught us? Forgive us as we forgive others. To harbor a grudge is to forfeit God's forgiveness."

Shemu'el sat in silence, thinking on Simon's words. What could he say? He had no rebuttal.

"Very well," Shemu'el said. "Samaria it will be."

## ~ 28 ~

*"Now those who were scattered went about preaching
the word."*

— Acts of the Apostles 8:4

Winter had come bringing cooler weather and rain. The sewing
group's meeting was subdued. The women kept their heads down
and concentrated on their stitching. Most would be leaving
Jerusalem in the upcoming days and weeks.

Rivkah glanced around the room with a heavy heart. The
friendship and support of these good women had enriched her
life and she considered each of them a dear friend. They had been
the one bright spot in her otherwise dreary existence and she
would probably never see any of them again.

She struggled to find words to tell them how much they
meant to her, but only came up with trite sayings and platitudes.
Noting the lack of conversation, she decided the others felt the
same way.

After all the hugs were shared, the tears shed, and many prayers
promised, Rivkah and Channah descended the stairway to
Aristopolus' atrium. Remnants of an earlier rain dripped from
the lathing above their heads, spattering against the flagstones.

Channah handed Rivkah her sewing bag. "Since we will
never be back, I'd like to visit the gardens for a few moments."

"Should I come with you?"

"It is where Stefanos walked, and I prefer going alone." She
gave her mother a reassuring smile. "I'll be back before you know
it."

Rivkah took a seat on a stone bench under the porch to
wait.

Channah followed the gravel path back to the garden area.
A wavering fog enveloped the grape arbors running the length of
the back yard. She stepped carefully, avoiding the sodden piles of

brown leaves raked aside and left to rot by the vinedresser. He'd anchored each pile by covering them with pieces of grapewood pruned from the nearby vines.

She touched the gnarled vines, black with moisture, and imagined Stefanos walking these same rows. Her eyes ran along the vines, searching for his marker. Her heart leaped when she saw the damp strip of weather-beaten cloth. It was at the end of the row beside the wall, just as he had said.

The cloth's bright red color had weathered to a soft pink. Several bunches of shriveled grapes still clung to the vine. The treats Stefanos planned to bring her were dried up and molding, encased in webs. She bowed her head and watered the vines with her tears.

A sudden gust of cool air raised goosebumps on Channah's arms. She sensed Stefanos beside her, imagined the reassuring warmth of his arm around her shoulder...remembered the depth of his gaze.

*Do not grieve, my love. Nothing is ever truly lost*, he whispered to her heart. *Someday we shall be together again.*

Then, quick as he came, he slipped away.

Taking a deep, cleansing breath, Channah removed a pruning knife from her purse. She moved down the row cutting off canes until she accumulated a thick handful. One by one, she counted three nodes up from the bottom and made a straight slice just below the bud. She checked each cane in cross section and discarded any that didn't have tight pith in the center and dense, light green outer wood. This left her a dozen canes all about a cubit long.

After making a diagonal cut at the bottom of each one, Channah wet a square of cloth and wrapped it around them. She pulled a supple piece of goatskin from her purse, rolled it around the damp bundle of canes, and tied it tightly at both ends.

She smiled. Stefanos' grapevines were packed and ready for the trip to Antioch where, one warm spring day, she would plant them in his memory.

Shemu'el frowned as he checked the growing pile of sacks and baskets stacked beside the donkey. The previous week had been a difficult one spent sorting and re-sorting their possessions. A small donkey cart only held so much. Size and weight determined what they could and couldn't take.

Some choices were automatic, things they couldn't do without like Shemu'el's medical kit and his carving tools, Rivkah's spindles, sewing basket and folding loom. And a few precious heirlooms...the glass suncatcher Sidonius gave her when she was a girl, the bowl Shemu'el carved that she'd found in a trader's bazaar, and a few momentos from his time with the Legions.

As the deadline drew closer, the decisions became increasingly difficult. This or that? These or those? In the end they jettisoned most of the accumulation of twenty-five years of married life.

Shemu'el stared into the distance with a faraway look in his eyes. "It will be strange to be in Antioch once again. So much has happened in the years since I left."

Rivkah read the mix of emotions in his face. It had been hard for him when Simon asked them to accompany him to Antioch. Especially so when he mentioned traveling through Samaria along the way. Shemu'el spent many nights tossing and turning beside her. The decision to return to the place where he once lived as a slave had not come easily.

She also had reservations about the trip, but for different reasons. It had been difficult enough to leave the little settlement where she'd spent her entire life and here they were on the run again.

Yet how could they stay? Yeshua had cleaved Judaism in half. The rift between the Jews who still clung to the Temple rites and those who followed The Way grew wider with each passing day.

Miryam had been right the day they watched the mob stone

Stefanos outside the Damascus Gate when she whispered, "*It has already begun.*"

And so it had. The Temple aristocracy refused to buy their lambs. People spit at them and called them vile names. Shops were riffled and burned. When away from home they clung to alleyways and glanced over their shoulder at the slightest noise.

But most of all, it was Sha'oul's relentless persecution that frightened believers. He had swept through Jerusalem and the surrounding area like an evil specter, dragging good people before the Sanhedrin. Their crime? They believed Yeshua was the *Mashiach.*

Now the High Priest was sending Sha'oul on wider missions. Rumors said he would soon be on his way to Damascus. What next? Would he appear in Antioch as well? Was there a safe place anywhere in the world?

Shemu'el turned to Rivkah as they rested on the front step. "I lost touch with Atticus the day we both left Antioch. All these years and his whereabouts remain a mystery. He did so much for me. Without him I'm not sure I would have survived."

She entwined her fingers with his.

A faint smile crossed Shemu'el's lips. "Atticus sailed for Thessalonica and Byzantium that day. Perhaps he is still there."

"The Citadel still stands next to the Tiberian Wall. And the Governor's palace remains on the *insula*, the island separating the two arms of the Orontes River. Surely someone there will know what became of him."

Shemu'el rubbed his chin and sighed. "Quirinius has not been Governor of Syria for twenty years now, and all of the commanders and officers of the Legions will have moved on."

"The years have changed us all," Rivkah said. "If you passed on the street, do you think you would still recognize each other?"

Rising, Shemu'el reached for a heavy goatskin cloth to throw over the load "The last time he saw me I looked and dressed as a Roman. The greater question is not whether I could recognize Atticus, but whether he would recognize me." He tugged his grizzled beard and shook his head.

"Nothing is hopeless." She walked to his side and kissed his cheek. "Pray. If it is the Lord's will that you be reunited with your friend and brother, Atticus, you will be."

Shemu'el looped the hemp rope into a knot and jerked it tight. "No, I'm afraid finding Atticus is a hopeless dream, my dove. That was not just another place and time, it was another life." He checked and double-checked the straps securing their baggage. "Ready to go?"

A tremor of fear rippled through her. She could not leave her daughter Hadassah behind knowing Yeshua had prophesied the coming destruction of Jerusalem.

She clutched Shemu'el's hand. "Come with me and speak to Hadassah before we leave. Ask her to go with us. She will not refuse you."

He shook his head. "We do not have the time and she would not listen."

"She always listened to you. She still would. We cannot abandon her."

"The decision is hers and she has made it." His tone indicated he'd discuss it no more.

"Then I will go by myself. One of my lambs is lost and I cannot abandon her." Rivkah spun around and dashed away, leaving him standing beside the cart.

## ~ 29 ~

Rivkah's heart felt like a rock in her chest as she trudged the narrow streets to Hadassah's home. She concentrated on the pavement, ignoring the merchant's shouts and the carts rattling past beside her.

Living closer had done nothing to enhance Rivkah's relationship with her oldest daughter. No matter how hard she tried, Hadassah steadfastly rejected Rivkah's attempts to bring her into the fold of believers. Now they were leaving Jerusalem, and she wanted...needed, to give her daughter one last chance to change her mind.

*You should be hurrying*, she thought. Shemu'el will be pawing the ground like an anxious camel when you return.

There would be time to hurry later on. For now, she needed to take it slow. Though it grieved her to admit it, her link with her daughter had always been strained. As a young woman, Rivkah longed for a daughter. When Hadassah came, she held her to her breast and dreamed of the close relationship they would someday have.

But it did not turn out the way she imagined. Even at a young age Hadassah was headstrong, easily riled and belligerent, resistant to her mother's loving advice.

She'd begged Shemu'el to come with her, but his stubborn pride prevented it. A mother doesn't put conditions on her love as a father sometimes might. She would happily humble herself if that was what it took to win her daughter over.

Still, she wished Shemu'el were at her side. He and Hadassah were always close. Unlike Rivkah, whom she rejected, Hadassah listened to him. Perhaps it was because they were so much alike and, as her father, he was the undisputed master of the household. Or maybe she sensed that he had the will and strength to force her into obedience. She never defied him and his steadying influence kept her in line as a young woman.

"Why has Abba not come with you?" Hadassah gave her mother a haughty look. "Will he no longer speak to his wayward daughter?"

"Your father will always love you and listen to what you have to say. But he is a man with a man's pride. I came alone to give you one final chance."

"And if I do not go with you to Antioch?"

"It is not good for us to be a world apart. When trouble comes, we will not be here when you need us."

Rivkah bounced her granddaughter, Sarit, on her knee as they talked. Before Sarit's birth, Hadassah feared she might die in childbirth as her grandmother had. Despite these concerns she had an easy delivery, though Rivkah could never have convinced her of it.

Little Sarit held the wooden ring her grandfather carved for her with both hands, vigorously chewing on it.

Hadassah toyed with a lock of hair, twirling it around her finger. "I have my own family now. Even though my father and mother forsake me, the Lord will take me up."

"No one is forsaking you. We are trying to protect you. Leave with us now while you can. The recent trouble will only increase."

She tossed her hair aside with a cocky grin. "Trouble? What trouble? Hebel and I are observant Jews. We are doing fine the way things are."

"Say what is on your mind."

"You have no one to blame but yourselves. If you and Abba gave up your fascination with Yeshua and *The Way*, your troubles would be gone overnight."

Yeshua once predicted his words would separate father and son, mother and daughter. Rivkah never imagined she might be one of those affected. "You know we could never put our beliefs aside."

"And why not?"

"To do so would be to turn our backs on God's Anointed One, the *Mashiach*."

"So instead you turn your back on your own flesh and blood and the Law given to us by Moshe."

"We cast nothing aside. Yeshua forged a new covenant between God and mankind."

"New covenant, indeed." Hadassah rolled her eyes. "Do not think I have forgotten the agape meal you forced us to attend? Everyone gathered around an altar pretending to eat a dead man's flesh and drink his blood. Have you and Abba lost your minds? Why have you aligned yourselves with a cult of cannibals?"

"Yeshua is not dead; he lives forever seated at the right hand of his father. You mock the sacrament that infuses his life into our hearts."

"And you mock our traditions. Have you forgotten the Torah command, '*If anyone eats blood, that person must be cut off from his people*'?"

"Since you quote Scripture to me, I will quote it back to you, '*Taste and see that the Lord is good.*'"

Hadassah tossed her head and curled her lip. "You people of The Way have nothing to complain about; you are getting only what the Law demands."

Rivkah bit her tongue, holding back the words she longed to throw at her. "This is your last chance. The family is leaving today. Put aside whatever differences we have. I beg you, come with us."

The tension between them began to upset little Sarit. Tossing her teething toy onto the floor, she fussed and cried. Rivkah patted and cooed to no effect.

"See what you have done? Now the baby is upset." Hadassah extended her arms. "Give her to me."

Rivkah moved Sarit to her shoulder, preparing to rise, but she did not move fast enough to suit her daughter.

"I said, let me have her." Hadassah jerked the infant out of her grandmother's grasp. Tugging her clothing aside, she put the child to her breast. Sarit settled into the crook Hadassah's elbow and ate contentedly.

"Your father and I cannot deny Yeshua. He is the son of the

Most High God. The one the prophets spoke of." Rivkah kept her voice quiet and controlled, trying not to upset her granddaughter as she nursed. "We have been over and over this. I've told you about his miracles."

"Stories and more stories. You ask me to believe unbelievable things...things which I never saw."

"What about the things you did see?"

"What about them?"

"You were there on Golgotha with me. You saw it all."

"Yes, I did." Hadassah shifted Sarit to her other arm. Her eyes grew cold as ice. "I watched three criminals die that day. Two were thieves, the third a blasphemer."

Rivkah covered her ears. "Do not say such things. Those are words of everlasting condemnation. If you deny him in this life, he will deny you before his Father in heaven."

"Why do you insist on quoting the sayings of a heretic?"

How dare she call Yeshua a heretic? Rivkah gritted her teeth until her jaw ached, trying not to create a permanent rift between them. Now, she could stand no more.

"Know this, as sure as I stand before you, Yeshua was no *sheker*." Despite her best efforts, Rivkah's voice trembled as she spoke. "I watched false *Mashiachs* come and go. They all had one thing in common. The message they preached was one of hate and violence. Yeshua preached only love and peace."

She rose off the stool. "Do not claim to speak of what you do not know. That *sheker*, Athrongeus, cost my Uncle Chayim his life. Visit their graves if you wish. Both Chayim and Athronges died and returned to the dust from which all men are made. All save Yeshua, who is risen in the flesh."

Hadassah concentrated on the baby ignoring her mother's words. When Sarit finished, she adjusted her clothing and rocked her.

"Very well," Rivkah said. "If you wish to stay, stay. Sarit is ready to be weaned. Give her to me and I will take her with me. Let her live with her *Savta*."

A look of panic swept over Hadassah's face. "So long as I am alive and healthy, she will not go to her grandmother." She clutched the child to her bosom and wrapped both arms around her. "Never! I will not allow you to tear my daughter away from me."

"Of course not, but that is what you are doing to me when you refuse to accompany us to Antioch."

Hadassah lifted her chin. "I am an adult now. I am no longer your daughter; I am Hebel's wife. You have no claim on me."

Rivkah clutched her chest as if a sword had pierced her heart. "I have never sought to control, only guide. As a young girl I ached inside because I had no mother to turn to. Yet when I tried to give you what I never had, you turned away from me. Why is that, Hadassah?"

"I have sometimes thought it would be better to have had no mother at all than to be subjected to your constant meddling."

"How dare you wish me dead." Without thinking, Rivkah slapped her daughter across the face.

Hadassah's hand flew to her cheek, rubbing the bright spot forming there. Her eyes narrowed. "It is time you left."

Rivkah tried to form an apology, but the withering look on Hadassah's face silenced her.

## ~ 30 ~

Hadassah's husband, Hebel, rushed out of his pottery shop when Rivkah descended the stairs.

She spun aside, avoiding his gaze.

"Imma Rivkah, I heard shouts." He took her by the shoulders and turned her around to face him. "And you are weeping."

His eyes grew wide with concern. He looked as sad as she felt. "It's Hadassah, isn't it? What has she done to upset you so?"

"It is nothing." She brushed a hand across her eyes. "Just a silly disagreement between women."

He clucked his tongue. "Once again you asked her to accompany you to Antioch, and once again she refused."

"Yes."

Hebel shook his head and glanced up the stairway she'd just come down. "When she makes her mind up, that daughter of yours can be as unyielding as a block of stone. I remain unsure about this Way of Yeshua you follow, but were it up to me we would leave with you. Little Sarit needs her *Savta* and, whether Hadassah admits it or not, she needs you too."

His words made her heart leap for joy. "Don't you see, Hebel, it *is* up to you." She took his clay-stained fingers in hers. "You are the husband."

"If only it were that simple." He sighed, remembering past battles fought and lost. "You and I both know our household does not work the way it should. I am the meekest of husbands. In the beginning I tried being forceful, but at heart I am a peaceful man." His shoulders sank as he massaged his temples. "You see, when Hadassah begins to shout it makes my head pound."

Fearing he'd said too much, Hebel quickly retraced his steps. "I am not saying she is not a good wife and mother, you understand. She is the one who encouraged me to leave Bethlehem and come to Jerusalem. Joining the potter's guild here has meant a better life for us. Without her constant urging, I would still be in my tiny shop in Bethlehem never amounting to a thing."

"You need not explain; I know her better than you."

They shared a look of understanding.

"Loving her more than life itself, I never tried to force her to do anything she did not wish to do." He gave a sheepish grin. "I prefer not to know what might happen if I made demands."

"Let that love overwhelm your meekness. Dangerous times demand bold action."

"The only way she would leave is if I bound her up and tossed her in a sack." He shook his head. "No. She would never forgive me...us."

Rivkah rested an arm on his shoulder. "Listen carefully. Hadassah will not leave today. I accept that. But the day is coming, and will soon be here, when the enemy surrounds this city and builds an embankment to besiege its walls. Men, women and children shall all die together—"

Hebel cut her off saying, "Imma Rivkah, calm down. You are letting your imagination run away with you."

She spun around and pointed at the Temple. Its white walls sparkled above the rooftops in the morning sun.

"Do you see those magnificent stones? When this time I speak of comes not one of them will remain stacked upon the other."

Hebel stared up at the Temple walls, tensely tugging at his beard. His bottom lip quivered. "How...how could this ever be?"

His eyes jerked about. From the Temple they followed the stairway to their tiny apartment, then down the alley to his little shop with its rows of finished lamps waiting for buyers. His brow wrinkled with pain. He massaged his temples with increasing force.

"You have sufficient time," Rivkah whispered, "but you must watch for the signs."

He drew a gasping breath. "Signs, Imma Rivkah? What signs?" Hebel's fingertips went white as he kneaded the sides of his head harder and harder.

Stepping behind him, she rubbed his shoulders and neck until he relaxed. "Do not worry, my son. You have sufficient time.

You are a clever man. Stay alert to the winds of change and watch what happens around you. When the buds swell on the trees, you know summer is coming. Likewise, when the violence increases and Jews begin killing Jews, you will know the time of which I speak is drawing nigh."

"I will do as you ask." He stood tall and straight. "Like a sentry at his post, I will keep the watch."

"When you see those signs, you must bundle Hadassah and Sarit out of the city...whether she wants to go or not."

Hebel's newfound confidence wavered. He rolled his shoulders and took a deep breath. "Yes. Whether she wants to go or not." He leaned forward and kissed her on the cheek. "*Shalom Aleichem*, Imma Rivkah. *Kol Tuv*."

"And may you also be well." She pulled her son-in-law into her arms and hugged him tightly. "Hadassah may not admit it, but she's lucky to have a husband like you."

"Wait." Hebel disappeared down the alley to his shop. A moment later he handed her a large bundle. "Here. For you and Abba Shemu'el with my blessings."

"What is it?"

"Several of the lamps I make. Their handles and wide base make them convenient for travelers. May they serve you well."

"I will say a prayer for you and Hadassah each time I light one of them." She clasped his hand. "You are a good man, Hebel. Take care of my wayward daughter and little Sarit. You must be their shield in the coming storm."

Rivkah found the children waiting with Shemu'el where she left them.

Shemu'el rose and untied the donkey's lead rope when he saw her. The children gathered around him watching her walk toward them.

He studied her puffy eyes. "What happened with Hadassah?"

"She will not be going with us."

"Did you two argue again?"

"What we did does not matter. I already told you she has chosen to remain in Jerusalem."

"What is in the bundle?"

"Lamps. A going away gift from Hebel."

"Ah yes, Hebel." Shemu'el smirked. "The *man* of the house."

"He was unable to convince her."

"Surely you are not surprised. He can twist clay into impossible shapes, yet his wife just as easily twists him around her little finger." He sighed. "Hadassah made her choice. Let her reap what she has sown. We will not speak of this matter again."

Shemu'el gave the rope a sharp tug. The donkey lurched forward and everyone fell into step. Their journey had begun.

Though Hadassah's decision left her with a broken heart, Rivkah said nothing more. She had read the pain in Shemu'el's eyes. Masculine pride wouldn't let him acknowledge his disappointment, but she knew he too regretted leaving her behind.

They left Jerusalem, heading north toward Samaria. As they passed through the city gate, Rivkah knew she would never miss this place the way she missed their little settlement outside of Bethlehem.

No tears would be shed over Jerusalem. They came there in desperation and never found a place. Life had been a constant struggle and the previous season's drought only made things worse. For the first time in their married life, she and Shemu'el knew real hunger. They had three children to feed and some nights Rivkah pretended not to be hungry so the children could divide her share of their meager meal.

Each time she visited Rachel arrived burdened down like a pack animal with fruits and vegetables from their friends in the settlement. During the harvest season Rivkah and the children had gone out into the countryside and gleaned the fields gathering stores for the coming winter. Without that and the packages of fish Yohan thrust into her hands each time she visited Miryam, they would have had to beg.

A slight smile crossed Rivkah's lips. In spite of the turmoil, the Lord had provided. They each had new sandals on their feet, a sturdy tent, and warm cloaks for the cool nights. She'd sold her jewelry to buy them, but that was of little consequence. The wedding ring Shemu'el gave her remained on her finger and she required nothing more.

Rivkah's thoughts turned to those they left behind. Leaders of the Jerusalem synagogue like Yaakov, a man even the Pharisees referred to as *The Just*. Their friends and neighbors. The hidden ones, like Claudia Procula, wife of Pontius Pilate, and Gamali'el, known to only to a select few within their group...and those special ones known only to Yeshua himself. Good people all.

They traveled in a group and many feet threw up clouds of dust. The children hardly noticed, or cared. Caught up in the adventure of seeing places he had never seen before, Yudah, their youngest, skipped along beside the donkey. Their oldest son, Yo'el, and middle son, Yaakov, came next. The two of them walked along each edge of the road, working as a team to keep the few remaining sheep herded.

The women brought up the rear. Yo'el's wife, Tzipporah, walked on Rivkah's right and Channah, Rivkah's youngest daughter, walked at Rivkah's left. Elpis, Channah's cat, came too. He rode like an infant, snuggled against her bosom in a small cloth sack she'd sewn for him.

"I'm tired of having that bothersome cat under foot," her younger brother had complained when she brought out the sack. "I don't like him. Why not leave him behind?"

Channah responded by suggesting a similar fate for Yudah.

Rivkah resolved the impasse by taking them both.

Their small band of travelers paused at the top of the first hill and shook the dust off their sandals before taking a final look back. Rivkah stared down at the walled city and drew a deep breath.

Persecution had forced them out again. This time they were running for their lives. A shiver crawled up her spine. Would they someday be forced to run from Antioch as well?

# ~ 31 ~

*"Now when the apostles at Jerusalem heard
that Samaria had received the word of God,
they sent to them Peter and John."*
— Acts of the Apostles 8:14

Big, brawny Simon marched at the front of the column with
Yohan bar Zebedee, on one side and Yohan Markus, the son of
Aristopolus, on the other. Simon's wife, Ruth, and their children
trailed behind.

Over and over in the time they'd lived in Jerusalem, Rivkah
watched Simon walk away from arrest and possible death without
a backward glance. Always smiling, he kept his shoulders back
and his head high. She envied his confident faith.

Like Shemu'el and Rivkah, most of the families had the
ragtag look of a defeated army limping away from the field of
battle. Living with daily slights, snubs, and outright hatred
damaged them all in mind and spirit. As much as it hurt her to
admit it, Caiaphas had won this round.

Whether they rejoiced or mourned, they always expressed
their feelings through the Psalms. Sensing the caravan's somber
mood, Simon sang out the opening words of Psalm 27, "The Lord
is my light and my salvation; whom shall I fear?"

Slowly at first the others joined in, their volume rising along
with their confidence.

The closer they came to Samaria, the more the tension lines on
Shemu'el's face deepened. Though he said nothing, Rivkah
sensed his inner turmoil. Years before he'd traveled this same
road chained to the other prisoners. Frightful memories lurked
behind every rock and around every bend.

Their first night out, they camped in a grove of trees. With
no friends or relatives close at hand, the small group depended

upon each other. Everyone from the youngest to the oldest had a job and each set about their assigned task with dedication. The younger boys scoured the area for firewood, the men busied themselves setting up tents, and the women concentrated on preparing the evening meal. The girls gathered wild greens, tubers and berries while the older boys left with snares in hopes of trapping quail or rabbits.

When it grew dark, Rivkah lit one of the special lamps Hebel gave her for the trip. Its flickering flame kindled thoughts of Hadassah, the wayward daughter she'd been forced to leave behind.

Channah had received permission from her older brother to share his family's tent so she could cuddle baby Shemu'el who was easily soothed by the purring of Elpis snuggled beside them. Rivkah and Shemu'el's two younger sons had drifted away to camp with friends, leaving Rivkah and Shemu'el alone.

After pausing to admire the myriad stars sparkling in the sky above them, Rivkah entered the tent and busied herself arranging the blankets. It felt strangely empty.

*When had they last slept alone?*

Not since the birth of their first child, she realized.

Shemu'el returned moments later.

Rivkah loosed her hair and shook it free. She extinguished the lamp and they settled into each other's arms. She rested her head on his shoulder and they kissed in the darkness. His arms tightened around her and they kissed again...and again.

As Shemu'el lifted her gown she closed her eyes and remembered their wedding night. It was a time of scented oil in the lamps, ointments on the table and crisp linens covering the bed. She'd worn bells on the hem of her gown and rings on her fingers then.

Now they slept on a fleece spread over the hard ground with only a goat hair tent overhead. Their muscles ached and they smelled of the road, but at that moment neither of them cared. They touched each other in familiar ways, entwined in the dark, and shared pleasures.

Afterwards she pressed her face into Shemu'el's neck, breathing in his familiar scent. They lay close and quiet. No words were needed to express what their hearts already knew.

Simon planned to make their first stop in Sychar. The town sat in a fertile valley between Mt. Ebal and Mt. Gerizim, where the Samaritans had their temple. Sychar was a small village, about the size of Bethlehem.

He joined Rivkah and Shemu'el while they ate their morning meal. Simon took the loaf Rivkah offered and swirled his bread in a dish of yogurt sweetened with *debash*, fruit syrup.

He glanced across the fire at Rivkah. "Phillip tells me many will be requesting baptism when he arrive in Sychar."

"Yes, I have heard. You and Yohan will be kept busy."

He took the cup of water Channah offered and caught Shemu'el's eye. Simon lowered his voice. "Can we speak privately? There is something I wish to discuss with the two of you."

Shemu'el nodded and stood up. Touching Rivkah's shoulder, he indicated a nearby grove of trees. She and Simon also rose and followed Shemu'el. As they entered the grove, Shemu'el asked, "What is it?"

"Now that we have left Jerusalem, our only companions will be each other." Simon ran his eyes around the circle of tents behind them. "This little group becomes our *ekklesia* and, like every congregation it must have leaders. As *episkopos*, I will be traveling to carry the Gospel to neighboring regions. While I am away, I need someone to act in my stead." His eyes rested on Shemu'el. "And I would like it to be you."

Shemu'el gave a start. "Me, an overseer? Are you certain?"

"I prayed about it and your name came in answer to those prayers." Simon turned to Rivkah. "When we reach Sychar, Ruth will need help baptizing the women and children. I plan to ordain you as our *ekklesia's* first *diakonos*."

Rivkah's eyes flew open wide. Shocked speechless, she nodded in agreement.

It didn't take long for Simon to gather all their group together and explain his intention. With everyone's support, he placed his hands upon Shemu'el first and then Rivkah, ordaining them into their new offices. In so doing, they accepted responsibility to and for the fledgling congregation. Shemu'el for the member's spiritual welfare and Rivkah for their material welfare.

From a distance Sychar seemed to be nothing but a nondescript collection of tan buildings formed of block and mud plaster. It was late in the afternoon and the townspeople gathered in the village square when they noticed their visitors approaching.

Shemu'el caught Rivkah's eye. "Keep walking as if nothing is wrong," he whispered. "Take the children and move them to the back. They gathered like this when the Romans marched us down this same hill."

"What is the matter?"

"You do not know these Samaritans as I do." His fingers tightened around the staff in his hand. "They could be preparing an assault."

Shemu'el studied the growing crowd assembling ahead of them. "If they attack, I do not want any of the little ones injured. Be sure to keep the donkey between you and the crowd."

"Channah," Rivkah quietly said, "bring baby Shemu'el over here. Tzipporah, gather the women and children into a group beside me."

Shemu'el reached into the donkey's saddlebag and eased out the handle of his shepherd's rod. He left the club hidden in the bag, but readily available if needed.

Simon's raised hand signaled a stop. They were a dozen cubits from the crowd.

Shemu'el stood stock-still, his fingers resting on the rod's handle. He kept his eyes on the Samaritan men spread in a semi-circle before them.

Rivkah scarcely breathed as she watched the events unfold.

A white-bearded man stepped forward.

Shemu'el's fingers tightened on the club.

"*Shalom Aleichem*. Welcome, my guests." He bowed. "I am Hadar, an elder of this village." His gaze settled on the big man at the head of their tiny caravan. "And you must be Simon." He spread his arms wide. "Come, we have been expecting you."

Hadar rested his arm across Simon's back and directed him to the village square. "Surely you are tired from your journey." He waved for the rest to follow. "Come to Jacob's well and drink of its refreshing waters. Wash away the dust of the road and sit in the shade. We have prepared a feast in your honor."

Shemu'el's hand slipped from the rod and his arm dropped to his side as he took his first tentative steps toward the Samaritans.

Women came from the village carrying bowls of fruit. Giggling children raced ahead of them with plates of sweetmeats. They moved among the group, kissing them as they introduced themselves and learned their visitor's names.

Rivkah noticed Shemu'el holding back as the others quickly washed and made their way to the waiting tables.

"Hadar seems like a nice man," she said, taking his hand. "You are tired from the journey. Find a shady spot to rest and I will bring you a plate of food."

He did as she suggested and found a place at the extreme edge of the group.

Rivkah appeared a few moments later with two plates. "Everything looked wonderful. I must be hungrier than I thought," she said, chuckling. She handed him a plate. "I got you a little of everything. Try the lamb, it is delicious."

Shemu'el remained distracted, picking at his food.

Rivkah licked a dab of sauce off her fingertip and brushed away the breadcrumbs in her lap. She turned and gave him a surprised look. "Why, you've hardly eaten anything at all."

He studied his plate for a moment then sneered. "It will take more than a plate of food to make amends for what this village did to me, to Yudah, and to all of the other prisoners."

Shemu'el grabbed a thick slice of untouched lamb and tossed it to one of the village's dogs.

The following day was a busy one. Rivkah assisted with baptisms while Shemu'el worked beside Simon and Yohan. He watched in amazement as the two laid hands upon the newly-baptized Samaritans. Clearly the Holy Spirit was in this place.

As was their custom, before the evening meal the two apostles gathered the converts for the Lord's Supper. Following the celebration of bread and wine which had become the Lord's body and blood, the women laid out another large festive meal.

After they'd eaten, the men gathered around a fire. A wineskin made its way around the group as dusk settled over the valley.

Hadar sat between Simon and Yohan.

Shemu'el sought a spot in the shadows far from the fire. Like the night before, he'd eaten little. When the wineskin reached him he passed it on without taking any.

"This is truly an historic moment," Hadar said. He lifted his cup in a toast. "Everyone here knows of the ill feeling the Samaritans have had for the Jews. Yet look around you. Tonight two ancient enemies have become brothers in the Holy Spirit."

Simon smiled and slapped Hadar on the back. "What you say is true, but we Jews have done more than our share of hating as well."

Hadar didn't reply. Growing pensive, he quietly stared into the flames.

An ominous silence settled upon the group as each man examined his own conscience.

Hadar slowly raised his eyes, swallowed hard, and looked from Simon to Yohan. "Truly there has been more than enough bad blood between us. Whatever you may have done, it is nothing compared to what some of us did."

Shemu'el shifted on the ground, struggling to control his

rising anger.

Simon waved Hadar's words away with a flick of his wrist. "Every man here has sinned. We have all fallen short of the glory of God."

"Undoubtedly we have," Hadar said as he rose. "But I feel compelled to confess one particularly egregious incident. It occurred when Quintillius Varus governed Syria...when Sabinus was Procurator in Archelaus' absence. Sabinus sent troops into the Temple court and they set fire to the cloisters."

Heads lowered in shame around the campfire.

Shemu'el's lips tightened. He crossed his arms and stared at Hadar like a judge preparing to pass sentence.

Hadar paced as he spoke. "The soldiers of *Legio XII* marched a line of young men through our village on their way back to Antioch." His voice quivered. "These young men were innocent of any crime. They'd been beaten and abused...forced to march chained together like animals. Did we offer them a dipper of cool water? Did we give them a morsel of bread, a piece of fruit? Did we so much as beat our breasts and implore God's mercy on their behalf?"

Deep in the shadows Shemu'el leaped to his feet. Shaking with anger, he stormed up to Hadar stood and kicked a log. Cartwheeling end over end, it careened into the fire sending sparks soaring into the dark sky.

" No!" Shemu'el shouted. "You did none of those things. Instead you spit on them, reviled them, and pelted them with rotted fruit."

For a moment Hadar looked shocked, then he sank to his knees in front of his accuser. He leaned forward, resting his elbows on his knees and hung his head. "What could I have been thinking? How could I have ever done such a thing?"

"Because you were a Samaritan and we were Jews," Shemu'el said as he loomed above him. "Just as I hated you that day because you were a Samaritan."

Hadar's head lifted.

Their eyes met.

"I have wronged you, brother," Hadar said. "I beg your

forgiveness. I have watched you these last two days and sensed your discomfort. Were you among those of whom I just spoke... one of those who passed through our village in chains?"

Shemu'el swallowed. "I was."

Hadar shook his head. "As I grew older I realized how wrong it was to treat you as we did. I began to pray for you each time I visited the temple on Mt. Gerizim."

Shemu'el's shoulders slumped and the anger drained out of his face. He looked tired and sad as he extended his hand.

Hadar took it and Shemu'el pulled him to his feet.

"I wish I could say I also prayed for you," Shemu'el said. "But I must confess I did not. Even though I accepted Yeshua's baptism, and swore to follow his commands, deep within me I hoarded a nugget of hatred in my heart. Forgive me, brother. The way to God is love, not hate."

Hadar placed a hand on Shemu'el's shoulder. "And yet, feeling as you did, you still accompanied Simon to our village and brought us the Holy Spirit. You have no need to ask my forgiveness. Your actions have spoken louder than any words."

# ~ 32 ~

*"Then Herod, when he saw that he had been tricked by
the wise men, was in a furious rage, and he sent and
killed all the male children in Bethlehem, and in all that
region who were two years old or under..."*
                                        —Matthew 2:16

After multiple stops in Samaria, the group continued on to
Galilee. The lush vegetation and cool sea air offered a welcome
change from the heat and dryness of the Jezreel Valley.

They followed the shoreline of Lake Gennersaret, passing
one fishing village after another until they reached their
destination, Capernaum. They stayed at this former base of
Yeshua's Galilean ministry for a week, resting and re-supplying
before heading to Antioch.

While in Capernaum, Simon took Rivkah to the home of
another of the Twelve, Mattithayu. His wife greeted them at the
gate and led them to a garden atrium where he waited. After
introducing Rivkah, Simon left to go about his day.

"It was kind of you to make time for this visit." Mattithayu's
soft voice matched his humble demeanor.

"Several people said you were anxious to meet me. It was
the least I could do."

"Ever since Miryam mentioned your name I have longed to
speak with you." He paused for a moment. "Are you aware, that
before the Lord called me from my booth to join his little band, I
was a *Mokhes*?"

Rivkah smiled. "Yes, Miryam mentioned Mattithayu, the
customs official, at various times when we lived in Jerusalem."

He smiled. "Before entering into a friendship, I always
make people aware of my background. Some find it," he
hesitated, smoothing his beard as he searched for the proper
word, "troubling...bothersome."

Tall and dignified with a thin face, he was older than some
of the Twelve she had met. For several years before the Lord

called him, Mattithayu managed the Capernaum customs office for the tetrarch, Herod Antipas. In the process, he grew accustomed to moving within the elite circle of the ruling class. He treated Rivkah with the courtesy and deference afforded to one of Ceasar's ambassadors. By the end of the afternoon she felt more like a princess than a former shepherd's wife.

"You may also know I am creating a list of the Master's sayings in Hebrew for use by the Jews to whom I preach."

"Yes. I saw one of your codices at the Synagogue of Rabban Yeshua *HaMashiach* in Jerusalem."

He smiled and brought his long fingers together as he spoke. "I have two scribes here in Capernum whose days are spent making additional copies. New congregations of believers are sprouting up everywhere. It is my hope that someday every *ekklesia* will have a copy. Before you leave, I will give you several to distribute on your journey."

As he spoke, Mattithayu rested his elbow on a portable writing desk on the bench beside him. "Now I have set my shoulder to a larger, more complex task. Those sayings I collected aid the faithful, but they lack depth and breadth. Let me show you what I mean. Suppose I told you David spoke these words."

Rising, he lifted a hand to the sky as an orator might. "The Lord who delivered me from the paw of the lion and the paw of the bear will deliver me from the hand of this Philistine."

Rivkah found herself wondering whether he chose this particular passage because he'd heard of her own encounter with a lion as a young shepherdess. "Noble words of faith spoken before he faced Goliath," she said.

Mattithayu put his hands on his hips and stared down at her like a rabbi interrogating a student. "Are they truly noble words? Or is it only because you know the context in which they were spoken that they have such meaning for you?"

"Well...I, uh."

He stood on tiptoes and waved his hand high above his head. "How meaningful would they be if you knew nothing of Goliath's enormous size?" He lowered his hand to knee level. "What if you imagined him a dwarf?" Casting wary glances into the treetops, he crouched and pretended to scoop stones for his sling. "What if you had no understanding of David's youth and inexperience in the ways of war?"

"What is it you intend to do?" Rivkah asked.

Flushed with excitement, he dropped onto the bench beside her. "The sayings I recorded may be wise and meaningful, but they are not enough. Sayings alone will not accomplish our task. Look at the Torah and the *Nevi'im*. Do the Law and the Prophets consist of only sayings without detail, merely pithy words? Of course not."

Too excited to sit still, Mattithayu leaped off the bench and strode across the stone patio directing the drama unfolding in his mind. "More is required. Sayings alone do not tell the whole story. They are like dry bones bleaching in the desert sun. Don't you see? We must gather up those dry bones and clothe them with sinews and flesh. Cover them with skin."

Rivkah gave a start when he smacked his hands together.

"They must live! Yeshua commanded us to go forth to all nations preaching and teaching. Until he returns, words are the only tools we have. Our words must put wind in the trees and clouds in the sky. The pages must echo with the roar of the sea and the smell of fish fresh out of the net, the crackle of firelight at day's end and the hope which rides on each morning's dawn."

He tapped a finger into the palm of his hand. "They must sing and dance, laugh and weep. Every nuance, every glance, every inflection must be recorded there."

He smiled apologetically. "Forgive me. As you probably noticed, I tend to become quite passionate about what I call the *Gospel*, the good news. It is incumbent upon those few of us who knew him to record the events of his ministry, so he can be known to others for all time."

Mattithayu shifted on the bench and looked at her straight on. "And you, Rivkah, have the honor of helping me in this momentous task."

He lifted the small writing desk onto his lap. Opening a drawer, he removed a fresh quill.

She recognized the white feather in his hand as one coming

from the tail of the sea eagles that soared high above the Judean desert.

Turning it, he chose a spot and made his cut. Mattithayu rolled out a fresh papyrus across the desktop, dipped his new quill and scratched several quick notes. "I understand from Miryam that you and your father were in the field tending your sheep the night they took Yeshua away to Egypt," he said without looking up.

Her cheeks warmed. "True, but she must have told you everything there is to know about that evening."

"Everything she could." Mattithayu rattled the quill against his brass inkhorn impatiently. "If one cannot experience something first hand, the next best thing is to hear it from the one who did." He swept his long fingers through the air. "I have heard many tales about these mysterious visitors form the east, but, other than Miryam and Herod, you are the only one who actually met them."

He gave a good-natured shrug. "In particular, when I heard about your encounter with them, I wondered why they came the way they did. What were they doing on the south road heading *away* from Jerusalem?"

Mattithayu dipped his quill and gave her an expectant look.

Rivkah took a deep breath and began. "Abba and I were in a tower watching the sheep when I noticed Miryam and Yosef coming down the south road. After they left, we checked the sheep and snuggled under our fleece cloaks."

"So it was a cold evening." Mattithyahu scribbled notes as he spoke.

"Yes, very cold. I fell asleep right away. When I opened my eyes it was morning and my cloak was heavy with dew. I heard horses coming toward us. Many horses."

He gave an understanding nod. "The Magoi from Parthia."

The two of them discussed the Magoi for about an hour. Rivkah answered his questions and relived her time with the Magoi. Mattithayu's hand flew across the sheet recording each word she said. He drew a breath, preparing to ask another question, but put his quill aside instead.

Looking up, Rivkah noticed his wife crossing the terrace with trays of food.

"It is noon," she said and handed him a tray.

She passed Rivkah the other and chuckled. "Do not let him overwork you. He can be as relentless as a prosecutor. If I did not intervene occasionally, his guests would find themselves hungry and exhausted." She waved a hand over the tray in Rivkah's lap. "Mattithayu eats neither fish, nor fowl, nor game. I find it easiest to serve our guests a similar fare. I hope you do not mind."

Rivkah assured her the meal was more than satisfactory and Mattithayu's wife left as quietly as she came.

Mattithayu sat his tray aside and brushed bread crumbs off his cloak. He returned the writing desk to his lap. "There is one other occurrence that I wish to discuss with you. One in which you were the sole witness."

"I cannot imagine what you might be referring to."

"A few days after the Magoi left Judea, your father's map in hand, Herod sent troops into the region around Bethlehem searching for the infant Yeshua."

The ground dropped out from under her. Tears formed in Rivkah's eyes. In that instant she became a little girl combing wool in the side yard. She recalled feeling the Centurion's rough hand grab the neck of her cloak and shake her back and forth as he demanded to know where her cousin, Yohan, had gone.

Rivkah took a deep breath and composed herself. "Their orders were to kill every boy child two years old and under. The soldiers began in the countryside north of Bethlehem. Abba had been forewarned and we were prepared for them by the time they reached our settlement..."

Mattithayu transcribed her words nearly as fast as she spoke.

Rivkah marveled at the speed with which he completed a line and commented. "I have never seen anyone write so quickly. It is quite a contrast to a scribe who labors over each and every character."

He smiled at the implied complement. "It is a method of speed writing. A series of marks that capture the essence of a thought without recording the entire word. Later, after you have gone, I will set my hand to this again and transcribe all that you said in exact detail."

"How did you learn such a thing?"

"Necessity is the best teacher. All manner of goods passed through my station when I managed the customs office for Herod Antipas. It forced me to take long inventories in a short amount of time."

Turning his head, Mattithayu surveyed an imaginary line of merchants waiting to pay their duties. "Few people enjoy paying taxes. I soon learned if they were processed efficiently and without delay, the procedure felt less onerous."

"Here, let me show you." He dipped his quill and made several cryptic marks in the margin. Spinning it in her direction, he pointed to it and read, "Six ewes, eight lambs and one donkey." Winking, he held out his hand. "Ten *quadrans*, please."

# ~ 33 ~

*"Now as he journeyed he approached Damascus, and
suddenly a light from heaven flashed about him. And he
fell to the ground and heard a voice say to him, 'Saul,
Saul. Why do you persecute me?'"*

—Acts of the Apostles 9:3-4

Leaving the lush valleys and maritime climate of Galilee behind,
Simon's band of travelers followed the King's Highway to
Damascus. Everyone speculated about the impact of Sha'oul's
persecution as they walked.

Traveling by the most direct route without delays and
stopovers, Sha'oul's small deputation undoubtedly reached
Damascus before them. Simon went into the city to make
inquires and returned accompanied by a stranger.

Simon waved his arm, gathering the group together. "Come,
everyone. This is Ananias. I want you to listen as he tells of
Sha'oul's visit to the city of Damascus."

They formed a tight circle never imagining the strange tale
they were about to hear.

"Sha'oul a believer? It could not happen," someone said
when Ananias finished.

Simon lifted his eyebrows and gave an elaborate shrug. "I
admit I was skeptical at first, too. That is why they took me to see
Ananias. You have heard him say the Lord sent him to cure
Sha'oul's blindness. And, that after regaining his sight, Sha'oul
began preaching in the synagogues saying, 'Yeshua is the Son of
God.'"

"Where is Sha'oul now?" someone asked.

"We smuggled him out of the city in a basket when the Jews
conspired to kill him," Ananias said. "He headed off into the
desert alone."

Sha'oul became the favored topic of conversation around
the evening campfire.

Channah held another opinion "I believe Ananias told us

the truth as he understands it, but Sha'oul is both shrewd and treacherous. This is another of his tricks to lure more victims into his snare. What better way to flush out his quarry than claim to be one with them?" She gave a mocking laugh. "Do as you wish, but I intend to have nothing to do with this evil man."

The road to Antioch followed a barren valley between two rows of chalky mountains. Dust from the road irritated their eyes and dried and cracked their lips. Because of the heat, they took to traveling at night with their cloaks pulled tight against the cold. After two weeks the mountains became low, rolling hills.

Shemu'el caught Simon staring at the setting sun. "Is something troubling you?"

Simon shook his head and smiled. "No, I was just thinking how pleasant it is to see a sunset without a mountain in my way." He brightened. "One of the camel drivers I spoke to said we will reach the oasis at Emesa tomorrow."

The following day they camped in a shady spot beside a stream-fed lake. Simon took the boys down to the water and showed them how to fashion fish traps from willow branches, reeds, and rope. Shaped like an Egyptian vase, the baskets trapped any fish that swam into them. Next, he had the boys pile rocks in the creek. Their makeshift dam increased the water flow between the rocks and directed fish into the boy's baskets.

Tired and damp, they strutted into camp with puffed-out chests carrying baskets of speckled fish in their arms. After dumping the catch at the women's feet, they swaggered off to join the men. While the boys told and retold their story, the women split the fish and mounted them on forked branches for cooking.

After they'd eaten, Simon rose to speak. He pointed to the Orentes Mountains they would cross in the morning. "My friends, soon we will be in Antioch. It is time we began to plan."

Shemu'el ran his eyes around the small group, counting. "Some of our fellow travelers stayed behind at each stop. The attrition is so great we no longer have enough for a *minyan*."

"We have what we have," Simon said. "We need not be bound by the rules of scribes and Pharisees. Besides, among the 3000 who believed the morning of Pentecost many were residents of Antioch."

"That may be so, but how will we find them?" someone asked. "And even if we can, do your words still burn in their hearts?"

Simon's confidence remained undiminished. "The Lord will lead us to them." He rummaged in the coals with a stick and smiled when flames burst forth. "Like this fire, those glowing embers of faith need only be prodded back into life."

The group lapsed into silence as everyone stared into the fire wondering what awaited them in Antioch.

Simon's voice broke the spell. "There is another thing I wish to discuss. We have left the world of Judaism behind. As we prepare to enter the Hellenistic world we must avoid offending those we meet."

His wife, Ruth, sat at Simon's side in the flickering shadows. He gave her a shy smile. "Since our very names single us out as foreigners, with Ruth's kind permission I have decided to change mine. From now on I wish to be called Simon Petros."

He lifted his hands when some questioned his decision. "Wait, hear me out. Our people have a long history of doing this. After all, didn't Avram become Avraham and Yaakov become Isra'el? When we traveled the roads and byways of Galilee the Lord often called me his rock. Many in Jerusalem addressed me as *Cephas*. But we are no longer in the land of our ancestors. A new life demands a new name."

Shemu'el warmed to the idea. "Simon is correct. We must meet people on their own turf rather than appear as outsiders. I will follow Simon's lead."

Rivkah leaned over and hugged his arm. Among his friends and family he would forever remain Shemu'el, but to the world at large, he became Evodius.

Like Simon, Shemu'el retained his *praenomen*, or given name, and paired it with the *cognomen* of his former master, becoming Shemu'el Evodius. Those who preferred could still address either of them by their given names, Simon and Shemu'el. But Greeks and Romans, accustomed to referring to each other by their *cognomens*, came to call them Petros and Evodius.

They arrived in Antioch after the *Shabbat*. Unlike Jerusalem, which sat high and dry, a pinnacle surrounded by valleys, Antioch lay in a wide, flat plain beside a river with mountains at its back. From their vantage point high on a ridge they saw the whole city spread out before them. Like Galilee, from a distance Antioch appeared lush and green.

The children eagerly squinted at the western horizon when Shemu'el pointed to a foggy bank of low-lying clouds. "There is the Great Sea, and beyond those hills lies the port of Pieria Seleucia, a single day's sailing down the Orentes River. Looking east, he showed them the Citadel, the garrison of the Legions, perched above the city in the foothills of Mt. Silpius.

They approached from the south and spent their first night camped outside the city near the Wall of Tiberius. Yaakov, their middle son and oldest child still at home, studied the wall with a look of disdain. "They call that puny pile of rocks a city wall? It would hardly stop a determined goat. I expected something magnificent...perhaps taller even than the Temple Mount. Look at them; they are not even aligned in regular courses. "

His older brother, Yo'el, wandered over to join the conversation. Hands on his hips, he stared up at the Daphne Gate. It rose higher than the wall by some measure, allowing it to admit caravans of loaded camels.

"The gate is not too bad, although the stone's edges remain rough and poorly cut." He clucked his tongue. "Not nearly as nice as the Water Gate near our former home. They should send their masons to Jerusalem so they can learn how to properly dress an ashlar."

Shemu'el joined them. "Don't be so quick to judge. Why build what you don't need? Antioch is flanked by mountains and faces the sea. Nature has provided all the protection it needs."

## ~ 34 ~

*"Now those who were scattered because of the
persecution that arose over Stephen traveled as far
as Phoenicia and Cyprus and Antioch, speaking the
word to none except Jews."*
                                        —Acts of the Apostles 11:19

The next morning, after everyone had eaten, bathed and donned
clean garments, the family set off to explore the city. They
entered through the Daphne Gate with Shemu'el leading the way.

Antioch's size dazzled the children. It was much larger than
Jerusalem, some said by as much as a factor of six or eight. The
children meandered along wide-eyed and gawking. They looked
from side to side and occasionally lagged behind to stare at
something they found particularly interesting.

"I had no idea Antioch would be so different," Yudah said.

"Was living here exciting, Abba?" Channah asked.

Shemu'el thought for a moment before answering. "In
certain ways, yes, but what I remember most is the loneliness."

"What was it like living among so many Gentiles?" There
was a hint of apprehension in Yaakov's voice.

"You act like you've never interacted with a Gentile before,"
Shemu'el said, chuckling. "They do not bite."

"Of course we saw them in Jerusalem, but it was different at
home. Other than the Romans and trading merchants, you
seldom saw a Gentile. Here," he glanced around the plaza
nervously, "they are everywhere."

*Yaakov's right*, Rivkah thought. In Jerusalem the city's
practices and customs were thoroughly Jewish. In Antioch,
though the number of Jews approached that of Jerusalem, they
remained a definite minority. Everywhere they turned they saw
another pagan temple dedicated to this, that, or the other god or
goddess.

Shemu'el tousled Yaakov's hair. "Trust me, you will
survive."

As for Rivkah, her most enduring memory of Antioch would always be the water. They passed several large baths with cascading pools arranged stepwise beside the entrances and every public square seemed to have a fountain. They'd rationed water in Jerusalem the summer after the drought. It felt odd to see water in such abundance.

Shemu'el explained that a series of dams and aqueducts captured the water coming off the mountains and directed it into reservoirs which fed the city as well as irrigation canals for the fields to the north.

Near the old Seleucid City Wall he pointed out the colonnaded walkway known as the Stoa of Herod and Tiberius. He stood beside a pillar and slowly ran his fingers along its polished surface the way he had many years before.

"I often stopped just to touch one of these pillars," he said, half-apologetically. "I was far from home, alone, and missed your mother terribly. I knew Herod taxed away the income of my countrymen to construct this walkway as a tribute to his patron, Tiberius." His voice quivered with emotion. "It was the closest reminder of home I had. Touching them brought me a measure of comfort."

Shemu'el sighed and walked on. They stopped again at the place where Herod's Stoa intersected with the covered boulevard called the *Via Caesarea*. "Like all Greek cities, Antioch is plotted on a Hippodamian Grid." He used his hands to demonstrate. "Notice how each street intersects its neighbors at right angles."

"Unlike Jerusalem where the streets go up and down the hills and snake off in multiple directions," Channah said.

"Yes. The Greeks believed it promoted social harmony."

"Here all this time I thought the High Priest caused the chaos in Jerusalem and now I find out it was the fault of the streets," Yo'el said, laughing.

Turning west, they followed the *Via Caesarea* to the bridge leading to the *insula*. Crossing an arm of the Orentes River to the small island, they walked among the official buildings of Roman Syria.

"There is the Governor's Palace." Shemu'el pointed to a

building atop a long row of marble steps. "The place where Quirinius gave Atticus and I our certificates of manumission."

"Is that a coliseum beside it?" Yudah asked.

Shemu'el shook his head. "It is a hippodrome."

The young boy's eyes sparkled with excitement. "Did you ever go there to watch a chariot race?"

Shemu'el rested his hand on his son's shoulder and turned him aside. "No, but I have treated the injuries caused by such races. It is nothing you wish to see."

Retracing their steps, they entered the marketplace. Shemu'el showed them the slave block where he and Atticus encountered their friend, Yudah, standing in chains; also Shemu'el's youngest son's namesake. He showed the children the goldsmith's shop where Yudah worked, and the place where the woodcarver's shop had once been.

Crossing the square, they stopped beside a stand with smoking braziers. He handed the proprietor a few coins and returned with roasted meat on skewers. He passed them out saying, "Atticus loved these more than anything."

From the market square they walked east toward Mount Silpius. In the distance the walls of The Citadel, the military garrison where Shemu'el once lived with his fellow slave, Atticus, and their mentor and master, Evodius Scipio, were clearly visible.

They stopped short of The Citadel to visit the *Museion*, a cluster of buildings which Shemu'el said were dedicated to the Muses. "As pagans, the Greeks and Romans believe inspiration and knowledge comes from various goddesses called Muses. We, of course, know all true knowledge comes from God." He gave them a keen look. "Whether they recognize its source, or not, the knowledge the pagans discover sometimes does much good."

Shemu'el led them past the library of Antioch, second in size only to the one at Alexandria. Bypassing other buildings devoted to learning, they stopped at a circular, domed building in the center of the complex. Leaving the midday sun, he led them into its shadowy interior.

"Close your eyes for a few moments to let them adjust," he instructed. "Then tilt your heads back and look up at the ceiling."

The children gasped in surprise and wonder when they opened their eyes.

Tzipporah tilted little Shemu'el's head back. "See the stars?" He looked around, clapping his hands and giggling.

"And the moon," Channah said.

Rivkah felt the same sense of motion she always got when staring up at the night sky. "I feel as if I am out in the fields on a summer's night."

The children began pointing to familiar stars and constellations, trying to see who could name them first. Somehow, the vault of the heavens with its moon and stars had been reproduced on a dome 100 feet above their heads.

On their way back to camp they encountered Simon Petros coming from the opposite direction. He noticed them at the same time and hurried toward them, breathless with excitement.

"I was on my way to your campsite to find you. I have wonderful news. I met a local resident, a believer named Loukas. He owns some land on Mt. Stauris and he said we could use it." A broad smile lit Petros' face. "We have our new home."

Rainfall greeted them the next day at Mt. Stauris. While the group settled in and tried to make a fire with damp wood, Petros set off to explore the area. He returned an hour later dripping wet and exhilarated.

Grinning, he leaned on his walking staff. "My friends, I have found our new meeting place."

"A synagogue here in the wilds?"

"A cave, actually. With space for us all and room to spare. Let me take you there. Leave what you are doing and come with me." He stopped and glanced back over his shoulder. "And be sure to bring some lamps."

He led them through the wet grass to a cleft in the hillside's dark rock where trailing vines and brush obscured a natural opening.

"It would have been easy to walk right past and never

notice. But the hand of the Lord turned my eyes." Grabbing a handful of vines and branches, Simon gave them a hard tug. Dirt and gravel cascaded down as they ripped out of the thin soil above the opening. He tossed them aside and grabbed some more. "Join me. It won't be nearly as forbidding with these out of the way."

The men tore away the greenery and their work gradually revealed a large opening. Overhung by the lip of the mountain, it provided natural protection from the weather.

He lit a lamp and ventured in. The others started to follow, but scattered when a flock of bats flew out the opening. Petros walked around the room holding the lamp high above his head. The floor, which was littered with bat droppings, rose to meet the ceiling and made the back half of the cave too low for anyone to stand up in.

"We can dig this out and level the floor." His eyes gleamed as he envisioned the finished room. "When complete, it will be larger than the synagogue we had in Jerusalem. And look!" He ran to a spot where a dripping spring had worn a natural basin in the rock. "We can baptize new converts right here."

Everyone moved their tents to Mt. Stauris. Over the next week the women swept and cleaned while the men dug out the back portion of the grotto and hauled the soil away in baskets. The men's digging exposed a large, flat mound of stone near the back wall, perfect for an altar. The boys spent their days chipping niches into the walls to hold lamps.

Their church in a cave became presentable in short order.

When they left Jerusalem it never occurred to anyone to wax their tent cloth. They had mistakenly assumed they would be in permanent housing before the rainy season began. The continuous rain saturated the fabric of their tents causing leaks. Petros suggested they celebrate the Lord's Supper in their new gathering place and then move into the cave to get out of the rain.

That night everyone hauled their bedrolls, blankets, lamps and other essentials into the cave. The boys discovered a smaller cave nearby. They cut saplings for a gate and converted it into a stable. The travelers stored everything not brought into the cave in this makeshift stable along with the animals.

The group extinguished most of the lamps after evening prayers and prepared for bed. The room was cool, its stone walls damp. Rivkah snuggled close, sharing Shemu'el's warmth. The children lay in blankets around them. The rain outside made the air heavy. Smoke from the fire pit at the center of the room hung in a cloud above them.

She glanced around the darkened cave at the other families huddled in similar bedraggled clumps. This was hardly how she imagined life in Antioch would be. Their path, it seemed, led ever downward.

They had left the familiar comforts of their little settlement for the scarcity and animosity of Jerusalem. Driven from their noisy house with its constant parade of camel caravans, they traveled for weeks only to end up living in a dank cave like animals. She knew they had much to be grateful for, but at that moment, Rivkah felt only disappointment.

A sudden gust swept around the room making the lamps flicker. She watched whirlwinds of light swirl across the rocky ceiling and remembered their comfortable synagogue with Shemu'el's beautiful carvings around the walls and on the altar. She missed Hadassah, Hebel and little Sarit, the day-to-day routines, and the friends and neighbors they'd left behind.

Somewhere along the way it had become easier to look back than ahead. Life seemed to be spiraling out of control and she felt powerless to stop it.

She sensed her faith waver. The more she tried to grab hold of it, the more it felt like snatching smoke out of the air. She struggled to pray, but the words eluded her.

Rivkah closed her eyes and tried to still her mind. One of Yeshua's sayings from Mattithayu's codex came to her. "*Come to me, all you who are weary and burdened, and I will give you rest.*" A weigh of the moment lifted and she drifted off to sleep.

# ~ 35 ~

*"...and in Antioch the disciples were for the first time
called Christians."*
— Acts of the Apostles 11:26

The next months passed in a rush of activity. The group
continued working on their grotto home, steadily making
improvements. Each *Shabbat* they rose early and prayed together
before splitting into groups and visiting the city's synagogues
where the men preached the good news of Yeshua's salvation.

Over time they re-established the routines and practices
that served them well in Jerusalem. The congregation elected a
group of elders to provide direction. People brought offerings
when they met and additional *diakonoi* were ordained to assist
with the daily distribution.

As things stabilized, Simon Petros began traveling to
outlying areas preaching and establishing fledgling communities
of believers. Shemu'el Evodius functioned in his stead. Whenever
he exercised his priestly functions, he wore a plain white robe of
bleached linen that Rivkah and Channah had sewn for him and
tied it at the waist with a woven girdle.

Shemu'el's fortunes took an immediate turn for the better
when Loukas, the physician who allowed them to use his land,
sponsored his introduction into Antioch's Guild of Physicians.
The physicians in Antioch viewed Shemu'el's experience with the
Legions very differently than those in Jerusalem had.

Thanks to Loukas, Shemu'el gained respect and a means of
earning a living. He and Rivkah found a modest home in town
and moved into it.

All the way to Antioch their group had preached only to the Jews
they met and, in their defense, members of the *ekklesia* could
always say the Hellenists never asked anyone's permission when
they began preaching the Word among the Gentiles. Not that

anyone opposed accepting Gentiles into the fold. As Petros said many times, "God truly shows no partiality. He accepts men from every nation who fear him and do what is right."

This influx of Gentiles altered the *ekklesia's* structure from a community of former Jews to a community of believers. In recognition of this wider mission, their terminology changed. *Yeshua HaMashiach* became *Iesous* the *Christos*. The Holy Spirit, *Rauch HaKodesh*, became *Hagios Pnuema*, and God the Father became *Theos*.

Though they no longer considered themselves a branch of Judaism, outsiders still asked, "You do not worship our pagan gods, yet seem not to be Jews either. What, or who, are you?"

They had no ready answer until one day Shemu'el Evodius replied, "We are followers of the *Christos*. We are...*Christianoi*.

As in Jerusalem, the *diakonoi* met in the grotto each afternoon to prepare the daily distribution. One of the wealthy women donated a wagonload of clothing, men and women's tunics and cloaks, gowns, scarves...even small items in children's sizes.

They spent the morning sorting the items, each of them taking what their clients could use. As the deaconess who ministered to the poorest of the poor, they allowed Rivkah first choice. She picked through this unexpected Godsend selecting something special for each of those she served.

"What do we have here?" Rivkah asked when she saw a corner of striped cloth. She thrust her hand down to the bottom of the stack and tugged...and tugged...and tugged. There seemed to be no end to the striped cloth.

The others watched, snickering as she pulled out more and more fabric.

Their laughter made her feel like an entertainer she'd once seen in Jerusalem. The man, part of a traveling troupe, untied a small scarf which proceeded to grow longer and longer as he tried to remove it.

She was up to her knees in cloth by the time the last of it

finally toppled off the end of the wagon. An inner voice whispered, *"Take it. This cloak was intended for you."*

"I'll take this one." Rivkah stretched to open her arms wide enough to measure its width.

Iola, another deaconess laughed. "Are you sure? We could use the material to make a nice tent."

Rivkah gazed down at the fabric piled around her ankles. Never had she seen anything so large. Who, or what, was it made for?

"Maybe we can find someone who will cut it down," Megaira said. "There's enough material there to clothe a family of four."

Grabbing the cloak by its shoulders, Rivkah lifted it as high as she could. Even standing on her tiptoes the bottom of the cloak still draped across the floor. "Who could ever wear such a thing?"

"Goliath," Gregoris suggested. "The only problem is David killed him."

Despite her misgivings and everyone's jokes, Rivkah kept the huge garment. She reached into the wagon again and came up with an equally large tunic. It joined the cloak on her stack.

With the clothing packed, Rivkah enlisted Shemu'el's help to carry it. Her daily allotment, two baskets of food, waited on the altar. She headed out anticipating the happy looks on her client's faces when they saw the clothing she brought.

Turning off the street of Herod and Tiberius, they passed through the crumbling gate and entered the original city of Seleucus I. Lengthening shadows stretched across the narrow streets where children played among puddles and potholes. The smell of a hundred cooking fires surrounded them as they wove between the homes and apartments crowded into the district.

They walked along a street bordering the riverbank. This was the poorest section of town, a place Rivkah knew well from her daily visits. Baskets dangled from both of her arms, filled with the day's portion allocated to the widows, orphans, and poor she served. Beside her, Shemu'el labored under a large packing basket similar to the ones camels carried. He glanced down one of the alleyways. "I hadn't realized how much worse this neighborhood has become. You should not be here alone."

"I never am. Yeshua..." Rivkah shook her head and smiled. "I mean Iesous, always accompanies me."

Something rustled the bushes on the riverbank.

They stopped and stared. The low light made it difficult to see clearly. Shemu'el put the heavy basket down and stepped in front of her.

Throaty grunts, followed by a shriek of pain came out of the brush.

The hair on the back of Rivkah's neck prickled.

She and Shemu'el stared at each other. Could there be a man in there? A man and what else?

The branches whipped back and forth as if animals were locked in mortal combat.

"What should we do?" Rivkah whispered. She sat her baskets beside Shemu'el's, freeing her hands.

Shemu'el straightened his arm, holding her back.

A mop of hair, dark, shaggy and matted, appeared between the branches for an instant then disappeared. Painful grunts and heavy breathing were followed by more thrashing.

Shemu'el searched the ground for a weapon. Settling on a heavy branch, he inched forward. He started to circle the bush, remembered Rivkah, and stopped. Glancing back, he raised a hand, giving the command "Stay."

"Who's in there," Shemu'el shouted as he rounded the bush.

A terrified scream came from the bushes followed by unintelligible mumbling. The branches below Rivkah sprang apart revealing a hulk of a man. His torn clothing hung around him in strips of dirty rags. Hunkered into a crouch, he watched over his shoulder for Shemu'el as he crept up the bank. This bear of a man clambered up the hillside heading  toward Rivkah.

Three-quarters of the way up the slope he turned and saw her. Dropping to his knees, he covered his face with his hands and quivered in fear.

Just then Shemu'el emerged through the tunnel of broken branches the man had created. He looked on in amazement as the huge man cringed in fear before his petite wife.

Rivkah approached the man and went down on one knee.

Shemu'el tensed, adjusting his grip on the branch.

"It's all right. You need not fear me," she said softly. She urged him closer with an outstretched hand. Rivkah's voice remained soft and lyrical, reassuring. She treated him like a small child, speaking as if he understood and never concerning herself whether he did or not.

The man sniffed and dragged the tattered sleeve of his cloak across his face. He shot her a furtive glance then quickly jerked his eyes away.

She continued speaking in soft, reassuring tones.

Shemu'el continued circling behind him with club raised.

The man appeared unaware of the threat Shemu'el represented.

"Are you hungry?" Rivkah took a barley loaf from her basket and offered it to him.

The man inched forward, but stopped short. He clearly wanted the loaf, but feared taking it. He kept his head low, shifting his eyes from side to side and avoiding her gaze.

She sat the loaf on the grass a few feet in front of him.

As soon as she stepped back, he leaped on it like a cat attacking a mouse. He snatched it up, hugged it to his chest, and retreated to his previous spot. He eyed his treasure in between stealthy glances at Rivkah.

She pantomimed breaking the loaf and eating it. "Go ahead. I have plenty."

The loaf vanished in the blink of an eye as he tore it into pieces and stuffed them in his mouth with approving grunts.

His roly-poly appearance reminded her of a bear gorging on honeycomb. She caught Shemu'el's eye. "Turn down the next alley. The first door is the home of Salome, a widow with two children. Tell her I sent you. Maybe she knows something about this man."

Shemu'el hesitated.

Rivkah gave him a reassuring smile "Go ahead. I am in no danger."

## ~ 36 ~

*"Truly I say to you, as you did it to the least of these my brethren, you do it to me."*
                                              — Matthew 25:40

By the time Shemu'el returned with Salome, Rivkah had coaxed the big man into the light of a nearby lamp. He sat cross-legged like a child happily munching the bunch of grapes she gave him. He removed each grape one at time, examined it for a moment, then popped it into his mouth. Besides the scrapes and scratches from the bushes, bleeding cuts covered his arms.

Salome rested her hands on her hips and frowned. "I thought as much when your man came knocking at my door. You have stumbled upon Pavlos the Giant."

"He has cuts everywhere." Looking closer, Rivkah noticed old scars from previous injuries. "What could have happened to him?"

"Who can say? He lives in the wilds and forages the refuse piles for whatever he can find. Children follow him to laugh and mock and pelt him with stones. The youngsters tell me he sometimes sits by the riverbank and cuts himself with sharp rocks."

"Can he speak?"

"He mumbles occasionally, but mostly he grunts and bellows like an animal."

A chill moved through Rivkah. She crossed her arms and hugged herself, rubbing away the bumps. "Can no one help this poor soul?"

Salome shook her head. "He has always been like this. A demoniac, clearly possessed by the worst of demons. His parents must have cast him away, yet somehow he survived." She made a face. "Do not waste time on him; he understands no more than a dumb beast."

"His wounds should be treated," Shemu'el said, "but I have nothing with me."

Salome shrugged. "Physicians are for the rich, and everyone in our district is poor."

"Is there no one close by?" Rivkah asked.

"Possibly," Salome said, after a moment's thought. "There is a *medicus*, a God-fearing man who operates a small clinic in our section of the city. He treats anyone who comes to him at no charge."

Seeing Rivkah's face brighten, Salome added a caution, "The Nubian comes only when he has time. He might help, but how will you get Pavlos to him?"

"Leave that to me." Rivkah tried to sound more confident than she was. Her rational side wondered where this sudden burst of confidence came from. But, like with the cloak, she'd learned to trust, not question.

Salome shook her head. "Easier you should drag an elephant than move this giant."

Rivkah faced a dilemma. Pavlos clearly required medical attention, but she had baskets of food to distribute, not to mention the clothing. Without the daily distribution, her charges would go hungry.

"Salome, you know the people I serve. Will you accompany Shemu'el and help distribute the food and clothing while I take Pavlos for treatment."

Shemu'el started to protest, but her resolute expression stopped him.

Rivkah handed her baskets to Salome. Shemu'el grabbed the bundle of clothing and heaved it onto his back.

"Wait." Rivkah dug through it and removed the over-sized outfit. "These were intended for him. I am certain of it."

Pavlos watched Shemu'el and Salome out of the corner of his eye as they left. Once they disappeared down the alley, he turned to face Rivkah.

For a brief moment, she thought she detected a spark of interest, but it faded so quickly she wondered if she'd wished it into existence.

She reached out and took his bear-sized hand.

He jerked his hand back as if she'd put a torch to his skin.

He cradled the hand, turning it, and staring at the spot she'd touched.

Rivkah leaned forward and stared into his eyes. "Pavlos, do you understand me when I talk to you?"

Though he refused to look her in the eye, the same spark of understanding she'd seen earlier flared in his sad eyes. More than ever, she became convinced this gigantic man understood more than anyone gave him credit for.

"You did not like it when I touched your hand, did you?

He grunted.

She took it to be an acknowledgement. "I did not mean to hurt you. There is someone who can help you heal. Will you walk with me?"

Pavlos hesitated for a moment then slowly rose to his feet.

"This way." Rivkah turned and walked in the direction Salome indicated.

Head bent and arms drawn protectively across his chest, Pavlos plodded along behind.

Lamps burned inside the building, but when Rivkah pushed open the door she found the room empty.

Pavlos lingered outside, pacing, looking around corners and nervously glancing over his shoulder.

"*Ave!* Is anyone here?"

"I'm in the *pharmacia*," a man's voice replied.

Moments later a smiling, dark skinned man with wiry gray hair appeared around the corner. He walked into the room wiping his hands on a blood-stained apron. Noticing her horrified look, he glanced down at the apron and gave her an apologetic shrug.

"Today is my day for surgeries. I have done this so long I no longer notice the mess. How may I assist you?"

"Are you the *medicus*?"

"Yes, I—" The sight of a huge man ducking his shaggy head and squeezing through the doorway rendered him temporarily speechless.

Pavlos' bulk seemed greater inside the tiny room. When he took a step forward, his bushy hair brushed the ceiling, raining down bits of plaster and dust.

"In all my days with Caesar's armies never have I seen anyone so large," the *medicus* gasped. "What happened to him? He looks like he's been set upon by a band of brigands."

"Can you help him?"

"I can try." He swept his eyes over Pavlos. "So the neighborhood giant is not a myth after all."

"You know of him then?"

"My patients have mentioned him and the children in the street sing a number of detestable rhymes about him. They alternately described him as a half-man half-bull Minotaur, or the embodiment of Ba'al-Molech. Either way, I assumed he was some sort of *shedu*, an ominous specter conjured up by their night fears.

He ran his eyes over Pavlos a second time and smiled. "Now I see how they could have come to that conclusion."

The physician studied the cuts visible through Pavlos' shredded sleeve.

The mute giant scrutinized the dark-skinned man's every move like a caged animal watching its captor.

The *medicus* reached out a finger to lift a scrap of sleeve.

Pavlos jerked his beefy arm away with a roar.

Quickly retreating, he lowered his hands and made placating gestures.

Rivkah stepped between them. "I should have warned you. He apparently does not wish to be touched."

"How long have you known this uh, uh...person?"

"A very short time. Salome, the widow of Fotios, said people call him Pavlos."

He chuckled. "A fitting choice for such a hulk of a man. His name, if that is what it is, means *small*."

"I found him hiding in the rushes along the riverbank."

"And so, having found him, you decided to keep him."

Rivkah stared at the floor. "He needed my help, what was I

to do?"

Pavlos' eyes followed the physician's every movement.

The *medicus* took slow, cautious steps, pausing often to assess Pavlos' reaction before continuing. "He appears to trust you," he whispered. "If I mixed a sedative, do you think you could persuade him to drink it?"

"I will try."

Satisfied, the *medicus* returned to the *pharmacia*.

From around the wall, she heard him softly humming as he worked.

Pavlos, who had begun to relax, snapped his head around at the sound of the pestle clinking inside its mortar.

His reaction convinced Rivkah he heard every bit as good as she did. She used the time spent waiting to explain things to him.

The physician returned and sat the cup aside. "We need to prepare ourselves first."

He drug two stout benches over to a corner of the room and placed them side by side. He stepped back, looked them over, and nodded with satisfaction.

"After he drinks the mixture, direct him to the benches. If he wobbles, we can lean him into the corner and once he falls asleep, they will serve as bed and worktable." He gave the cup a final swirl and handed it to Rivkah.

She extended it to Pavlos.

He took the cup in his big hands and sniffed its contents.

Rivkah cupped her hands around an imaginary cup, lifted it to her mouth, and pretended to drink. Then she looked from Pavlos' sad eyes to the cup in his hand.

He raised the cup with both hands and downed it in a single gulp. After returning the cup, he belched loudly and gave her a childlike grin.

She and the physician waited in silence, hoping the potion did its job.

## ~ 37 ~

Rivkah grasped Pavlos' beefy hand and led him to the benches.
A few moments later his eyelids drooped and he began to sway
from side to side. Sensing his oncoming loss of consciousness, he
shot her a terrified look. He began waving his arms in circles and
struggling to rise from the bench.

Moving quickly, Rivkah cradled his dirty face in her hands.
She outlined the *signum crucis* on his forehead, closed her eyes,
and whispered a prayer.

Sweet calm settled over the giant. He relaxed and eased
back onto the benches with a sigh. A moment later the rhythmic
sound of his heavy breathing filled the small room.

The physician laid out his instruments and began removing
Pavlos' clothing. "What kind of sorcery was that?" he asked as he
worked.

"I laid my hands upon him, blessed him with the *signum
crucis* and prayed for God's peace to descend upon him."

"The sign of a cross? How strange. In all my years I have
never seen anything like it. Where did you learn to do it?"

"My husband and I are *Christianoi*, followers of Iesous the
Christos. It is the mark of his immortal cross. I asked our Lord to
be with Pavlos and comfort his fears."

"Hmmm." The physician left and returned with a bucket of
water and a cloth. "Now I understand." He squeezed out his cloth
and bathed Pavlos as he dozed. "You are one of those who
migrated to Antioch from Jerusalem, a member of what is called
The Way. I have heard rumors about you people."

She sat beside him while he worked. "You speak about us in
sinister tones. We are simply spreading the good news. The
*Mashiach*, the *Christos*, promised to the Jews has come. His
salvation will reach to the ends of the earth."

The physician listened as he worked.

Watching him dress Pavlos' wounds reminded her of the
way Shemu'el worked.

He tied off a bandage, straightened, and looked in her

direction as he reached for another. "But to get this eternal life one must first accept this Yeshua as their Lord and be baptized."

"It appears you, a Roman, have already heard our message, Sir."

"I am what the Jews call a God-fearer. Some men came to our synagogue one *Shabbat* speaking the name of Yeshua, the one whom they executed in Jerusalem."

"But he rose from the grave; he now lives."

"So they said. But if that be true, why have I not seen him?"

"He lives enthroned in heaven at the right hand of God, yet remains beside us every moment."

"Interesting. No one ever explained it quite the way you do." The physician smiled. "By the way, I am called Atticus."

"I have heard of one named Atticus."

"Good things, I hope."

"Very good things. What are you doing here?"

His white teeth gleamed when he smiled. "Most of the people in this district cannot afford a physician. I come whenever I can to treat their injuries and illnesses." He applied salve to Pavlos' arms and covered his lacerations. "So, is that how you know of me...from your friends?"

"I never heard of you until Salome directed me to this place. The Atticus of whom I spoke was once the slave of Evodius Scipio, the *Medicus Cohortis* to *Legio XII Fulminata*. Receiving his freedom from Quirinius when Evodius died, he accepted the position of *Medicus Ordinarii* with *Legio V Macedonia*."

He dropped his tools on the tray and listened with rising interest. "That is me. How have you come to know these things? Who are you?"

"I am Rivkah, wife of Shemu'el bar Yo'el, once the slave known as Marcus."

He surprised Rivkah by pulling her into his arms and hugging her tightly. "So many years I prayed he would find you. And it appears he did. Welcome, Sister." He kissed her cheek. "Is my brother Marcus here in Antioch as well?"

"Shemu'el will be overjoyed to see you! He's distributing food and clothing to the poor as we speak. He will return soon."

"Speaking of clothing..." Atticus nudged the pile of torn cloth he'd removed from Pavlos with his toe. "These filthy rags are not fit to wear."

"Let not your heart be troubled. The Lord knew his needs and provided fresh garments." She dug in her bag and produced the enormous striped cloak and tunic she'd removed from the pile that morning.

Working together, they managed to roll and turn the big man enough to get the clothes on him. They left Pavlos quietly snoring in his new outfit.

"Do you have a shaving blade?" Rivkah asked. "I could trim his hair and beard before he rouses."

Atticus disappeared into the back room and returned with what she needed.

She had nearly finished Pavlos' hair when the door opened and Shemu'el entered.

Atticus' brow knitted as he gazed at the bearded, graying man blinking in the light. An instant later a broad smile of recognition crossed his lips. "Marcus!"

A startled look came over Shemu'el. He stared at the dark-skinned man coming toward him with his arms outspread.

"Atticus?" He took a step. "Atticus!"

The two men embraced. Questions spilled from their mouths at unintelligible speed. Deep in conversation, they ignored Rivkah and Pavlos and walked arm-in-arm into the *pharmacia*.

Rivkah grinned when she heard them laughing and talking as excitedly as young boys at play.

"So," Shemu'el said when they returned to the treatment room, "how is your patient?"

After Atticus's quick review of Pavlos' injuries, Shemu'el wandered over to gaze down at the sleeping giant. He ran his eyes up and down the big man's huge frame. "Gives you a much greater respect for young David and his sling, hmm?"

Pavlos tossed his big head from side to side and groaned. His fingers went to his head, pressing against his temples.

Rivkah waited by his side while he regained consciousness.

He glanced up at her in confusion, eyes wild with fear.

Touching his hand, she spoke his name. The men gathered near her offering protection, but she shooed them away.

Pavlos ran his eyes around the room.

Leaning into his line of sight, Rivkah smiled reassuringly. "You have been asleep." She repeated her pantomime. "Remember the cup the physician gave you?"

Pavlos' brow knitted as he searched his memory. Sighing, he looked around the room again, trying to make sense of his situation. He froze when his fingers accidentally brushed the fabric of his cloak. Pavlos inched the tips of his fingers along the new cloth. The more he stroked its nap, the more excited his expression became. Lifting an arm, he dangled the sleeve and flipped the striped cloth back and forth.

"No more rags for Pavlos," Rivkah whispered. "The one who watches over you provided new clothing."

For the first time since they met Pavlos looked directly at her. His eyes glistened for an instant before he jerked them away and turned to face the wall.

"Would you like to sit up?"

Pavlos lifted his arms expectantly, reminding her of the children when they were young.

"I cannot do this alone." She laughed. "You must help."

With her help, he rocked into an upright position and placed his feet flat on the floor.

Atticus glanced from Shemu'el to Rivkah. "You must come to my home for dinner. I will not take no as an answer. We must celebrate. Too much time has already slipped through our fingers. Bring your children. Meet my wife and family." He crossed the room with long strides. "Come, let me draw a map."

When they left, Pavlos followed them out the door. The empty camel's basket waited by the door. Shemu'el grabbed the strap and threw it onto his shoulder with a grunt.

Pavlos reached for the basket and took it away from him. Easily tossing the heavy basket onto his shoulder, he tagged along behind them as they walked back to the grotto. Rivkah, it seemed, had found a new friend.

# ~ 38 ~

*"The church at Antioch, also, now flourishing and
abounding in members and the greatest number of
teachers coming there from Jerusalem..."*

—Eusebius' History, Book 2, 3:3

Atticus' directions led Shemu'el, Rivkah, and their family to a
large home in the foothills. The house sat amid gardens and
rolling meadows where peacocks wandered free.

Shemu'el rang the bell. A servant appeared and led them to
the front entrance where Atticus and his household waited.
Having never seen such luxury, their children marveled at the
opulence.

An indoor fountain, lined with blue tiles and mosaic fish,
burbled and splashed in the entryway. A side doorway led to an
adjacent bath and an indoor pool.

Atticus had clearly prospered in his years with the Legions.
Moving up in rank, he amassed both wealth and power. After
time in Byzantium and Thessolinica, he returned to Antioch
where he served as *Medicus Primus*, chief medical officer and
supervisor of the medical staff serving the four Syrian Legions.

After introductions, Atticus escorted them to the *triclinium*.
Frescos decorated the walls and ceilings of the dining room, and
the smell of roasting meats filled the air. Servants bustled in and
out, arranging silver table service, candelabras, wine goblets, and
platters heaped with fruits, nuts, sliced melons and other tidbits.
Bread, still warm from the oven, arrived in large baskets.

The room followed the classic Roman design with six *klinai*
arranged in a U-shaped configuration around low tables. Each
dining couch served three diners. On the floor in the open center
between the tables was a pair of large mosaics. These *trickinia*,
decorative figural panels for the diner's viewing pleasure,
displayed fruits, vegetables and herbs on the left and game and
domestic animals on the right. Above them, aligned to face
someone entering the room, was a row of three smaller mosaics.

A series of arched windows ran across the *triclinium's* exterior wall providing a view of the distant mountains. Yaakov and Yudah stood at the windows admiring the vista until Marcelina, Atticus' wife, took them by the hand and led them to their places around the table.

Several empty plates waited at each place. Made of molded glass, they had images of seashells pressed into their underside and visible through the translucent glass.

After the meal servants appeared and cleared the tables. Atticus invited Shemu'el to join him in another room. Marcelina ordered wine sent to the men and suggested her children entertain their guests.

Channah left with her daughters amid much chattering and giggling. A servant brought a dish of flat, polished black and white stones and a *Latrunculi* board. A game of war and strategy, *Latrunculi* was played on a board of squares with game pieces that moved, jumped, and captured each other. Yaakov and Atticus' oldest son sat opposite each other preparing to play. Yudah and their youngest boy sat cross-legged rolling dice beside the familiar oblong playing field of Hounds and Jackals.

Marcelina invited Rivkah to a walk in the gardens so they could become better acquainted. Like Atticus, Marcelina was of African descent. She had creamy brown skin, several shades lighter than her husband, delicate features and a charming manner.

They sat on a bench beside a grape arbor. Dusk was fading and servants provided torches for light and a brazier to dispel the cool night air. After Rivkah told her story, she asked Marcelina how she met Atticus.

"It is a long tale." Marcelina smiled. "Are you sure you wish to hear it?"

"Absolutely."

"He found me on the auction block in Thessolinica," she began. "The ship my family and I were sailing on was set afire by pirates. They plucked me from the sea to sell as a slave."

"What a horrible experience."

"The worst, and yet the best, of my life. Atticus happened past and stopped."

"And you assumed him to be just another lecher come to stare at your nakedness?"

"I did until the auctioneer opened the bidding. He set the minimum at 30 silver *denarii*."

"The standard price for a slave."

"I was younger then, of course, and the auctioneer clearly thought because..." Marcelina lowered her eyes. "Because of my beauty I would command a premium. Before anyone had a chance to bid, Atticus offered eight gold *quinarii*."

"Did anyone have the nerve to bid against him?"

"No, his audacity stunned the crowd. He was in full dress uniform and looked resplendent. He offered me his hand and, when I stepped down, immediately threw his crimson cloak around me."

"What did you think when this Roman officer bought you?"

"I was young and attractive; he was strong and virile. What would any woman imagine? However, things did not go the way I anticipated." She stared at her hands folded in her lap. "On the way to his home he stopped and purchased a wardrobe for me, tunics, cloaks, gowns, veils, sandals...everything a woman needed to be properly attired. When we passed the goldsmith's shop he had the driver stop and bought rings for my fingers and a necklace."

"I can imagine what must have been going through your mind."

Marcelina gave her a wry nod. "I had visions of being paraded into banquets to provide entertainment for him and his fellow officers." A bright smile broke over her face. "Happily, I was mistaken. Over the evening meal he laid out the terms of my servitude. He said I would live with him for the next two months, keeping his house and preparing his meals. He showed me my room and vowed to make no incursions or untoward advances."

"After the two months, what then?"

"At the end of this trial period he promised me my certificate of manumission. As a free woman, he said, one of two things could happen. If we were both willing, he would take me for his wife. If, for any reason, I did not wish to marry him, I could leave his home with all the goods he had given me and he would provide passage to the destination of my choice."

"Shemu'el often spoke of Atticus as an honorable man."

"Words cannot begin to describe the depths of his kindness," Marcelina whispered.

"You've done well for yourself," Shemu'el said, leaning back in his seat.

"I have much to be thankful for, Marcelina and the children, a good reputation, financial security. And you?"

"My life has not always been easy, but I would change nothing."

Atticus sighed. "In some ways I envy you, my friend. What I wouldn't give to be a simple physician again."

"But so many depend upon you."

"Do they? Instead of healing patients I've become an administrator. Me, an administrator! I never aspired to be a shuffler of dispatches and reports. The only thing I mend now is rifts between the quartermaster and the pharmacist."

"Surely you still have some patients."

"You mean the petulant wives of Roman officials who come to me whining about imaginary ills?"

Shemu'el chuckled. "Is it really so bad?"

"It's worse. What I wouldn't give for a real illness. Instead, I am inundated with people to whom an ingrown toenail constitutes a medical emergency." He pounded his fist on the chair arm. "Give me a laceration to stitch or a broken bone to set and let Rome keep its dispatches."

Shemu'el smiled as he listened to his friend complain.

"It seems you have caught me on a bad day." Atticus swirled his cup and grinned. "So what happened to the two of us? How did we suddenly end up old men?"

The visit left the children excited. Rivkah sent them to bed, but instead of sleeping, they jabbered to each other about the evening's experiences.

She entered their rooms with a lamp. Rather than chide, she asked, "Did you have an interesting time?"

They all spoke at once, commenting about anything and everything...especially the lavish lifestyle.

"Yes," she admitted, "Atticus and his family have been richly blessed. I want you to think about something. On the day they received their freedom, Quirinius offered your father a commission equal to the one he gave Atticus. Perhaps now you realize how much he gave up when he relinquished the opportunity and returned to me in Judea. It is a measure of his character that he chose to tend sheep in our little community when he could have been living in luxury."

Unbeknownst to Rivkah, Shemu'el stood outside the doorway listening. He tiptoed up, slipped his arms around her waist, and kissed her neck.

She shrieked in surprise.

The children laughed nervously and got the half-pleased, half-embarrassed look they always did when their parents became affectionate.

"But I have the greatest treasure of all." Shemu'el winked. "Remember children, whenever life gives you a choice between love and money, always pick love. It is priceless."

The relationship between Shemu'el and Atticus went through a series of stages. In the beginning they spent hours telling each other stories of what had happened to them since their parting twenty-five years earlier. They shared meals and then became so involved in discussions about old times that their food remained on their plates, cold and uneaten.

Over time, Shemu'el's perspective shifted. While they were both slaves, he had exposed Atticus to the truths of Judaism. Now he became determined to convert Atticus to The Way of Iesous.

Having worked equally as hard to convert their daughter, Hadassah, Rivkah understood how he felt. She prayed he would succeed where she had failed. Just as it nearly broke her heart when Hadassah rebuffed her overtures, she knew Shemu'el would be devastated if Atticus rejected Iesous.

The two of them spent many evenings discussing the prophets and prophecies. They spoke of the meaning of Iesous' crucifixion and resurrection. Shemu'el told him of the angels that appeared in fields outside Bethlehem and the miracles he witnessed.

One happy night Atticus announced he and his household would convert. They went to the grotto in the foothills of Mt. Stauris and were all baptized. The Holy Spirit came upon them and, following the Lord's Supper, Atticus and Marcelina made a startling declaration.

"My friends, new brothers and sisters in Iesous, I have an announcement to make. I have heard that in Jerusalem, after one joins The Way, they sometimes divest themselves of their worldly goods. New members donate some, or all, of these proceeds to the community of believers for the common good."

Atticus walked among the group as he spoke, pausing to touch shoulders. "I am told a holy man called Barnabus, whom I have never met, sold a field and gave the proceeds to the Twelve."

From his place at the head of the table, Simon smiled and nodded.

"People say the company of believers is of one heart and soul and no one claims what he possesses as his own. Marcelina and I have discussed how we might best honor this tradition. We asked ourselves, what are the needs of the *ekklesia* here in Antioch? How could we best facilitate the work of the Lord?"

He took his wife's hand and pulled her to her feet. "More than anything, this community requires an adequate synagogue, a base of operations from which you can reach out to the community. Our home and compound is larger than we require. Therefore, we have decided to present it to this *ekklesia* so it may serve as a place of prayer, worship and study."

In one fell swoop, Atticus had changed everything. Now they had space and resources adequate for their mission. The base of their operations shifted from the grotto to his compound. Their outreach to the poor and helpless grew with room to store additional foodstuffs and clothing.

The *ekklesia* quickly set about adapting the home to their use. The pool became a baptistry, the *triclinium* their sanctuary, and the other rooms were converted to multiple uses.

Atticus' baptism also opened a door to the Legions. In other places members of Rome's Army had already chosen to follow Iesous, but Atticus was the first in Antioch. His fellow officers respected him for his competence and honored him for his integrity. His conversion gave The Way newfound credibility.

Basking in the warmth of sudden good fortune, everyone anticipated a bright future ahead. They had turned a corner. Jerusalem and its persecution lay behind them. Good things were clearly in store for them in Antioch.

# ~ 39 ~

*"We do not expose our children, and you are well aware
how so many of the little ones that have been left out to
die have been rescued by Christianoi and given a home...
We protect and defend human life."*

—Marcus Minucius Felix *The Octavius*

Rivkah discovered an unused implement shed on Atticus'
compound and converted it into a home for Pavlos. Though
small, it proved adequate for his needs. He lived on the grounds
and accompanied her each day when she made the daily
distribution, freeing Shemu'el for other work.

The lower section of the main house became a storehouse.
Vitellius, a stonemason in the *ekklesia*, constructed grain bins.
They were built round, without corners where grain could be
trapped and spoil. He built them of stone, each one carefully cut,
fit and mortared. Then he troweled plaster over them, inside and
out. Each bin had a heavy, tight-fitting lid at the top. The bottom,
made of poured concrete, sloped to a chute making the bins self-
emptying.

The growers of grain in the congregation tithed a portion of
their fields. After the ripe grain had been cut, threshed and
winnowed, the young men set a ladder against the sides of the
bins. Balancing heavy bushel baskets on their shoulders, they
climbed the ladder and filled the bins. They had two large bins,
one for wheat and one for barley, and smaller ones for millet,
spelts, and lentils.

The weather had cleared after several days of rain, leaving Pavlos
and Rivkah in a cheery mood when they set out on their rounds.
Their baskets were heavy with produce and Isaias the donkey
trailed behind at the end of a rope.

As a young girl Rivkah played a game with Miryam's

husband, Yosef. Each time she and her father visited his carpentry shop in Bethlehem, Rivkah gave Yosef's donkey a new name. She'd labeled his donkey Isaias the evening they met them on their way to Egypt.

It caused Yosef to lose his composure. Already worried because Herod intended to kill baby Yeshua, hearing her call his donkey by the name of their greatest prophet upset him.

Yosef had rested with the righteous for a number of years. So, when Atticus offered them a donkey, Rivkah suggested they name him Isaias in Yosef's memory.

They left later than usual on the days when they had the donkey and cart because Antioch's roads were closed to wagons and pack animals during the day. Isaias plodded along behind them, his cart laden with their bi-monthly allotment of oil and wine. Each deacon distributed oil and wine on a different day, allowing everyone to utilize Isaias and his cart.

In its former life the cart hauled baggage for the Legion. One day, as the troops returned from maneuvers, it broke free and tumbled down a ravine. The Centurion deemed it not worth repairing and abandoned it where it lay.

Men from the congregation clambered down the steep slope and salvaged it using ropes and pulleys. After repairing the cart, they presented it to the group and Atticus kindly blessed them with a donkey to pull it.

Shadows were lengthening by the time they turned off of the *Via Cesearea* into Herod's Stoa. Rivkah, Pavlos, and Isaias walked through a gate in the old city wall of Seleucus I, entering the oldest and poorest section of town.

As usual, neighborhood children joined them as they walked, laughing and petting Isaias. They came for the sweetmeats Rivkah carried. At each stop she placed her hand atop the children's heads and blessed them. Then she dug into her bag and handed them a sweet treat.

Pavlos waited with the cart, paying no interest to children. Suddenly his happy face turned grim. He cocked his head, intently listening.

Handing Rivkah his basket, Pavlos rushed down the bank

and into the brush. The dense foliage swallowed him in an instant. Branches shook and snapped as he shoved them aside. Grunting, he rooted through the underbrush heading for the river.

Back on the street, Rivkah waited with the donkey.

Pavlos' sudden scream caused a shiver to run up her spine. His terrified wail rolled along the Orentes River, reverberating off the houses. Hidden by darkness and foliage, Pavlos sobbed.

Rivkah tracked his progress by the swaying branches and prayed he hadn't encountered a wild animal.

A moment later the top of Pavlos' head appeared over a bush. The top of his head was soon followed by his shoulders. Tears poured down the big man's rough cheeks. He made blubbering noises as he walked toward her shaking his head and wailing. Pavlos carried something in his hands. A small, mottled clump of dirty rags.

Stepping closer, Rivkah recognized it for what it was. A newborn infant.

Pavlos dropped to his knees in front of her and lifted the child, offering it to her as if before an altar.

It was a girl child, tiny and weak, with its umbilicus fresh and still attached. Rivkah brushed dirt from her sweet face and picked insects and crawling things off her tiny body. Closing her eyes, she marked her with Iseous' cross and commended her to his almighty care. When she cradled the baby to her bosom, the child's little lips made instinctive sucking motions.

Pavlos stared up at her hopefully, his wet cheeks glistening in the lamplight.

Rivkah drew her cloak around the baby to warm her. Leaving the donkey and baskets behind, she ran down the alley and pounded on Salome's door.

She showed her the newborn baby. "Pavlos found an infant. If she is not nursed soon, she will surely die."

Salome nodded gravely. "Another abandoned one. People throw their unwanted children over the bank, leaving them for the elements and wild dogs." She glanced down at her bosom and sighed. "I have been widowed five years. I cannot help you."

"And Yudah, my youngest, is nearly twelve. We must find someone with a child at her breast. Someone who will help us save this little girl's life."

"That will not be easy. Most Jewish women will refuse you." Salome shrugged. "Why should they want more *Christianoi* in Antioch? And the pagans will do no better. They are the ones who throw their unwanted babes away."

They went from door to door like beggars seeking someone, anyone, who would take pity on this helpless infant and give her a tiny bit of warm milk. Rivkah knew she could find a young woman in their congregation to act as a wet nurse, but the baby wouldn't survive the trip home without nourishment.

"Corella is our last chance," Salome said. "I know of no other nursing mothers in the district."

Rivkah prayed as she knocked.

Mumbling and the shuffle of feet sounded on the other side of the rough plank door. A young woman opened it and lifted her lamp, illuminating their faces. "What do you want?" she asked in a harsh, unfriendly voice.

Rivkah stepped forward and folded back her cloak. "I have an infant here who must have milk to survive. You have that milk. Will you help us?"

She looked down at the child and sneered. "What is she to me? Why would I want another dirty urchin crowding our streets?"

"This beautiful little girl is weak and near death. If you do not feed her, she will surely die before I can get her home."

A baby cried inside the small house. "I have my own children to take care of." Corella's face remained a mask of defiance. Hearing her child's cry caused her milk to flow. Damp spots formed on the front of her tunic. Milk the baby in Rivkah's arms desperately needed.

"You have more than enough," Rivkah said, pointing. "Your breasts are heavy with milk. A newborn requires very little."

Corella smacked her hand away. "Go. I will not do what you ask." She turned away and swung the door shut.

The door had almost latched when Rivkah asked, "What if I

paid you?"

A spark of interest flickered in Corella's eyes. She opened the door wide and inched closer. "What do you offer?"

"I have foodstuffs, bread, fruit and vegetables."

She shook her head. "We have already eaten."

Rivkah heard the plodding steps of Pavlos and Isaias at the end of the alley. "I have wine...good wine. And oil also."

She watched the young woman's mind work and nibbled her lip as Corella weighed the offer.

A sly look crossed Corella's face. "No, I do not want wine or oil." She stuck out her palm. "I want money; give me coins."

Rivkah glanced at Salome.

Salome lifted her shoulders and shook her head.

"If I had money, I would give it to you, but I have none." Rivkah lowered her eyes, humbling herself like the beggar she was. "Please. Choose anything you wish from my baskets. Take as much as you like."

Corella lifted her chin. "If you have no money, then I have no milk to give you."

The baby whimpered inside Rivkah's cloak.

Corella's expression remained cold and distant.

Rivkah stared into her eyes, seeing neither love nor empathy, only greed. She had no one left to turn to except Iesous.

*If you want this child to live, you must tell me what to do.*

Something drew Rivkah's eyes to her right hand. On her finger was the gold band Shemu'el placed there the day he asked to take her as his wife. It had never been off her finger in the twenty-five years since. She knew what she had to do, but still hesitated.

*What would Shemu'el say?*

What he said did not matter. If this infant was to live it had to be done. "Will you take this gold ring? It is worth more than 50 *denarii*."

Salome grabbed her arm. "No! Not your wedding ring. This is foolishness. She asked for coins...a few *sisterii*, perhaps. Not two month's wages." She pointed to the lump in Rivkah's cloak. "Infants like her are tossed away without a thought. How do you know this child was not intended to die?"

"Perhaps she will, but not because of any decision I make. I must do all I can to preserve her life."

"You are making too much of this," Salome said. "Midwives routinely kill the unborn babies of pagan women."

"Does that make the life of this child worth any less? I cannot save them all, but this child I *can* save."

"I say again, you make too much of this."

"How could I face Iesous and tell him I held the life of one of his precious ones in my hands and let her die? And for what, a piece of gold?" Rivkah pushed Salome aside and turned to face Corella, "Will you do it?"

The woman nodded in agreement. Inside the house the infant's cries grew louder.

Rivkah pointed to the small, still form in the crook of her arm. "She suckles first and for as long as she likes."

Corella extended her hand. "The ring. Give me the ring."

It didn't want to come off. Rivkah licked her finger and still had to tug and twist to get it over the knuckle. Even her finger, it seemed, balked at the bargain she'd made.

Corella slipped the ring onto her finger and held it to the light. She grinned, delighting in her cleverness as she admired her new treasure.

Rivkah glanced down at the stripe of pale, bare skin where her ring had been. Its absence made her feel incomplete...almost naked.

"Give her to me," Corella said with a frown. She sat on a stool beside the door, exposed a breast heavy with milk and reached for the girl. The infant had to be coaxed, as all newborns must, but in a short time she began eating with vigor.

Pavlos tiptoed over. Smiling, he hugged himself and rocked from side to side. Watching the baby nurse felt like a holy moment.

Eventually named Sousanna by her adoptive parents, she was the first of many foundlings rescued by the *ekklesia*.

# ~ 40 ~

Rivkah mashed the parched wheat cooked to porridge between her fingers, further softening it. "Ready?"

Errikos opened his mouth wide and she scooped it in. He chewed, swallowed and stretched out his little arms for his cup. He took a sip of goat's milk and grinned at her. "More, Maia. More."

Little Errikos had more mothers than he had fingers to count them on. One of their women discovered him when she went to the trash heap to discard her garbage. He lay among the refuse weak and nearly starved, his body covered in crusty, oozing sores. She wrapped him in her scarf and brought him back to the compound where Shemu'el applied healing salves.

He stayed with them until the sores healed, then they moved him into the nursery where he lived with other foundlings awaiting adoption. Every woman who cared for Errikos became another of his many Maia's.

He swallowed the last of his porridge just as Shemu'el entered the room. He waved his arms in the air and shouted, "Patros!"

Though little Errikos had many Maia's, he had only one Patros. Most likely because his earliest memories were of Shemu'el's healing touch. He continued calling for Patros while Rivkah washed the cereal off his hands and face.

Shemu'el crossed the room, swept him up and spun him around.

Errikos squealed with delight and clapped his hands.

Packing the boy on his hip, Shemu'el walked to the counter and began flipping through his correspondence. He stopped every once in a while to steal Errikos' nose or tickle his ribs. Shemu'el had an easy way with youngsters and the children of the *ekklesia* loved him.

The muscles across Shemu'el's shoulders tightened as he read and reread one of the epistles. Atticus had forwarded the letter to him by courier the night before. Shemu'el had read the text by lamplight, pondering its meaning before he slept.

He arose looking more tired than when he lay down. Now he'd gone back to the scroll like a dog searching a previously gnawed bone for a missed scrap of meat. He sighed deeply and shoved it aside.

Errikos patted Shemu'el's shoulder with his tiny hand. "Patros sad?"

"Nothing for you to worry about," he said, forcing a smile. Shemu'el sat Errikos on the counter in front of him. He took the boy's hands in his and they tugged each other back and forth.

Rivkah slipped an arm around Shemu'el's shoulder. "Is everything all right?"

"I've been reading the report Atticus sent about an attack on a century from *Legio III Gallica* along the Parthian frontier."

"Why would anyone attack Roman troops?"

"The Centurion who wrote this report did not know. He, and the hundred men under him, were on a routine patrol and had no contact with the local population." Shemu'el tapped the open scroll. "I've read this three times and it's finally beginning to make sense. When the troops gave pursuit, their attackers retreated to a small settlement of *Christianoi*."

Errikos fussed to be put down. Shemu'el lowered him to the floor and he toddled around the room as they talked.

"You are confusing me," Rivkah said. "You seem to be saying the instigators were *Christianoi*."

"I never said they were *Christianoi*, only that they retreated to the *Chriatianoi* settlement. When the soldiers responded, the instigators melted away."

"One might conclude their intent was to draw the soldiers to the village."

"My thoughts exactly."

"But *Christianoi* would not engage Roman troops in battle."

"No, but they would protect their families from what they perceived to be an unprovoked attack."

Errikos wandered the room looking here and there. A red lamp, one of those Hebel gave Rivkah when they left Jerusalem, sat on a table behind them. Its bright glaze caught the little boy's eyes and he reached for it.

Rivkah saw him out of the corner of her eye and shouted, "No!"

It was too late. One instant his chubby fingers were curled around the handle. The next instant the lamp crashed to the floor and shattered.

Errikos' eyes widened. A look of terror swept across his face. He stared down at the red shards in the widening pool of oil. Twisting his hands one over the other, he burst into tears. "Errikos sorry, Maia." He looked over at Shemu'el and wailed, "Not mean to, Patros. Not mean to."

Hiding her anguish over the loss of her treasured lamp, Rivkah opened her arms to him. The little boy leaped into them and she wiped away his tears. Handing Errikos to Shemu'el, she knelt to gather up the pieces.

Though she'd treated each of them like precious jewels, one by one the lamps they brought from Jerusalem had been broken. Now the red one would join the others on the trash heap. This was the last one she had. Like her relationship with Hadassah, it had been reduced to nothing but shards.

After Rivkah disposed of the lamp and cleaned the floor, she returned to Shemu'el and the repentant Errikos. Shemu'el was rereading the scroll yet again.

"Do you have any idea who the troublemakers were?"

He shook his head. "They may have been Zealots. You can never rule them out. The attack occurred near the border and the report says some of them dressed as Parthians. It's very confusing."

When Rivkah was a child, Melchior—one of the *Magoi*, the Great Ones of the Upper House and an advisor to the ruler of the Parthian Dynasty—told her Yeshua would conquer not with war, but with peace and love. He predicted Yeshua would find allies among the Parthians.

"I have trouble believing they were Parthians," she said. "In his most recent epistle Thomas spoke of the many converts he has made throughout Parthia."

"True enough. Thomas converted many descendents of the

Babylonian Jews who chose to remain behind rather than return to Jerusalem with Ezra. But you know as well as I that for every person who accepts the Word of salvation there are many more who reject it. Throughout the Empire...Jerusalem, Alexandria, Damascus, here in Antioch...even in Rome itself, bad blood exists between Jews and Jewish *Christianoi*. The same is surely true of Parthia."

"How bad was it?" Rivkah asked, chewing at her lower lip.

"A number of men in the village died fighting. The remainder, along with the women and children, were enslaved. Their livestock and possessions are gone, their homes burned."

"This is so unfair. Through no fault of their own they've become spoils of war."

Shemu'el stared out a window, watching a tree branch sway in the breeze. "The soldiers are marching them to the *Legio's* encampment. Atticus and I plan to meet with the *Tribunus*. If we are unable to negotiate their release, Atticus intends to pay their ransom."

She touched his shoulder. "As a former slave I know how difficult this must be for you...for both of you."

His jaw tightened. "It is strange how God uses our most trying experiences to strengthen us so we can minister to others undergoing similar trials." He rolled the dispatches and stuffed them into his pocket. "Marcelina has agreed to make the trip. Can you accompany us as well?"

He needed to say no more. Rivkah understood why they wanted the women along. In times of conflict it was more dangerous to be a woman than a soldier. By now the troops would likely have ravished every woman and girl in the village.

"Of course I will go. Channah can manage the daily distribution until we return." She began making plans. "We should also take one of the midwives with us."

Shemu'el agreed. "Atticus will pack medical supplies."

"There is clothing in the *ekklesia's* cupboard. I will have the women sort and organize it. We can also draw down our pantry, taking dried fish, fruit and other things that are light to carry and will keep."

"I plan to walk to the Citadel to meet Atticus. We'll bring a wagon back to the compound and load what you have."

Shemu'el latched his well-worn traveling case and sat it near the door alongside his bedroll.

"There's something I'd like to discuss with you before you go," Rivkah said.

He glanced up with an expectant look.

"The night Pavlos and I searched for someone to nurse the waif he found on the riverbank, Salome the widow reminded me that midwives routinely kill babies the pagan women do not wish to bear."

"It is hardly a secret."

Placing a foot on a stool, Shemu'el leaned forward and grabbed the laces of his *caligulea*, the thick, hob-nailed sandals worn by the Roman soldiers. He snapped them back and forth in practiced moves and tied them around his lower calf.

"Well," Rivkah said hesitantly. "I have been thinking perhaps we could begin to talk to the midwives of the city and try to end this horrid practice."

He kept his eyes on the laces. "Midwives? I know nothing of midwives. This is women's business. The last thing they want is condemnation from a man's lips."

Putting his foot on the floor, he reached for his cloak.

"I did not expect you to know or do anything. You are right; this *is* women's work. I only wanted your permission to seek them out and minister to them."

He grasped her by the shoulders and kissed her. "You need never ask, Rivkah. Go where your heart leads you and act as the Lord instructs you."

Shemu'el tousled Errikos' hair and kissed his forehead before walking to the door. "I'll return with the wagon in a short while."

## ~ 41 ~

Any hope Shemu'el had of a simple country outing with his old friend evaporated when he arrived at the Citadel. Long years away from the military allowed him to forget the pomp and ceremony that accompanied their every move. He and Atticus would ride with the Legion's flags and insignias flying, accompanied by a full military escort.

Atticus cast Shemu'el a sidelong glance as they passed under the Citadel's archway and headed in the direction of the compound. "You seemed a little taken aback." He glanced up at the banners snapping in the breeze above their heads. "Does any of this bother you?"

"No, of course not," Shemu'el said over the clop of hooves and clink of armor. "Actually, it brings back memories of traveling with our mentor, Evodius, when we were both slaves."

Atticus fell silent for several moments, recalling times long past. "I seem to remember you speaking about the condemnation of graven images. Is it no longer a problem for you?"

"As *Christianoi* we have no Temple to be defiled except the temple which is our own bodies." He tapped his chest. "What lies inside the heart of man is of far greater importance than what lies without." Shemu'el swiveled his head, examining the regalia of the Roman Empire and shrugged. "As Iesous said, 'Let Caesar have the things that are Caesar's, and God the things that are God's.'"

A shiver ran up Rivkah's spine. The condition of the prisoners was worse than she had imagined. The century's slaves, dirty, ragged and bloodied, were huddled inside a picket enclosure.

Although he still retained the nominal title of Centurion, Atticus supervised the medical care of all Legions within the Province of Syria and reported directly to Lucius Vitellius, the Syrian Governor. In truth, as *Primus Medicus* Atticus wielded power equivalent to a *Tribunus*.

While Atticus negotiated for the slaves' release, the others worked with the prisoners. The children wandered aimlessly with blank stares. The adults stood downcast and frightened, shrinking back and avoiding their eyes as Rivkah and the others passed among them. They had the hollow, frightened look of someone who had witnessed a great evil.

By prior agreement, the men and boys remained in the compound with Shemu'el. Marcelina, Phaidra, the midwife, and Rivkah relocated the women and girls to a small building which Atticus commandeered. In the privacy of those four walls the women huddled together, seeking comfort with friends and neighbors.

Marcelina answered a rap at the door and opened it a crack.

Several of the camp commander's slaves waited outside holding pots of warm water. Additional slaves stood behind them, arms piled high with towels.

"Do not enter," Marcelina said. "I will take them from you one at a time."

She waved the women and girls to one side, placing them out of sight while she and Phaidra set up space for temporary baths.

While Marcelina stacked towels, Rivkah unloaded the new clothing they brought.

Once everything was ready, Rivkah stepped to the center of the room. "Welcome, sisters in Iesous. I am Rivkah." She motioned toward the two women who were busy sorting the clothing by size. "And this is Marcelina and Phaidra. We are pleased to be your servants. I can barely imagine the pain and grief each of you has experienced." She lifted her arms to the ceiling. "But the Lord Iesous is here among us and he longs to take each of you into his healing embrace."

She glanced around the room, looking into the eyes of each woman.

"Never forget, purity lies in the mind, not the flesh. As women, we sometimes cannot control what happens to our bodies, only how we react to it. A woman's purity is not lost because a man violates her. Where the spirit resists indecency, the body is sanctified."

She crossed the room and took Phaidra's arm. "Phaidra is a midwife. She came along to tend to those of you who suffered injury at the hands of the soldiers. She will help you any way she can. I say this especially to the young girls among you, do not be afraid, she seeks to help, not hurt. She understands a woman's body and has the gentlest touch."

Phaidra moved to the opposite side of the room. "Since we have no walls or curtains, out of respect for your sisters I ask that you turn your backs while I work."

Pointing to the water pots, Rivkah said, "As you can see, our benefactor, Atticus, requisitioned warm water and towels. After Phaidra has completed her examination you may all bathe. Throw away the dirty rags you have been forced to wear; we brought enough clean clothing for all."

Marcelina formed the women into groups, those who required Phaidra's help and those who did not.

"Come, my sisters," Marcelina said to the second group, "shed your rags and wash away the grime. Warm water, soaproot, towels and clean clothes await you."

The women stayed where they were, giving each other wary, sidelong glances.

Marcelina scooped a handful of water and let it drip between her fingers. "Hurry. Do not let the water cool."

The women hemmed and hawed like a flock of frightened sheep. Finally a gray-haired woman grabbed a toddler's hand and pushed to the front. She undressed her granddaughter, then tugged her stained tunic over her head and tossed it aside. After removing her loincloth and baring herself in front of all, she took her granddaughter's hand.

"Come little one," she said, in a voice loud enough for everyone to hear. "We have shed our filthy garments, now let us clean ourselves so we may become respectable once again."

The other women quickly formed into a line.

An old woman, slow of step and stooped with age, motioned Rivkah aside. Cocking her head, she stared up at her. "Bless you my child. This is a wonderful thing you do. I am Cybele, wife of the village elder."

"Is your husband with the men in the enclosure?"

Cybele shook her head and brushed a frayed sleeve across her eyes. "No, the Roman dogs killed him when he tried to stop the violence." She took a deep breath. "But I did not seek you out to speak of my woes."

"There is something you must understand." Moving close, Cybele began to whisper. "Each and every woman here carries the shame of what they did to us. The soldiers attacked our women repeatedly. Some until they died, others until they wished they had. Two of our sisters have already taken their own lives. More will surely follow if you do not intervene."

The old woman's directed Rivkah's gaze to what could have been mistaken for a ball of dirty rags crammed into the darkest corner of the room. Looking closer, Rivkah picked out a woman's shape. She sat with her legs pulled tight against her chest, quietly sobbing into her knees.

"Everyone suffered, but none more than she." The old woman's hand tightened around Rivkah's elbow as she led her toward the corner. "Though you cannot tell it now, Eleana was once the most beautiful woman in our village. Her betrothed died at her feet trying to protect her. Because of her beauty she became a target for the soldiers, someone to be fought over. The one we dubbed *The Red Man* defeated the others and claimed her for his own. When she refused to submit to him, he dragged her into the village square and brutalized her in front of everyone. She has not been the same since."

"Who is this *Red Man*?"

"Though I do not know his name, you would recognize him the instant you saw him. He is a devil., a big brute of a man with a ruddy complexion and hair the color of fire." She spat. "He searched out the youngest girls and derived pleasure from their screams, but he saved his worst torments for Eleana. Each day he dragged her back to the village square and each day she fought him. She hears the call of the next world more strongly with each passing hour. Mark my words. If nothing is done, she will be the next to leave us."

## ~ 42 ~

Rivkah tiptoed over to Eleana. Kneeling beside her, she whispered her name.

Eleana remained rigid, unresponsive.

"Eleana, can you hear me?"

She slowly turned. Her veil covered all of her face except for her swollen eyes. "The one you seek is not here. Eleana died in the village square."

"Do not punish yourself for what happened. You did nothing to merit this."

She let her veil slip aside.

Rivkah's stomach lurched. Eleana's swollen face and cracked lips were worse than anything she'd ever seen. She tried to mask her shock, but Eleana read it in her eyes.

"Do not be ashamed," Eleana said. "I know I am as repulsive as a bloated corpse. When I refused to submit, the Red Man beat me senseless. By the time I awoke, the damage had been done. Each night I begged God not to let me awaken the next time." She gave Rivkah a cold stare. "I prayed the Red Man would kill me."

She winced in pain when Rivkah touched her shoulder.

"He used his fists on my face and a strap across my back."

Looking closer, Rivkah noticed rows of oozing scabs beneath her torn tunic. The shreds of cloth had imbedded themselves into the scabs, sealing the garment to her flesh.

"We cannot remove your tunic without tearing open your sores. I must get my husband. He is a physician; he will know what to do."

"No men. I never want to see another man as long as I live."

"He can help you. He will treat your wounds."

"All men are the same. He either wants to leer at my nakedness, or ridicule my ugliness."

"I understand your reluctance, but none of us here know how to deal with your injuries. If he does not treat your wounds, they will fester. You could die."

"I would be happy to die. If I died, I could rejoin my beloved Kyros."

"Please, I beg you, let him help you."

Eleana glanced across the room. Head down, Phaidra knelt between a young woman's knees. Against the other wall, Marcelina stood with girded loins assisting several nude women as they bathed.

"You propose to bring a man in here?"

"No. I must take you to him."

"Take me back to the enclosure so I can be humiliated yet again before the men of my village? I think not."

"We have a wagon tied just outside the door. It will shelter you while Shemu'el does his work."

Eleana remained unconvinced.

"I know this is difficult for you. Despite all that has happened, I ask you to trust me. You must see a physician. I promise to stay with you every moment. Phaidra, the midwife, will too. No one will expose you or take liberties; we will not allow it."

Shemu'el placed his medical bag on the floor of the wagon and rapped on the door twice.

Rivkah and Phaidra led the once beautiful Eleana out the doorway. She limped as she walked, favoring her left foot.

Shemu'el noticed and asked how long her ankle had been sore.

"Just a few days. I tripped on the pavement when I tried to escape the Red Man."

"We'll deal with it later. First, let me see your back."

Eleana turned.

Shemu'el did a brief examination then stepped away shaking his head. He poured wine into a cup, swirled in a generous pinch of the medicine he kept in the vase shaped like a poppy pod and handed it to Phaidra.

"Have her drink this. It will relieve some of the coming pain."

Eleana stared at the ground, refusing to take the cup.

Rivkah took the cup from Phaidra. "Please, Eleana. Drink this, it will help you."

"It will make me sleep. I know what men do when a woman cannot protect herself."

"There is not enough in it to make you slumber," Shemu'el said. "I came to tend your injuries, not gawk at your nakedness."

Rivkah stared into Eleana's eyes. "He is a good man. Phaidra. I will remain by your side the entire time."

Eleana took the cup with shaking hands. She hesitated for a moment, swirled it, and drained the cup in a single gulp.

"I have done what I could," Phaidra whispered to Shemu'el. "She has been sorely used."

"The medicine takes effect quickly," he said. "I will need warm, clean water and rags."

While he waited, Shemu'el made cuts on each side of Eleana's ragged tunic from just below her shoulders to her waist. He made a horizontal cut below the collarband and at her waist. The remaining garment exposed her back, but not the front and lower portions of her body.

He dipped a cloth in the warm water and dampened each spot where fabric adhered to her wounds. He patiently dabbed the material again and again until the scabs softened and he could remove the fabric without damaging them.

"Now I must apply healing salves to you wounds. This may hurt."

Eleana steeled herself for the promised pain.

Shemu'el removed the seal from a large clay jar. Using a cloth, he scooped out a glob of ointment and began dabbing it on her back.

"My back has burned like fire for days," Eleana said with a sigh. "For the first time it feels...cool."

"Yes, this salve has a cooling effect."

"Why? What do you put in it?"

He continued patting it on as he spoke. "Mentha and myrrh, hyssop, aloes, oil of myrtle, palm wax and sweet almond oil. The almond oil helps reduce scarring."

"And that is all?"

"Except for a blessing which I say over every medicine I mix."

"How did you learn these things?"

Shemu'el held up a square of cloth, testing its size against that of her back. "I spent eight years as a slave to a physician who tended *Legio XII Fulminata*."

"You, a military physician? How very odd."

He trimmed the cloth to size. "Yes, the Lord truly works in strange and mysterious ways."

Atticus returned to the wagon after his meeting with the *tribunus,* and assured them all went well. "Do you need help here?" He glanced at Eleana's injured back spread with salve and, knowing she could not see him, gave a look of disgust.

"Check her ankle and then see to the men," Shemu'el suggested.

Atticus removed his Centurion's helmet. After sitting it in the bed of the wagon, he loosened his armor, leather girdle and straps. He leaned his *gladius vitis,* the short, thick staff all Centurions carried, against the wagon's wheel and knelt to examine Eleana's ankle.

A man laughed behind Atticus. "Be wary, she's a tiger,"

Eleana quivered at the sound of the Red Man's voice.

Rivkah put her hands on her arms, offering support.

Atticus looked back over his shoulder into the face of the brawny, redheaded legionnaire. "This area is off limits. Why are you here?"

"Thought I would come by and watch you work." He grinned and pointed out a series of red stripes running the length of his cheek. "Watch her fingernails. She tried to claw my eyes out. Needed a taste of the whip before she finally submitted." He gave a deep belly laugh. "But in the end, I taught her what it's all about."

"Get out of here before I have you removed." Atticus gently

flexed Eleana's swollen ankle, asking where it hurt.

Tears streamed down her cheeks.

"I could remove her clothing for you. I've had plenty of practice."

Atticus' hand moved toward the wheel. His fingers slowly closed around the *vitis* he'd left there. Without a word, he rose out of his crouch and spun around. Striking like a cobra, he laid the *vitis* across the Red Man's face with all his might.

The soldier's head snapped around. His hands went to his face and he screamed in pain. Staggering back, he fell in the dirt. The Red Man suddenly found himself lying on the ground choking on the blood that gushed from his nose and mouth. Glaring up at Atticus, he made a twitching motion as if he might draw his sword.

Atticus slammed the *vitis* down across the man's hand.

Eleana softly chuckled when the Red Man yelped in pain.

"Go ahead, try it," Atticus snarled. "I'll have you drawn and quartered and your severed head mounted on a pike as a warning to anyone foolish enough to challenge my authority."

The Red Man dug his heels into the ground and retreated by scraping along on his back.

Eleana's cracked lips formed a crooked smile as she watched the Red Man skitter away like a half-smashed beetle.

Once he'd put sufficient distance between himself and Atticus, he rolled onto his knees and rose. He stumbled back to camp cradling his broken hand with blood dripping from his face.

Atticus tossed the *vitis* aside and resumed his examination as if nothing had happened. He wrapped a bandage around Eleana's ankle and down and over the bottom of her foot.

Shemu'el rested his hand on Eleana's head and blessed her. "Time and medicine will heal your body, my daughter, but only Iesous can heal your heart and soul. He will, if you allow him."

# ~ 43 ~

Atticus requisitioned a second wagon so no one would have to walk back to Antioch. They packed its floor with clean straw and spread blankets so the badly injured could lie down on the trip.

They took their guests directly to the compound where the congregation waited to greet them. After a festive meal, they celebrated the Lord's Supper together.

Some of the people left to stay with other members of the congregation. The few intact families camped on the grounds surrounding the compound. Those with injuries slept inside the building.

Over the following weeks they began reconstructing their lives. Some joined extended families elsewhere. Others found jobs and settled in Antioch.

Eleana, injured in both body and soul, had no family and stayed on in a small room at the compound. Rivkah and Shemu'el visited each day so he could dress her wounds. His tender touch gradually won her over and, though she remained moody and withdrawn, she no long resisted his efforts as she did on that first day.

Rivkah encouraged her to participate in the *ekklesia's* activities each time they visited. Most young women enjoyed being in the nursery with the youngsters, but Eleana found excuses to remain in her room.

Over time her features returned to their former beauty. Despite her progress, Cybele's warning lingered in Rivkah's memory. So long as Eleana remained cooped-up, the urge to take her own life would never leave her.

One evening, after visiting Eleana, she went to Channah's room. Her daughter sat cross-legged on the floor weaving a girdle on a small loom.

"I have someone I would like you to meet."

Channah concentrated on her work. "I am not ready for a man in my life, Imma."

"I meant Eleana, a young woman about your age."

"The one whom the Red Man shamed in the village square."

"So you have heard?"

Channah shrugged. "Stories make their way around. You know how it is."

"Yes, unfortunately I do."

Channah glanced up at her mother. "Why do you want me to make her acquaintance? I cannot just show up at someone's door and say, 'Here I am, your new friend.'"

"You two have much in common. Perhaps you also heard her betrothed died at her feet trying to protect her from the Romans?"

Channah stared at the far wall and swallowed hard. "Just as Stefanos insisted I go into the trees where I would be safe."

"Will you do it?"

"Give me some time to think about it."

Channah arrived at Eleana's door with her sewing bag slung over her shoulder. She knocked twice, got no response, and tested the door. It swung aside at her touch. The drapes had been pulled making the room dark even at midday.

"Eleana?" She paused, waiting for a response. "It is Channah, Rivkah's daughter. Are you here?"

When her eyes adjusted to the darkness, she spotted Eleana standing in the shadows holding a spindle. A ball of yarn lay in a spinning bowl behind her.

"I do not wish to have visitors." Eleana focused her attention on the spindle as it dropped.

"Please, may I stay a short while?"

"It appears you offer me no choice. Very well, stay if you must."

Channah pulled up a stool and sat down. She slipped the bag off her shoulder and sat it on the floor. "I brought my sewing. While you spin, I can sew."

Eleana continued working the spindle with a sullen expression.

"Must we work in the dark? I will surely jab myself with the needle."

"Darkness is the only friend I have." Eleana sighed in resignation and swept the curtain aside. Sunlight flooded the room. "There. Happy?"

They blinked in the sudden brightness. Though the swelling in Eleana's face had gone down, remnants of dark bruises rimmed her eyes making them look as if she'd painted them with kohl.

Feeling Channah's gaze, Eleana lowered her face. "Did you come so you could stare at my injuries?"

"We all have scars."

"Perhaps, but most are not as obvious as mine." She jerked an arm out of her cloak. "Very well. I will show you my back. Then you can tell your friends all about what the Red Man did to Eleana."

"I would never do such a thing. I came to offer friendship and support."

"So your mother told you how sad it is that poor Eleana has no companions and sent you here to befriend me."

"You must release the notion that I came because of my mother."

"If I need a friend, I will find one for myself," Eleana said with an angry snort.

"I told my mother the same when she suggested I visit you."

"Yet here you are. Why did you come?"

"I came for you...and for myself." Channah chuckled. "Although, since you wish to display your back, I must tell you Abba gave me a bottle of oil to apply to your scars."

Eleana's expression softened. "Forgive me. Your father is a kind and gentle healer. Both of your parents have been very good to me."

Eleana sat the cloak aside and pulled her tunic over her head. She sat on a stool with her back to Channah. Leaning forward, she rested her elbows on her knees.

Her father's warning had not prepared Channah for what she saw. The scabs had fallen away as the wounds from the Red

Man's whip healed leaving a crosshatch pattern of bright pink scars running across Eleana's back.

Channah took a deep breath and poured a small amount of oil into her shaky palm.

"Did you bring sweet almond oil?"

"Yes. How did you know?"

"I conversed with your father each time he treated my wounds. I have learned quite a lot about medicinal compounds. The last time he visited he said I no longer required the salve. Instead, he suggested regular applications of almond oil to help reduce the scarring."

Channah patted the oil onto Eleana's back. Afraid of accidentally causing her pain, she brushed her fingers across the skin with feathery strokes.

"Are you afraid you will hurt me?"

"Yes," Channah admitted. "Abba is the physician, not me. I have never done this sort of thing before."

"I am not a piece of antique pottery ready to crumble at the slightest touch." She rolled her shoulders. "A firm touch feels better. What you are doing tickles." Eleana glanced back over her shoulder and grinned. "If it hurts, I will let you know."

Channah poured more oil into her hand and rubbed it in, making sweeping motions across Eleana's back. "Better?"

Eleana sighed with pleasure. "Much."

## ~ 44 ~

Channah returned the following day carrying a round, lidded basket. She took a seat and balanced it on her knees.

Eleana pointed to the basket. "If you brought food, I have already eaten,"

"The only thing in my basket is Elpis."

"Elpis? You carry hope around in a basket?"

Hearing his name, the cat began to squirm.

Eleana stiffened. "Your basket is...it's moving."

The lid lifted a bit and two yellow eyes peered out at her.

She leaped out of her chair and backed up against the wall. "There is some kind of creature in there," Eleana shrieked. "What have brought?"

Elpis shoved his head out, toppling the lid onto the floor. Over the years the tiny ball of gray fluff that attacked Channah's toe beside the aqueduct had grown into a sleek gray cat.

"It is a wild animal." Eleana retreated into a corner making shooing motions. "A cat."

Elpis stood up. Arching his back, he stretched and glanced around the room.

Channah waved her back to the stool. "It's all right. Come sit down."

Eleana tiptoed part way, grabbed the stool, and slid it to her. She tapped her foot and chewed a finger, never taking her eyes off of the large gray animal in Channah's lap.

Without warning, Elpis leaped out of the basket and into Eleana's lap.

She gave a startled cry. "Help! Do something before he attacks me."

"Elpis will not hurt you."

Ignoring Eleana's frenzied attempts to brush him away, the cat circled her lap before curling into a ball. He snuggled in and began purring contentedly.

"What is this strange sound he makes?"

"He is purring. He does it whenever he's happy."

Eleana relaxed a bit, but continued eyeing the cat suspiciously. "I know the Egyptians keep cats, but I have never touched one before." She glanced down at the mound of gray fur in her lap. "I thought cats hissed and bit and scratched."

"Only when they fight. Most of the time they are very calm. I brought him with me from Jerusalem. He has lived with us for several years now."

"Were you afraid the first time you touched him?"

"Oh, no. He was very tiny then."

"How did you come to own him?"

Channah sat the basket on the floor beside her. "It is a very long story. Are you sure you want to listen?"

"I have nothing but time." Eleana tentatively brushed her fingers along the Elpis' back. His tail twitched and she jerked her hand away.

"Stefanos must have loved you very much," Eleana said when Channah finished the story of how he was wrenched away from her.

"As your betrothed, Kyros, cared for you," Channah replied. "We both lost good men whom we loved."

"Why did you bring your cat?" Eleana marveled at the rough texture of his tongue when Elpis licked her hand as she stroked the thick fur on his chest.

"I am not certain why I brought him. I suppose because he plays a part in my confession." Channah shifted on the stool and swallowed hard. "You see, I have not always been as you see me today. In the days after Stefanos died I thought my heart would never heal. Believing his death must be avenged, I purchased a *sicarius* and haunted Jerusalem's streets searching for the one I believed responsible for his death."

"You killed a man?"

"I wanted to, but in the end I could not do it. That is where Elpis comes in. I grew despondent and felt I had failed my beloved Stefanos." Channah's voice sank to a whisper. "I decided to use the *sicarius* to end my life."

Eleana rocked forward. "What happened?"

Channah told the story of her failed attempt on Sha'oul's life, of plunging her hand into the aqueduct, and of Elpis' timely appearance. "I believe Stefanos sent him to give me hope. Hope enough to work through my pain one day at a time. Hope that there were happy days ahead, and proof of the blessings life still held." Channah gave her a self-conscious shrug. "So that is my story."

Eleana smiled down at Elpis dozing in her lap. "It is a good story and a comforting one. Thank you for sharing it with me. You have been a friend to me and I enjoy your visits." She took a deep breath. "I too have secrets to share."

**Jerusalem—**

Wearing nothing but a sweaty loincloth, tired and dirty from a long night at the kiln, Hebel staggered out of the alleyway and vomited into the gutter. When he straightened, his legs quivered and jerked as he stumbled to the steps. Holding his pounding head with both hands, he trudged up the steps to the small apartment where he, Hadassah and their daughter, Sarit, lived.

"There is water on the table. Drink it," Hadassah commanded when she heard the door open behind her. Five years as a potter's wife taught her the effect heat had on the human body and the importance of hydration in warm climates.

She swept a sleeve across her forehead and continued kneading her dough. "I could feel the warmth of your fires all the way up here."

She noticed his hand shake when he returned the empty mug and put aside her work to refill the glass. "You look like a man who has wandered in the desert too long."

Little Sarit glanced up from her dolls and smiled at her father.

Hebel managed a weak smile and a short wave, then gulped down more water.

At the counter, Hadassah concentrated on preparing the

day's bread. "How are you feeling?"

"Do not fret over me; I will be fine."

"You should plan your work so you do not have to fire pots in the month of Aviv. The weather is always too hot."

Hebel grabbed a generous pinch of salt from the bowl. He tossed it onto his tongue and sucked on the larger chunks. Refilling the empty glass, he gave a deep sigh and up-ended it a third time.

"I will." He swiped the back of a hand across his mouth. "As soon as you arrange it so we do not have to eat during the month of Aviv."

"Do as the caravans do. You do not see their camels out in the desert sun. This time of year they travel only by night."

"Have you forgotten me slipping away last night? I kindled my ovens by moonlight. This was my last load. I cannot abandon my work just because the sun comes up." He staggered slightly and grabbed the table for balance. "The next time you speak with the Almighty tell him, 'Do not let your sun rise while Hebel has pots in the oven.' I am certain he will do as you tell him. Everyone else does."

Hadassah shook her head and fished pickled cucumbers out of a crock on the floor. "You need to take better care of yourself."

"I drank vinegar water all night, but even it can only do so much." Hebel loosened the rag he'd tied around his head to still his throbbing brain.

"Your noonday meal will be ready in a mo—"

The smile slipped from her lips when Hadassah turned and saw her husband's flushed face. Droplets of sweat dripped from his beard and clung to wiry hairs on his bare chest. Hebel's damp hair hung around his face limp as a mop.

"You do not look well, my husband."

Hebel insisted he was fine.

"Quick," she said, setting her work aside. "There is cool water in the bedroom. Go in and swab yourself down."

He thumped the glass down on the table and traced a wavering path across the room.

"Hebel?"

He leaned against the doorframe and glanced back.

"Slip on a light tunic when you come to the table." Her eyes went to Sarit playing on the floor and then back to him. "That damp loincloth conceals nothing."

Stripping off his loincloth, Hebel soaked the rag in cool water and squeezed it until it no longer dripped. He sighed with pleasure as he moved the cloth over his fiery skin. After washing away the sweat and grime of the night's work, he swabbed his body again and again. He didn't bother to dry. Instead, he stepped in front of the open window and spread his arms.

A midmorning breeze fluttered the sheer curtains. The air carried the sooty smell of the last, dying embers burning out in his kiln. Hebel closed his eyes and sighed with pleasure as the wind cooled his body. Dogs barked in the next alley over and the clop of donkey's hooves competed with merchant's cries as they hawked their wares on the streets below.

When the wind died away, Hebel tugged a fresh tunic over his head. The dry cloth against his skin felt as comforting as Hadassah's caress on a moonlit night.

## ~ **45** ~

**Antioch—**

"Now I shall share my secret with you," Eleana said.

Channah scooted her stool closer.

"Two moons have come and gone since I received a woman's regular time."

Quivers of fear churned the pit of Channah's stomach. She felt the onset of dizziness as if she might faint. Trying to appear unconcerned, she said, "I would not worry, many things can disrupt a woman's cycle."

She gave Eleana a reassuring smile.

"Neither of us can pretend the truth away. I am tired all the time, my breasts have grown tender, and I awake each morning feeling sick to my stomach."

"You are with child," Channah gasped. Her hand went to her mouth as if she could retrieve the words as they left her tongue.

Eleana took a deep breath, lowered her eyes, and nodded. "Yes, my friend, I apparently carry the Red Man's child."

Channah's mind raced to find a way to somehow make things better. "Were there others?"

"Other soldiers besides the Red Man, you mean?"

"Yes." Every fiber of Channah's being wanted to scream, *"Spare me the details. Do not describe what I never want to know."*

She waited, scarcely breathing. How strange, she thought, to wish there had been others. But without them, the Red Man was the only one who could have fathered Eleana's child.

Eleana cupped her chin and tugged at her lip, deciding how much she wished to share. She had struggled to purge all memory of those times from her mind and now, despite the pain they brought, she was forced to relive them. She rested her head in her hands and rubbed her temples.

"No one else," she said, avoiding Channah's eyes. "The Red Man kept me for himself alone."

"I'm sorry." Channah gasped. "That's not what I meant. I only thought..."

"I know what you meant." Moving to the window, Eleana slid the drape aside and stared out at the mountains. "You once admitted contemplating suicide. I now confess, like you, I considered doing away with myself."

"You speak of it as the past. What changed your mind?"

"I came to realize harming myself would be unfair to all the people who showed me kindness. You, your parents, Atticus and others here at the compound, friends...even strangers. I could not disappoint you all and so I chose life over death."

Channah smiled when she heard this.

"I no longer plan to end my life. Instead, I now contemplate something much, much worse. I intend to snuff out the life of this innocent child living within me."

"No! You cannot."

"But I must. I hoped you of all people would understand."

"I understand that killing this child is murder as surely as if I had stabbed Sha'oul through the heart."

Eleana toyed with a strand of her light brown hair. "Try to imagine how difficult it has been for me. This on top of everything else? I could never bear the shame."

"Shame? There is no shame when a woman is forced to submit. You cannot do this. Hands that shed innocent blood are an abomination to the Lord."

"I am not strong like other believers."

"You are as strong as you need to be. God never asks more than we are capable of."

Eleana tossed her hair aside. "Believe what you like. My mind is made up."

"Phaidra, the midwife, will not do it. She refuses to destroy unborn babies."

"There are others who will."

Channah watched tears trickle down Eleana's cheeks. "Do you wish you had not told me?"

Eleana shrugged. "I had to tell someone. At first I tried to wish it away, but with each passing day I became surer and surer.

Now that I know for certain, I need your friendship more than ever." Her face clouded. "Although I suppose you will run to your mother and tell her."

"If I did, you might destroy yourself to destroy the child."

"And who could blame me? I will never find peace until I rid myself of this..." she tugged at the tunic stretched tight across her abdomen, "this horrible thing growing inside me."

"Nothing horrible grows within you. God placed that child within you and killing it will bring you torment, not peace."

"How strange to hear God is the one responsible," Eleana said with a wry laugh. "And all this time I blamed my troubles on the Red Man."

"Do not twist my words. We both know a man and woman must come together for her to conceive, but God alone decides when a man's seed takes root."

"So why is he punishing me by allowing this evil man's child to grow in my womb?"

"You have not been punished; you have been blessed. Regardless of the circumstances of conception, all babies are good. God pronounced it so on the last day of creation."

"Good or bad, the child still must go."

"Both of you are innocent. This child no more deserves to die for what happened than you do. I beg you, do not place the stain of taking an innocent life on your soul."

"What choice do I have? I cannot manage alone."

"You will never be alone. You have me. My parents will help you." Channah spread her arms wide. "The whole assembly will assist you."

**Jerusalem—**

Hebel felt better after he ate. He sat on the floor with his back resting against the wall and motioned to Hadassah. "Come, my wife, sit in my lap."

"I have dishes to put away."

"Leave them."

"It is the middle of the day." Glaring at him, she lowered her voice. "What about Sarit?"

The little girl's head popped up at the sound of her name.

"Sarit, do you mind if Imma sits in my lap?"

"No, Abba," she said and returned to her dolls.

He opened his arms and waved Hadassah to him.

Though she hadn't intended to sit in Hebel's lap, Hadassah found his touch relaxing. She rested her head on his shoulder and he massaged her neck. Lifting her bangs, he kissed her forehead.

She smiled.

"Your forehead is damp, my love. Perhaps we should go into the bedroom and I will swab you with a cool cloth."

She kissed her fingertips and touched them to his lips. "I think not."

"Did you hear the *shofar* blast from the Temple last evening?"

"Mmm-hmm." Hadassah's voice had the faraway sound of someone fighting midday drowsiness. "It is *Rosh Chodesh*," she said sleepily. "The first day of the new month."

Taking his wife's hand, Hebel folded back one of her fingers then another. "Funny thing. A second moon has come and gone, and still no *niddah* for Hadassah."

She gave him a prim look. "Since when have you begun tracking my monthly cycles?"

He shrugged. "A husband notices."

"So you miss the times we must stay apart?" she asked with a girlish giggle. She turned in his lap and gave him a long, sensual kiss. "Have you grown tired of me already?"

"Never, my love. I only wondered if, perhaps, there was something you wished to tell me."

"Tell you?" She wrinkled her brow and pretended to search her memory. "What could I possibly have to tell you?"

He stared at her square on.

She kissed him again and, putting her lips very near his ear, whispered, "Yes, my husband, you have guessed it. I am with child."

Hebel's eyes gleamed. He rocked her in his arms, kissing

her again and again. He eased her off his lap. "I am so happy I must dance."

"You need to dance in our front room in the middle of the day?"

"Yes. For everything there is a season, a time for every matter under heaven." He pulled her to her feet. "And this is the time to dance."

He tapped his foot on the floor, setting the beat and hummed a melody. Together they spun around the room hand in hand, beaming at each other across the circle of their arms. Hadassah loosed her braids and leaned her head back as Hebel spun her. When the air whipped through her locks she laughed for the sheer joy of it.

Hebel's heart swelled remembering the glow she'd gotten when she carried Sarit. Something about the process of childbearing made Hadassah happier, less moody, a better companion and more suitable wife. Not so bossy. He looked forward to watching the changes the new life inside her would bring. And, though it seemed profane and slightly paganistic, he looked forward to being freed from the restrictions of *niddah*, their time of monthly separation.

Sarit watched them for a moment, then tossed her dolls aside and jumped to her feet. She clapped and giggled and skipped in and around her parents as they circled the room. They each grabbed one of the little girl's hands, and together the three of them swirled until they grew too dizzy to stand.

Laughing and grinning, Hebel collapsed onto the floor and pulled Hadassah back into his lap.

Sarit shrieked when he gave her a strong tug. She spiraled toward them and plopped into her mother's waiting arms.

"Why are we so happy, Abba?" Sarit asked, between gasps for breath.

"We are celebrating because God has chosen to bless our family with another child."

Sarit's eyes widened. "A baby?" She stared at her mother's stomach. "When, Imma? When?"

She patted the girl's head. "Not for many months."

Sarit's face sank in disappointment. "Why must it be so long?"

"God's ways are not our ways. Things like this cannot be hurried." Hadassah opened her daughter's hand and traced each line and crease in her palm. "Just as we do not know where the wind comes from, we do not understand how God forms bones in a mother's womb."

She kissed the tip of Sarit's nose, making her laugh. "Each of us is fearfully and wonderfully made. Day by day the Lord God patiently knitted us together inside our mother's body."

Sarit swelled with sisterly pride. "Now I will have a baby brother or sister just like my friend, Michal,"

"Yes, but with one difference." Hebel slipped an arm around the little girl's shoulder. He drew her close and whispered, "If it is a little boy, he will be stronger, braver, and more handsome than any of your friend's brothers. And, should it be a girl," he lifted her face, "like my precious Sarit, she will be more beautiful than any of their little sisters."

"Hebel!" Hadassah jabbed her elbow into his ribs. Their eyes met and she shot him a look. "Listen to yourself. Have her talking like that and she will have no friends."

He patted his daughter's head. "What I have said is true, but you must remember one thing. Your friends might not like it if you told them this. You see, even though Imma and I know you are the smartest, most beautiful little girl in all Jerusalem, we never tell anyone."

"Why not?"

He tapped his chest. "It is a secret we hold in our hearts. You must never speak of these things outside our home. Do you understand?"

Sarit gave him a solemn nod. "I understand, Abba. I will be a good big sister and keep our secret."

Hebel rested his hand on Hadassah's belly. The place where she carried his child. His eyes misted. God willing, maybe a son this time, he thought, blinking back tears.

The baby would come in early spring. What could be better than that?

## ~ 46 ~

*"Throughout every city and village...churches were
rapidly found abounding and filled with members
from every people."*
                                   —Eusebius' History, Book 2  3:2

When Rivkah went to the compound to harness Isaias the
donkey, she found him limping with a sore foot. She washed his
foot and applied a poultice of herbs wrapped in a bandage.
Lowering her head, she held his foot between her hands and
asked Iesous to heal this friend who played such an important
role in their ministry. Without him they could not use the cart.

Big Pavlos solved the problem by putting himself in the
donkey's place. He wrapped his huge hands around the cart's
staves, which would have been buckled to the donkey's harness,
and with a mighty grunt tugged it on its way. He spent the trip
pulling the cart like a pack animal.

The skies had grown dark by the time Rivkah and Pavlos
completed their rounds. They returned to the compound late and
footsore. Pavlos trudged back to the barn where he dropped the
cart's staves with a weary groan and, without a backward glance,
ambled away to the little building where he now lived.

Shemu'el, Petros and Yohan Markus were visiting the
communities at Pergamum and Ephesus in Asia. They had gone
by sea, sailing down the Orontes from Antioch to Pieria Seleucia.
From there, they would cross the Great Sea to Ephesus where
Iesous' beloved disciple, Yohan, now lived with Miryam.

The children loved traveling with their father and
accompanied him whenever possible. While everyone was away,
Rivkah stayed behind in Antioch to tend those she served.

She opened the stable door and re-checked Isaias. The foot
seemed better, though he still favored it. From the barn she went
to the house, stopping briefly to chat with Eleana before locking
up. She found herself puttering around and doing busy work to
avoid going home to an empty house.

When she could find no more to do, Rivkah headed out the gate. As she turned to latch it, something rustled the bush beside her. Startled, she cocked an ear and listened. Expecting to find an injured animal, she held out her lamp and tiptoed closer following its circle of light.

A battered and bedraggled slip of a woman threw a protective hand across her eyes when the light hit her.

Rivkah dropped to one knee beside her. "Who are you?"

The woman coughed and spit blood. "I am called Zeeta." A foreign accent blurred her words.

"What happened to you?"

"Some evil men beat me."

Rivkah pushed aside clumps of matted hair and brought the lamp closer, examining her face. One eye had nearly swollen shut and her cheek bore a bright red welt. In the light she saw that her ragged clothes were ripped and torn, exposing her to shame.

"How can I help you?"

"Someone once told me the *Christianoi* feed beggars."

"Are you hungry?" What a ridiculous question, she thought as the words left her tongue. Of course the woman needed food; she was hardly more than skin and bones.

Zeeta bowed her head. "Yes,"

"Come with me." Rivkah slipped an arm around her. "We can go to my home and I will feed you."

Zeeta's eyes widened with fear.

"You will be safe there. My husband and children are away. It will only be the two of us." She helped her to her feet. "Come. It is not far."

Zeeta sat on a stool beside the table glancing around their humble home and tugging the torn scraps of her clothes together in an attempt to cover herself.

Rivkah worked in the kitchen preparing their meal. Placing a cake of dates on a platter, she surrounded it with several loaves, a small bowl of spiced oil for dipping, some dried fish, cheese and olives. She sat the platter on the table and went back for juice.

Zeeta eyed the food with eager anticipation.

"I have some freshly-crushed grape juice," Rivkah said over her shoulder. Purple-pink bubbles formed around the rim of the glasses as she poured. She sat at the table and bowed her head in prayer.

When she finished Zeeta gave her a questioning look.

Rivkah nodded.

Zeeta attacked the food like a hungry dog.

After they ate, Rivkah drew water and prepared a bath. She pulled the hides tight across the windows and snuffed one of the lights, leaving the room in soft shadows.

"I will tend to your injuries when you have bathed."

Zeeta washed and wrapped herself in a towel.

Rivkah examined the marks on her face. "How did you receive these injuries?" she asked as she applied Shemu'el's salve.

"I was on a street corner begging when a man came up to me. He was young, not the kind to show interest in a hag like me. He said if I came to his room with him he would give me roasted meat and cakes with wine when we finished. An inner voice warned me," Zeeta lifted her shoulders in a hopeless gesture, "but I was hungry, and so I went."

"Do you know this man's name?"

"His name is not important. He was sent to lure me to where several others waited. The leader of the group was a man they call Gamma."

"Gamma?"

"Yes."

"His name is *Three*?"

Zeeta took Rivkah's hand and covered the thumb and smallest finger with hers, leaving only the middle three fingers visible. "Gamma," she said firmly. "He has no thumb or small finger on either hand. They cut them away in Sparta when he was caught stealing."

Leaving Rivkah's fingers curled like the talons of a hawk, Zeeta rested her forehead in her hands. "Gamma is an evil, evil man. The men had their way with me, but when they finished there was no food. Instead they began ridiculing me and cursing me, calling me despicable names. Then the one called Gamma beat and kicked me. They tore my clothes for sport and cast me back into the street."

Rivkah reached out and rubbed her bony shoulder.

Zeeta's eyes grew wide with fright and tears came into her voice. "Gamma said the next time he would kill me. I knew I must hide, but I had nowhere to go. I limped to your compound and hid beneath the bush until you came out."

"The Lord guided your footsteps."

Rivkah hummed as she combed Zeeta's thin gray locks. Opening an alabaster jar, she applied a small amount of spikenard to her hair. The air grew thick with its heady aroma.

Zeeta spun on the stool. She jerked the comb from Rivkah's hand and threw it to the floor. "I see you are more subtle than the young man and his companions. Rather than strike me with your fists, you anoint me with costly Nardos and pretend I am a fine lady." Her eyes narrowed. "*Meretrix. Zonah.* Whore...Harlot. Every language has its word for women like me. I do not need you to remind me; I know what I am."

"Forgive me," Rivkah said. "You have been ill-used and injured. I felt with food in your stomach and a warm bath, the scent of perfume in your hair might refresh your spirit." She tipped the alabaster jar, proving it was new. "This was given to me by a friend. She intended it for my use. Instead I saved it, knowing someday someone would need it more than I."

The burden of gratitude became more than Zeeta could bear. She looked away, refusing to meet Rivkah's eyes. "When you have been hurt as often as I have, it becomes second nature to distrust even the most innocent gesture."

Rivkah picked up the comb and began again. Zeeta quietly sobbed as she platted her hair and tied it with ribbons. When she finished, Rivkah offered Zeeta one of her tunics, a multi-colored girdle Channah wove, and a linen cloak.

Zeeta shed the towel and raised her arms to slip into the tunic. Her gaunt figure accentuated old stretch marks across her belly.

"You have had children?" Rivkah asked.

"Just one," Zeeta said, smoothing the tunic. "And you."

Rivkah grinned. "Five...and two grandchildren now."

A tentative bond formed between them. For the first time they were just two women doing what women did best, talk about their children.

"Do you have a son or a daughter?"

"A son," Zeeta said with a telltale shift of her eyes. "It was not the same for me as with you. I sold my body to anyone with coins in their purse. I consoled myself by pretending I offered love." She shook her head. "I did shameful things. There has never been love in my bed, only lust. And now, old and alone, the names and faces are forgotten, but the degradation lingers."

Her shoulders sank under the weight of past sins. Zeeta shot Rivkah a sidelong glance. "You are a good woman, does hearing these things shock you?"

"No. I recognized your name as soon as you spoke it. I have heard of you before...from my husband."

Fear arced across Zeeta's face. She raised her arms, steeling herself for a blow that never came. "Please do not strike me. If I served your husband, it was only out of need, never love. I swear it, never love."

"You went to him, but he turned you away."

She appeared shocked. "He turned Zeeta away? When?"

"Many years ago. Twenty-five, perhaps more."

A sudden gust sucked the air out of the room. The hide flapped against the window frame, sending eerie shadows dancing across the walls. Rivkah watched the demon of pride enter the old woman's soul. Zeeta now wrestled not against flesh and blood, but with the hosts of darkness.

She reveled in what, only moments before, she had lamented with tears. The lamplight glinted off her green eyes. She flung her head back, tossing her hair aside like a young girl.

"Your husband lied to you because he did not want you to know. In those days men begged for Zeeta's charms. I was young and beautiful. No man could resist me."

"That is nothing to take pride in."

Grasping her shoulders, Rivkah stared into Zeeta's startled

eyes. She placed her hand alongside Zeeta's face and traced the immortal mark of Iesous' cross on her forehead. "In the name of the Son of God and all his angels," she shouted, "release her. Be gone, Demon!"

Zeeta's head snapped back. She blinked in fear. Her eyes swept the room searching for the presence she felt there with them. Lifting a finger, she cautiously traced the mark of the cross on her forehead.

"Think," Rivkah said. "Think and remember. Many years ago, Evodius Scipio was *Medicus Cohoritis* to *Legio XII Fulminata*. He came to you and gave you money to lie with his assistant, a young slave named Marcus. You went to his room in the Citadel where you tried to seduce him and failed."

Zeeta's brow furrowed as she revisited times long past. She sucked in her bottom lip and nibbled at it. After several minutes of silence, Zeeta smiled and nodded.

"I recall Scipio...and Marcus as well. He was a young lad who had never been with a woman." She chuckled. "Oh yes, do I ever remember Marcus. Believe me when I tell you he desired what I offered. Ached for it. Yet he quaked at my touch and refused to have anything to do with me."

Zeeta hugged herself and rocked on the stool.

"When he threw me out, he called me *Daughter of Satan*." She glanced up at Rivkah. "He was right, you know. That is what I am, a she-devil, a curse upon all whom I touch."

"And yet you came to the gate of the *Christianoi*. Why?"

"I was driven to it. I had no where else to go. Look at me; I am a hag. I wander the street wearing rags. Children throw sticks at me and call me dreadful names. I beg for coins and eat what others cast away."

Rivkah stretched and yawned. "Enough for now. Tonight you shall stay with me. In the morning we can talk some more."

## ~ **47** ~

*"If we confess our sins, he is faithful and just, and
will forgive us our sins and cleanse us from all
unrighteousness."*

— 1 John 1:9

"How did you come to be in Antioch?" Rivkah asked the
following morning.

"I was born in Albania, in the foothills of the Caucasus
Mountains. A lovely village beside the Caspian Sea." Zeeta gave a
self-conscious laugh. "Would you believe Zeeta, the whore, was
once pure as a Vestal Virgin? As a maiden, I tingled when young
men in our village caught my eye and smiled."

Saying nothing, Rivkah broke off a piece of bread and used
it to scoop cooked cereal out of her bowl.

As quick as it came, the lyric tone in Zeeta's voice
disappeared. Girlish dreams and happy memories were swept
away in a flood of rage and resentment. She grabbed her bread
and ripped it apart.

"But the gods chose a different fate for me. We were poor
and my father sold my sister and I. She went to a wealthy family
in the next town to become a house servant, perhaps even a wife
for one of the Master's sons. I was sold to a traveling merchant
named Cretorius. I imagined he, too, might make me his wife."

Zeeta shrugged and scooped out the last of her porridge.
"Not the future I envisioned, but at least I had a future. Instead,
Cretorius became my procurer, selling me for a night's pleasure
in every town we visited."

She paused, staring at the shredded remnants of her loaf.
Her voice softened. "Then we came to Trapezus, in Cappadocia,
where a rich old man coveted an evening with the young Zeeta."
She looked up and winked. "Like all men, his reach exceeded his
grasp. The doddering old fool could not have satisfied a woman
his own age. What did he plan on doing with a hot-blooded young
filly?"

Zeeta's eyes narrowed. "His fantasies were his undoing... and the key to my freedom." Her chuckles became laughs. "The excitement proved too much for him. We had barely begun when he collapsed on the bed clutching his chest. Rolling him aside, I grabbed my clothes and quickly dressed."

"And what became of the man?"

"I grew tired of his wheezing and pathetic pleas for help. I wanted him to die. I needed him to die." Her fingers curled into a tight fist. She smacked it into the palm of her other hand. "So I made a fist and punched him in the chest with all my might."

Rivkah sat, saying little and listening much.

"His eyes popped open wide. He gave a final gasp, and then closed them forever. I knew it would be hours before Cretorius came to collect me. Leaving the man in his bed, I ran."

"And so you were free."

"Yes, but I had to decide what to do with my freedom. I could not go back home. The young men of my village would shun me and, even if my father took me back, he would only sell me again. So I headed south. Along the way, I worked when I could or kind strangers fed me. When neither sufficed, I knew how to get whatever I needed."

Rivkah began clearing their dishes. "Last night you mentioned a son."

"I named the boy Orion. I imagined him someday becoming a great hunter. Had I known the future, I would have named him *Abaddon* instead."

The dish slipped from Rivkah's hand and clattered onto the counter. "*Abaddon*? The angel of the bottomless pit, the gatekeeper of *Gehenna*? How can you say such a thing?"

"Because that is what he was, a *gryllos* sent to torment me. A big, lumbering oaf of a child." She sneered. "Much like the soldiers who tapped on my door at night."

"Perhaps he required your understanding."

"Understanding, what understanding? He could neither hear nor speak. All he wanted was be left alone. He spent his days tucked into a corner hugging himself and sucking his thumb as he rocked and moaned."

"What became of him?"

"He never fit in. The other children either avoided him, or they encircled him yelling insults and taunts." Zeeta's lip curled in disgust. "I told him to fight back. He could have easily beaten them all, but he never did. Instead he covered his head and whimpered like a sick puppy."

Zeeta adjusted the skirt of her tunic, smoothing the cloth like a young girl expecting a suitor. "I had youth and beauty then. Men desired me. I could pick and choose, offering myself to only those who had silver enough to afford me."

"Who was the boy's father?"

Zeeta stared into her hands for a time. When she looked up again her mouth had become a tight line. "There are four legions in Antioch. Count them. That is over 24,000 soldiers plus the merchants, staff and traders who accompany them. Select one," she said with a flick of a finger, "any of them could have fathered him."

"I am so sorry." Rivkah instinctively reached for her hand.

Zeeta pulled away. "I do not need your pity. What is done is done." She took a deep breath and brushed aside a tear. "It was my own fault. I was drinking heavily and missed taking my herbs. Oh, I could have gone to one of the midwives. They know how to deal with such things." Her voice sank to a remorseful whisper. "I *should* have gone to one of the midwives."

"But you did not."

Zeeta sighed. "No I did not. While he lived in my womb I dreamed of making a new life for us. Imagined going to a place where no one knew Zeeta, the whore. Where I could be like other women with a home and children and a man who wanted me for who I was, not the pleasure I gave."

"Why did you never leave?" Rivkah asked from the other side of the room. Hoping to calm her nervous fingers, she'd pulled out her wool and begun to spin.

"While my belly grew I spent my days...sometimes two or three at a time, lying in my bed drunk on cheap wine. Then he came and, though I believed things could not get worse, they did. Orion failed to thrive like other children."

Rivkah looped her thread around the spindle and smiled at her. "Still you kept him alive. You must have done something right."

"It was nothing I did." Her cheeks flushed. "Sometimes at night I stood over him while he slept, my fingers clenched into a fist, wondering if a blow to the chest would kill him as it had killed the old man."

"You never harmed him, did you?"

"Harm him? I harmed him by allowing him be born," she screamed. Her hands trembled as she spoke. "Sometimes when I lay in bed in a drunken stupor he would creep beside me, pushing and shaking me, begging to be fed. When I could no longer stand his pestering, I'd roll onto my side and offer the little monster my breast."

Zeeta shook her head trying to drive away the memories. "But my milk sickened him. And, when he spat it up, I had to rouse out of my bed to clean him." She pounded the table, rattling the dishes. "Yes! I struck him in anger...many times."

Rivkah put an arm around her thin shoulder.

Zeeta panted like a runner. "Orion survived because some force stronger than my hatred willed it. For all the good it did." She wept deep, wrenching sobs. "Though he neither heard nor spoke, his eyes missed nothing. Over and over I told him, 'When the men visit, do not watch.' Yet each time I looked up, there he was in his corner chewing his fingers, his face a mask of stone."

She buried her face in her hands. "He was there watching... always watching."

Rivkah brought her a cool rag for her face and urged her to rest. But a lifetime of regret demanded to be spoken. Her sins needed to be confessed, and so Rivkah listened. Iesous had her in his grasp now, and wouldn't let her go.

Zeeta clutched Rivkah's hand in hers, squeezing until it hurt. Her lips quivered. "I explained to him I only cried out to please the men, but he never understood. He thought they were hurting me. As he grew bigger, Orion took to leaping on their backs and pounding them with his little fists."

Despite her best efforts, the image made Rivkah chuckle.

"They did not like that, did they?"

"They would cuff him alongside the head. Time and time again he flew off the bed, rolled across the floor, and crashed into the wall."

"And then?"

"Those who were able cursed him and continued. Those who could not, demanded their money back and stormed away, cursing us both."

She glanced up, catching Rivkah's eyes and holding them. "Can't you see, he left me no choice. I had to bring the men home or I had no living. It was him or...or them. I could not have both." She turned aside. "And so, I chose the men over my own son."

"What did you do?"

"I took him down to the riverbank and turned him out."

"The place where they throw unwanted babies to die?"

Zeeta glared at her. "Would you prefer I plunge a knife through his heart, or smother him with a pillow? If a ship is sinking, something...someone, must be thrown overboard. It was harsh, I know, but sometimes one must be harsh to survive."

"And did you? Survive, I mean."

"I told myself I did. For a little while I might even have believed it. But inside, a piece of me died. Eventually, I became what you see before you...a specter, a walking corpse."

Her tears flowed freely washing out the pain.

"All he wanted to do was protect me," Zeeta said, sniffing. "Yet I set my child out as food for wild dogs and jackals. I deserve to die for what I did. Yesterday, when the men were beating me, I decided if the men didn't kill me I would throw myself in the river."

"But instead you came to the gate of the *Christianoi*."

She seemed perplexed. "Yes, and I do not know why."

Rivkah leaned forward and kissed her damp cheek. "I do."

## ~ 48 ~

*"If anyone purifies himself...then he will be a vessel for noble
use, consecrated to the master of the house, and ready for
any good work."*

—2 Timothy 2.21

"What god's do you worship?"

A wistful look filled Zeeta's eyes. "In my home village we
made offerings at the temple of Targitoas, offspring of Zeus and
founder-god of the Scythian people. The women and girls also
went to the shrine of Tabita. The Greeks know her as Hestia and
the Romans call her Vesta. She is the goddess of the home and
hearth."

"And now?"

"Since the day Cretorius took me away from my village, I
have believed in nothing. The gods men make have no power
except what they give them."

Zeeta seemed surprised when Rivkah agreed. "No matter
how ornate, those gods all come from people's imagination. Man
can never breathe life into metal and stone."

"So why bother to ask?"

"Because if these man-made gods did not create this world,"
Rivkah asked with a sweep of her hand, "who did?"

"I sense you believe you know the answer."

"Suppose there was an Almighty Being of indefinable power
who spoke the heavens and earth into existence? Created every
plant, animal and person. A God who knows our every thought...
whose power surrounds us like the air we breathe?"

"I would hope with all my heart there were no such being."

"What a strange thing to say."

"Is it? Gods judge people's lives and actions. Nothing could
be hidden from such a being. That is a terrifying thought."

"Fear of the Lord is the beginning of wisdom," Rivkah said.
"Instead of a frightful judge, suppose he was a loving Father who
wanted only good things for his children and craved their love?"

"Even if such a god existed, how could we ever be worthy of his love?"

"We could not. We call ourselves *Christianoi* because of our belief in a man, Iesous, who was the *Christos*, the Anointed One... to the Jews, the *Mashiach*. He was the Son of God who came to us so we might know his Father and have eternal life."

"That is all well and good for you, but he would want nothing to do with the likes of me. Would such a God approve of the things I have done?" Zeeta shook her head. "No. I turned my son out. I was no more a mother than I was a wife."

"He will forgive you everything."

She patted Rivkah's hand. "It is a kind thought, but I am undeserving of forgiveness."

Rivkah told her stories of Iesous. She spoke of his atoning death and his promise of eternal life to those who believed in him and kept his commandments.

Zeeta smiled as she listened, but when Rivkah offered him to her she shrank back.

"Check the central registry," Zeeta said through her tears. "My name is on the list of *licentia stupri*. I am a registered prostitute. Once entered, only death removes a name from the list. It is a brand I will carry to my grave. There is no forgiveness for one such as me."

"There is forgiveness and joy and peace, if only you will accept it. Iesous knocks at the door to your heart. Open it and let him come in."

"Do you renounce Satan and accept Iesous as your Lord and Savior?"

"I do."

The *ekklesia* usually demanded more preparation before a person's baptism, but Rivkah chose to make an exception in Zeeta's case. The Lord came upon her in a rush once she opened the door to him and, sensing her readiness, Rivkah took her to the pool reserved for baptism.

Rivkah girded her loins and waded in beside her. She

anointed her forehead with blessed oil and gently pressed her under.

A moment later Zeeta emerged a new woman. A light burned in her formerly lifeless eyes.

"I have a surprise for you," Rivkah said while Zeeta dressed. "There is someone I would like you to meet. He lives here on the compound and helps us with our work. He is called Pavlos and he also accepted Iesous' love."

Zeeta grinned as she knotted the girdle around her waist. "Anyone with such a name must surely be a dwarf."

"I will let you be the judge."

They left the Baptistry and followed the path leading to the former tool shed where Pavlos lived.

Rivkah knocked.

He opened the door, saw Rivkah, and smiled.

Zeeta gasped when she saw the huge man in the doorway. Her earlier gaiety vanished. She began to tremble.

Pavlos' eyes narrowed and the smile faded when he noticed the woman standing beside Rivkah.

He sometimes grew agitated when encountering unfamiliar situations. Rivkah saw his brooding expression and prayed she hadn't made a mistake.

Zeeta gave a piercing shriek of recognition. She took a tentative step toward Pavlos, then another. Dropping to her knees on the small stoop, she crawled to him, bowed low, and kissed his feet, washing them with her tears.

Pavlos shot Rivkah a terrified look.

She smiled her reassurance.

The big man's face gradually softened into a grin. He bent down and lifted Zeeta's face.

Between sobs, she repeated apologies and regrets and begged his forgiveness.

Pavlos shook his head and placed a finger over her lips, silencing her. He dried her cheeks with the hem of his sleeve and effortlessly scooped her into his huge arms. He held her close and rocked her like a baby.

Wracking sobs shook Zeeta's body.

Pavlos put his hand alongside her boney cheek and laid her head against his chest. He carried her over to a bench under the shade of a myrtle tree and sat down.

Rivkah left them there and headed back to the main compound. It was time to join the other *diakonoi* in preparing the daily distribution. As she turned the corner, she glanced back a final time.

Zeeta looked like a child snuggled in Pavlos' big arms. He continued rocking her, pausing occasionally to blot away her tears.

Rivkah waited until evening to tell Shemu'el what she had done. It didn't seem like something he should hear the moment his ship docked.

"Zeeta, the whore?" Shemu'el stroked his beard and grinned across the table at her. "This is a joke, yes?"

"No, it is not a joke. I did it while you were away at Ephesus."

Eyes dancing, he shook his head and chuckled. "I cannot believe you actually baptized Zeeta, the whore. My old nemesis is now part of my flock?"

"I worried you would be angry with me. But you said, 'I never need ask...go where my heart leads me and act as the Lord instructs me.'"

Shemu'el took her in his arms. "Angry? No, no...no. I could never be angry with you, my dove. The things you do never cease to amaze me." He laughed. "If that lion had any idea who he was up against, he would surely have chosen another flock to raid those many years ago."

Grinning, Shemu'el leaned his head back and stared at the ceiling. He spread his arms wide. "Did you hear the news, Lord? While I was away Rivkah baptized Zeeta, the whore. I didn't believe it at first either. What next? Will I someday come home to find she has charmed the Emperor himself into our humble Baptistry?"

## ~ 49 ~

"Have I been forever damaged?" Eleana tied her loincloth and ran a hand over her swollen belly. She reached for her tunic wishing it wasn't so tight. She'd begun sewing new, larger ones. They seemed big as tents when she turned the fabric in her lap.

Phaidra wiped her hands on a towel. "Despite the abuse, it appears you suffered no permanent damage."

"Easy enough for you to say."

"I was referring to your body, not your spirit." Phaidra motioned her into a chair. "We need to talk."

Eleana settled into the chair and nervously adjusted her cloak.

"Have you ever asked yourself where the essence of womanhood lies?"

Eleana admitted she had not.

"There are many stages in a woman's life...girl, young woman, wife, mother, grandmother. The characteristic in all of these is nurturing and caring. This is the true essence of the female species. Did your mother celebrate the day you received your womanhood?"

The memory brought a smile to Eleana's face. "My friends and I had cakes and spiced wine."

Phaidra nodded. "But were you truly a woman on that day?"

Eleana admitted she was not much different than the day before.

Phaidra took Eleana's hand. "You are poised on the threshold of understanding the secrets of the universe. Only by giving birth can you truly understand how special it is to be a woman."

Eleana appeared less than convinced.

"Let the men drink their wine and boast over their puny accomplishments; it is all they have. As daughters of Eve we are the truly special ones, the creatures through which God brings forth new life. Not even the angels in heaven can do what a woman does."

Phaidra gathered her materials and packed them in her bag. She paused to glance back from the doorway. "You know, destroying this child will only bring you further grief."

Anger flashed in Eleana's eyes. "I see Channah told you of my plan even though she promised not to."

"She said nothing. I have been a midwife long enough to know what goes through a woman's mind in a situation like this." She returned to kneel beside Eleana. "Nothing happens by chance. You have been given a gift of indescribable worth. I beg you do not do what you know in your heart to be wrong."

"I've grown tired of being told what to do." Eleana tapped her foot and fidgeted in the chair. "Everyone keeps saying 'Eleana do this; Eleana do that.'" She waved a hand in the air. "'Go here. Go there.'"

She covered her face and sobbed. "Why does no one ask, 'What would you like, Eleana?'"

Phaidra reached for her, but Eleana shoved her away.

"Do not be ashamed because you weep. Carrying a child intensifies a woman's emotions and you struggle under a difficult burden. God placed this life within you for reasons known only to him. At a time such as this it is not what Eleana wants, but what God wants. Let us pray and reason together. There may be a solution, an alternative."

"There is only one answer to my problem."

"Give God time to speak to your heart. I said there may be another path." Phaidra caught the young woman's eyes and held them. "I never promised it would be an easy one."

**Jerusalem—**

"What do you mean you cannot attend me when I deliver my child? You are my midwife; that is what you do."

"I already told you, I will be away," Siphrah said. "I am going to stay with my younger sister in Joffa for a month."

Hadassah's voice grew whiny with disappointment. "But you were with me when Sarit came. I counted on you being here for this child as well. I do not feel safe without you."

Siphrah patted Hadassah's shoulder. "You worry needlessly. Idriya is the one who trained me in the art of midwifery. Trust me, she will attend to all your needs."

"I do not want someone new. Things went so well with Sarit. My mother has gone to Antioch; I want you here with me again."

"Ah, but we do not always get what we want." Siphrah concentrated on packing her bag. "Idriya's skills are second to none. Ask around, your friends will tell you what I say is true. She has delivered half the children in Jerusalem."

Hadassah sighed in resignation. "Since there is no way to change your mind, I suppose what will be, will be."

Siphrah smiled from the doorway. "Relax. You had no problems with Sarit's delivery. This one should be no different. When I return to see the baby you can tell me how easy it went. We will look back on this day and laugh."

**Antioch—**

Channah went directly to the compound when she returned from her trip to Ephesus.

"Come, I have something to show you." Eleana led her to the windowsill. "Here are my bowls of grain."

Channah wrinkled her nose.

"You do not know what they are for, do you?"

"I have no idea."

Eleana laughed. "Why should you? A few days ago I would not have known either. Phaidra told me to put a scoop of soil in each bowl and plant kernels of wheat in one and kernels of barley in the other."

"And then what?"

"Each morning when I pass water I catch some of it and use it to water my grains."

Channah arched an eyebrow. "Well, that explains the odor. What purpose does this serve?"

"Phaidra says they will tell me the sex of my unborn child. If the barley germinates, I am carrying a girl." She lowered her eyes and her voice dropped to a tight whisper. "Wheat indicates it is a boy."

"Does it matter which germinates?"

"Very much. I refuse to bear the Red Man's son." Eleana lifted her chin and tossed her hair aside. "I will carry this child to term only if it is a girl."

"Have you told Phaidra this?"

"No."

Channah saw the resolute set of her friend's jaw and knew any plea she made would fall on deaf ears.

Eleana caught Channah's hand as she turned to leave. "Pray with me over my bowls of grain before you go."

"Wouldn't it be better to pray over your womb? That is where the baby is."

"True, but the key to my future lies in one of these bowls."

## ~ 50 ~

*"Do not repay evil with evil or reviling with reviling, but on the contrary bless..."*
— 1 Peter 3:9

Zeeta moved into the converted shed with Pavlos. She had what she'd always dreamed of, a life free from prostitution spent caring for her son. For his part, if such a thing were possible, Pavlos seemed to walk a little taller with Zeeta around.

It surprised Rivkah to one day hear the sound of conversation as she approached their modest dwelling.

"I thought I overheard you conversing with someone as I came up the walk," she said when she and Zeeta were alone.

She smiled. "Yes, Pavlos and I were talking."

"He speaks?"

"In a way only I can understand. But, yes, when no one else is around he sometimes speaks." She bit her lip. "He trusts me because I am his mother." Zeeta took Rivkah's hands. "I am so blessed. This is more than I dared imagine."

Rivkah's first inkling of coming trouble appeared in the form of Xenia, one of the Jewish women in her district. She noticed Xenia watching her come down the street and stopped to greet her.

Xenia returned her *"Shalom Aleichem"* with a snort and spat at Rivkah's feet. "I watch you come and go each day. You arrive here with baskets overflowing and leave with them empty."

"I distribute food to widows, orphans and the elderly, those who cannot fend for themselves. This is as the Law demands."

"Law? What right do you have to speak of the Law? The Law was given to the Jews and you distribute your goods to *goyim*."

"I distribute to the needy without prejudice."

Guessing Xenia's motives, Rivkah motioned Pavlos to her side. She drew back the cloth covering one of the baskets he carried.

Xenia's eyes widened when she saw the rows of fresh loaves neatly stacked in the basket. Uncovering another, Rivkah showed her an assortment of fruits and vegetables. They seldom had meat, but today's allotment was particularly generous. Rivkah's son, Yo'el, donated several lambs from his flock and her basket held meaty pieces fresh from the spit.

"We have plenty. Would you like to take something home for your family?"

Xenia lifted a hand as if she might reach into a basket, hesitated for a moment, then pulled it back. Her lip curled into a sneer. "Everything you have is unclean, fit only for heathens. I would not defile my home with provisions from that brothel you call your compound."

Rivkah grappled with her words before their meaning became clear. After Zeeta settled in with Pavlos, she began slipping out some nights to mingle with the city's prostitutes. She told them her story and the good news of Iesous' transforming love.

Several of these women had accepted Iesous' call, left their life of sin, and were baptized. They now lived a new life at the Christianoi compound where they cooked and baked, wove cloth and cared for the young children. Perhaps because of experiences during their time of service, these women exhibited a special tenderness toward the orphaned, abused and abandoned.

"We offer love to all and salvation through Yeshua," Rivkah said. "The women you refer to have sinned and repented as we all must."

Xenia covered her ears. "Do not speak to me of that *sheker*, Yeshua. When the true *Mashiach* comes he will sweep you away like dust before the wind."

"The way of God is love, not hate."

"Why don't you go back where you came from? They drove you out of Jerusalem because of your heresy so you came here telling your lies. You visit the synagogues and abuse our hospitality by trying to draw our people away. Though a Jew by birth you consort with all manner of Gentiles...even members of the Roman army."

"Jew or Gentile counts for nothing," Rivkah said. "We are all children of the same loving Father. Our leader, Petros, says God accepts all who fear him and do what is right."

"I have watched your people scour the riverbanks for infants. Do you think no one knows what you are up to? You scavenge these castaways and take them into your group, filling their heads with your strange beliefs so you can increase your numbers."

"If it bothers you to see this, why not rescue them yourself? Judaism is a legal religion under Roman law. You have the same rights we do."

"What will you do when your stores are depleted and your baskets empty?"

Rivkah told Xenia the story of Yeshua feeding the 5,000. "So you see," she said as she finished, "with Yeshua the basket is never empty."

"Enjoy it while you can. Do you think you can mock the Most High forever? HaShem is patient and slow to anger, but he will exact his retribution.

Rivkah's encounter with Xenia remained on her mind. She mentioned it the following day while they sorted the daily distribution.

"It is no wonder we face animosity from some of the Jews," Eleana said. She'd begun helping them every afternoon. "When the Christianoi came to our village they drew away members of the synagogue. Lifelong friends shunned us. People refused to trade with us. That is why we established our own settlement. Even today, with my parents dead, and after all that has happened, my three brothers refuse to speak of me."

"Many pagans have joined our community as well," Channah said, "including a number of slaves. Even though we preach obedience, it has to make their owners uneasy. These slaves now profess a higher loyalty to Iesous than that of a slave to his or her master."

Zeeta lugged over a basket filled to overflowing and plopped it onto the bench. "Three evenings a week I visit the city's harlots. Each time one accepts the Word of the gospel, that is one less woman to serve the base desires of pagan men."

Marcelina glanced up and shook her head. "You may drive up the price of pleasure, but you'll never shut down the trade. The world's oldest profession will continue to flourish so long as men reject truth in favor of gods who romp and cavort like rutting stags."

"We must learn to accept the tares among the wheat," Rivkah said.

Her heart swelled as she thought about the good things they'd accomplished in their time in Antioch. She looked around the room with pride. "We really have made a difference here, haven't we?"

Everyone agreed the future looked bright. Women were gradually being shown the dignity due them. Masters no longer abused their slaves with impunity. *Christianoi* performed good deeds with no expectation of return.

Rivkah busied herself arranging vegetables in the baskets. Yes, she thought, things truly had changed for the better.

"By and large, the members of our congregation are upstanding, loyal citizens...virtuous, hardworking husbands and wives. Yet the nonbelievers still hate us," Zeeta said.

"Let them," Marcelina replied. "We're an army on the march, gaining new ground each day. Look around you. Believers serve in Caesar's legions, produce utilitarian items for everyone's use, and our merchants provide honest weights and measures. The kingdom of God flourishes."

# ~ 51 ~

The rhythmic tap of Channah's sandals echoed in the narrow corridor. She reached Eleana's room and knocked. "Eleana? It's Channah."

No answer.

A sense of foreboding rippled through her. Eleana seldom left her room except to walk in the garden or help the *diakonoi* in the kitchen.

She knocked again. Getting no response, she tried the door. It squeaked as it swung aside on its hinges. The smell of stale urine wafted out to greet her. She squinted into the room's shadows.

"Eleana, are you here?"

Walking by memory, Channah crossed the room and groped for the drapes. In the darkness her foot struck something on the floor. Shards of broken pottery clinked against each other.

She threw open the drapes and studied the broken bowl lying at her feet. Icy fingers of fear tiptoed up her spine. Channah knelt and poked among the shards. Her stomach dropped when she moved aside the clump of soil the bowl had contained. Pale green sprouts poked out from the tips of swollen kernels of wheat.

*Eleana was carrying a boy.*

Channah leaped to her feet and ran back down the hallway. She checked the sanctuary as she passed, but found it empty. She hurried into the kitchen.

No Eleana.

She left the building and dashed across the lawn, scattering peacocks. She checked the gardens, didn't find her, and headed for their favorite bench beside a grove of cedars.

No Eleana.

Turning, Channah ran down the drive and headed for town. She roamed up one street and down the other, desperately

searching for Eleana. Fears, prayers, and gruesome images
crowded her mind as she walked. Time was running out. She
couldn't visit every midwife in Antioch.

She stopped at a house. Blotting her damp forehead, she
took a deep breath and knocked. "Eleana," Channah blurted out
when a woman opened the door. "I'm looking for a young woman
named Eleana. Has she been here?"

"I have seen no one by that name."

The woman called her back when she turned to leave.

"Why do ask? Does someone require a midwife?"

"No." Channah lowered her eyes. "Eleana does not wish to
have the child she carries."

"Hmm, I see." The woman stroked her chin. "Desmos does
that sort of thing," she said and gave her directions.

Channah scanned the streets for Eleana as she jogged to
Desmos' home. She turned a corner, glanced up the street, and
came to a halt. Far down the street Eleana headed toward her.
Channah slipped into an alley.

Head down and her veil pulled over her face, Eleana came
toward her taking long, purposeful strides. She approached the
alleyway and slowed before crossing.

Channah stepped out to block her path.

Eleana took a posture of defiance, chin set and arms folded
across her chest. "What are you doing here?"

"Shouldn't I be asking you that?"

"It is no secret why I am here. Get out of my way."

When she tried to push past, Channah grabbed Eleana's
arm and fell into step alongside her. "I went to your room. I saw
the wheat."

"Then we have nothing to talk about, do we?"

"This baby is not yours to keep or throw away as the mood
suits you. All life belongs to the Lord."

"Surely you do not think I want to do this. I have no choice."

"Of course you have choices. Just because you do not wish
to keep this child does not mean you must kill him. There are
those who will take him, train him up, nourish and love him."

Eleana ceased struggling against Channah's grip. She stared

her in the eye. "The Red Man's son will never suckle at my breast."

"He doesn't have to."

"This isn't your problem. Go back to your mother where you belong." Eleana shoved her aside and continued on her way.

Channah chased after her. "In your heart you know this is wrong. A mother cannot forget the child of her womb. This will haunt you the rest of your days."

"What chance do I have of ever forgetting the Red Man if I do not rid myself of his child?"

"I know you are a Hellenist and grew up speaking Greek. In Hebrew we have a word for God forming us in our mother's womb, *raqam*. It also has a second meaning."

"And what would that be?" Eleana asked with a frustrated sigh.

"It refers to fine needlework or embroidery." Channah touched her friend's shoulder. "Don't you see? God carefully weaves each of us into this tapestry of life. It would be a grave sacrilege to pluck a single thread from the curtain that guards the Holy of Holies. The hands of men made this beautiful work which hangs in the Temple. The hand of God formed life within you. How much worse would it be to tear *his* handiwork apart?"

Spinning away from her, Eleana begin walking again. "Why won't you leave me alone?"

"Because I want you to understand that a child in the womb is a holy spark, a sanctification. God is using this child to draw good from evil."

Eleana rested her hands on her hips and glared at Channah. "Suppose our roles were reversed? What would you be doing and saying then?"

"You want me to say I would also destroy the life which lived within me. Well, I will not say it. If such a thing happened, I pray I'd have the strength of character I now wish for you."

Channah begged God for a solution and one came to her.

"What if you never had to see the boy? Let me assist when it is your time to deliver. I'll take him from Phaidra, wrap him in a blanket, and spirit him away."

Eleana shook her head. "You are grasping at straws. There is no way you can feed him."

"True, but a wet nurse could." She took her friend's hands in hers. "Eleana, women die trying to rid themselves of an unwanted child. Your life, and your baby's life, are both too precious to throw away like this. Don't do it. Together we can work this out."

Shemu'el pulled Rivkah aside. "Should I go with you?"

"No. Petros is busy; you are needed here."

He frowned. "Others have reported confrontations. Tensions in the city are on the rise."

Putting a hand to his cheek, Rivkah stretched up and kissed him. "You worry too much."

"You should not go into the worst parts of town unprotected."

She laughed. "Unprotected? I have Pavlos beside me."

Shemu'el's lips tightened. "You know I have reservations about the big man."

"Nonsense, Pavlos is my friend, my security."

"No one knows what goes through his mind. He's a demoniac who can't speak and doesn't respond to those around him. Petros has anointed him and prayed over him to no avail. This demon Pavlos carries refuses to relinquish its hold on him."

"You worry needlessly." She rechecked her basket and folded a cloth over it. "I must go."

"Take someone with you."

Rivkah smiled. "I always do, Pavlos."

Dark clouds gathered on the horizon as Rivkah and Pavlos strode the *Via Caesera*. The afternoon light had a peculiar cast to it and the air smelled of earth and moss. She whispered a quick prayer, asking God to allow them to complete their daily distribution before the rain began. Preoccupied with the threat of a coming storm, Rivkah failed to detect the danger lurking in the next alley.

She thought of Shemu'el's comment about the rising

tensions in the city as they walked. The *Christianoi* had come offering love and peace, yet at every turn encountered hatred and violence. Their preaching and conversions angered as many as it saved.

Phaidra's outreach among the midwives diminished the practice of infanticide and Zeeta moved through the meanest neighborhoods without fear, seeking out women trapped in the web of prostitution.

But the wives of influential men still whispered against them. To Rivkah, these murmurs and gossip felt hauntingly familiar. That was how it began in Judea. They'd been persecuted in Bethlehem, encountered it again in Jerusalem, and now it had found them here in Antioch.

Yet all was not gloom and doom. Eleana's baby was due any day. Thinking of it sent a tingle of excitement rippling through her. She felt as if she were about to become a grandmother again.

Rivkah tried to understand why their efforts to rescue unwanted children raised people's ire. The pagans of the city treated these babes as if they had no value, tossing them away like spoiled fish or rotting vegetables for dogs and vermin to eat. Yet they resented the *Christianoi* rescuing them.

In their heart of hearts these men and women knew better. Since the *Christianoi* came, they were forced to face the truth. Now each time they saw the robust youngsters the *ekklesia* had rescued and they must ask themselves, "*Is that boy mine? Could that lovely girl be the daughter I tossed over the embankment?*"

Rivkah smiled. Despite the opposition, they'd made a difference. The gnawed bones and bloated corpses of unwanted children no longer littered the riverbank and trash heaps. Fewer women degraded themselves in the beds of strangers. They had proclaimed the sanctity of life, the dignity of women and children, and the honor of all men, slave and free, just as Iseous commanded.

## ~52 ~

*"Do not wonder, brethren, that the world hates you."*
                                        — 1 John 3:13

Pavlos disappeared into the bushes, heading for the riverbank. He might have heard the whimper of an infant, or perhaps he had to relieve himself. Either way, he did this often enough that Rivkah paid no heed. She continued on her rounds knowing he'd rejoin her momentarily.

Rivkah had gone only a short way when she heard a child whisper her name. Turning, she noticed a youngster lingering near the entrance to an alley.

"Did you call to me?"

The child gave her a mute stare.

She transferred the basket she carried to her left arm and approached him. "Do I know you?"

The boy inched back as she approached. At the corner he slipped down the alleyway.

"You need not be afraid. Are you hungry?" She quickened her steps, hoping to catch up with him. "What is your name?"

Rivkah scanned the deserted alley. The child had vanished. Could she have imagined him? She was still squinting into the shadows when a hand shot out of a doorway and snatched her wrist.

Rivkah tried to jerk free, but spilled the items in her basket instead. "Now look what you've done," she snapped. "There are hungry people waiting for that food."

She tried to lean over to retrieve the goods she dropped.

Her arm was twisted, forcing her back up.

Rivkah cried out in pain.

Footsteps reverberated in the alleyway. Another set of hands grabbed her from behind.

"This is the one he wanted," a man's gruff voice said.

Rivkah's heart pounded in her chest. She glanced around, desperately searching for Pavlos. Where was her protector?

They tore the basket from her arm and flung it aside. The man holding her other arm wrenched it against her back.

Rivkah sensed something moving toward her in the shadows. An ominous figure materialized out of inky darkness. The other two fanned back as he approached. The man stopped a few feet from her. He leered at her with a sinister grin.

"Who are you? What do you want?"

"All in due time." He looked her over and chuckled deep in his belly. "You're a good *Christianos* woman, not one of those whores from the compound. We'll have to teach you how to please a man." He winked at his partners standing behind her. "Many men, hmm?"

Rivkah began to tremble. She swallowed hard and whispered a prayer.

The men laughed and made crude suggestions.

Rivkah struggled to free herself from their grip.

"You won't need this." He grabbed her veil and whisked it away.

Rivkah started to protest, but a fist crashed into the side of her face before she got the words out. Stars and bright colors flashed in her left eye. Wincing in pain, she staggered and collapsed against the men holding her arms.

They caught her and pitched her back up.

She struggled to see her assailant's face. Tears poured out of her left eye, making it impossible to focus. Her head throbbed. She trembled and begged the Lord for strength...and for Pavlos, her security.

"Why are you doing this?"

"Some people in this city have grown tired of you *Christianoi* and your strange ideas. Since you are so eager to convert the prostitutes, they decided you might enjoy being one yourself." He reached for the binding on her cloak. "Let's see what you have under here."

Scarcely breathing, she watched his hand approach. Her right eye focussed on the man's mangled hand and his three claw -like fingers.

*Gamma!*

Running footsteps and heavy breathing sounded on the main street. The dark outline of a hulk of a man filled the alleyway.

Rivkah saw Pavlos' image reflected in Gamma's eyes.

A look of terror swept across his face. "Quick! Kill her," Gamma shouted.

One of the men released her arm and bent to pick up a club.

Pavlos barreled into the man holding Rivkah sending them both sprawling in the alley. He threw himself over Rivkah, taking the blow intended for her.

Sheltered beneath him, she heard the hollow thump of the club crashing against his back.

Pavlos leaped up. He grabbed the man who'd been holding Rivkah and flung him against the wall of the building.

The man smashed into the bricks, swayed, and collapsed. He lay on the ground moaning and holding his head.

Pavlos spun to face the other man. He yanked the club out of his hand and snapped it in two.

Gamma rushed over. Leaping onto Pavlos' back, he began pummeling him.

The other man grabbed one of Pavlos' arms.

Pavlos pulled Gamma over his shoulder and slammed him to the ground. He spun around to deal with the man gripping his arm.

Bleeding and disoriented, Rivkah tried to crawl away.

She'd gone only a short way when Gamma overtook her. He shoved his hand into the neckline of her tunic and ripped it open.

She grabbed at the material, trying to cover herself.

Dropping to his knees, Gamma began punching her.

Covering her face with both arms, she rolled on the ground. She knew she must escape Gamma's fists. Ignoring her pain, Rivkah pushed herself up and tried to run.

Gamma snatched her ankle in his claw-like grip and jerked her foot out from under her.

The pavement flew up to meet her. Pain exploded inside her head. For an instant, she imagined her skull splitting apart like an eggshell.

Then everything went black.

Pavlos turned and saw Rivkah lying unconscious on the ground. He let out an ear-piercing shriek and headed for Gamma.

The man's eyes widened in terror. He scrambled to his feet and raced down the alley.

Pavlos pursued him, but the smaller man outdistanced him and escaped.

Ignoring Rivkah, the other two used the big man's absence as an opportunity to flee.

Pavlos prowled the maze of alleys growling and flexing his fists as he searched for Gamma. When he realized his quarry had eluded him, he retraced his steps and returned to Rivkah's crumpled form.

Pavlos dropped to one knee and gently shook her.

She didn't respond.

Rolling her over, he brushed back her disheveled hair and dabbed her bloodied face with his cloak. He softly tapped her shoulder. He waited a moment and, when she didn't respond, tapped again. Only then did he notice that her ripped clothing had fallen aside leaving her almost completely exposed.

Taking the jagged edges of her torn tunic in his fingers, Pavlos carefully fit them together. He sat back against the wall and lifted her into his lap. After smoothing her tunic a second time, he rocked back and forth and sobbed.

That was how he was when the soldiers found them.

## ~ 53 ~

The Legionnaire saluted. "We have an injured woman. Where do you want her?"

Atticus swung the clinic door back. "Over there on the table."

A man entered cradling Rivkah's battered body in his arms.

Atticus gasped. "What happened to her?"

"We found her a few blocks from here in an alleyway," the commander said. "We have her attacker."

"What about him?" Atticus pointed to Pavlos who stood in the street, head down, shackled between two soldiers.

"He's the one who did this to her. We were headed for the city's prison when I saw your light."

Pavlos lifted his head for an instant, gave Atticus a pleading glance, then resumed staring at the ground.

"Dispatch one of your men to the compound of the *Christianoi*. Tell him to seek out Shemu'el Evodius and send him to me at once."

Atticus acknowledged the commander's salute with a quick nod and began assessing Rivkah's injuries.

Shemu'el burst into the surgery. His face glistened with sweat and his eyes were wild with fear. "I came as soon as I heard. How is she?" Still panting from the run, he approached the table to stand beside Atticus.

"*Koma*," Atticus said, "caused by *contusio cerebri*."

"Are there fractures?" Shemu'el slipped his fingers beneath his wife's hair and probed her scalp for injuries.

Atticus took his hand and gently removed it. "Hippocrates warned of the inherent danger in treating those whom we love."

"I cannot stand here and ignore her condition."

"You can and you will." Atticus' tone made it clear he gave

an order, not a request. "I have done a thorough examination and treated her injuries. Remain calm so I can provide you with my diagnosis."

He pulled aside the sheet exposing her nearly nude body. A lamp hanging from the ceiling cast a golden glow over her skin. Averting his eyes, Atticus said, "Her clothing was ripped and torn when the soldiers brought her in. Her loincloth appeared undisturbed so I made no examination. Phaidra can make a determination later."

Atticus tilted the lamp on its chains, illuminating various parts her body. "As you can see, she has scrapes and bruises on her arms and legs. I cleaned and bandaged them as needed."

Lifting her right arm, he loosed the wrappings and pointed out three curving welts on her swollen wrist. "Someone apparently restrained her by the wrist. My guess is she twisted it when she attempted to break free." He re-wrapped the sprain and swept the sheet back over her.

Rivkah's arms and legs suddenly went rigid. Her breaths turned to pants. Her eyes moved rapidly beneath closed eyelids and her head jerked from side to side as she convulsed.

"Hold her legs!" Atticus shouted. "I'll get the shoulders."

The two men held her down as she shook and trembled. After what seemed like half a lifetime, Rivkah's muscles relaxed and her breathing returned to normal.

The men's eyes met over her now still form. They released their hold in unison.

"*Spasticus*," Atticus said in reply to Shemu'el's unspoken question.

"When did it begin?"

"Best we sit down." Noting Shemu'el's hesitancy to leave Rivkah, Atticus rested his arm on his shoulder. "Come, my brother. We have time. The previous two were a quarter hour apart."

Shemu'el slumped forward when he sat. He dropped his elbows onto his knees and waited to hear what Atticus had to say.

"We must make provisions for her treatment. I can recommend several competent physicians from the *medicus* guild."

Shemu'el stared into his friend's eyes. "If I can't treat her, then I want it to be you."

Atticus bit his lip. "I am hardly dispassionate. I love Rivkah as a sister."

"That said, you are still the most experienced physician in Antioch. Put aside your reservations and do it for her."

Atticus seemed at a loss for words. He took a deep breath and let it out slowly. "Is this truly what you want, my brother?"

"It is. I would trust her to no one else."

"Very well, then it's settled." Atticus sighed. "She has severe trauma to the right side of her head."

"Is the skull fractured?"

"No, but her convulsing indicates pressure on the brain. She will require surgery to relieve it."

"Outside of a compressed fracture, I have never operated on the skull," Shemu'el said. "What about you?"

Atticus shook his head.

"With rest a contusion can heal itself," Shemu'el said in a low voice. "Perhaps we would be better served to wait."

"Several years ago I traveled to Rome and spent time studying with Cornelius Celsus."

"The renowned brain surgeon?"

"The same. I believe Rivkah's seizures are caused by an internal, bleeding bruise. Celsus treated such cases by opening the skull with a *trepannes* and allowing the fluids to drain. While in Rome, I observed several such procedures."

"You want to drill into her skull?" As a physician, Shemu'el understood the risks of such an operation.

"Her condition leaves us no choice." Atticus reached out and touched Shemu'el's hand. "She won't last the night seizing every quarter hour. With no way to anesthetize her, we'll require additional men to hold her down. You can assist, or observe, whichever you prefer."

"I will assist." Shemu'el thought for a moment. "Even with the surgery she will remain in a *koma*."

"And the strongest succumb in less than a week," Atticus

said, finishing the thought.

Rivkah moaned on the other side of the room.

Both men snapped to attention. They leaped out of their chairs and ran for the table when her arms stiffened.

They brought Rivkah home late in the evening. Petros came, anointed her and prayed over her.

The *ekklesia* began a vigil of fasting and prayer for her recovery.

Rivkah lay in the bed, her head swathed in a lopsided wrap of bandages. After penetrating her skull, Atticus had packed absorbent pads against the right side of her head to wick away the drainage. He stayed the night, changing her dressings each time they became saturated with a pinkish mixture of blood and cerebral fluid.

The flow diminished as the night wore on and by dawn the fluid ran clear. The immediate crisis had passed. Atticus tacked the scalp in place with sutures, placed a clean pad over it and re-wrapped her head. Having done all he could do, he began gathering his instruments.

Phaidra arrived and, after a whispered consultation with Shemu'el and Atticus, called Channah aside.

"Since you are the only woman in the household, you must be your mother's caregiver. Come, I'll show you what to do."

They went into the bedroom and Phaidra closed the door behind them.

Rivkah lay on the bed lost in deep slumber.

"Fold back the blanket and raise her clothing," Phaidra instructed.

Channah carefully eased the blanket aside. She lifted her mother's gown to the knees and glanced at Phaidra for approval.

"Higher."

She eased it up a few more inches.

Moving Channah aside, Phaidra said, "All the way to her waist. Watch now." She slipped an arm under Rivkah's knees, raised her lower body off the bed, and bunched the gown around her waist.

Channah stared in disbelief. "Why is she swathed like an infant?"

"The body continues to function even in a *koma*." Phaidra loosened the cloth around Rivkah's midsection and extracted a wad of damp rags.

Channah's hand quivered when Phaidra passed them to her.

"Take these to your father. He wishes to examine them."

Her cheeks turned shades of red. "Why would he ever do such a thing?"

Phaidra gave her an indulgent frown. "Being in a *koma* is like wandering in the desert. Your mother passes water, but drinks nothing. By studying the amount and color of her urine, a physician can estimate how near she is to death."

Channah left the room to make the delivery and returned wiping her hands on a towel.

Phaidra had a pad of folded rags waiting on the bed. "Use only the cleanest rags," she said, "and fold them as you would for a newborn. If they are pressed tightly against her body, the bed will not become soiled. Check often and change them each time she passes water. I will try to stop in several times a day."

She gave her an expectant look.

Channah took the pad and leaned over her mother. "I can do it."

Despite Zeeta's protestations of his innocence, Pavlos, had been flogged and chained in a dungeon. If Rivkah died, the Governor announced he would execute the big man for her murder.

To Shemu'el the circumstances of the attack felt all too familiar. This was the way it had begun in Jerusalem. A muttered curse here, an unkind word there. Someone's shop vandalized. He recognized this attack as the harbinger of things to come.

Bad things.

# ~ 54 ~

While Channah sat with her mother, Simon Petros gathered the elders at the compound to formulate a strategy. "Powerful forces are aligned against us. This attack on Rivkah is not an isolated incident. My experience in Jerusalem tells me others will follow."

Opinions were voiced around the table.

"We must be more careful in the future," one of them said.

"We should not be so open in our preaching."

"If someone is in danger, they need a way to find a safe house."

"How can we know who is trustworthy? We must develop a method to identify ourselves."

"I may have stumbled upon a way to do that," Shemu'el said. Rising from his seat, he took a piece of charcoal and drew two swooping lines on a piece of papyrus. His lines crossed then curved back up to meet at a point. He held it up, displaying the stylized image of a fish.

Head scratching and confused looks greeted his drawing.

"Watch now." Taking the charcoal he wrote the letters ΙΧΘΥΣ in a column beside the fish and spun it around for all to see.

"*Ikthus*," someone said. "Fish. What is it supposed to mean?"

Rather than give them the answer straight away, Shemu'el decided to let them solve the puzzle themselves. He aligned the scroll on the table and went to work. Starting at the top, he wrote additional letters alongside the first.

Using the *Iota*, he created the word Ιησους. Iesous.

The group watched with keen interest.

Using the next letter, *Chi*, he made the word Χριστος.

"*Christos*," someone said.

A sense of expectancy filled the air as Shemu'el scratched out another word. Beside the *Theta* he wrote Θεος.

"Theos." God.

The only sound in the room was Shemu'el's charcoal stick

marking letters on the scroll. He leaned aside so they could see. Using the *Tau*, he'd made Υιος.

"*Uihos.*" Son.

Shemu'el began the final word. Starting with the *Sigma*, he wrote, Σωτηρ. "*Soter.*" Savior.

Shemu'el held it up and moved his finger down the string of words. "Iesous the Christos, God's Son and our Savior." He glanced around the circle of elders. "He promised to make the Twelve *fishers of men*. What better symbol for *Christianoi* than a fish? We can use this as means to identify ourselves."

After the meeting Shemu'el retired to the sanctuary to pray. He lit a single lamp and knelt in the flickering darkness with his head bowed low. He'd been there only a few minutes when footsteps padded up behind him.

"What is it, Zeeta?"

Kneeling in front of him, she touched her forehead to the marble floor. "I am sorry to intrude, but I must speak to you about Pavlos. I came to beg for his life."

Shemu'el rocked back into a sitting position and rested his elbows on his folded knees. "I'm afraid there is very little we can say about Pavlos other than that he's guilty as charged. I tried to warn Rivkah, but you know how trusting she is."

"He is innocent. I swear he is. Pavlos would never harm your wife."

"So you've said again and again, but the facts speak for themselves. The soldiers caught him in the act."

Zeeta began to weep. "Don't let them take him away from me now that I finally have him back. Pavlos loves it here. He...we, are grateful for your generosity. Look at the progress he's made. He would never do anything to jeopardize what's been given to him."

Shemu'el tugged at his beard and sighed. "I suppose there's no way we can ever know what set him off."

"Let me have a few minutes with him and I can make sense

of this for you." She grabbed Shemu'el's hands. Wetting them with her tears, she kissed his fingertips. "Please. I beg you. Speak to your friend, Atticus. The magistrate will let me in if Atticus requests it. If I could just have some time to talk with Pavlos."

"Talk, Zeeta? Everyone knows Pavlos does not speak."

"But he can. Believe me, he can."

Shemu'el untangled himself from her grip. "With all due respect, there isn't time for these fantasies. Rivkah is at death's door. Right now I wish to be alone. If you truly want to help her, join the others in prayer."

"Have you been you talking to her?" Shemu'el asked when he returned to the house.

"Just as you instructed me to," Channah said. "How can you be sure she hears me?"

"People who have had head injuries and recovered say though they lay unresponsive and seemingly dead, they could still hear each word spoken beside them. We must keep her mind awake at any cost." He lifted Rivkah's hand and released it. It dropped like a lead weight. "Her body has already gone to sleep. If her mind slumbers, she will surely die."

"How was your evening?"

Shemu'el thought for several moments. "Informative."

He leaned over the bed and pressed his fingers against the arteries in Rivkah's neck. Her pulse beat harder now than it had in the morning. Straightening, he said, "I've had no supper. Carry on as you were while I eat."

"I'm running out of things to say. I've told her every story I know."

"Make up new ones. Sing Psalms. Pray. It makes no difference what you say, only that you maintain her interest."

Channah nodded and returned to her place beside the bed. She brushed a sleeve across her forehead and took her mother's hand in hers. "It is warm this evening, Imma. I will swab your face again." She swirled the cloth in a basin of cool water, squeezed it out, and patted her mother's face and neck.

"Have I ever told about the time Yaakov ate so many of the cucumbers you preserved in the crock that it made him ill?"

She smoothed her mother's hair and sat the basin aside.

"And you never knew, did you?" She chuckled. "Of course I will tell you about it. That is why I am here. It happened shortly after Hadassah married. It was market day and you had gone to Bethlehem taking Yudah along with you. Abba went to the field with the sheep as usual. Yo'el was away somewhere, leaving Yaakov and me at home alone.

"He dipped into the crock, pulled out a big cucumber and ate it. Then he ate another and another. He loves your pickled cucumbers. I told him he should not eat so many, but he ignored me. You know how boys are."

Channah leaned closer and lowered her voice. "Well, after the sixth one he..."

# ~ 55 ~

The change in Rivkah's appearance frightened Channah. In just three days she'd become a different woman, someone her daughter barely recognized. Having lost its tone, her skin shriveled and sagged. Her hollow cheeks resembled a corpse. And despite the emollient Channah applied to her mother's lips, they grew dry and cracked.

Every morning Channah boiled myrrh in white vinegar, filtered it, and scrubbed the floor to minimize the odor of sickness permeating the room. She spent her days dipping a cloth in cool water and patiently squeezing it drop by drop into her mother's mouth.

Despite these efforts, Rivkah's tongue swelled. Her breath stank. Her parched skin felt hot to the touch and she lay on the bed panting for each breath.

Atticus and Shemu'el entered the room.

Channah rose from beside the bed and stepped aside.

They examined Rivkah without comment, lifting the skin on the back her hand and watching it sag back until sinew and bones showed through. They placed their fingers alongside her jaw, felt her heart race, and tested her burning forehead.

Atticus loosened the wrapping wound round her head and checked the bandage covering the incision. He eased it back, allowing Shemu'el to see. Like the night before, it held only the tiniest hint of blood.

Shemu'el acknowledged him with a smile and a nod. Believing Rivkah could hear them, they never discussed her condition within earshot.

Channah handed them the latest pad when Atticus finished re-wrapping Rivkah's head.

They gave it a quick glance and left the room to confer.

Channah glanced at the pad they left on the table. The first few had been heavy with dampness and a pale, citron-yellow. As time went on they grew drier and darker, darker than she would have believed possible.

The door opened a crack and Atticus motioned her out. "I don't think I have to tell you your mother is dying," he whispered.

Channah sobbed.

He took her in his arms and she rested her head on his shoulder. "It is all in the Lord's hands now."

"How much longer does she have?"

"If not today, she will surely succumb tomorrow. Should she begin to convulse, send for your father immediately and gather your brothers."

A frantic knocking on the door came just as they finished their morning meal. Channah conferred with a youngster from the compound, then returned.

Her father glanced up with an inquiring look.

"It was a message from Eleana," Channah said. "Her travail has begun."

A look of panic swept across her face. Unsure what to do, she glanced into the room where her mother lay dying and then to her father.

"Summon Phaidra and go to your friend's side," he said. "That is what your mother would want. I will keep watch over her."

Channah hesitated a moment longer, then gave her father a quick kiss and raced away.

"Why isn't Phaidra with you?" Eleana asked.

"They told me she hasn't returned from an earlier call. A woman in distress."

"And what of me?" Eleana grimaced and clutched her abdomen. "Am I not also in distress?"

"Things seem to be progressing normally. There is nothing to worry about."

Eleana shook a finger at her. "I can hardly wait until you deliver your first child. See how you feel then."

She looked from Channah to the doorway and back again. "Where is Phaidra?" Eleana pounded her fist on the chair arm. "She should be here when I need her."

"She's assisting another. You will do fine until she arrives."

"I'm afraid, Channah. So very afrai—" Eleana squeezed her eyes shut and gritted her teeth when the contraction began. After it passed, she took a deep, cleansing breath and shook her head.

Channah stepped behind her. "Let me rub your shoulders. It will help you relax."

Eleana slapped her hand. "I am relaxed. Now get your hands off of me."

Channah caught her hand and tugged Eleana out of the chair. "Then let's walk around the room."

They'd only taken a few steps when Eleana clutched her stomach and slumped against her. "It hurts more than I ever expected it to," she groaned. She shot Channah an angry look. "This is all your fault. If I hadn't listened to you, I would not be going through this agony."

Channah led her to the bed and eased her into it. "Your attitude can't be helping. Try to stay calm. You have me here with you."

"For all the good it does me." Eleana choked on her laughter. "You know less about this process than I do."

"That's not true. I have delivered more lambs than you can count."

"Do I look like a ewe?"

"No. They never complained the way you are."

Eleana sucked in her breath and grabbed Channah's hand, squeezing with all her might.

"Focus on your body," Channah said.

"I am," Eleana moaned through gritted teeth. "And my body hurts!"

Channah folded a cool cloth and laid it on her forehead. "Remember what Phaidra told us about controlled breathing? On the next pain we will try breathing in unison. It will help. I know it will, just you wait and see."

Eleana muttered skeptically.

Channah prayed Phaidra would arrive soon.

*What if she did not?*

Channah briefly considered leaving to search for another midwife, but decided against it. She had promised to stay with Eleana, and she would no matter what.

**Jerusalem—**

Hebel wrapped Hadassah in his arms and kissed her. "Good morning, my lovely bride. Did you sleep well last night?"

She pushed him away with an angry grunt and rolled toward the wall, turning her back to him.

He stretched out his arm and stroked her shoulder. "It is not good to push your husband away." Hebel scooted close beside her and curled around her.

With some effort, Hadassah rolled to face him. She put both hands on his chest and shoved him away. "You know what happens when you lie close."

Hebel frowned. "Nothing happens which the Lord God did not intend when a man lies beside his wife."

"Another time, perhaps, but not now." She patted her swollen belly. "The midwife said no husband this close to my delivery. Until my purification, I am *niddah*."

Hebel spun in the bed and slammed his feet on the floor. "I only wished to hold my wife in my arms and tell her I love her. Unless of course, Idriya the midwife, has prohibited that as well."

As he did every morning, Hebel turned to face the Temple. He swung his *tallit* over his head, raised his arms, and recited the *Sh'ma*. Next, he prayed for his family, then that this day be a productive one. And, as he folded the prayer shawl, under his breath he begged HaShem, *Please let it be a son this time.*

I am a humble man, he thought, as he returned the *tallit* to its place on the shelf. I ask for very little. Surely the Almighty can do this one thing for his faithful servant.

Hebel extended his hand to his daughter. "Come Sarit, time for your morning meal."

He settled the girl at the table, giving her several small barley loaves, a cup of water and clabbered milk flavored with *debash*, grape juice boiled to a thick, sweet syrup.

"Will today be the day we get our new baby, Abba?" Sarit made swirls in the yogurt with her bread.

"If it is God's will, little one." He kissed her forehead. "Stay here and eat your food. I must check on your mother."

"Turn aside."

"Has the midwife also made it forbidden for a man to watch his wife as she dresses?"

"I am as big as a cow; I do not want you to see me. Besides, when you stare at my nakedness it makes me feel like a *zonah*."

"Then come to me, my beautiful harlot." Grabbing her from behind, Hebel chuckled and gently rocked her from side to side. "My Hadassah. You are the loveliest woman who has ever lived, more beautiful than Rachel or Ruth."

She rolled her eyes. "Such nonsense."

He lifted her chin and kissed her. "Your beauty would shame even the Lady Bathsheba."

Hadassah sighed and removed her gown.

Hebel sat on the bed giving her appreciative glances. Catching her hand, he tugged her close and rested his cheek against the bare roundness of her belly. "Your time is very near, my love." He kissed the place where the child grew.

She ran her fingers through his tangled hair. "I felt twinges during the night."

## ~ 56 ~

The merchant rocked the lamp in the palm of his hand, admiring its shiny turquoise glaze. "Very nice, and I like the wide base."

"I have other colors." Hebel raced into his shop and pulled down identical lamps in bright green, red and black. He lined them up on the table in a row for inspection.

"How do you get such lovely colors?"

Hebel beamed at the compliment. "All my glazes start out the same— sand, *pumicis*, seashells ground to powder and, of course, clay and water." He scooted the turquoise next to a green one. "These two are half-brothers. They both derive their color from powdered copper. For the turquoise I add wood ash, for the green I mix in powdered lead." He put the red lamp beside the black one. "The same with these. For the black I use iron filings; for the red, scrapings off a rusty piece of iron."

"Few potters bother to glaze something as commonplace as a lamp."

"I make them plain, too." Hebel scurried back to his shop and returned with several similarly shaped, terracotta lamps.

The merchant cupped his chin as he studied them.

"I will let you in on a little secret." Hebel leaned his elbows on the table and lowered his voice to a conspiratorial whisper. He spun his finger in a circle above the lamps. "I charge more for these colored ones because they take additional time and materials, but the wealthy ladies prefer them. They like to match the color of my lamps with the wall hangings in their rooms."

He straightened and shrugged. "And why not? What is money to them, heh?"

"I'll take six of each. Tomorrow my caravan heads south to Idumea and Nabatea. We shall see if the ladies there have the same vanities as those in Jerusalem."

The merchant's coins still jingled in his purse when his friend, Eli, arrived.

"How are you this fine day, my friend?" Hebel busied himself filling the empty spots on the shelf with more lamps and bowls. "You are not smiling, why?"

"Jepthah, the wine-seller, was found dead on the floor of his shop this morning."

Hebel gazed up the street in the direction of the wine-seller's shop. "He seemed well enough when I saw him last. How did it happen?"

"How do you think? Jepthah supplied wine to the Centurion's household."

"Well, of course he did. The Romans drink far more wine than the Jews ever will." Hebel shrugged and resumed stocking his shelves. "Why should he not sell to any who wishes to buy?"

"Because the *Sicarii* consider anyone who deals with the Romans a traitor." Eli pretended to grab someone by the neck and made stabbing motions with his hand. "They slip up from behind and thrust their blade between your ribs."

Hebel rubbed his chin as he reflected on this. "Then the High Priest and his cronies had best watch their backs. They have been in Rome's pocket for years."

"They know their names are on the list. Why do you think they surround themselves with armed guards everywhere they go?"

"List? What list?"

"The roster of those the *Sicarii* have marked for death." Eli shook his head. "How did it come to this, my friend? At night the city cowers behind locked doors, God-fearing men are afraid to leave their homes after dark. Oh, everyone seemed happy enough when the Romans and the Zealots battled it out in the countryside. Things are different now that it has become Jew killing Jew."

*Jew killing Jew.*

The words pierced Hebel like a double-edged sword. In the back of his mind he heard Imma Rivkah speaking those same words the day she left for Antioch. He'd promised her he would watch the signs and guard Hadassah and Sarit. He swore to be her sentry...then dozed at his post.

He glanced around in terror. They must leave Jerusalem right away.

Hadassah's voice intruded on his thoughts. From the doorway she said, "Hebel my time has come. Quickly, now. Take Sarit to the neighbor's and summon Idriya, the midwife."

"Listen to that lusty cry," Idriya said with a satisfied smile. "A healthy baby boy. Your husband will be pleased."

Her travail forgotten, Hadassah extended her arms. "Bring him to me. Let me hold my new son." She took the child from the midwife and put him to her breast. As he suckled she whispered a prayer of thanksgiving for her safe delivery.

Yes, she thought, Hebel *would* be pleased. Where was he? Midwives usually brought the husband in right after the birth so they could see that everything had gone well and beam with fatherly pride as the infant nursed for the first time.

Had Idriya even bothered to tell him he had a new son? Hadassah imagined Hebel huddled on the stoop, hugging his knees and praying. It didn't seem right for him not to know.

She didn't like Idriya's pinched face and domineering manner. "*True, she is old, but she has good hands,*" her friends had assured her "*She's caught more babies than any midwife in Jerusalem.*" One of them patted her shoulder. "*You will like her.*"

Well, Hadassah didn't. She would never call the old prune again.

"Why have you not brought my husband to me?"

"I will bring him in so you can tell him he has a son, just be quick about it." Her next words sent a quiver through Hadassah. "Do you know someone who can care for your baby?"

"I am his mother; I will care for him." She smiled and kissed the tiny infant in her arms. "Look, he's eaten his fill and sleeps soundly."

"I will fetch your husband now." The old woman wagged her finger. "But only for a short while, and then you must find someone to take the infant."

# ~57 ~

**Antioch—**

Eyes squeezed tight against the pain, Eleana rocked and moaned on the low birthing stool. Her contractions came quickly now, one melting into the next.

Channah stood behind her with her arms looped through Eleana's armpits whispering encouragement. "Soon...soon...soon. It will all be over soon."

Phaidra's voice came from somewhere near the floor. "I see the head. Now push."

Eleana rose in Channah's arms, sucked in a deep breath, and pushed with all her might.

The head emerged and Channah watched the midwife rotate the infant slightly.

Its shoulders followed.

Phaidra said, "Push again."

Eleana drew a breath and bore down a final time.

The baby slipped into Phaidra's hands and Eleana collapsed against Channah.

When Phaidra finished, Channah helped Eleana into bed. She settled back against the sheet and sighed with fatigue.

"The baby," Eleana said, glancing up at her friend with urgency. "Remember our agreement. You must take the child away."

Channah padded over to Phaidra and extended her arms.

The midwife knew of their agreement and handled her the bundle without a word.

Channah folded the blanket back. She found it impossible not to smile at Eleana's newborn son.

Eleana nervously watched from the bed.

Something urged Channah to look more carefully. The baby instinctively turned to her making sucking motions with his little mouth when she reached down and smoothed his hair. Turning her back to Eleana's anxious gaze, Channah slipped her hand into the blanket and caught a squirming foot. An instant later she sighed a prayer of thanksgiving.

Channah extended the wiggling bundle. "I have brought you your new son,"

Eleana turned to face the wall. "You have broken our agreement. Do not think you can change my mind. I will not have him. Take him away as you said you would."

"Hold him for just one moment. Then, if you ask me to, I will whisk him away. Do not reject this gift without knowing what it is you would be throwing away."

"You promised you would take him away." Eleana pounded her fist on the blanket. "Now do it!"

"Do you recall the day you spoke to me of Kyros, son of Telamon?"

Eleana gave her a wary look. "Yes...I remember."

"And how we spoke of how we dreamed of lying with our beloved and making love."

"Yes," Eleana said with growing hesitancy. "I said that. We both did."

Channah grinned. "But you did more than dream, you acted on those impulses."

"How dare you speculate about things which you cannot know. Kyros was a good man, I will not allow you to besmirch his memory. He would never intentionally lead me into sin."

"But you did, didn't you?"

"Why must you badger me like this?"

"It was before the Red Man came. But not too much before...a week, perhaps...no more than ten days." Channah gave her a hard stare. "When was it?"

"Yes, if you must know. A few days earlier we were walking in the meadow and..." Eleana's cheeks flushed deeply. "And one thing led to another. Neither of us planned it. We were caught up in the moment and lost our heads. Afterwards I was too ashamed to even look him in the eye. Then Red Man came and Kyros was dead. There. I've confessed; are you satisfied?"

Channah extended the bundle, forcing Eleana to take the baby.

Eleana held him at arm's length, resisting the urge to nestle him to her bosom.

The little boy stretched and flexed his fingers, reaching for his mother.

Channah knelt beside the bed and folded back the blanket, revealing the boy's face. "Touch his soft hair," she whispered. "And here on his chin, see the cleft? Now look at his little foot."

Eleana's fingers shook as she pulled out her newborn son's foot. At Channah's urging she spread the tiny toes revealing delicate webs of pink skin. She stared for a moment, frozen, then she gave a wrenching sob and kissed the tiny foot. "My little *batrachos*."

"The time in the meadow was our first time," Eleana said while little Kyros nursed. She swallowed the lump in her throat and gazed down at the newborn infant in her arms through joyful tears. "I never imagined anything could come of it. After my terrible experience with the Red Man, I pushed all memories of my time with Kyros out of my mind."

She squeezed Channah's hand. "Thank you, my friend. Were it not for you I would have thrown away the most precious gift anyone could have given me."

**Jerusalem—**

"My head is pounding, can you give me something for it?"

"Not now," Idriya snapped. "Lie still." She removed the rags she'd pressed between Hadassah's legs, cursed, and tossed them aside.

Hadassah glanced down at the floor and gasped. The rags were soaked through with bright red blood...her blood. She had not bled like this after Sarit's birth.

"What is happening to me?" Her choked voice was but a frightened whimper.

Idriya looked up from the bowl in which she'd caught the afterbirth. "The bleeding has not slowed as it normally does. Did you feel the womb contract when the child nursed?"

"Yes, but I remember it being stronger with my daughter."

The midwife grunted in acknowledgement. "Sometimes the afterbirth fails to pull away as it should and causes bleeding." She continued shaking her head and poking at the mass of tissue in the bowl. "This looks fine. I see nothing out of the ordinary."

"Then what is wrong?"

"I do not know." Idriya frowned. "Lie back in the bed and raise your knees."

Another wad of rags slapped against the floorboards.

Hadassah smacked at the midwife's hand. ""Stop! You are hurting me."

"Be still you little fool. I am trying to save your life."

"I cannot tolerate this pain."

Rising, Idriya rested a hand on the sheet beside Hadassah's head and leaned forward until they were eye to eye. "Do you imagine this is pleasant for me? At this point, we have no choices. You *can* tolerate the pain, and you will. I must massage your womb. It is the only way I have to stench the bleeding."

Returning to her place at the foot of the bed, Idriya oiled her hand a second time. "Take a deep breath and let it out slowly. Good. Again now. Relax and let my fingers pass."

Placing the other hand atop her abdomen, Idriya kneaded Hadassah's womb like a ball of stiff dough.

Hadassah squeezed her eyes shut. Clutching the bedding, she moaned in pain. Her complaints must have angered the midwife, Hadassah decided, when she felt her prod with increasing force. Why else would she hurt her so?

Idriya had rushed Hebel in and out before he could say a word and packed him off to their neighbor's house carrying his newborn son wrapped in a blanket.

She needed someone there to protect her from this awful woman. Hebel surely must have returned to his stoop by now. If I scream, Hadassah thought, he will hear me and come to my rescue.

She snatched up the thin blanket and stuffed it in her mouth, chewing on it to muffle her cries of pain. She could never look him in the eye again if Hebel saw her like this.

Blood gushed onto the sheet when Idriya removed her

hand. She grabbed more rags and packed them in place.

Hebel heard the latch on the door and jerked around. "How—"

"I need water," Idriya said.

He stepped inside to get the water jug and was shocked to see the midwife wiping her hands on a bloody towel.

If the midwife looked like this, what must Hadassah be like?

Idriya ran the cloth around her fingernails, scraping blood from under the cuticle. "And hurry," she commanded.

Hebel drew the water and rushed back.

"My wife," he begged. "How is my wife?"

The midwife finished dipping water into her bowl and shook her head. "She is not good. All women bleed after giving birth, but it quickly subsides. Hers has not. Nothing I have done seems to help."

Panic twisted Hebel's gut. "But you are the midwife, you know about women and birthing. Surely there is something else you can do."

"I have done all I know how to do." Idriya shrugged. "God gives and God takes. You have a healthy baby boy, a namesake, an heir. Be grateful."

"Can I see her?"

Idriya shook her head. "Not now. She is dozing. I will try again after she has rested."

Her next words made Hebel wince.

"Pray I succeed. She cannot last much longer bleeding as heavily as she is."

The old woman turned away and Hebel returned to his stoop. Each day for months he prayed for a son never realizing the price he would be asked to pay. Exchanging the life of his wife for a son was not a trade he wished to make.

Hebel suddenly leaped up, grabbed his cloak and dashed away.

# ~ 58 ~

Hadassah watched the midwife cross the room through heavily lidded eyes.

Idriya rested her hands on her hips and stared down at her. "The bleeding has not slowed. I must massage your womb again."

Hadassah gave a soft moan and turned her face aside.

Idriya removed the sopping rags and tossed them away. She began swabbing her right hand with oil. "Try to relax,"

Hadassah sucked in her breath when the midwife began. Pressure, then sharp pain, shot through her. Sweat poured off her face and ran down the small of her back. The room began to spin; spots danced in front of her eyes.

Waves of fright rippled through her. A sinister presence seemed to have sucked the air out of the room. It became increasingly difficult to breathe. She opened her mouth to scream, but no sound came out. Her eyes flicked around wildly, looking, watching, hunting for the presence looming around her.

*I know who you are. Show yourself!*

Though she couldn't see him, she felt his icy fingers wrap themselves around her heart. With no strength left to fight, Hadassah relinquished herself into the hands of the *Malakh HaMavet*, The Angel of Death.

Somewhere far, far away, Idriya, the midwife, sweated and kneaded and cursed, urging her to fight on.

Hadassah thought of her daughter Sarit and the nameless baby boy she would never know. Salty tears dripped from her closed eyelids and dribbled down her cheeks as she slipped deeper and deeper into darkness.

**Antioch—**

Channah took her mother's hand. "It's me again. Phaidra had

another call and for a time it appeared I might have to deliver Eleana's baby alone." She laughed. "Fortunately she got there in time. Eleana had a little boy. She is going to keep him. I will tell you the rest later."

She lifted her mother's frail hand to her lips and kissed it. Channah's eyes misted as she spoke. "I never really understood what you went through to give me life. This probably sounds silly, but I just never knew. I was so young when Yudah came that I never gave it a thought. Only now do I understand. Thank you, Imma. Thank you for everything."

Channah squeezed her mother's hand. To her surprise, she felt Rivkah's fingers tighten around hers.

Had she really felt it, or only imagined it?

Channah's heart swelled to bursting as she watched her mother's eyelids flutter and her cracked lips curl into a crooked smile.

**Jerusalem—**

Fear gnawed at Hebel's stomach and bitter acid scorched the back of his throat. He whipped through Jerusalem's narrow streets like the wind ignoring his burning lungs screaming at him to stop.

He pushed himself harder, running faster than he would have believed possible. The specter of impending doom hung over him, matching him step for step. The winner of this race would lay claim to Hadassah's soul. And no matter the cost, Hebel swore this was one race he would not lose.

How could he tell Imma Rivkah he let her daughter die? She'd entrusted Hadassah and Sarit to his care. Asked him to shield them. And what had he done? *I am as worthless as a broken pot*, Hebel thought.

He ran into an intersection without looking, heard hobnailed sandals clattering against the pavement, and snapped his head around in time to see a Roman detachment bearing down on him. His sandal caught on the uneven corner of a paving stone when he leaped aside, sending him tumbling into the gutter.

Undeterred, Hebel pushed himself up and brushed himself off. In seconds he was on the move again, careening through the crowded streets. He reached the Synagogue of Rabban Yeshua *HaMashiach* and pounded on the door with all his strength. A startled woman opened the door a crack and peered out. He laid an elbow against the heavy door and swept her aside.

Against all odds, he had made it. There was still a chance. Hebel stepped into the entryway and slumped forward, exhausted. Resting his hands on his bent knees, his chest heaved as he gulped in air.

Hebel glanced around. The Synagogue, surprisingly enough, appeared no different than any of the others he had visited. Holy scrolls in a cabinet, a few *tallits* hanging from hooks on the wall, rows of wooden benches, a table, altar, at the front. Somehow he had expected something more, something... different.

The dimly lit room was empty.

Hebel's heart sank.

A few years earlier this Synagogue had been a hub of activity, but no longer. Forced out by persecutions, none of the Twelve remained in Jerusalem. Simon Petros, their appointed leader, was now Bishop of Antioch. Yohan bar Zebedee, Yeshua's beloved disciple had quietly slipped away to Ephesus to protect Miryam. Mattithayu remained at Capernum in Galilee preaching to the Jews and laboring on his gospel. The rest of the Twelve had scattered far and wide, carrying the good news of Yeshua to the ends of the earth as he instructed them to do. Control of the Synagogue and the Jerusalem church now rested in the hands of Yaakov, known to all as *The Just.*

Hebel turned to the woman. "Yaakov," he gasped. He brought his hands together and bowed as he said the name. "The Holy Man. I must see him right away."

"He is praying."

"Please, this cannot wait. It is a matter of life and death."

At home Idriya urged Hadassah to fight, to hang on...to live.

She lay motionless in the bed, oblivious to the drama unfolding around her. Idriya's voice blurred and blended into the murmur of the street noises coming through the open window. Sheno longer felt the pain, or even the bed beneath her.

For an instant Hadassah felt all alone, more alone than she ever dreamed possible. In those depths of nothingness only her thoughts and memories remained. Memories that made her wish she could go back and change things. Live her life over. Better. But she knew it was too late now.

She recalled the hurt look on her mother's face the day she left. A hurt she had deliberately chosen to inflict on a woman who, right or wrong, never ceased loving her. Everything seemed so clear now, so simple. She should have gone to Antioch as her mother wanted her to. If she had, this evil midwife wouldn't be tearing her apart.

Why do we make so many bad choices, hurt the people we love, fight battles that don't need to be fought? Hadassah silently sighed. It no longer mattered.

Nothing did.

The woman led Hebel through the Synagogue and into the back of the building. They turned down a hallway and walked toward an open door. As they drew closer, Hebel heard a man's voice murmuring familiar words of prayer. They stopped at the doorway and she waved a hand toward the reed-thin man kneeling on the stone floor.

Hebel stepped in. He glanced around the sparsely furnished room as he waited for him to finish.

Seemingly unaware of his presence, Yaakov continued praying.

Hebel was surprised to hear his name, and Rivkah's and Hadassah's. How could a man whom he had never met be praying for his family? A few moments later Yaakov chanted a solemn, "*Omein.*"

He rose from his knees and hobbled toward him, smoothing

his plain tunic. "Stiff from kneeling," he explained with a humble smile.

Their eyes met and Hebel felt a loving warmth wrap itself around him. He threw himself at Yaakov's feet, hugged the man's ankles, and wept.

Yaakov touched him on the shoulder. "What troubles you, my son?"

"My wife lies dying. I came to ask you to pray for her safety."

Ya'akov helped him to his feet. "Tell me, have you come because you truly believe I can help, or because you have no other hope?"

"You have seen through me. I am not a member of your Way." Hebel hung his head, avoiding the man's piercing eyes. "I came because I had nowhere else to go."

His mother-in-law believed enough for them both, Hebel thought. Her belief was all he had to offer. Did that currency have value here?

"Imma Rivkah once told me some of your people have the power to heal the sick."

They walked the dim corridor side by side, heading for the door. "By Imma Rivkah do you mean the wife of Shemu'el who now resides in Antioch?"

"Yes. She is my wife's mother." Hebel grasped the holy man's hands. "Will you come? Can you help me?"

"Of course I will come and pray over Rivkah's daughter. Though I must warn you I have no control over life and death. Such power resides in God's hands alone."

Hebel could not look him in the eye. He bowed his head and confessed, "Imma Rivkah encouraged us to follow The Way of Yeshau, but we resisted. I am not worthy that God should grant me this request."

Yaakov threw an arm around Hebel's shoulder and grinned. "That is the miracle. None of us is worthy, yet God loves us anyway." He grabbed a walking staff leaning against the wall. "Show me the way."

Unseen hands supported Hadassah in the darkness. It reminded her of a day when the family went swimming. She was just a little girl and her father told her to lie back in the water. Though she was afraid, she followed his instructions and felt his strong hands beneath her. Trusting her father's strength, she relaxed and stared into the cloudless sky. Before she knew it, she was slowly drifting away from him.

Indriya slapped Hadassah's cheek. She shook her shoulders and called to her.

It was too late. The current had already carried Hadassah away.

290 E. G. Lewis

## ~ 59 ~

*"Is any one among you sick? Let him call for the elders
of the church, and let them pray over him, anointing him
with oil in the name of the Lord...and the Lord will raise
him up."*

— James 5:14

The smell of burning incense met them when they opened the
door of Hebel's modest home.

Leaving Yaakov in the front room, Hebel entered the
bedroom alone. What he saw made his knees buckle. The room
looked more like a slaughterhouse than a bedroom. Bloody rags
lay scattered across the floor.

The midwife's tunic had bloody smudges and smears all
over it.

Hadassah lay on the bed uncovered, arms at her side, eyes
closed...unmoving. She seemed to be sleeping peacefully. Then
Hebel noticed the wide, dark stain surrounding her hips. Blood
had wicked through the towel the midwife wrapped around her
and saturated the sheet.

Idriya stood beside the bed with her eyes closed, swaying
and mumbling strange incantations. She'd arranged smoldering
bowls of incense around Hadassah's limp form and placed a clay
image of Asherah, the Earth Mother, on the bed beside her. The
old woman raised her arms and let out a piercing wail.

Hebel gasped.

Both of her hands were covered with blood...Hadassah's
blood.

Idriya's eyes snapped open at the sound of Hebel's sobs.
"It's about time you came back. Your wife died. I could not save
her."

"You are no midwife; you are a butcher." Hebel pointed to
the bowls and statue. "Why are these here? What are you doing?"

"I'm helping her cross the great divide between the worlds."

"First you kill my wife then you defile my home with idols?"

Hebel grabbed the night pot and circled the bed, dumping the smoldering incense. When he had it all, he smothered it with water. The scented embers vanished in a cloud of steam with a hiss.

He grabbed a thin blanket and swept it over Hadassah's lifeless form. "Could you not at least have covered her? It is not decent to leave her exposed like this."

Yaakov entered the room and stepped around them. Kneeling in a corner beside the bed, he began to quietly pray.

"We do not need this," Hebel shouted. He snatched the statue of Asherah off the bed and flung it against the wall, shattering it.

Ignoring the screams, shouts, and shards flying about the room, Yaakov bent low to the floor and continued praying.

The old midwife curled her lip and eyed Yaakov suspiciously. "Who will prepare your woman for burial?"

"Not you." Hebel pointed to the door. "Be gone."

"Sometimes they do not wish to live." Idriya shrugged and gathered her things. "I did what I could. At least I gave you a healthy a son," the old crone muttered as she hobbled away.

Hebel knelt beside the bed and took Hadassah's hand. Her cool skin made his stomach clench. She seemed whiter than the bleached cloth on which she lay. He studied his wife carefully as Yaakov prayed, searching for even the tiniest sign of life. He licked his finger and held it above her blue lips, but detected nothing; the breath of life had left her.

His Hadassah was gone.

On the other side of the bed, Yaakov lifted bony fingers to the sky and threw his head back. The veins in his temples bulged and sweat beaded on his forehead.

Hebel rested his head on the bed beside his dead wife and wept. If only they had not arrived so late. Why hadn't he run faster, left sooner, tried harder?

Feeling a hand on his shoulder, Hebel lifted his head and stared into Yaakov's soft brown eyes.

"Faith, my son. Never loose faith." Yaakov rested a hand on Hadassah's forehead and traced what Rivkah called, *the mark of*

*Yeshua's immortal cross.* Taking her hand, he said, "Hadassah, in the name of Yeshua, Son of the Most High God, I command you, awake!"

Hadassah lurched on the bed. Her lips moved. She coughed, then sucked in air like a newborn taking its first, gasping breath.

A tingle of excitement surged through Hebel as he watched her chest begin to rise and fall in a steady rhythm. A healthy pink tone came back into her cheeks. He touched her hand and smiled. It felt warm.

Hadassah turned her head. She opened her eyes and glanced over at him with a surprised expression. "What are you doing here?"

Fright and confusion washed over her face as she ran her eyes around the small room. "What happened? Where am I?"

"Here with me where you belong," Hebel said, blinking back tears of joy.

"I...I don't understand. I left this room and went to the place of light." Her brow furrowed as she tried to piece together the confusing sequence of events. "And she was there...waiting to greet me."

"She? Waiting? Who was waiting?"

"My mother's mother, my namesake." Her eyes gleamed. "She told me of my mother, and of life. She was so beautiful, more beautiful than anyone I have ever seen. When I looked at her I saw Imma's love for me. There were others there too, many others." She sighed. "But now..." Hadassah brushed aside a strand of hair and gave him a bewildered smile. "Now here I am with you."

Hebel laughed and kissed her.

She gave a sudden start and patted her hands around the bed. "Where is my son? Tell me he was not a dream."

"He is fine." He touched her cheek. "Michal's mother is caring for him and little Sarit."

Hadassah rubbed her eyes and stretched as if awakening from a refreshing night's sleep. "How did I get here?"

"I brought Yaakov, the holy man from the Synagogue of Raban Yeshua. He prayed over you and summoned you back from the world of the departed."

Hebel glanced over his shoulder expecting to see the tall, gaunt man standing beside him. But he did not. Yaakov had done his work and slipped away.

Hadassah took his hand and pressed it to her lips. "Thank you, my love."

Hebel knelt and gathered the rags off the floor, dumping them on top of the ashes from the incense.

Hadassah watched from the bed and protested "Stop. That is woman's work. Besides, the blood will make you unclean."

He lifted his head and smiled at her over the edge of the bed. "A trifling price to pay for the blessings God bestowed upon us this day." He glanced around the chaotic room. "It would greatly disturb little Sarit to see the room this way. I will scrub the floor until it shines."

When he finished with the floor, Hebel carried away the scrub bucket and returned with a towel draped over his shoulder. One arm circled a basin of warm water. He had a large glass of cool water in the other hand.

He slipped an arm under his wife's shoulders and gently lifted her. He put the glass to her lips. "Drink, my love. You must be thirsty."

Hadassah took a long sip, then put the glass aside to massage her temples.

"Do you have an ache?"

"Just thinking." She took the glass and drank again.

"When you drink your fill," Hebel said, "I will change the bedclothes and bathe you."

Their eyes met over the rim of the glass. He expected her to protest; instead she gave him a confident smile. "That would be very kind. You are my husband. It is appropriate for you to see and touch me."

"Have you ever wished you had another wife?" Hadassah asked as Hebel bathed her.

"Another wife?" He disappeared from view for a moment when he bent to dip the cloth in the basin. Twisting it, he squeezed the water out and smiled. "Such a foolish question." He held her foot and swabbed the cloth along her leg. "I am a simple potter. How could I ever earn enough to support a second wife?"

She gave him a playful slap on the back of his hand. "I meant a different type of wife, silly. I wondered if you were displeased with me."

Hebel plopped the rag back into the basin without a word. He ran his hands down his legs, drying them on his cloak then took her face in his hands. Leaning forward, he gave her a long, lingering kiss.

"I knew what you meant. Do not trouble your mind with inconsequential worries. I will always love you more than words can tell."

"What about my moods and the times I complain?"

"What about when I come to supper hot and sweaty, smelling of the kiln?"

"Why should that bother me? I love you just the way you are."

Their eyes met.

"My point exactly."

After he changed the bedding, Hebel settled her back into the bed and covered her with a soft blanket. He was on his way out to retrieve the children when Hadassah called his name.

He paused in the doorway, looking back.

"I want you to know that I am sorry."

"Sorry? Sorry for what?"

"Sorry for everything. I will be a better wife from now on." She paused and stared at her fingers. Lifting her eyes, she gave him a tentative smile. "Things will change. I promise."

**Antioch—**

Rivkah made a slow, but steady recovery after she awakened.

She was unable to speak for several days due to her

dehydrated state and communicated with notes and hand signals. When she finally did speak, the first word she gasped was "*Gamma.*" The attack left big gaps in her memory, but she pieced events together well enough to have Gamma arrested and Pavlos exonerated.

Zeeta and Pavlos stopped to visit Rivkah the night they freed him from prison. He arrived carrying the soiled veil Gamma had torn from her head the night of the attack. He'd plucked it out of the dirt when he returned to find her unconscious and kept it with him in prison.

The big man's lips quivered when he saw Rivkah sitting up in the bed. He fell to his knees and they both wept while he kissed her hand and she patted his head.

Satisfied, Pavlos rose and quietly shuffled away.

Shemu'el stopped him at the door. "I...ah..." He cleared his throat and took a deep breath. "We should talk. Your mother tried to convince me of your innocence, but I ignored her pleas. Had I listened to what she had to say, you would not have spent so much time in a jail cell. I am deeply sorry and ask for your forgiveness."

Pavlos rested his beefy hand on Shemu'el's shoulder and gave it a soft squeeze. When he removed his hand he stared into Shemu'el's eyes. For an instant a wispy trace of a smile curled his lips then the big man's head dipped in a deep, respectful nod.

Turning, he left the house walking as he always did, head down and hands clasped in front of him.

## ~ 60 ~

*"...by the benign and gracious providence of God, Peter,*
*that powerful and great apostle, who by his courage took*
*the lead of all the rest, was conducted to Rome..."*
                              —Eusebius' History, Book 2, 14:6

"Can we walk in the garden?" Petros asked. "There are things I wish to say."

Shemu'el put aside his work. The two men crossed the compound's wide porch and followed a gravel path across the lawn. Sunlight filtered through the trees casting dappled shadows at their feet.

Petros took a breath of spring air and released it with a happy sigh. The former fisherman slowed to point out swallows soaring and diving above the meadow.

He'd seemed distracted for several weeks. Seeing him now, Shemu'el decided Petros must have been reconciled to whatever had caused his distress.

He gave Shemu'el's arm a friendly squeeze. "We've been through a lot together, my brother, haven't we?"

Shemu'el agreed they had.

"In Jerusalem you were the congregation's physician, tending our wounds and healing our hurts each time Eleazer and his guards sought to beat us into submission. Forced to leave, we traveled the road to Antioch together sharing our joys and sorrows. Do you remember sweating side-by-side as we dug out the grotto on Mt. Stauris?" Petros grinned. "And those bats. Who could forget the bats?"

"I'll always remember the women snapping their veils as they fled in terror."

Both men laughed.

Petros gazed across the grassy field, as if seeing the grounds and buildings for the first time. He moved his hand in a wide, sweeping arc. "And now, a few short years later, look at everything we've accomplished...the progress that's been made."

His weathered face crinkled. "With your help and God's blessing we've gone far beyond anything I imagined."

Apprehension tightened Shemu'el's throat. "A man embraces nostalgia for only one of two reasons. Either he thinks his work is complete, or he believes he is dying." He looked him straight in the eye. "Which is it, my friend?"

"As usual, your diagnosis is correct." Petros gave a nervous laugh. "Though if I were dying, I imagine you would be telling me, not the other way around." He paused, taking a moment to arrange his thoughts. "Truthfully, I feel my work here in Antioch has reached its conclusion."

"But there is so much yet to be done."

"There always will be. Do not misunderstand, I am happy with our achievements, but happiness breeds contentment. And contentment is like a ship at anchor, though it rises and falls with the tides, it never goes anywhere." A sudden urgency came into his voice. "Ruth and I talked and we agreed it would be best if we moved on. I felt you deserved to be the first to know."

"Where will you go? Jerusalem is not safe."

"True enough. Though I occasionally slip in and out of the city undetected, returning to Jerusalem would be a step backwards. I asked the Lord where he wanted me. When the answer came it was Rome."

"Rome?"

"Yes, Rome. A rather large city in the west." Petros poked him in the ribs and chuckled. "You have heard of it, haven't you?"

"Meet the lion in his den, heh?"

"The Lord left us a great task. Never forget he said, '...and to the ends of the earth.' I plan to start at the center and work out."

Simon Petros announced his decision after the next agape meal. The first step in implementing the change, he said, was choosing his successor.

The assembly proclaimed Shemu'el Evodius their next *episkopos*, by acclamation. He demurred at first, but with urging

accepted the post. The group planned a festive gathering the
following week to wish Petros well as he and Ruth prepared to
leave for Rome, celebrate Shemu'el Evodius' ordination as
Bishop, and offer thanksgiving for Rivkah's recovery.

They set up banquet tables outside. Members of the
congregation brought breads and desserts, dishes of cooked
vegetables, spiced and pickled treats, fruits and wines. Atticus
contributed a yearling calf that they roasted over coals.

It reminded Rivkah of a wedding feast. People served
themselves from the tables and reclined on the lawn to eat with
their families. As honorees, Petros and Ruth, Shemu'el and
Rivkah and their family ate on the porch overlooking the
grounds.

A lull settled over the group as the day drew to a close.
People rose and moved about. They revisited the tables, stopping
for second helpings, mingled with friends, talked and shared.

"Why don't you and Channah visit your friends?" Rivkah
asked Eleana.

Now considered part of their family, Eleana had joined
them on the porch.

Rivkah extended her arms. "Give baby Kyros to his Yaya. I
need to become better acquainted with this new grandson of
mine. He'll be fine until you return," she said, waving her away.
She pushed the infant's downy hair aside and kissed his forehead.

Kyros responded with a sleepy yawn.

She moved him onto her shoulder as Channah and Eleana
descended the stairs. Rivkah listened to Kyros' regular breathing
as she watched Shemu'el and Petros move through the crowd
clasping hands, pausing to bless children, and accepting hugs of
congratulation.

"The *eclessia* made a wise choice," Petros said.

"I am not sure I am fit to task."

"None of us are. You will learn, as I have, to move ahead in
faith always trusting the Lord to provide the necessary strength
and resources."

Shemu'el gave him an uncertain nod.

"Here," Petros said, "I have a departing gift for you." He

handed him his staff.

"This is the staff I formed for you from olive wood when we left Jerusalem."

"And it has served me well. You made it and I want you to have it as a reminder of our time together."

Shemu'el turned the staff in his hands, testing its heft. "You are about to undertake a long journey. What will you do for a staff?"

"I have a new one." Petros gave him a broad grin. "Your son, Yaakov, carved it for me. In case you haven't noticed, he's become quite the artisan. His father trained him well."

Shemu'el planted the staff. Taking a step, he cast Petros a sidelong glance. "There is still time to change your mind. Are you certain?"

"As certain as I am that I am leaving my flock in the best of hands."

"I wish I were as confident of my skills as you seem to be."

"The Lord delights in exploiting our weaknesses." He clapped Shemu'el on the back. "The ones I worry about are those who confess great self-confidence. You are a shepherd by trade." He swept his arm in a wide circle. "These people are now your sheep. Provide them the care, guidance and attention they require and all will be well."

A child's shriek echoed across the grounds. On the porch Rivkah turned in time to see four-year-old Sousanna break into a giddy dash and head straight for where Pavlos and Zeeta sat.

"Ready or not, here I come," she cried. "I'm going to get you."

The little girl leaped onto Pavlos' back. Giggling with delight, she climbed him like a mountain.

Pavlos remained still as a statue, letting the child clamber onto his big shoulder.

Sousanna paused just long enough to catch her breath then pitched forward shouting, "Catch me!"

At the last possible instant Pavlos threw out an arm and arrested her fall. He tumbled her against his chest, gave her a soft hug, and rolled her into his lap.

The little girl rose grinning.

Her foster parents arrived to collect their errant daughter before she tired the big man out. Sousanna stretched onto her tiptoes and planted a kiss on his check before taking her mother's hand and skipping away.

Pavlos had an aversion to being touched and went to extreme lengths to avoid even a handshake. Sousanna was the sole exception to this rule. Their love affair began the day he picked her up along the riverbank. She idolized her giant friend and didn't care who knew it.

Sousanna was the first of many children the *eclessia* rescued from ditches and dumps. Pavlos' simple act of decency had launched an ongoing ministry to the most vulnerable of Antioch's citizens.

For reasons known only to God, Pavlos had been born different from the rest. Different. Not better, not worse. When he first appeared, some believed his handicaps were manifestations of demonic possession. Very few in the *ekklesia* still held to that notion.

For her part, Rivkah had always respected his simplicity, gentleness, and humility. She watched him sitting beside his mother and smiled. God was surely pleased with Pavlos just the way He made him.

Atticus and Marcelina passed by the porch and waved. They crossed the lawn hand-in-hand. They'd been so instrumental in the church's success. Others might have demanded the position of *episkopos*, or at least a seat on the council of elders, as their due for donating the compound. But Atticus asked for nothing. He never sought accolades and preferred his contributions go unnoticed. Both he and Marcelina continued working behind the scenes enabling and encouraging.

Seeing Phaidra with Eleana, Rivkah searched for Channah. She found her beside a tree with Darios. Handsome in the classic Greek way, he was a metalworker by trade and spent his days forming precious metals and rare stones into fine jewelry.

She watched them converse, smiling and laughing. When Channah turned to leave, Darios called her back. His hand disappeared into a pocket.

Unable to see what his open palm held, Rivkah could only watch and wonder.

Channah extended her arm and Darios looped a silver bracelet around her wrist.

After a nod of thanks, they parted. Channah took a few steps, paused, and shyly glanced back over her shoulder to wave good-bye.

Darios crossed his arms and leaned against the tree, smiling as he watched her walk away.

Kyros squirmed in Rivkah's arms, stretching toward his mother. "You timed that just right. He's been searching for you."

Eleana patted her bosom and grinned. "His Maia always knows when it's feeding time."

She took him inside, leaving Rivkah alone on the porch.

The sun had begun its long slant in the western sky and, though trees blocked her view, she knew it would soon be sinking into the blue horizon of the Great Sea. Coals in the fire pits burned themselves out sending ribbons of smoke into the pink sky. Women clustered around the tables packing up the last of the day's feast.

Rivkah sighed contentedly.

One of the women placed a lamp on the table beside her. Its flicking flame reminded her of the lamps Hebel had given her. *All broken now, just like her relationship with her oldest daughter*, she thought with regret. Since awakening from the *koma* thoughts of Hadassah frequently crossed her mind.

She noticed Petros' bulky frame silhouetted in the fading light. Soon he and Ruth would be gone. She'd miss his booming voice, easy laugh, and childlike enthusiasm as much as his steady, unwavering faith. He'd been aptly named. Without a doubt, Petros was the bedrock upon which their church had been built.

It worried her that he and Ruth planned to return to Jerusalem and sail to Rome from Caesarea. Judea was rife with turmoil. Herod Agrippa had recently come to power and seemed eager to flex his muscles. She'd heard rumors that some of the priests now considered Agrippa Israel's long awaited *Mashiach*. Understandable perhaps since he'd re-united the divided kingdom of his grandfather Herod the Great.

Gazing across the meadow, Rivkah spotted a man in a traveler's robe plodding along the road. A woman with a babe slung across her chest and a child at her side walked beside him. They paused outside the compound's gate, apparently debating whether to enter. After long hesitation, they started up the drive.

*Who were these strangers?*

Rivkah had the sudden feeling that something wonderful was about to happen. She squinted, but dim light and distance made it impossible for her to discern their faces. Suddenly her heart leaped in her chest. Hebel and Hadassah were coming up the drive!

*Or were they?*

Since the *koma* her mind sometimes played tricks on her. Rivkah blinked and rubbed her eyes. Could her imagination have run wild, causing her to see what wasn't there?

Hadassah glanced up at that instant. Her eyes met her mother's and she grabbed Hebel's arm. Together, they and little Sarit raced toward her. Hadassah spread her arms wide calling, "Imma, Imma," as she ran.

Rivkah rose and threw her arms around them. Only when she felt Hadassah in her arms could she be certain it was not a dream. Glancing over her daughter's shoulder, she noticed tears of happiness in Hebel's eyes.

She touched his arm. "You've done well, my son. I knew I could count on you."

*—The End—*

## Author's Notes

I hope you enjoyed reading DISCIPLE as much as I enjoyed writing it. Because of the enthusiastic response to the Author's Notes that I included in WITNESS, the first book of the Seeds of Christianity Series,™ I decided to continue the trend of sharing some of my research. My goal has always been to entertain, educate and (hopefully) inspire by presenting a story that is Biblically *and* historically accurate.

Except for the natural compression of time necessary in a novel, I adhered to the historic sequence of events. Everything is portrayed as my research indicated it most probably occurred. When introducing historic personages, I exploited the existing gaps in the record and deduced what cannot be known. Here are my thoughts on a few of the many topics covered in the book:

### Stefanos

Acts tells us very little about Stefanos – Stephen. Tradition says he trained in the School of Hillel under Gamali'el. We know he was a Hellenist from Alexandria. Luke describes him as "full of faith and the holy spirit," and says he did "great wonders and signs among the people." We know of his ongoing dispute with some of the synagogues, that false witnesses accused him of blasphemy, and he was dragged out of the city, stoned and later buried by "righteous men." Last, but not least, we know Saul of Tarsus participated in his murder.

It seemed reasonable to make him approximately the same age as Saul. As a young man, whom I've assumed to be unmarried, it also seemed reasonable for him to have a love interest in his life.

The traditional place of St. Stephen's martyrdom has always been placed outside Jerusalem's Damascus Gate where the Church of Saint Étienne (Stephen) stands beside the famous *École Biblique.*

### School of Hillel

At the time of Christ there were two primary "schools" of

thought in Jerusalem, the School of Shammai and the School of Hillel, founded by Rabbi Hillel. Leadership eventually passed to his son, Simeon ben Hillel, and then to his grandson, Gamali'el ben Simeon. Luke speaks of a Simeon who waited in the Temple for the "consolation of Israel"— the *Mashiach*. Are they one and the same? The co-incidence of the names was too great an opportunity to overlook.

In the book, Gamali'el relates two other intersections of his life with the life of Christ. Surely Herod would have included him among the chief priests and scribes he questioned about the prophecies. And, as a leading mover and shaper of Pharisaic thought, he most likely would have been one of those questioning the boy Jesus in the Temple a dozen years later.

### Gamali'el and his Tomb

We need to approach this like a detective. Nicodemus and Joseph of Arimathea seem the most likely suspects as the "righteous men" to have buried Stephen. Both are known to have been secret followers of Jesus and they went to Pilate and asked for his body after the crucifixion. Without question they had already formed a *Chevra Kadisha*, or holy society, as Jewish burial societies are known.

Many in the early church considered Gamali'el a secret follower who remained a member of the Sanhedrin for the purpose of helping his fellow Christians. According to Photius, he was baptized by Sts. Peter and John. In Acts 5:34 Luke gives us his impassioned speech by which he freed Peter and the other apostles. Both the Roman and Eastern Church considered him a saint. His feast day was celebrated on August 3rd.

In an interesting side note, fragments of the apocryphal Gospel of Gamali'el have been found written in Coptic, Greek, Ethiopic, Garshuni (Syriac transcribed in Arabic script), and Syriac.

Now about that matter of the tomb...

In the year 415 a certain holy priest in Capharganda named Lucian was awakened one night by a venerable man appearing to him clothed in white. He called him by name and bade him go to

Jerusalem and tell the bishop to come and open the tombs, in which lay the remains of several servants of God, together with his own.

Lucian asked who it was who spoke to him. "It is Gamali'el," the figure replied, "the one who instructed Paul the apostle in the law." He told the priest that the body of St. Stephen would be found in his tomb along with that of Nicodemus.

Not wanting to be seen a fool, Lucian prayed that if this was a true apparition, Gamali'el should come a second and third time. Sure enough Gamali'el appeared to him twice again. Now terrified, Lucian hurried off to Jerusalem. The Bishop allowed him to search for the grave, which he eventually found. Inside were three coffins...most likely, ossuaries or bone boxes. They were labeled in Greek with the names of Stephen, Nicodemus, and Gamali'el. When the coffin of Stephen was opened a sweet fragrance filled the air, and many miracles took place at the tomb. Early Fathers of the Church testified to the authenticity of the story.

### The Synagogue of Rabban Yeshua *HaMashiach*

I'm sure we've all seen Biblical movies such as *Ben Hur* or *The Robe* in which St, Peter or some other disciple says, "The Master told us..." There are three forms of the Aramaic word *Rab*. The first, *Rab*, means "Master" and was used by slaves when addressing their owner. Wives also often used it when addressing their husband. The second form, *Rabbi*, means either "Teacher" or "My Master"...as in my instructor or leader. The third form, *Rabban,* denotes the highest respect and means "The Master," that is, the ultimate authority or wisest person. So the actor's actually saying "Rabban said..."

*HaMachiach*, of course, means *the Mashiach*. We know from history and tradition that the apostles and followers of The Way had a meeting place in Jerusalem. At first it was in the famous Upper Room in John Mark's father's home where they had their last supper. By the time of the Council of Jerusalem, they met at a location close to the Temple where James the Just, the first Bishop of Jerusalem, presided. To the Jews a meeting place for worship was, and still is, called a synagogue.

## Rivkah's Meeting with Matthew

My research into the work of expert papyrists who've examined early scrolls and codices indicates that the gospels were written earlier, instead of later, than previously believed.

So, how did they come to be? What and who were the evangelists' sources? We know how John gathered his information; he witnessed the events first hand. Peter affectionately called John Mark "my son," and his gospel most certainly reflects Peter's teachings. Matthew, also an apostle, had firsthand knowledge and Luke was an early convert from Antioch.

We've all heard of the three synoptic gospels, but there's a second way to classify them. John and Mark mention nothing about Jesus' birth and early life, whereas Matthew and Luke do. Granted Matthew was an apostle, but he only knew Jesus as an adult and Luke never met Jesus at all. Where did the birth narrative, the Wise Men, the flight into Egypt, the murder of the Innocents, etc., come from? Mary pondered all these things in her heart. Was she their source? Perhaps, but what about the things Mary couldn't know like the slaughter of the innocents or the return of the wise men by a different route?

Luke tells us in his letter to Theophilus: "However, it occurred to me that it would be well to recheck all these accounts from first to last and after thorough investigation to pass this summary on to you..." — The Living Bible, Luke 1:3.

I'll go on record as saying I believe Matthew, Mark, Luke and John wrote the canonical gospels that carry their names, and would argue that both Matthew and Luke consulted someone with personal knowledge of those events as they prepared their gospels. Someone such as Rivkah.

## Rivkah as a Deaconess

The history of women taking an active role in the early church is well documented. A number of women are mentioned in the Acts of the Apostles and various Epistles. Literary sources have left us ample records of deaconesses in different parts of the Byzantine Empire. Constantinople's main cathedral, the Hagia Sophia, counted among its clergy 60 priests, 100 male deacons and 40 deaconesses. (Justinian, *Novella* 3.1) The early church's practice of baptizing converts by full immersion in the nude – a symbolic rebirth into the life of Christ – made the presence of deaconesses a practical necessity.

Some of these women are known by name because of their association with other notable members of the early church. These few undoubtedly represent unnamed thousands whose contributions have been lost to history.

Olympias in Constantinople, ordained by Bishop Nektarios, friend of St. Gregory of Nazianze and later of St. John Chrysostom. Anonyma who ministered in Antioch during the persecution of Julian the Apostate. Procula and Pentadia, two deaconesses to whom St. Chrysostom wrote letters. Salvina whom St. Jerome knew and who later became a deaconess in Constantinople. Deaconess Anastasia whom Severus, Bishop of Antioch, mentions in his letters. The deaconess Macrina, sister of St. Basil the Great, and her friend and deaconess Lampadia. The deaconess Theosebia, wife of St. Gregory of Nissa.

The names of others have been preserved on their tombstones. Sophia of Jerusalem, whose Greek inscription reads: "Here lies the servant and virgin of Christ, the deacon." Theodora of Gaul carried this Latin inscription on her tomb: "Here rests in peace and of good remembrance Theodora the deaconess who lived about 48 years." In Delphi, Greece, a tombstone dating to the 5th century remembers a certain Athanasia. "The most devout deaconess Athanasia, established deaconess by his holiness bishop Pantamianos after she had lived a blameless life." Another tombstone in Jerusalem remembers the deaconess Eneon who ministered to the sick.

Notice also that the ordination of deaconesses was not restricted to only the early church; it continued well into the later centuries.

## Pavlos, the Autistic Giant

Autism, a condition that seems to be taking on epidemic proportions in recent years, has probably always existed. The practice of the early church sheltering people considered to be Demoniacs, that is possessed by a demon, is well documented. In that era mental illness was attributed to possession and these poor souls were turned out and shunned much like some of the homeless people we encounter wandering our inner-city streets and babbling to themselves.

Pavlos is also portrayed as injuring himself with sharp rocks. This pattern of self-abuse is recognized by psychologists as a way of externalizing emotional pain. Some self-injurers are punishing themselves for having strong feelings which they could not express as children, or for a sense that they are somehow bad and undeserving. His acceptance by the *Christianoi* and his reconciliation with his mother, Zeeta, alleviated these negative feelings, but his autism continued to limit his ability to interact in social situations.

## A Few Final Thoughts

It is well-documented that early Christians rescued babies who'd been abandoned, orphaned, or otherwise exposed to die. They drew criticism for doing it and a number of Romans historians mention the practice. The Christians also ransomed slaves whenever possible. Their commitment to life...the unborn, the outcast, the crippled and injured are part and parcel of who they were as followers of Christ.

The extent of their outreach becomes more amazing when one considers that most Christians belonged to the lower social classes and didn't possess great wealth or power. In spite of this they accomplished great things. Their continued dedication to the Gospel civilized a generally uncivilized world and eventually overturned the world's greatest empire.

To follow in their footsteps is a privilege. To emulate their faith and fidelity is a challenge faced by every Christian.

*—Peace and Blessings*

## *The Seeds of Christianity find fertile soil—*

Follow the lives of Rivkah and Shemu'el as they continue to spread the good news in Antioch and beyond.

Sha'oul, now renamed Paulus, returns before leaving on his first missionary journey accompanied by Barnabus and Yohan Markus. The church in Jerusalem suffers a mortal blow when Herod Agrippa executes Yaakov bar Zebedee making him the first of the Twelve to suffer martyrdom.

In Rome the Emperor Claudius tires of the ongoing conflict between the Christians and the Jews. Believing Christianity to be a sect of Judaism, he expels all Jews from Rome. Simon Petros is forced to leave his flock behind as he carries the Gospel to new lands and peoples.

When all seems lost, Atticus is promoted to the office of *Tribunus Medicus Militum,* placing him in command of all of the army's medical corps. He and his family travel to Rome to fill the gap left by Simon Petros' departure.

Meanwhile, the beloved disciple, Yohan, has relocated to Ephesus for Miryam's protection. He brings Shemu'el Evodius a new convert named Ignatius and asks him to mentor the young man. Though surrounded by chaos, the church in Antioch grows in size and influence under Evodius' competent leadership.

# APOSTLE
Book Three of The Seeds of Christianity™ Series.

*"News of this reached the ears of the church at Jerusalem, and they sent Barnabus to Antioch."*
— Acts of the Apostles 11:22

Rivkah's fingers slid across Shemu'el's neck and shoulders massaging his tense muscles with long, soothing strokes. "Why have you taken such a defensive posture? No one questions your authority in these matters."

"He has not come all this way from Jerusalem to offer his

congratulations."

*Why now, Lord?* She wondered. *He has only been* episkopos *of Antioch for a few days. Are you testing him?*

He drummed his fingers on the table. "If this narrow-minded thinking prevails, it could undermine all the progress we've made."

Rivkah kissed Shemu'el's check. "Why do you worry so?"

"I must be ever vigilant. As Bishop, the *orthodoxia* of our teaching and practices rests in my hands. I am responsible to the Lord for my flock here in the church of Antioch."

Barnabus spent the next week inspecting all they'd accomplished in Antioch. He accompanied Rivkah and other *diakonoi* as they made the daily distribution of food for the poor, met some of the new converts, observed the mission among the midwives and prostitutes, and visited the compound's nursery filled with happy, healthy children the *ekklesia* rescued from abandonment along the riverbanks and in the city dump.

When he finished his review, they organized a dinner in Barnabus' honor. All of the *presbyteroi* and *diakonoi* attended, with their spouses. As *episkopos,* Shemu'el Evodius presided.

After they'd eaten, the women cleared the dishes and went into the kitchen so the men could discuss Barnabus' conclusions.

Shemu'el leaned back in his chair and motioned to Barnabus. "Repeat that message you relayed to me so they all can hear."

He rose and cleared his throat. "Many in Jerusalem feel the message I bring to be of great importance. They have heard that you carry the message of salvation to the Greeks and Romans as well as the Jews of your city. This practice makes them uneasy."

Shemu'el shrugged. "I fail to see why this should concern anyone. Simon Petros was well aware of this practice and endorsed it. After all, do not the Psalms say, 'Praise the Lord, all nations! Extol him, all peoples?' and elsewhere, '...let *all* the peoples praise thee?'" He scrutinized his guest. "Tell me, brother, are you among those who feel uneasy about this practice?"

Barnabus sat and studied the wine in his cup as he gathered his thoughts. "My feelings are of no import. I am merely a messenger delivering a message. In all honesty, I must say I do not know how I feel. Before I arrived, it concerned me quite a bit; now, I am not so sure." He frowned. "The Spirit clearly moves among this *ekklesia*, yet salvation belongs to the Jews."

Shemu'el slammed his cup down on the tabletop. "On this you are mistaken!" He scrambled to his feet, looming over Barnabus as he spoke. "God may have chosen the Jews, we however, like you, are mere messengers. Salvation was never intended for us alone. We were told, 'Go and make disciples of all nations.' How can we do this if we exclude the gentiles?"

Barnabus started to speak, but Shemu'el's raised finger silenced him.

"Hear me out. We are not innovators in this matter. In Caesarea, after Simon Petros baptized all in Cornelius' household, did the Spirit not descend upon those gentiles?"

"Yes," Barnabus admitted, "but Cornelius was a Godfearer."

"A Godfearer, and by definition, therefore not a Jew." Lowering his voice to a more conciliatory tone, he rested a hand on Barnabus' shoulder. "My friend, we are both sons of Avraham. It is not my intent to raise anyone's ire. Yet while he trod our soils did Iesous not visit Tyre and Sidon...the Decapolis? When the Ethiopian requested baptism, did Phillip refuse his request?"

Shemu'el spread his arms wide. "This *ekklesia* has grown forty fold since we arrived. Antioch blossoms even as the flock in Jerusalem withers." He swept his arm over the elders gathered around the table. "We have established a strong foundation here. With all due respect, the future of the movement resides in Antioch, not Jerusalem."

Barnabus shifted uneasily in his seat.

"You have walked among us. Do we not remain steadfast in the breaking of the bread and infuse each and every catechist with the teachings of Iesous? We endow all of them with the prayer the Lord gave to his disciples and the creed the Twelve ordained. How can God's hand not be in this?"

"I have seen, and I agree that the Lord's hand is at work

here in Antioch. Still, some traditions must be respected."

"Traditions? What traditions?"

"Most particularly, that all men admitted as believers should be circumcised."

Shemu'el laughed.

Barnabus' eyes narrowed at this perceived insult.

"At last, the truth comes out," Shemu'el said, wiping tears from his eyes. "It is not a question of adhering to the principles of Iesous. All this fuss is over an insignificant bit of skin."

Barnabus straightened in his chair. "What you call '*an insignificant bit of skin*' marks a command given to our father Avraham. It seals our covenant with Almighty God."

Channah came out of the kitchen with a pitcher in her hand. Ignoring the men's conversation, she moved around the table refilling their cups.

* * *

"How are things going out there?" Rivkah asked when Channah returned.

"I cannot believe it; they are arguing over circumcision."

"Men!" Marcelina said with a derisive snort. "One way or another, they have only one thing on their mind."

The women chuckled and nodded knowingly.

"I shall never forget the times Shemu'el cut our sons," Rivkah said. "Their painful shriek was like a knife piercing my heart. And then, to make matters worse, he brought them to me, still bleeding and hysterical, while he left to share wine with the men of the village. While they laughed and clapped each other on the back, I was left to bandage my sons' tiny parts and put them to my breast in the hope of comforting them."

* * *

Shemu'el gave Barnabus a keen look. "You, my friend, have spent too much time in Jerusalem surrounded by the Pharisees. Just as a sponge absorbs water, their preoccupation with rules and regulations has unwittingly seeped into you." He shook his head. "Do you not see what a great irony this is? You, the Hellenist, have become the conservative and I, the Hebrew, am now cast as the liberal."

Barnabus' cheeks colored. "Because you, the Hebrew, would have us toss away two thousand years of tradition."

"*Jewish* tradition. We *Christianoi* are developing new traditions."

"Barnabus smoothed his cloak and shook his head. "Call yourselves whatever you will. A new name does not absolve you from the traditions of centuries."

Resting his elbows on the tabletop, Shemu'el leaned forward opening his palms to Barnabus. "You seem to say that acceptance of the practices of Judaism is a necessary stepping stone to becoming a *Christianos*. We are talking about gentiles here, brother. Is it not enough that they have turned their backs on the gods of Rome and broken faith with their families and friends? You are familiar with Roman prejudices. What does circumcision accomplish other than subject these men to pain now and ongoing ridicule when they go to the public baths?

"In Judea you preach among those who have already been circumcised. Like you and I, choosing to follow Iesous is an intellectual decision for them. How would you be received if you went about preaching with a scroll in one hand and a knife in the other?"

Barnabus began to nod in agreement. His expression changed from one of skepticism to one of understanding.

"Circumcision is a mark of the old covenant," Shemu'el continued. "The night before his death, the Lord Iesous established a new covenant. The mark of this new covenant is Baptism...available to both men and women, girls as well as boys. Why must we pile additional requirements upon these new converts until they groan like an overloaded camel?"

"What would you have us do?"

"Make no unnecessary demands on the converts. If the Jews reject us for this, let them. Our days upon this earth are numbered. The Lord entrusted us with a cache of seeds to be sown. Should we not plant them in the most fertile soil we can find so they yield a bountiful harvest for generations to come?"

www.ingramcontent.com/pod-product-compliance
Lightning Source LLC
Chambersburg PA
CBHW072101020726
47501CB00003B/663